RING OF STARS

RING OF STARS

Richard Sanford

*To Sara —
With much love,
Dad*

Odeon Press

I remember America

I remember America.

John Stewart, songwriter

O starry-spangled shock of mercy the eternal war is here.

Alan Ginsberg, poet

PART 1

Chapter 1

Walker Beale considered his options where he halted on the downslope, under the dark trees. He could barely make them out in the thickening air.

One was a twisting ravine that hooked out of sight toward the base of the hill. The second went higher, up a trail as wide as two shoes between knuckles of scrub oak. The last was a rubble road of smooth stones, a dry creek bed that could take them to the lake.

He was still trying to locate the others. They never should have been playing. Crazy. Adults playing hide and seek. He had no idea where they were now. If he shouted their names, he would give up his position. They would come if he could give them a reason. They would follow him if he could show them the way.

Walker scoured the slope for them again. Between the trees the air was pearl-gray and translucent, obscuring as much as it revealed. He wanted to believe it was fog that clouded his view of the wooded hill and the escape routes, but he knew otherwise. He had known for some time before understanding completely. He had begun to know with the first hint of creosote bush and dry grasses, the raw scent of combustion.

The smoke had spread over the top of the hill and down the front, in the direction of the lake. Although he could not feel it where he stood, he realized there must be wind, carrying the fire toward them from the back of the hill where it might have consumed itself. Smoke had tumbled silently over the trees, changing the sun. Bands of light splayed around the limbs.

They were being burned out. The creek bed of dry stones was the best option against fire, but that would put them in the open, clear targets from any vantage point on the hill. He had not seen or heard a gun, but he could expect the worst. He knew enough about them: the madness, predatory, bestial. Even if he followed the ravine, he could be leading them into a trap. The pursuers could have torched the hill and circled its base. By now they could be waiting at the bottom.

If he could find the others, something they could say might make the difference. He wanted their thoughts unencumbered, direct as fear. He needed their counsel.

Ready or not...

He could not search the burning hill for them.

Ready or not...

He could not decide for all of their party. What did he know of them really? They were the ones he would name if asked, who are your closest friends? Memory was an unrecoverable blur of conversation over food and alcohol through years in what could have been another lifetime. They all may have wanted more, in the days that had dispersed. That was nostalgia, he thought, comforting indulgence, but useless. All he knew for certain was the sharpening smell of burning.

He was circling the decision which in seconds became inevitable. He must risk revealing their position, otherwise he would have no way to lead them. If he did not lead he would only be running, and that he could not do. He would call the first name. He drew a breath and nearly gagged. It was the acrid air, but only in part. Something else was blocking him. It was in himself, or in the names.

Their lives together had come to this. They had only minutes. He clamped his eyes shut and tried to ignore the firing in his chest and his mouth as dry as a glove and focused only on his memory of a trace of light through branches. He knew what he could not do, for the rest he could only believe. He would be able to do it. He believed he could shout without names. His mouth fell open and he tried to haul the words up from the gut to the bottom of his lungs.

"Here I come," he would shout to their hidden ears. He would call out to them in the next second, just beyond the wall in his throat.

"Here!" he called, too weakly. "Here!" he shouted.

Walker snapped awake, close to praying that he hadn't been heard. He felt suspended without control, like a pilot in free fall, and it occurred to him he could have wet his pants. He glanced around for the others.

Lynne was sitting cross-legged, closest to him, her back turned. The sun hurt his eyes. It struck shockingly bright on her hair, chrome and gold. On her right Karen was smiling below her wraparound ski shades. Laughter came from Lynne's other side, Margo's laugh. From prone position Walker craned his neck to see her. Her healthy laugh was like a reassuring breath. He could just make out a slice of her left side where she sat facing Lynne, blue pullover with the tie-dye burst on the shoulder. Sharp laughter may have wakened him, he was coming to realize mercifully. He had not shouted himself awake.

He glanced up to reconfirm the sky. Over them all stretched immense blue with the half-wet brush strokes of cirrus clouds, the same sky he had seen before falling asleep. He felt a wave of thanks for the same clear day in early March in the Spring Mountains.

He rolled onto his right shoulder. Rob lay flat-out, hands on his stomach, thirty feet or so above them in the clearing on the gently rounded summit. So that was it, the girls were going strong and the guys went out after sandwiches and cheap Chablis. He remembered two cool refills of his thermos cup.

As he sat up, he could not resist doing an irrational thing. With reality in plain sight, he sniffed the air. Then he drew a deep breath. No smoke. He listened for any crackle of fire under the lilting conversation of the ladies. Fool, he confirmed with great relief, but he still felt a shadow from the dream. *Angels of Fury*, he realized, or *Furious Angels*, depending on the translation of the Portuguese. The Brazilian film they had downloaded over the weekend. "The makings of a cult classic" the review had said. Lynne had checked out after half an hour, but he had stuck it out. The visual effects and music explained the cult status, but Walker recognized the story as a rehash of *The Treasure of the Sierra Madre*. The chase in the mountains he had filed away somehow. It was clearly the source of his dream.

The women's talk bubbled up then effervesced into laughter, Lynne first and then all of them.

"Hey, a man can't get any sleep around here." Rob was rising into a long, arduous sit-up, clearly against his will. He shook out the clouds, squinted at the blue horizon like a pioneer getting his bearings, then grinned. He rolled to his knees and began rummaging in his backpack. In a moment he had it.

"All right, who's up for brainball?" he asked, rising to his full height. He held his extracted treasure, a sponge football, bubblegum pink. He slapped it against his other palm. "It's the thinking man's game," he explained.

"Hey!" Margo objected and the other females chimed in.

"Sorry, sorry. Thinking *person's, persona's*." He lobbed the sponge ball into his partner's back. Karen's sunglasses dropped on her nose and she sent him a look. She lunged for the ball a few feet behind her in the grass, but Rob snatched it first, then started dropping casually back.

"Twenty-five, twenty-six, cube root of two fifty-six K, hike."

Karen was on her feet. Rob launched an easy arc with no wobble. She hopped to her right and snagged it. It popped out of her hands like a pink bird but she recaptured it.

"Yea!" Margo shouted and the others applauded. Inspired by Karen, all including Walker staggered to their feet.

They shuffled in anticipation, eyes on Karen. She feinted left then right, overdoing it, delighted to see her receivers reacting. Then Walker broke left and threw up his arms. She heaved the foam ball in his direction, but it wobbled against her will toward Margo. She lunged, but it glanced off the back of her hand. The new arc favored Lynne and she grabbed it. Delighted and surprised, she bounded away from the others.

"Guys against gals," Rob announced.

The females looked dubious.

"Come on," he argued, "you guys are great at interceptions, obviously. Besides, it's two against three, you've got the ball—what more do you want?"

"Okay, huddle up," Lynne called, taking charge. Her authority could have come from the fact that she was holding the ball, but Walker knew she would have been the quarterback anyway. He loved her core of energy, wishing only rarely that he could dampen it.

They huddled for a second then broke, and Margo and Karen took their places on the line. Margo worked her fists like a boxer warming up. Karen's cap was turned backwards, giving her with the shades an inner-city Venus look. Walker and Rob dropped back.

"One potato," Lynne barked, holding the ball at arm's length at the line of scrimmage. "Two potato. Yeah!"

She retreated and the receivers pranced out. Walker and Rob ghosted them, close enough for interception. Suddenly Lynne tucked the ball and came straight up the middle. It had never been done in any of their games. It was understood that every play would be a pass.

Rob broke toward the middle and Lynne halted. She bounced to her right and put up a simulated pass, more of a shot put, over his head.

Walker watched the pink balloon hang for an impossibly long second at the top of its parabola against the blue and then drop toward Margo. She clutched it to her breadbasket with both hands. He broke behind her on a diagonal. Karen was squealing for her to go. In the moment that it took her to regain her balance and pivot to run, Walker tagged her two-handed on the back. He smelled a billow of her body-heated perfume. They both laughed nonsensically, and then they were all laughing at the brilliant success that had begun with Lynne's stratagem. Rob held his head in mock agony.

Patting Margo on the shoulder, Karen rallied their side with a cheer of "Girls, girls!"

They reassembled loosely around the new scrimmage line. The men checked the uncomfortable distance to the end zone, the spot where the grassy clearing ended and the tall grass began.

Walker grinned as he watched their opponents huddle. The combination of waking from the disturbing dream into the clear blue day and the unlikeliness of Margo's grab filled him with a sense of well-being. He saw them in their other worlds: Margo, whom they all loved, in her classroom in the Waldorf school, former spouse of an engineer living in Dallas. She was the only one of them doing anything of value, he realized, and she had the poverty-level salary to prove it. Karen incognito, doing web design for Rus-sellWorld, really ready at any minute to hop into the ancient green VW bus with Rob and head for the far corners of their dream together.

Even approaching what had been known in earlier days as the big four-o, Rob and Karen had kids still trapped inside, close to the surface. It was a big part of why Walker and Lynne, at the other end of the forties scale, cherished them. For Walker they were a connection to a previous lifetime, something that no longer made any sense to try to relive on his own.

He settled last on the opposing quarterback, his mate of twenty plus years. She broke from the huddle and stepped to the line.

"Red," she called and held the pink pig at arm's length.

"Blue." She shook her head, flipping her tinted blond hair, shorter now. A long-ago memory brushed by him of her flipping it the same way when it was longer before some blinding bright pool.

"Green!" She dropped back and her receivers broke from the line. Walker backpedaled, staying with Karen, then realized he had to cover them both. Rob was heading straight up the middle, targeting the passer.

Lynne froze a moment, as shocked as the others. She had broken the unspoken law on the last down. Now all was fair. She hopped back, tucked the ball, and tried to break to the side. Rob cut on an angle. In two of his long-legged strides they intersected.

Whether he had meant to tackle her was debatable. It could have been more of a trip than a tackle, and it seemed to Walker that Rob grabbed at her to break her fall. Whatever the intent, they went down in a tangle. Walker laughed and applauded, entertaining the thought that Rob had gone for the partial tackle as an opportunity to squeeze his wife's ass which, though a few years older than his and Karen's, was still an admirable bundle. He checked the hand position—mid-thigh.

"Quarterback sack," Walker reported as they jogged in. Lynne pounded Rob on the shoulder and he rolled over laughing idiotically, arms straight out in *mea culpa* position.

"Loss of ten, loss of ten," he crowed.

"More like one," Margo summarized. "What a man." She extended a hand to pull him up. Lynne was sitting up too, and as Walker reached for her hand, they all heard it.

The rumble was oddly discordant, out of place as thunder in a blue sky.

"Jeez," Rob said.

They checked one another then Walker glanced up, sweeping the sky for any source of a sonic boom. Even as he did, he knew it was not. He could deny it rationally, but the concussion felt like dynamite. It made no sense to him that there would be blasting in a state park on a Sunday afternoon in March.

"What *was* that?" Margo asked the rhetorical question.

Walker thought of saying something reassuring, but he pulled Lynne to her feet instead, and they all went to the edge of the summit. They looked out over the green foothills of the mountain and beyond, the tan and olive valley floor. The pristine afternoon revealed natural Nevada, sun-dried space with green patches under a blue haze. Walker spotted the glint of a tiny lake in the distance and assumed it was a golf course water hazard.

"Don't say heaven on earth," Margo ordered. "I want to know what the shit that bang was."

"Shitty shitty bang bang," Rob reported, but he was staring too, searching for the source.

Walker was curious, but if pressed, he could not say that he cared what had happened down there. He was envisioning the population of the valley in concrete bungalows and ranch homes with spreading lawns and in motor vehicles foreign and domestic on oil-dark strips of roadway. He imagined the Babel of transmissions vibrating speaker diaphragms like the wings of electronic insects. They were carrying news of the rescued faithful, mindless enticements to buy, putrid vitriol of the political process, and strident bombast of all kinds. Someone was blasting down there, displacing earth on the planet. He took a quiet breath and only appeared to join the others who were full of concern. He could stay where he was forever.

Chapter 2

"It's a road or a tunnel or something," Lynne said. It was a note of realism they all needed.

"Right, right." Karen nodded. Her sunglasses were off and she was peering into the expanse.

"It sounded like a gun to me," Margo said. "Maybe a hunter."

"More like a cannon," Rob said.

Not so crazy, Walker was thinking but didn't say.

"It's just blasting or something," Lynne persisted. "A road or a subdivision. Maybe it's that, what is it, Moonraker Estates."

They stood in silence for a while.

"Let's get outta 'ere," Walker said in mobster voice. "It's second and twenty."

They all glared at him. Undeterred, he headed back to the scene of the tackle. The others lingered a little longer then followed, Rob and Karen glancing backward.

Walker lobbed the ball to Rob, but what followed was not the game where they had left it. No one seemed quite able to find it. Instead the boys circled the girls, tossing air balls over their heads, inviting a block. Margo and Lynne stood talking, and Walker knew they were processing whatever it had been. He bounced the ball off Lynne's folded arms, and it wobbled a few feet away in the grass. He didn't like the inevitable way the melodrama had taken over, puncturing the game. Rob picked up the brainball and heaved it straight up like a last hurrah. Margo said she wanted to get back.

As they wound their way down to the parking lot, they met two other groups of Sunday hikers descending, passing one and being passed by the other. In the lot they started looking for Rob and Karen's VW bus, the green classic they usually took, including the last time to Vegas for the Oldies

Auction. This time they had opted for comfort, so they piled into Walker's Outlander wagon, Lynne in the front and the others in the back. Soon they were on the on-ramp to Highway Ninety-three west.

They debated lazily whether to stop at Little Delhi, to save them all from making dinner. Walker was reasonably sure he had the take-out menu in the glove compartment and asked Rob to look. When he refocused on the road, the white SUV in front of them was suddenly close. He hit the brakes and hands hit the backs of the seats. The dry surface was the difference between a screeching stop and airbags and a breakaway engine on the pavement.

"Jesus, no brake lights!" he exploded with the obvious when they were stopped.

"Moron," Rob confirmed.

"Where's the highway patrol in this state?" Margo added, still shaky after catching her breath. "Why don't these hicks ever get pulled over?"

"Your Boston's showing," Lynne jibed.

"They'd be in jail in Boston."

Walker leaned his head out the window until he had a view of the next half mile.

"It's a line of brake lights. They're barely moving. We could turn around and get off on Hemenway."

"So we'd cut over on Pacifica at the end?" Lynne asked.

"Another twenty minutes, maybe half an hour."

"I vote we keep going," Margo said. "It could clear."

Rob and Karen agreed, and they stayed with the creeping line. Rob found a classical station to settle them down, and they inched along. It may have been five minutes but felt like thirty before they saw the first red-and-yellow rotating beacon. White flares lined the shoulder.

"Is it an ambulance?" Karen asked.

"Can't tell, it's just sitting," Rob said, his head as far out the window as it could go.

They were passing orange cones on the asphalt, the white ash of flares between them. They spotted the source of the lights, a hulking tow truck with a long flatbed. In front of the truck a patrol car sat angled toward the road, its red-and-white lights spinning, adding to the riot of lights.

In the opposite lane a state patrol officer was standing, blowing his whistle, waving cars around. The gawkers crept, unable to resist staring.

"Jesus," Rob said, reacting to the lights in the foreground and the others, white and red and blue in various frequencies of rotation that came from farther down the shoulder. In another moment they were inching past the tow truck and the squad car, and the gawkers' target came into view under a cloud of mixed smoke and steam.

Half an hour, maybe less, Walker guessed from the fresh vapor and wide patch of water on the shoulder and the highway surface. A full-sized sedan. A Sonora was likely, or maybe a Cadmon. He could make out a wave of the silver body color on the lower doors and trunk. The wheel covers were intact, but the front wheel on the driver's side was splayed, resting on a flat. The top half of both doors and the front fender were scorched, a gradient from silver to carbon film to charcoal black at the line where the windows had been. All that remained of the window glass was a ragged outline. The roof over the front seats arched open and curled backward, the front edge jagged, black on the underside. It reminded Walker of an exploded pop can. The hood stood open from the wrong end, the hinged back canted up over the gaping hole that had been the dashboard. Yellow police tape separated the vehicle from the road.

He glanced around for an ambulance then realized it must have come and gone, probably as they were descending. Behind the burned-out car the tow truck operator was on his knees, hooking up. On the shoulder two officers of the state patrol flanked a wiry buzz-cut in a suit with a cell phone at his ear. Between them and the slowly rolling Outlander, smoke and steam misted up from the exploded shell of the vehicle of someone who must have been, Walker imagined, regardless of affiliation or place, much more like than unlike themselves.

"It smells like powder," Rob said. He was closest to the wreckage, but they could all smell it. It was the fireworks scent mixed with the sour aroma of burned polymers of dashboard and door padding, carpeting and electronics.

An image blew past Walker in an instant, less a vision than a shutter click in a black and white dream, a frozen frame of an ancient newsreel. Alamogordo. A crash dummy in a steel chair, burned black by an unnatural wind. The seated dummy charred by a blast of air.

"God, was it blown up?" Karen asked.

"What else..." Margo trailed off as they passed the car.

They rolled past the first patrol car throwing white and blue beams from the roof, and then the next. Finally they approached the last car in the line, a dark gray sedan. Walker tried to focus on the lane and the state patrol officer waving traffic through, but his eyes swung irresistibly to the right and the gray car.

He could see two clearly behind the windshield, close-cropped and officious looking. The one in the driver's seat was staring straight ahead behind dark glasses. The other was looking down, reading or writing. The squads and the tow truck were Nevada state vehicles, clearly marked. The charcoal sedan carried no front plate or marking.

Recognition that began in the brain cascaded down to adrenal glands and sweat glands. He was hoping no one would ask.

"Check these dudes," Rob said, wasting no time. It hung in the air like a caption.

Walker's foot was toying with the accelerator. The white off-road the size of a cape buffalo sat in front of them, no brake lights. *Silver State* said the plate. *I heart my Yorkie* said the frame. The patrolman on their left was blowing a whistle, waving at the moronic consciousness at the wheel who could not tear himself away. Walker was breathing small, tight breaths. Dots were swimming like tiny satellites in the corners of his eyes.

"What are they, FBI?" Margo asked, and although he loved her on some level, to Walker she could have been his doctor asking if the blood in his stool was black or red.

He checked the side mirror, cranked the wheel to the left, and gunned out of line. The tires squealed for an instant and then he was around the hulking Cadillac Adonis. The trooper blasted his whistle. Walker threaded the needle between the uniformed human being on his left and the steel behemoth on his right. The cars before him were unevenly spaced, light opening briefly between them as some picked up speed. In his lane, perhaps fifty yards down the blacktop, a flagger was holding the oncoming cars.

"Walker," Lynne said, and he heard the tension. The others were silent, too shocked to react. What was he doing with their lives in his hands?

He hit the gas harder and felt the rush, the thrust latent until he needed it. The flagger picked him up for the first time, staring down the empty lane that was closing between them. He showed no sign of moving. To their right Walker caught a glimpse of a woman in a red Daewoo Leganza, face blank. He swung into the widening gap in front of her.

"Yee-ha!" Rob burst out, then slumped back in the seat.

"Jesus," Lynne added.

"We're fine, we're fine," he reassured them all, chest pounding, wondering who could have been talking. They were well past the flagger who could only watch them as he receded in the mirror. They all began to breathe again. He could feel their questions hovering around him. He wanted to explain but knew he could not.

"Maybe it's in the news," Karen ventured, and it felt to Walker like rescue. He touched the first AM station.

... giant bucket of spicy wings
Press.
... fifty-inch HD TV!
Press.

They stayed with the last AM station through the weather, prerecorded on Saturday, and into a piece on the Las Vegas student arrested for punching his English teacher into a coma. He touched on/off and the radio was silent again.

"You hear about car fires," Margo said. "What causes those?"

"Can be wiring," Rob said.

"It couldn't have been just a fire," Karen countered. "You saw the roof, right?"

Stony silence.

Walker couldn't see Margo sitting directly behind him, but she had seen what they all had and she was quiet.

"It was what we heard," Lynne said. "Up on the mountain. We heard it explode."

Walker watched the traffic ahead beginning to stretch out. He sensed that they were about to talk about the bomb and the victim and what it meant. He imagined they all had the same feeling behind the solar plexus, like dropping in an elevator fall. He leaned forward, toggled to FM this time, and pressed once.

The six o'clock alarm would never ring.
But it rings and I rise,
Wipe the sleep out of my eyes.
The shaving razor's old and it stings.

As Davy Jones launched into the chorus, they did begin to theorize about the explosion, and Walker stayed connected just enough to nod along. But the more he filtered out the subject and tuned to the decades-old music, the finer he felt. By the time they regained highway speed, his chute had opened. Soon they would all be back on solid ground.

Chapter 3

Lynne had said nothing about it after they dropped the others off. He was fantasizing she might let it pass.

"I thought you were going to get pulled over."

She spoke through the open bathroom door as he was drying his face. At her bedroom mirror she stripped the cinch off her ponytail, and her hair fell shoulder length. She shook it out.

"The constables had their hands full," he said. "They weren't going anywhere." He crossed the bedroom and wrapped her from the back, testing the waters. "Did I weird you out?"

She turned and they were front-to-front.

"No more so than usual." She stared frankly back.

"Weirdsmobile," he said, one of their keywords, this one from Bing in *White Christmas*. "Sorry."

"You're a wild guy," she said. "That's why I married you." She was trying to be light, but he sensed there was something more under the surface. He worked her two steps sideways then tackled her backward onto the quilt. They both laughed and Walker felt the tightness release.

"It was supposed to be touch and he tackled me," she pouted.

"Easy to see why." He planted a kiss on her cheek and squeezed the seat of her jeans, his property if he could believe they were the property of each other, contractual, consensual. He was thinking of doing more.

"God it was strange, wasn't it?" He saw sudden wrinkles between her eyebrows.

"Well, I would have to say no. Just because we don't drive past it every day..." Walker rolled over and focused his thoughts somewhere just under the ceiling. "Remember when it *was* strange?"

Lynne rolled toward him and he folded his arm around her. He felt her nod into his shoulder. In the silence he heard her breathing and after a moment, a tick in the hall that he almost imagined was Sophie's footstep, until he checked himself.

"It's still horrible," she said.

He squeezed her and released, as though imparting some strength of character or equipoise that he could not claim. He was still seeing the gaping gash in the roof. He tried to dismiss the memory of the smell. The aftermath of flaming components even settled on the tongue, plastic and fabric and gasoline and in its core, the ghost of gunpowder.

"I feel like calling Sophie, just to check on her," she said.

"We just talked to her yesterday. She's perfectly safe; it's Madison, Wisconsin." He was repeating what they said whenever they had similar floating concerns, as though Madison did not have its share of poisoned psyches and depressive sons of advantage who were bringing their Uzis to campus because that day they had forgotten their meds.

"Do you think the lake is safe?"

"Of course. It's not like these things are random." He had meant to reassure, but everything he said seemed to have double edges. He considered trying again but decided instead on another aspect of the lake. "How's the design going?"

"Okay, I'm on the studios." Her tone shifted to the adult Lynne. "I'm thinking of rotating them on the east end of the house. The windows would get more light."

He heard the difference. For both of them it felt solid to talk about Lynne's design project—the retirement house on the Lake Mead property. He saw the lake, a hundred miles long and a dozen marinas. His fly line arced and dropped.

"When can I see it again?"

"How about after dinner?"

"Little Delhi's still an option."

"No more driving today. Besides, we still have enchiladas and I want to get a shower."

Lynne curled forward and then she was standing and popping her blouse matter-of-factly over her head. She had gone from momentary vulnerability back to the things of the world, smooth as a diver slipping in without a splash. That quality scared him a little. He was still back with the emptiness of the ravaged car. But he also cherished it, her ability to recover, see things as they are, and move on. They had discussed her as the responsible kid at age thirteen when her father died, but how she came to be was less important to Walker at that moment than who she was, between the bed and the closet with her blouse off, her back limned with the fine line of her white bra strap. She shook out her hair, still blond, only lightly highlighted—still young he had to admit, perhaps younger than the year between them. A trace of Chanel, warm and cured by a day, lingered on his shirt where she had been. Losing Lynne could kill him, he realized for an instant, then dismissed the thought.

She dropped her blouse into the laundry chute, and then she was in the bathroom and the door closed behind her. Walker flashed on Sophie and Lynne's question and his feeble assessment of their daughter's safety.

"Shit!" she spat from the bathroom, and it matched his feeling exactly.

On the dresser her cell was going off. Walker groaned at the idiotic ring tone, customized by the caller. He tried to remember when phones would just ring. He had not particularly cared for that either.

Lynne took it wrapped in a bath towel.

"No, that's okay, what is it? Right, I need you to check the pressure in the duplex on Gaviotas. We had to replace fixtures in both the units and one's leaking again. The faucet, the kitchen."

Walker rolled to his feet and headed for the living room. No escape for property managers, he knew. He felt restless.

A malformed feeling of trepidation was with him in the hall. Sophie was in there, with the ghost of a burned-out sedan.

He entered the living room and kept going. He didn't see the tan sectional, the low tables of hardwood and hand-painted tile, the huge Baja-toned seascape opposite the sofa, or the sweep of glass that opened on the flat natural yard with jacaranda and junipers. After a dozen years of living in the house, these had disappeared for both of them except for the rare times that they reminded themselves of their good fortune.

He passed through to the kitchen, popped the cork on a half-full bottle of Zinfandel, and filled a bistro glass. Back in the living room, he retrieved the remote, clicked, and savored the first aromatic mouthful.

"The unique Astroflex Toning System—"

Click.

"It cleans itself—"

Click.

"I just want to IM my friends—"

He punched through the frequencies, huge images in hideous colors hitting the screen like tropical bugs against a windshield. He stopped at Las Vegas channel eight. Over the Breaking News banner, Stacy McGuinn was roadside with her mic. In the background he saw a dark sedan and rotating red and blue lights. Barely visible behind them was a blackened shell he recognized. Walker sat down on the sofa and raised the volume.

He took another drink but he didn't enjoy it. The report annoyed him. He emptied the glass and watched Stacy, and despite her comely body in a smart tan pants suit that seemed to be the screen's only way to apologize for its content, he was more than annoyed. He was close to rage, with the paralyzing knowledge that there was nothing he could do.

He became aware of the weight of the glass, bottom half an inch thick. Stacy was nodding her serious nod, and then they cut to the station anchor. Dan Greene was announcing an interview with the governor whose thumbnail-sized picture appeared over Dan's left shoulder. The phone call began, and the voice of Governor Cruz was pledging justice for the victim's family and redoubled efforts to ensure the security of all.

What would it take, Walker wondered, for the man inside the governor to say what he was really thinking? Something had gone wrong out there. It seemed to have its own life, grotesque, self-protective, like a disembodied laboratory eyeball swiveling away from the light.

He stopped listening. Part of the reaction was his standard recoil from platitudes, but if he had to be honest, more was fear. Not fear for himself but for Sophie in the far-off Midwest, and for Lynne. What could be done with fear? In his right hand was a glass grenade. With his left he seized the remote, punched Mute, and held down the next channel button. The silent images flashed by, stroboscopic, inane. After twenty or so he clicked them off.

It was only one glass of wine but enough to bring clarity. He saw himself rising, crow-hopping, and firing the bottom-heavy bistro glass through the broad picture window. He felt the release like a charge of dynamite. A bird took flight. He heard his heart in his ears. His palms were sweating. He stood up.

He could hear Lynne's voice in the bedroom, still on her cell in her cool business tone, working the problem. It was the sound of sanity, and it stopped him. Saved from himself, he thought, like so many garden-variety lunatics. He stepped to the window and the warm bands of sunset that were beginning over the horizon. He raised his fingers to the glass.

He did not know what protected them, what the dependencies were. He could not risk breaking the imperceptible netting around them. Other lives were with him in the room.

Walker was trapped, and as usual, he accepted it. He would not get out. More to the point, he would not let the outside in. Things were moving along as they always had. Today was a detail, an incinerated shell on the evening news. He would not compromise whatever shield protected them, which as far as he knew, was as fragile as a diaphragm of glass.

Chapter 4

"Want a glass?" Rob was in the kitchen with their organic jug wine.

"It would put me to sleep," Karen answered from the living room. "I will with dinner. You hungry yet?"

"Nope." Rob took a sip on the way to the leather sofa which, though not quite cracked and battered, had been with them a number of years and had a comfortably creased look. He picked up his WyPad, punched on the tuner, and switched to jazz, cool guitar, light as rain.

"That was fun," he said.

"Until we saw the car." Karen closed her eyes. She was leaning into the corner of the sofa, one hand behind her head. Her top button was open, and her breast strained the flannel shirt. He reached over and undid the second button. Startled, she mock-slapped his hand.

"Pervert. I'm talking about death here."

"In the midst of life, we are...where were we?" His fingers slipped under the edge of her bra.

"Incorrigible freak." She tilted his way but seemed more cuddlesome than arousable. His arm slipped around her and he enjoyed the dark, fresh smell of her hair.

"Do you think Margo likes me?" she said suddenly. He stared at her.

"Margo? Of course, what do you mean?"

"She seems nervous around me. Not just today, I've sensed it before. She disapproves of me or something."

"You're crazy. She bought your Mexico picture. It's in her place."

"I know, she's always been perfectly...nice. It's just something."

"Maybe you turn her on."

"What are you talking about?" Karen checked him for a joke. "*You're* crazy. She had a husband."

"So. She could be bi, you never know. I've thought so before. And you know she's wired underneath, but that's okay." Rob was referring to Margo's outré side. She had a natural capacity for intensity about causes and people that she considered important, and it expressed itself in effusions. Her anxieties and concerns were equally obvious. These were traits that they all found endearing but which, they also suspected, were not the easiest to live with.

"They had a bad break-up, didn't they?" she asked.

"Yeah, I think Walker's the only one who knew him, at the other company, in the days before Xynapse. Margo worked there too, HR or something. She and the Beales go way back."

"What about the way Walker peeled out today? That was definitely different. He's kind of a spook sometimes."

"I think the whole scene really gets to him."

"The political..."

Rob went back to his drink and she took it as a yes.

"I know Lynne's planning on him retiring in two years. She's all into designing their house. She's forty-nine, he's what, fifty-one or two." She thought back to the dinner for his five-oh and tried to remember whether it was a year ago or two. "I guess if you're planning like that it's hard..." She drifted off, looking squarely at the charcoal sketch of the woman on the side wall, her image in the mirror half-bird, no longer quite seeing it, like all of her works that vanished until someone praised them or she forced herself to focus.

"He's been talking retirement already. He wants to fish."

She raised her eyebrows.

"It's part of a grand plan. He wants me to go out with him in Baja."

"Where did that come from."

"East coast, remember?"

"Right. He's from...Florida?"

"North Carolina, Durham. But he wound up in Florida, somewhere like Tampa. He did major fishing all the time he was growing up. His dad took up with another lady while he was a kid, I don't know how. He told me he went to some school in the south, not Rice, maybe Emory? Anyway, his mom remarried and he split at some point. Knocked around for a long time, like into his thirties. I think he was in this country band for a while in Chicago. Played Merle Haggard, 'Mama Lied' or 'Mama Tried' or something, he told me once."

"Was he stoned?" She was grinning, bemused.

"A bit, on rum and Coke as I recall. He told me great country songs were like sonnets, they were that tight."

Electric guitar notes, subtle punches and harmonics, drifted sweetly downward in the room.

"That's from Lenny Breau Live in Toronto," the DJ said.

"It's kind of funny," she said.

"What?"

"That he wound up with Lynne. But I see it. She's the anchor." Karen wondered what would happen if Walker lost her, if the fishing boat would drift around like a toy in the bathtub.

"You think so?"

"If he lost her he would...fill in the blank."

"What, be sad? What are you saying?"

"Purely hypothetical."

He was speechless.

"Go to pieces."

"No way," he said.

She considered a moment.

"Well, I guess you know him better."

"How do you know anything like that? If I lost you, for example, no prob."

"Mm." She hummed two syllables instead of punching him. "It almost happened."

Thunderous silence.

"You or Lynne?"

"Lynne, idiot," she clarified.

He half-nodded and took a slug of *vin ordinaire.*

"She told me almost a year ago. This happened before, like maybe five years, and she was feeling guilty because it was their anniversary. Walker didn't know. But while it was going on this insane thing happened. He pulls up right beside them at a stop light. This guy—some real estate person—is driving, and she's in the passenger seat. And Walker sees them and everybody waves and they just go on. Lynne told him the guy was an agent she had to deal with, and of course it makes sense because she's in property management. No questions, nothing. But she calls because she's wracked with guilt five years later."

"What did you say?"

"I told her to think about telling him, just because she was feeling so tortured. But she never has. So I guess ignorance is bliss. But that's why I wondered what he would be like if she took my advice and told him."

Rob took another slug and looked into the ceiling. The station had gone to pseudo-jazz, studio quality sax and rhythm, not at all bad. "The Shadow of Your Smile."

"You wouldn't tell him, would you?"

"Of course not," he said.

"It was really nothing. She said she hasn't seen him again. I think she and Walker were going through something at the time."

"Maybe," he said and took another, calmer sip.

Karen imagined he really knew what had happened.

"I'm sure guys hit on her," she said. "What are you thinking?"

"I'm thinking it's funny you're saying that about her. It's you."

"Shut up."

"You're the sexpot. Look at you." With her shirt halfway undone, the evidence was hard to deny.

"*You* hit on her. You tackled her, as a matter of fact."

"Let's not confuse brainball with...other matters."

"Who's confused? You seemed to be enjoying yourself."

He ceremoniously placed his glass on the table at the end of the sofa then went for the midriff, tickling mercilessly. She fended him off, swiveling on the sofa and shoving with both feet. He found them, encased in white athletic socks, like the rest of her, irresistible. He trapped her bare foot under his arm and pulled off one sock. Then, grinning, she dropped her resistance and he wrestled the other off.

His hand was in her shirt, the other behind it, working the flannel off her shoulder. She shrugged under it, assisting, and he felt like thanking her, like laughing. He slipped her sports bra over her head, and the shock of dense, dark waves brushed his arm. He touched her and felt her nipples firm, drawing his tongue.

"Would you be doing this if we were married?" She was joking, but he heard her breathing harder. He removed his mouth, leaving a wet ring.

"Hell no."

Saxophone tones were swimming around them. They undid their jeans and tugged them off. She was standing before him in white elastic panties, Riviera crescents on her hips. Then she was kneeling.

At first he held her dark shock of hair close to him. He smelled the day's aromas, sweet and dusky. He cradled her head like a gift. She was drawing on him like an undertow at the bottom of his spine.

Jazz filled the spaces, wrapping them in a stream, and it felt to Rob like a continuum, a single flowing memory of all their times. He lay back and let the long, fluid moments roll together. Eventually he sat up, his signal of enough, and she rose, face flushed. Her crescents of elastic moon were the last thing separating them.

He reached for the target, but as his arm swung from its position on the sofa back, it struck something alien. He realized dimly he should have put it in the safety zone on the floor.

Someone was speaking in the room, a male voice, familiar.

"...Highway Ninety-three in the Spring Mountains area."

The news station, Rob realized. Across the room by the bookcase lay the WyPad. The impact with his arm or the floor had changed stations. He got up and stooped toward the micro-thin device that had humiliated him. Karen stopped him with a hand on his shoulder. He glanced at her, checking for sanity. Then he heard what she was hearing.

The reporter's voice was compact and modulated, almost musical. Rob wondered as he stood naked, impulses frozen, if somehow they could pick up where they left off. But the voice was not music, and its message was not conducive to preserving the moment. He and Karen listened to the report of what they had seen, standing in their living room in their primeval state but not, as they understood full well, in paradise.

Chapter 5

Margo Selman's townhouse lay across Boulder City from the Beale's desert ranch in one of the rare cul de sacs with deciduous trees, small live oaks. The spot felt to her like a sheltering lagoon far away from turbulent backwash. After her divorce from Ken, she had sold the house that had become increasingly cavernous and chosen the scaled-down but newer place of her own. It was arguably the nicest in a cluster of six, farthest from the street with windows facing the stand of live oaks. Being less than two miles from the school, it was also in sync with the sustainable style of her new life. On many days of the school year before it was too hot, and if she did not have more than her backpack to carry, she could leave her hybrid in the garage.

The townhouse suited her perfectly in most ways, but as she pulled the door closed behind her and faced the inside of home, she sensed something unpleasant but familiar, difficult to place. If she had forced herself to focus on it, she might identify the silence that occupied the rooms, the way it owned the space, the outward expression of emptiness.

Margo crossed the living room to her silver tuner that resembled an alien craft, surrounded by house plants. She punched the power button, and harpsichord and strings freshened the room. The orderly tones settled on her like leaves, the beginnings of calm.

The purple folder on the sofa reminded her that she had work to do. Twenty or so papers to go, some science, some English. She would start during dinner and be done before nine. That felt good too, an anchor, a reminder of who she was. If she needed proof, it could be found any time of day on the wall beside the hall, although she no longer saw it. The caption below the framed photo read, "Golden Apple of the Sun Award, Teacher of the Year 2009, Margo Selman."

She was receiving a plaque from the president of the board of Boulder Ridge School. The photo that she did not see hung on the left side of the entrance to the hall. On the right side, the painting caught her eye. The double image of a woman, one blond and black-eyed and imperious looking, the other, her image in a mirror, owl-headed. Karen's painting was making her uneasy. She recognized the problem and lifted the corner a touch until it hung straight.

She hauled her backpack toward the bedroom, quizzing herself on the way. Handel? Not exactly, probably Scarlatti. A concerto for strings. She wasn't positive, but she could live with it.

The backpack went on the bed, and as she unhooked the water bottle, she glanced automatically at the answer phone. The red light was blinking. One call, one message. She sat on the edge of the bed, stared at the blinks for a moment, then punched the play arrow.

"Hey, Hon, it's Cathy. Just hoping you're all right. If you'd answer this like a normal person instead of a granola-head, I'd be feeling okay by now."

She sounded tense. Margo was touched.

"Spring Mountain Road is all over the news, so I hope you were out of there when it happened. When you get in, *give me a call, please.* Plus, I've got a classic Sigourney Weaver for download. We could snuggle, or just hang out, I know you've got class tomorrow. But so do I—you could be home by ten. Anyway, *call me.*"

Margo was smiling at her maternal side, the flip-side of the Fremont High softball coach with the tight butt and flat abs. It felt like a trace of confirmation that their getting together was a good thing, even in their secret second life. But it was complicated. She didn't feel any false sense of immorality or similar queasiness. It was the sense of complication that weighed on her enough to postpone the call. She needed to be in her own place that night. She would let Cathy know, but not right away. She left the backpack on the bed and headed back down the hall into the Scarlatti.

At the end of the sofa sat two stuffed animals, a koala and a kangaroo. Beyond them on the end table lay the remote. One button under her thumb silenced classical FM, another switched on the TV. A VedaStore ad fired at her in half-second cuts. She punched hard and held and the stations rolled. She found it, reversed.

"...state police, as well as FBHS. The road was completely closed following the incident, and as you can see, it has been reopened, but traffic is crawling past here." In the middle distance on the shoulder of the road, engulfed in squad car lights, the charred shell of the vehicle was visible. Over the reporter's shoulder the line of cars stretched to the vanishing point. The reporter was the exquisitely packaged Stacy McGuinn, whom Margo could not stand.

She punched again and once again, and another reporter, Charles Attica, appeared before the same car. The view was straight on and close. The video crew had maneuvered into position on the opposite shoulder, and between the cars that rolled on bumper to bumper, Margo caught glimpses of the burned-out sedan. She focused on Charles.

"...has been identified as James Canliss, an Oklahoma City pastor and spokesperson for the Union-Fundamentalist Council. Canliss was reportedly on his way to a rally tonight in Henderson. Another person was driving the car at the time of the explosion, and it has been rumored but not confirmed that this person was Canliss's bodyguard. He has also been confirmed dead.

"Canliss himself was known among fundamentalists as a firebrand speaker. His followers tell us that some of his most passionate speeches were delivered from the pulpit of the Kingdom Tabernacle in Oklahoma City, where he was pastor. We're going now to KOCO, our affiliate in Oklahoma City, where Eldon Davis is at the Canliss home."

Eldon was speaking into his microphone, but Margo was not hearing him exactly. She was distracted by his tie. The picture on it was not an animal, she knew. That could not be on evening news. But what else the ochre blob on a gray field could be, she didn't know. It caused her to watch closely but hear nothing, or it may have been that she did not hear because the home of the late pastor in the background with shades drawn was sufficiently eloquent, and she knew full well that no statement by family members, however grief-stricken or vitriolic, would be forthcoming. She preferred not to hear Eldon or see the pastor's dismal house. She didn't care for the late Pastor Jim or his ilk. She didn't care for U-F and most of what it stood for, but that was not the point. She was tuning Eldon out because a human interest tragedy told by an Oklahoma reporter with a bad tie would only upset her more. The afterimage of the burned-out car lingered, and the raw smoke smell. She retreated to the sofa and sat on the end.

Her eyes were starting to tear, and she was surprised. Why should she be watching a moron from Muskogee? People were incinerated. She sensed an ad coming and raised the remote. Instead the report cut back to Charles Attica beside the road.

"Already acts of reprisal have been reported. In Houston a Parents Services clinic is on fire in what appears to be arson. In Indianapolis a spontaneous gathering of protesters turned into a confrontation with police. Here in Sparks, two men have been arrested in connection with a bombing at a Democratic Party headquarters. The state awareness level has been raised to red. In Las Vegas, police presence in the streets has been increased. For a report we go to Tiffany Zin, who is with Police Chief Greg Imholtz."

They seemed to be standing on one end of the strip, traffic behind them active for a Sunday evening. The chief was in uniform and Tiffany was her animated self. Margo saw no squad cars. Instead she noticed a car parked behind them, towncar-sized, slate colored or a smothered brown. In an inappropriate corner of her mind, she was anticipating a calamitous event. She saw it erupting from the dull car, spiriting the chickie reporter and the chief upward and outward far beyond the camera. Her heart was racing. She could smell it, the burnt essence of gunpowdered plastic and gasoline.

She rose with the remote and killed Tiffany and the images of all. She turned to the end of the sofa and the furry creatures of comfort, bear and kangaroo. She considered taking one. Instead she let herself feel what she had not since arriving home, and she let the tears come.

Instead of using the remote, she crossed the living room and pressed the button on the tuner. It was appropriate to contact Scarlatti only by touch.

"Forget your debt. If you have credit problems, or no credit at all, we can help. Call one eight hundred—"

She hit the power button again, and the room was still except for her own sniffling. She looked out the window, and the trees were swimming. The lack, she thought. Of decency. Kindness. The random horrors.

She closed her eyes, and the papers on the sofa reappeared in her mind's eye. She remembered why she had them and thought of the kids whose pencils had scratched them out. Her thoughts drifted to Cathy and the call she would make. She opened her eyes and clung to these reminders and cycled through them until the window cleared and she saw nimble oaks again and she was smelling nothing.

Chapter 6

"I'm just wondering," Jamal began, pen oscillating beside his ear, "do we really need a visual identity here? I mean, do we need to brand this product?"

The youthful design director had hit the end of the diving board and was unfolding from tuck position, a moment before noting that the pool was empty. The audience was still. Walker checked Ivan at the head of the conference room table. The CEO was staring impassively at the tiny black Cyber Ball, spinning it on the veneer. He would not put Jamal out of his misery. He was deferring to one of the others. It was Walker's domain. Ivan's little black ball was bouncing squarely into his court.

"I think we have a branding story with every product," he said. "Anyone close to our space knows Xynapse, I think we can say that now. They think games, and if we're lucky they think bleeding edge and quality, and I believe they do. The brand is already there for every consumer who knows us or knows of us. We didn't create it as something separate. The brand is a network of associations, and we can leverage that, for every product."

"We need to do it." The project manager of *Spectrus* spoke quietly, with palpable restraint. Below his buzz-cut, the face of Don Karpos betrayed no emotion. A voice stress analyzer would be challenged, but to Walker, the stifled rage in his voice was clear.

"We're doing it," Ivan confirmed quietly, the ball folded in his hand.

Walker checked Jamal who was expressionless also, but now his pen was point-down on his portfolio pad.

"And the focus here is quality," the Ukrainian chief continued.

Walker watched Medha, bless her heart, begin keying dutifully on her netbook. He was amazed by her youth. He tried to put it in perspective, her seriousness with the luminous black sheen of her hair even under the conference room fluorescents and the delicate tapers of her fingers to the nails the color of dark blood. The project manager in training.

"Quality is the thing here. That is confidence. Why should DoD have confidence in Xynapse? Our quality." Ivan's black eyes ticked around the table, checking them all. His lean face tapered into a goatee. He turned his attention to the ball and rotated it between his fingertips and the table.

The action, and his imperious silence, which intimidated the youth at the table, nearly made Walker laugh. He was recalling Ivan in the early days when the company was a mad Ukrainian, his sister Roxie, his backer Kevin fresh from Wells Fargo Bank, Dave Montoya and Ray Silver—the programmers of *Roswell*, the monster hit that started it all— and Walker. In those days he was project manager and general pitchman. They could have been a garage band. Xynapse was nothing in those days if not the shambling spirit of freedom itself.

"We need to lose the trivia," Ivan went on, "and focus on quality." He stared at the ball for final inspiration. "And we need to think about the serious aspect of games."

Walker was still recalling the long-haired freak from the Omega user's group who had the idea of starting a game company. Now he was the CEO speaking with Ukrainian gravitas about the serious side of gaming, taunting them all with an expression that asked, "Which is..."

Medha looked up from her pad. Jamal looked down. Karpos shifted in his chair. Silence.

"Survival," Walker ventured.

Ivan said nothing. He folded the black ball into his palm. He removed his hand from the table, no further inspiration required. Obviously pleased, he sat back to let the team take it from there.

"I'll open a charge line," Jamal put in.

"I'll get with Walker on the schedule," Medha added. Walker suppressed a grin at her jargon.

They went over action items. Walker would work with Don Karpos with support from Medha. Having put the machine in motion, Ivan excused himself. The others passed a few marketing platitudes. As soon as acceptable, Walker pushed his chair back and was standing at last, the *Spectrus* kickoff at an end.

As he did, he felt overtaken. In the serene air conditioning, he felt a chill. At this party he knew no one. He did not know how it would all turn out, but he had a sense. *Spectrus* for the DoD had allowed Xynapse to go public, with a commensurate boost to the fortunes of all. The significant boost went to the circle of founders, himself included. There would be no turning back. He himself had helped to sell the deal as the proposal process had played out over more than a year. The visualization and optimization that set Xynapse games apart could take training for urban warfare to a new level. *Augmented realism*, Ivan had dubbed it. Proposal, presentations, demos scalable from headsets to full screen. Walker had sold the quality and would go on selling, as expected. He was glad they had not put Rob on the project. They still had games to create and sell.

In the long moment that he monitored the chill and then let it pass, he came to realize he was stalling. He nudged his chair back under the table with his knee. Hoping to avoid eye contact, he waited to move toward the door until Karpos had turned from the table. But escape was not to be.

"Got a minute?" the *Spectrus* project manager was holding the door with the stolid face of a college jock and incongruous enthusiasm around the eyes that confirmed to Walker he was right to be nervous. Not yet forty was the PM, and brimming with ambition. They stepped down the hall in the opposite direction from the main offices.

"Walker, do you know what this can do for Xynapse?" Don pumped a breath, and his chest rose and fell inside the tan Tattersall shirt with the double-thread sheen, open at the button-down collar.

"For, or to?" Walker was piqued with himself. He had not meant to reveal that corner. He had a long way to go with Karpos, formerly of U.S. Technologies. Ivan had needed a point man with Defense experience and had recruited him. It was all right, Walker realized, Karpos wasn't listening anyway. He probably knew already where they stood, and what he needed to do.

"You wouldn't believe how far this company can go now. The same talent and this new vision piece. There are inside lines at the DoD. We're hooked into one, but only one. This is just the beginning. Walker, it's time to take Xynapse to the next level, and only people from the senior side of the house, like you, can lead that."

Karpos had been on the job less than two weeks, and it was the first time he had cornered Walker. He was being hustled by a newbie. Worse, he was being forced to smell his cologne with its sweet under-fragrance like baby powder. He took a step back before he responded.

"The company is going to change, I don't disagree. But it may not be the way you think." He checked Karpos for a beat. The hooker appeared moderately hooked.

"We were talking about branding. A brand is really associations, fuzzy ineffables, but they run deep. There are roots here that run deep, shallow, all kinds. There's always an issue with change, but you need to understand there are a lot of people here who are thinking about this change. They're asking themselves something." Walker checked his young hopeful. He seemed to be on hold.

"They're asking themselves where they come down. Because sometimes that's the question. You ask your-self...where do you come down."

Walker was waiting for a question, but Karpos seemed to know what he meant.

"How do you tell, Don?" he went on. "It's in the gut, isn't it?"

Karpos was impassive, the thrill gone from his eyes.

"Walker, I don't doubt you know your team. But as you say they need to decide, everyone with skin in the game. They're with us or they're not. I believe Ivan brought me here to open some eyes, to show what can be done. I know he expects that. Some may not agree with where we're going. A certain number. They may need to get off. The others...the others are the ones that are going to count."

"You're right, Don. You're the PM. You're the expert on teams, what it takes to build them. But overall, what I'm saying is that in the company, in the big team, it's numbers too, isn't it? And everybody counts."

Walker nodded, reinforcing his point but appearing just positive enough to preserve the thread. He grinned and gave his young buzz-cut in baby powder a beat to respond, which he felt was more than enough. He turned and headed back down the hall, taking one deep breath and then another, surprised at the spike of adrenalin that must be fueling the firing in his chest.

Back at his desk, face to flat panel, he appeared to be concentrating, but he was seeing Karpos. A piece of work, but not in a good way. Just outside his door, Nate and Jodi were chattering about an occult TV series that was shot, it sounded, in public bathrooms. He did not wish to be included. He checked his online calendar, then started capturing what he would need from the meeting in one of his *Spectrus* files.

Key concepts: nimble, responsive, optimum, adaptable, leading edge.

"I was like, what do you do with him? He's a snag."

Jodi stifled a giggle. Nate was scoring points. Walker put on his headphones.

Precision, envision, responsive, predictive.

His default was KRNG, classical FM. He focused for a moment on Vivaldi, or Geminiani. He and Lynne hearing Geminiani in an Internet café in Venice, e-mailing Sophie at school. Two years gone. He felt the encroachment of heartbreak, dismissed it.

GPS, global deployment, topography, aggregation, mobile, distributed, peer-to-peer.

He opened the video window and clicked through the stills of urban fighting. He stopped on a street backed by a scorched apartment building, mattress on the sidewalk, at the end of the block a smoking steel drum and an ancient van that could be hiding anything.

Perimeter, range, detection, protection. Survival.

Fear, defense.

Danger, fear.

Fear. Greed.

Product. Positioning. Karpos.

Shareholder. God.

That evening at the usual time, Walker pressed the remote, watched the garage door rise steadily, rolled in, and rotated out of the car. As he lifted his laptop case from the back seat, he remembered a story an engineer had told him about passing out at the wheel. He said it had felt like a flat calm. He woke up in an intersection where he had rolled, unconscious, against a red light.

It seemed something like that to Walker, how he had been typing the words and had then left his desk because the words and the desk and his position in space and time had rendered him unable to focus, sweating. He had taken the steps through the back door and over the grassy median to the lot where he always parked; he remembered that much. He had climbed into the Subaru and pulled the door shut. He remembered feeling grateful for tinted windows. He reclined the seat and breathed back into it. That was all he remembered before waking, sweating against the leather-

ette. Time had passed, but nothing to cause alarm. He
hadn't been spotted.

He was walking on his own drive, and the scent of
verbena came to him across the desert as he neared the
front door. Lynne was inside somewhere, the pin to his
tether. He stood at the door for a long moment.

He had left his car and gone back in after a time in the
wet of his sweaty, quiet benediction. He had cleaned his face
and aired out his shirt in the men's room, then returned to
his desk. He had greeted the screen saver and raised his
finger to clear it and scanned again with an odd sense of
relief the *Spectrus* key terms where he had left them, the
terms he would shape into a campaign.

He remembered those facts, enough of them. As he
raised his key to the lock, he tuned to the waveform of the
day until he could begin to understand it, to feel it coursing
through him again like water, outward bound.

"Hey there," he said as he went in. In a moment he
realized she was in a remote place in their cool, vast home
and could not hear him.

Chapter 7

"You're going to shoot birds. With a gun." Lynne was reflecting what she had heard, incredulous. "You don't have a gun."

"Dale's bringing one for me, a four-ten."

She stared.

"A shotgun."

They were in the kitchen where he had taken the call from Dale. He saw the concern.

"I shot quail when I was a kid, I thought I told you that. Same thing, four-ten, no big deal."

"Sounds fabulous."

"Don't knock it—it could come in handy. You're at Whole Foods one day—no more chicken.... I'm not saying hunting would be my first choice, but what am I going to say?"

"Because of the fishing, you mean."

It was mostly because of the fishing, he had to admit. The trip on the Humboldt River in the fall had been his idea, and all had gone well; they had made out. But it made it impossible to refuse when Dale proposed the quail hunting gig.

"Is anybody else going? Maybe you could have to work." She wasn't giving up. Clearly she thought it was a bad idea.

"Don't think so. Just us two, *contra naturam*. We'll pop off some wildlife and bear it home. How's your quail cacciatore?"

Walker replayed the work option a couple of times before Saturday, but not seriously. Dale was valuable. He moved him off his square. He was the only one of their friends who wore a cap with an Air Force insignia. As Walker stared at the glove box door, he realized he was the only one with a Right to Bear sticker. The only one with a Chevy pickup.

They were riding across flat prairie broken by an occasional arroyo, Joshua trees, and creosote bushes. Hedgehog cactus with their audacious purple blooms. They saw one jackrabbit. The last town they passed was Troublesome. The sun had been opening the sky for half an hour at most, highlighting a few bands of clouds. They had nearly reached their destination, a looming clump of foothills. Generic male country played low on the radio.

"You said you were here what, last fall?"

"October," Dale said. "Fall's supposed to be the hot time for quail, but spring can be better." Despite himself, Walker felt a ripple of anticipation. "Some use dogs, English setters and pointers, but you don't have to."

"I'll follow you. I don't want to spook them."

Dale shook his head, grinning.

"These birds don't spook. Believe me, if you remember how to aim and pull the trigger, you'll do all right."

"Ready, fire, aim."

"Right," Dale confirmed. "Great."

Walker trusted him explicitly. The fishing trip aside, that was why he had decided to go. He was what he was, a cowboy in a camouflage vest and khakis out to shoot birds. Walker thought he was about forty, maybe five years older than Marianne. He had that funny switch in the genes that made him preternaturally mature, then flipped as everyone else began sliding downhill. He was their mechanic, and if you entrust the car of your daughter and wife, you trust explicitly. Walker had not thought of it that way always. It changed the day of their breakdown in Potosi Pass.

It was the time of high soccer. Sophie was a sophomore in Boulder High, and they were returning from a regional match with Laughlin on the east side of the mountains. It was a season-ending loss, and the parents were trying to raise spirits. Walker had an Audi wagon then, and they had crested the summit in gray drizzle and were heading down. They had been coasting, and as he returned to the gas he felt nothing, no acceleration, just a glide, even as he pumped the pedal and the engine revved. In a moment it died.

He rolled to a partial turn-out on a curve and braked. He tried a couple of restarts and pointless shifting, then remembered the glove compartment and the cell phone, the size of a steam iron in those days. It had sat in the car for months, for emergency purposes only. He had fully intended to charge it the weekend before, before one thing had led to another. He dropped the compartment lid and tried the power button to no response.

On the wide downhill curve, cars and RVs coasted, banking like bobsleds. Walker turned on the flashers, got out, and stood in the drizzle trying to flag one down. Two bighorn sheep were staring at him from the opposite crest. Any other time he would be hailing the site none of them had see. Now it felt like a mockery. Lynne and Sophie wanted to join him, but at first he insisted they stay in the car. Eventually he caved in, acknowledging the advantage. By then the bighorns were gone.

When the silver Dodge Ram seemed to slow and Walker saw brake lights, he thanked God, something he had rarely done since adolescence. As the truck backed up the hill, he imagined a nonspecific beef-headed male out for a better look at Lynne in her soaked pullover. When the truck pulled even, he was surprised to see a woman behind the rain-pearled passenger window.

The driver was down and walking toward them, not tall but solid looking, sandy hair under a cap, tan chamois shirt. He introduced himself and offered to check the engine. Walker had been hoping for a cell phone or a lift and was happy to oblige to get either. He popped the hood and the guy tugged a belt then spent some time behind the radiator. He dropped the hood and came back with his diagnosis: timing belt.

Walker thought the damsels in distress may have been the main factor. Whatever the reason, Dale offered to tow them down. Walker insisted on paying him, but his only request was that they tow to his garage. He could do the job the next day.

Walker understood that nothing outstanding would happen for the rest of the year. This was his ration of luck. A mechanic had appeared in a vision. Dale trudged up the curve above them and placed a flare, then backed the Ram into position and hooked them to a tow hitch.

The lady on the passenger side was his wife Marianne, who balanced Jessie, nearly two, on her knee. They all squeezed in, Walker and Sophie in the rumble seat.

In twenty minutes they were down the mountain and inside Roadrunner Motors. After dropping the Audi, Dale concluded by driving them home. The next day Walker and Lynne ordered a weekend getaway package for them at Caesars Tahoe.

That was the beginning of the friendship. While she was in high school, Sophie sat a few times for Jessie. The Beales and the Wilsons shared a dinner or two, but they shared less common interest than a simple bond. Walker wanted to keep that alive.

"That it?" he asked.

"That whole stand. And around to the left there."

Walker saw a broad span of junipers interspersed with clumps of silver-green creosote. Not a bird in sight. Behind the trees foothills tumbled back toward the mountains.

They pulled up in a flat of tumbleweed and climbed down. The air was still cool, fresh with earth and plant smells. He looked up at the foothills washed in morning light, the colors vivid: tan, sienna, and spring green.

"This one's yours," Dale said from the back of the truck with the tailgate down. He was extending a belt and what

Walker recognized as a shell pouch. Dale opened a box of four-ten shells and Walker filled it. Then Dale turned to one of the two black scabbards, unzipped it, and drew out one of the shotguns.

"Remember how to load?" He grinned, handing it over.

Walker took the long weight in his hand and glanced along the perfectly straight barrel, sleek, the greyhound of shotguns. It smelled of oil.

Dale had his belt on, and he drew his gun out of the bag. He closed the tailgate softly. Then he slipped the strap of the canvas game bag over his shoulder and led the way toward the foothills and the junipers.

When they reached the trees, they stopped and focused on the sounds. Behind the insect jabber they heard cooing. Dale grinned and nodded. It reminded Walker of fishing at sun-up, cruising on glass and spotting a ruffle of baitfish in the distance. They loaded quietly then worked their way into the creosote bushes dotted with yellow blooms and then into the trees.

Just inside the cover of branches they crouched down, six feet apart. Walker was heady with the pure air that smelled rich with morning earth and dew-moist green. He checked the safety. Still on.

They heard cooing again in the distance and Walker scanned the trees. They looked empty, nothing moving. Dale was scanning too.

Walker had the sudden unsettling image of his shotgun blowing up in his face. What if it misfired? He had no idea what he was holding, an alien gun. It could be any machine randomly selected for human targeting on the basis of one defect. He trusted it only because his mechanic had put it in his hands.

Dale was down in the posture of the hunter, squatting with his thunder stick. He was in his element, Walker saw, watching the trees under his Air Force cap. If his four-ten went up in his face, he would adjust. They had different concepts of danger, as though they were different words, in parallel worlds.

Dale's arm went up suddenly. He was pointing at a tree in the front of the stand.

"Bottom limb," he whispered.

Walker picked out the small dark body on the bare limb. He guessed sixty or seventy yards away.

"Look under."

In the brown grass and hackberry below the limb, Walker could make out several other dark forms the same size bobbing and righting themselves, foraging.

"You want him?" Dale whispered. Walker guessed he meant the one in the tree.

"Go ahead," Walker said.

"Okay, when I shoot that covey's going to flush. You'll have your pick. All right?"

Walker nodded.

Dale turned back to the limb and the shotgun barrel came up. The safety clicked off.

Walker raised his gun quietly and peered through the rear notch to the front brass bead sight to an approximate square above the grass. The second stretched into more. He glanced at Dale who seemed to be waiting until he was one with the gun, crouching, still as a held breath.

The blast went through Walker like cold lightning. Knowing it was coming was no defense. He saw a burst of dust and feathers on the limb and the quail's body tumble down. The brown grass erupted with half a dozen birds churning into the air.

He was rising with them, charged with adrenalin from Dale's shot. He tried to steady the gun. He picked up a darting body, wings beating furiously, arcing away. It was in the sight, crossing the sight. Lead him, he thought. He squeezed the trigger.

That nothing at all happened was puzzling only as long as it took the brain to interpret the trigger, nonfunctional, frozen under his fingertip. In the moment that it took him to curse himself and click the safety off, the quail had dispersed. Immediately two more rose in the target zone. He swung the barrel toward one heading for the trees and fired. The blast and recoil hit him and he stood stunned, as though looking for a hole in the sky.

Dale was laughing insanely. "What is this, shoot and release?"

Walker waited for a rejoinder in the midst of humiliation. It did not come. "I figured it was too easy, watching you," he said.

The air was full of the powder smell. Dale was shaking his head, still laughing. He uncoiled to his feet.

"Let's get him," he said and started across the field. Walker reset the safety with sickening humility and set out through the grass. He wondered about his hearing after the fusillade and tested it against the grasshoppers and crickets. Still there. He and Dale searched in the grass under the limb.

"Not a monster but okay." Dale presented the chestnut body the size of a medium takeout cup. The perfectly circular black spot on its breast merged with blood. Its head lolled back.

"Gambel's quail, highly okay. Baked, stuffed with some rice pilaf. We'll have you over." Dale flashed a smile and Walker tried to catch his enthusiasm. He lifted the flap on the game bag and settled the quail in.

"Now let's get about half a dozen more," he said. "We can go in here and set up. They'll be around."

Dale headed for another crescent of trees behind heavy grass. They waded in past clumps of columbine and settled in between junipers and live oak and waited.

This time the birds came to them. Dale and Walker picked them up at the same time, fifty feet or so in front of the tree line. Dale's gun came up, then Walker's. He clicked the safety off and checked it.

"Take yours out of the left side," Dale whispered. "I'll go right, try to flush them. They like to stay on the ground. On three." He counted down. Walker had his bird in his sight.

Three was a sharp whistle that cut across the grass, and the quail were running briefly and then they were up. Dale might have fired first, but Walker's shot was like an echo. Other birds ran and fluttered out of the ground. Lead it, he thought, lead it. He pumped and fired again. Two birds went down, one on each end of the covey.

"Hey, hey!" Dale praised. As they walked in, Walker felt a disconcerting mixture of relief and exhilaration. He hefted the compact weight of feathers with its wing blown off, limp neck, black plume on its head, and tried to imagine how he could have hit it. If he bagged nothing else all day, he could still claim victory. He passed it to Dale who dropped it matter-of-factly into the bag on top of his.

"They say fall's the season, but there's three in twenty minutes. Not too shabby."

Walker nodded, knowing that he with his gun was a paper titan. As he had blown down the quail, so might the great blind archer take him down. He thought of going as the quail had gone, in a heartbeat. It was better to vaporize than linger. Better to rock than rust.

"There's a place around that bend. It's an indent, fan-shaped. There's a grassy patch there. That covey came through there first."

They headed for the end of the tree line, and Walker was on the lookout for birds now that he knew what to look for, dark bodies in the straw grass. The hunter had been wakened. He checked the ground by his shoes, his leg, for any corkscrew rustling in the grass. Rattler. They were a ways out, fifty yards or so from the point of trees. Could be worse than nerve death by venom in a grassy, godforsaken country of birds. It was their territory anyway, long before humans or prehumans. He was watching for the slithering and the diamond head in the grass when he heard it.

At first the low rumble seemed like drumming inside the mountain. Then it changed to a low frequency throbbing.

"Where is it?" Walker asked, even as it was coming to him. The answer was coming like thunder in the heavy whip of helicopter blades.

The chopper swung over the low end of the mountain, behind the spot where they had fired first. In a second it was over them, two hundred feet or less, thundering pulses.

They dropped back. Walker was thinking of heading for the trees, but the white State Police lettering on the dark blue body stopped him. The helicopter hung over them, and it was suddenly clear to him that it would pass them by, racing on to its real target. As expected it yawed, tilted its fan, and banked away. But as they watched, it turned and looped back under the path it had taken out. Walker felt horror rising as it approached them dead-on. It was setting down. When the bank of compressed air and dust hit them, they nearly buckled.

It was on the ground a safe distance away, but the blades continued their thundering spin, chewing air, flattening the grass around them and whipping their clothes. In the cradle of Walker's elbow, his shotgun drifted sideways toward Dale and he pulled it back. The blades settled into a lazy rotation.

"This is Nevada State Patrol." The blast from the chopper's bullhorn froze them. "Put your guns on the ground and step back."

It felt to Walker like penny-ante intimidation, and he knew how to deal with that based on his resources and friends, property, an attorney he had used once, and his rights as a citizen. He had done nothing wrong. He could nail them. He could also comply for the same reasons. Dale was laying his gun down. Walker was surprised and pleased that he had not been the first. He laid his on the grass, out of the sand.

"Step away from the guns." The bullhorn blasted again and they stepped back.

The door swung open and a patrolman climbed down, khakis and cap. A second followed. They advanced on Walker and Dale, hands on their pistol butts above black holsters. They stepped around the shotguns.

"Do you have ID?" the one on Walker's side asked. He was the stockier of the two, heavy arms below short sleeves. Football at state, Walker imagined. They both wore black aviator goggles under tan caps with Texas-style white stars.

"Why? What's the problem?" Walker said.

"What are you guys doin' out here?" the other asked, louder. My question, Walker heard, is bigger than your question. He also heard a note of southwest, Texas or Oklahoma hick.

"Quail hunting, that's all," Dale said. "Right here." He reached for the game sack, and the officer lifted his pistol butt a perceptible inch. Dale raised his right hand, open palm. He lifted the top of the game bag with his left and turned his hip toward the officer. They both glanced in.

"ID, please," the linebacker repeated.

Walker extended his wallet.

"Take it out, please."

He removed it and Dale did the same. As the officer studied them it occurred to Walker that he could easily ask for hunting licenses next. Dale would have his, of course. What would the fine be, fifty, a hundred? Under the long moment he became aware of the blades' final rotations, guttural.

After a long, officious study by the first officer and then the other, they returned the plastic squares. They stared back at the hunters, black-eyed, bug-eyed.

"What's the deal?"

Dale had opened the door.

"We live in this area," Walker said, "as you can see." He held up the license like a flashcard. "So if there's something happening here that we should know...this would be an excellent time."

It was enough. He had not gone too far. He was within his rights and they were kids, punks.

"There are two fugitives loose in the area," the smaller one said. "They hit the containment camp at four in the morning, released a lot of prisoners. Enemy combatants. We got all those right away, but there was five intruders total. We got three."

Walker flashed on the holding compound. Since it was put into service, it had been a magnet for exposé. The pipe beatings had graduated to another level. A death had been under investigation for months. Terrorists. The euphemism for undoc aliens.

"Good luck," Dale said.

"We'll flush 'em," the linebacker said, and Walker nearly appreciated the hunting metaphor, then realized it was only dumb. The two turned and stepped around the shotguns. The chopper blades restarted as they neared and ducked, and then they were inside.

Walker and Dale felt the blast of air and watched the helicopter rising out of a bloom of dust. The chopper banked around the far side of the mountain. They stooped to retrieve the guns.

"Sand?" Dale asked. He blew on the action.

"Looks pretty clean." Walker blew a few grains off the magazine. "That was different. Nothing like being pulled over by a swat team to scare you shitless."

Dale didn't respond. He was inspecting the four-ten. Then he looked up, shook his head, looked away toward the trees. He seemed different.

"They need to get..." He trailed off.

Walker watched him move a few steps to the side. He was looking at the trees in such a way that Walker had the strange sense he was seeing the simple light in all of its colors.

"Not animals," he said. "We might say those kind are animals, but that's wrong. Hawks don't let the snakes loose. We've got kids." He was searching. "How do we handle it..." He raised the shotgun.

Walker watched the barrel come up parallel to the ground, aimed toward the mountain. Before he could pick out the target the shotgun blasted, and a branch dropped from a live oak at the front of the stand. He fired again and a branch powdered. Again. When he lowered the shotgun, they watched the maimed tree emerge from the fog of smoke. After a long moment Dale turned.

"Let's pack it in," he said.

They rode most of the way back without talking.

"That place was shot to hell," Dale said finally. "With that chopper it might not be any good until fall." It sounded weak, but whether it was true or not, Walker had no way to know. But he was right, there was no going back.

When they reached Dale's house, Walker spent longer than he would have chosen being sociable, hanging onto a beer. They rehashed the state patrol episode for Marianne, and although Walker quickly confirmed Dale's opinion that there was no danger, he was thinking about Lynne. He declined the invitation to stay for lunch, and when he could excuse himself, he left his lonesome quail in Marianne's care.

On the way home he called and she answered, no tragedy. He told her to keep everything locked as an extra precaution. He ended the call, punched the radio, and half-listened on the way home.

Less than a mile from his garage it was there, the breaking story. He pulled over, killed the engine, and boosted the volume.

Following a chase on the ground and by air, two fugitives were killed in a gun battle with Nevada State Patrol.

The group responsible for storming the Goodsprings containment camp were all accounted for, in custody or dead.

As Walker rolled into the garage under the rising door, he wondered if Lynne would notice the smell of gunpowder smoke on him. It seemed to be everywhere.

Chapter 8

Margo inspected the shiny blue fenders and twin chrome tailpipes of the Mitsubishi Freelancer for another two seconds, which was two seconds more than she could stand. She closed the issue of "Road and Track" and reconsidered the choices on the end table. "Extreme Specialties: Trucks," "Sports Afield," "Guns and Ammo," flyers from MusicMaster Audio for car stereo systems. The choices had not changed in the three minutes since "Road and Track" had been the least bad option.

She rechecked her watch against the clock behind the counter. Five twenty-six. Bob Conlin, one of the sixth-grade teachers, had dropped her off at five past five. Her car was supposed to be ready. She heard a phone hang up somewhere, in a back office or the shop. There was muffled conversation, possibly about her car. She listened, holding her breath. Nothing. Then the door in the rear of the office opened.

"Okay, Margo," Dale began. "We've got a new water pump. We replaced the belt, and you had a cracked radiator hose."

Easy enough to believe, she thought as she perused the invoice. Her radiator hose could indeed have been cracked. It sounded to her like a country song. She presented her card and fingertip for scanning.

Dale watched the scan and waited for her confirmation and receipt. Margo noticed that they were almost the same height. Sandy-haired, handsome in a grubby mechanical way, he smelled like oil. Her eyes drifted past him to the back wall past a framed American flag to a photo of a monster truck. It reared over a smashed barricade, leading with a six-foot tire, cab wrapped in roll bars. Overcompensating for penis size, she mused. A cliché, but one she could live with.

Why was she in Roadrunner Motors at all? It was embarrassing. On Walker's recommendation, of course.

"Hybrids," he said. "They always take longer. But we got yours done today."

"That's great, I really appreciate it." She forced the enthusiasm, but she had to admit it could have been worse. Dale had done her a favor by slipping her in that morning and had finished if not under the wire, at least around it. She was half-expecting it to dribble over to another day with the hassle of another connection. Luckily, the part had come in and it was the right part, twin miracles. The things she wound up being thankful for.

Margo worked her key back onto her ring and thanked her cowboy mechanic again on the other side of the counter. Soon Roadrunner Motors was in her rear-view. Five thirty-five.

She picked up the two-lane county line road that was the shortest route to Cathy's place. She would be there by six if the car behaved, and it seemed fine. He was a redneck but he could fix cars. Would she rather have a redneck mechanic and a purring car or a well-intentioned kindred spirit and another trip to the garage? It had happened before, she recalled. She had picked her mechanics on intuition. Now, for a saner experience, she had Walker to thank.

She found his friendship with Dale implausible. Lynne was more skeptical, she knew that. Walker himself was hard enough to figure. Margo had liked him from the start, even felt smitten a bit in the early days. He had worked with Ken at Vericom, and their friendship with the Beales began by the pool of Margo's old house, the suburban sprawler that never fit her East Coast idea of a home. She liked Lynne, her energy and good sense, but she appreciated more what Lynne saw in Walker, even if that was difficult to say exactly.

She imagined it was what most women saw in him, an open door. Part of him seemed rootless, incomplete in some yearning way. To any woman up for a challenge, that could be irresistible. The first thing Ken had told her about him was that he was a smart guy, creative. The second was that he could seem distracted but not to take it personally, it was just his way.

She was anything but offended. In fact she was charmed, so that she caught herself thinking about him at random moments. Those thoughts were soon obscured by the smoke of her own life with Ken, which had already begun to smolder destructively. But after all of those combustible days, it was still the charming part of Walker she thought of first, the one that resisted decoding and that pulled you in. She was well aware there was an odd one in there too, the one scratching off around the blasted car and the line of gawkers as though he had been scorched by the same fire. So be it, she knew, she felt.

The forty-five-mile-per-hour traffic tightened to twenty, then to a stop. The reason was several cars lengths ahead, on foot. An unlikely troupe of pedestrians emerged from between the cars onto the shoulder. The traffic was rolling again, and in a moment she saw them. In shabby clothes, they were half-stepping from the shoulder down onto the plain, two men and a woman with two small children in tow. She glanced past them across the flat and saw what she already knew was there.

Nearly a mile in from the road lay Settlement City. Tents and homes made of scavenged lumber and sheetrock looked like a scattering of irregular blocks on the plain. The five were heading home, from where or what Margo couldn't tell, probably from foraging, probably not from jobs, however menial. She tried to recall when those kinds of encampments had become common. They were like a breakout that healthy minds repressed, blemishes below consciousness. She could recall when a band of squatters in a park in Las

Vegas made the news. Now they were a factor in every city, in parks and streets and doorways and wherever an abandoned building could be found. Delhi, she thought for a moment. Jakarta.

Traffic was picking up speed. In a few moments the tent city was behind her in one of the many zones of discomfort that she could visit but do nothing about. She took a breath of the air off the plain, warm but fresh through the window. She focused on Cathy's place and rolled on through the flawless evening.

As she turned off the county line road, she was excited as a kid. In a few moments she was in the patch of trees that overhung the road, the sudden bower she anticipated, the portal to the underworld of things impromptu and thrilling. Beyond the trees the road rose gradually, and then she was on the home stretch. She spotted Cathy's building, one of two white tri-level structures, condo pueblos, sitting starkly at the top of a short hill.

"Hey, Baby." Cathy gave her a wraparound squeeze at the door at the top of the steps. As inviting as her firmness and bright smile was the waft of air conditioning. Margo entered the cool grotto, undercover life. She could claim innocence no longer. She knew where she was and she accepted it, welcomed it.

"Long week?" Cathy asked, relieving Margo of her overnight bag. She carried it briefly to the bedroom. "Same here. We expelled a kid today." She flashed a deadpan smile. "He put a video of himself on the Net mutilating a stuffed toy, life-sized. It was an effigy of Deke Willis, his physics teacher. All his own work, mind you. Very creative."

"I don't know how you do high school."

"I'd say it's a living, but... Listen, sit. I've got Viña Undurraga, should be almost frozen by now."

Margo grinned at the thought of the funny greenish wine. It was a topic when they first met, at a conference in Albuquerque. In the anonymous Sheraton, they had shared trips to Spain in earlier lives. They had both loved it. Cathy focused on Ibiza and Formentera, the sun-blazed islands the white of communion wafers, her first year out of college. Margo recalled her ultimate city, Barcelona, its fantastic gothic boulevard of bird cages and *tableaux vivants*, the exotic counterpoise to the Boston outskirts of her youth. In those days the Chilean Viña Undurraga in its squattish bottle had thrilled them both.

Margo watched Cathy heading toward the kitchen in her burgundy T-shirt and white drawstrings that fanned gracefully around her strides. The sight of her brought back the feeling of her firmness, a sense of her natural poise. Margo saw her as a rock climber, defying gravity as her forty-year-old body had.

She went to the picture window and gazed out and down over the greening hill toward the access road she had just driven. It was a panorama compared to her own foreshort-ened view of live oaks. The whole feel of Cathy's condo was different too—southwest style, red, black, ochre, and burnt orange, a leather sofa and the leather-covered bucket chairs, tan *equipajes*, made tolerable for sitting by red cushions.

The main difference between Cathy's place and her own was a double negative, no emptiness. Despite the spare landscape and white walls with O'Keefe prints, Cathy's world brought connection and comfort. Even before the split from Ken, and decidedly after it, despite students and affirmative parents and awards, and stuffed animal surrogates, she had been in a long *pas de deux* with emptiness. Cathy had cut through it emotionally and physically, and it was an amazement to Margo to be the object of someone's desire again on both levels.

Cathy joined her with the greenish yellow wine in her green-stemmed German wine glasses that she called fascist. They went to the sofa and commiserated over their common grief, students and the entrapments of their times. Margo bemoaned cursing and sniffing aerosol cleaners. Cathy focused on the knife fight in the high school parking lot and the bomb threats that seemed to start earlier each spring. And the tedium of grading was lessened, like it or not. The district was sending more to India. They talked through another glass as the sun declined in an orange blaze. Cathy's legs were akimbo as she half-reclined.

They sat down to an antipasto glittering with oil, dried tomatoes, black olives, cheese, camponara, and crustini bread. Margo felt the strain of the week dissolving. Cathy's face was replacing it, her blue-gray eyes with tom-boy wrinkles at the corners. She wondered what Cathy saw in her. *She* was the athlete, the physically cultured one. What did Margo bring but support that she would call motherly, even though there were only four years between them. She preferred to imagine herself as the older sister Cathy never had.

"Okay, you ready?" Dinner was done and Cathy was gleefully aiming the remote at the TV, bare feet far apart on the rug like a gunfighter.

"What do we have?" Margo asked, moving to the sofa. They had both finished three glasses, and she was feeling a warm oneness with the air.

"I know you're not crazy about scary movies, but this is not horror, I promise."

Cathy had clicked and the title was already coming up.

Panic Room, Margo read.

"It's retro. You haven't seen it, right? Good, it's primo Jodi Foster. Wait 'til you see her."

As they both knew, Margo did not care greatly about Cathy's cinematic objects of desire. That was in the realm of their mutual acceptance. She relished much more sitting next to her on the sofa in the dark as Jodi, trim and terrified, outpaced her attackers with agility and cunning.

Their shoulders were together and Cathy's hand was on her thigh.

"She's wearing drawstring pants like you," Margo said.

Cathy glanced at her sideways a moment, then she stood up.

"Not anymore," she said. She pulled the end of one string and then they were off. She was standing before Margo as she had never stood before anyone but had wanted to, pantyless and trim, the curves of buttocks and thighs irreproducible in any form other than human flesh or marble.

Margo wanted to reach out and touch the perfection at the same time that she was awed by it. Cathy moved first. She bent down and opened the tie on the front of the blouse that Margo had worn purposely, in anticipation of that very moment. Then she felt Cathy's hand slip inside her bra, and she was bending close, the scent of her shampoo, and as her breast was lifted over the light cup, the first touch of Cathy's tongue on her nipple. Margo was more voluptuous than her partner, and it felt so strangely wonderful. She raised Cathy's head, gently but steadily pushed her shoulders back, and relished her surprised look. Then she pulled open the buttons on the bottom of her blouse and slipped it off. She unhooked the bra and let her breasts fall. Cathy was on them hungrily, delightedly, on the sofa beside her.

As usual, Margo was hesitant, but then she reached behind Cathy and took her buttock in her hand. As she had before, she closed her eyes and allowed herself to imagine it was a man's, and in a moment she was comfortable enough to ease into its smooth, supple firmness. When she was ready, she filled both hands. Then with Cathy on her and her heat against her, Margo dropped her last resistance. She was outside herself finally, the reason she had come.

In the last minutes before they turned out the lights, and with Cathy in the bathroom, Margo took a silent moment to study the photos on her dresser. She had seen them before but not closely.

The first was an outside shot with her mom and dad, obviously years ago, Cathy in her girlie pullover with flowers, much to Margo's amusement. Iowa, she assumed, where by her own admission Cathy had floundered through Davenport High. The photo beside it was a fuzz-headed guy smiling widely under dark ski shades with Yosemite's El Capitan in the background, which he looked well prepared to scale. He fit the description Cathy had given of her brother. The photo on the other side was a more enigmatic black and white of two subjects. One was clearly Cathy, although perhaps a decade younger, hair longer. Beside her a curly-haired brunette with a strong, self-assured expression, nearly diffident. Not a sister, Margo knew that much.

She thought of leaving the light on for Cathy but decided to kill it. As she slipped under the sheet and white cotton blanket, she tested why. It may have been that she felt comfortable enough to do what she wanted, which was to lie there in the complete dark. Or it could have been the adrenalin shot triggered by, what else could she call it but jealousy? As she started to wonder *how could she possibly*, Cathy was out of the bathroom.

"Oh," she said.

"The light was so fucking bright," Margo said partly drunk, partly freed by her revived senses and out of character. They both laughed and Cathy was in bed then, kissing her firmly and with her tongue in recognition of the new bit of freedom that had sprouted between them. They rolled onto their backs and chatted quietly before sleep. Margo was smiling to herself. She had been right to kill the light, jealous or not. It was a true act. For that knowledge of rightness she thanked the lovers of the past, in history and at peace.

When Margo woke, chest pounding in the darkness, she was sure it was something she had heard. She checked Cathy. She was turned away, curves of shoulder and hip, lying still.

She held her breath and tuned to the lightest creak or any sign of movement. Only the smooth rotation of the ceiling fan. Then behind the fan, a dull murmur, barely perceptible. She fastened on it, the slightest hint of a deep drone that seemed to be receding. Extra-terrestrial. In the pit of the night, that seemed suddenly plausible. If she had gone on sleeping, would it have abducted them? She needed to get a grip. She propped on one elbow and squinted over Cathy at the numerals. One-forty.

She settled onto her back and listened again to the fan. There was nothing else. The aliens had come and expressed no interest. But as she knew all too well, that was only part of the equation. The few times that Margo and Cathy had slept together were not enough to go from a hard wake-up to relaxed. They had an agreement, which Margo had proposed. Either of them was free to leave in the night, at any time. It was an expression of the core principle of their relationship—freedom, especially from expectations. It was somewhat unrealistic, they both knew, but they shared it as one piece of a great undimensionable ideal.

She wanted to stay, to show Cathy they were close. At the same time she knew that she would lose a couple of hours, probably more. She preferred not to be catatonic on Saturday. It occurred to her that both options were selfish, perhaps one more than the other. She thought of her own place and the loneliness that drove her to Cathy in the beginning. The emptiness had been filled, at least for a while. She could return and get a good sleep. She listened again for any sound beyond the ceiling fan until she was wide awake. She uncovered quietly and slipped from the bed.

She gathered her clothes and shoes and bag, checked and focused in the quiet on anything else she may have left, then found her way downstairs. Irrationally, she went into the bathroom, too bright, chrome and frosted glass. When she had dressed she wrote a short note, signed with a sketch of a teddy bear, a joke they shared. She climbed back up to the hum of the fan and left it just inside the bedroom door.

Back downstairs she unlocked the front door quietly and stepped out. She reset the lock, pulled it shut, and tested it. Cathy would be safe. Less safe than behind a cyber lock like her own, but it would have to do for the four hours until sunrise when all demons were dispersed.

She checked the sky for alien spacecraft then crossed the gravel to her car, silver and dew-filmed under the pale light from a slice of moon. In a moment she was back on the two-lane road descending toward the patch of trees. Her window was down and the night air bathed her, cool and fresh. In another few minutes she was on the county line highway with one distant set of tail lights ahead.

She had the odd sense that she was a free adult, answerable to no one else. She had gone into her otherworld and was returning, eyes open. Her own apartment seemed anything but hollow, even inviting. The next day, Saturday, she would sleep late.

She heard a rumbling sound and thought first of the car, but it was somewhere outside the car. It was like water, a heavy wave, distant. Then it was building like low thunder, sustaining itself. A burst of white light hit the road in front of her. Before she could brake or swerve, she was in it. On either side of the car the road shoulders glared chalk-white.

She felt the pulsing of the thunder in the wheel and seat and the pedal. The painful brightness kept pace with her. She had gone out too far. The natural order, which cared nothing about how good a person you were in your own trifling system of values, would have its revenge.

In the next second as she hit the brake, she understood. It was the same frequency laid bare, unmixed with any other, as though the sound man had dropped all tracks but one. It was the same droning that had wakened her, softened then by the ceiling fan. The raw beat of the helicopter weighed down on her solitary, halted car, flooding it relentlessly with light. The blinding white source poured through her windshield. She clamped her eyes shut.

In a few moments the light on her lids changed. The thunder weakened and the white light dropped, and as she opened her eyes and adjusted, she saw red warning lights on the tail and struts of the chopper. It floated higher to the top of the windshield then banked away. She watched until it was gone. In seconds Margo was sitting in silence except for the engine's hum.

Which agency? she wondered. At one time, perhaps even last year, she would have assumed state, probably transportation. Now Fed Sec was more likely. One of the recon choppers everyone read reports of but rarely saw. They were looking for somebody, but not her. She played through the possibilities: secessionist bomber driving a hybrid, Union Fundamentalist avengers of the good reverend who-the-hell Canliss, one of a thousand high-school-age kids sleeping in doorways and alleys, a south LA refugee in the exodus from the race war wanted for cracking windows in Vegas Heights or Xanadu.

Headlights appeared far back in the rear-view. Margo was off the brake and onto the accelerator gingerly, rolling and then picking up speed. She wanted the news and reached for the radio buttons, fast-firing through the ads and talk. She hit Off and rolled and tried to breathe deeply, at the bottom of the lungs. Instead of tuning to the news outside, she tried inside, her own body, which was tightening.

Changes, nearly imperceptible, until all had changed. Not the same country, even at its most struggling and quarrelsome. Changes, she realized simply, rationally. She could adapt. She had. She could survive in the world of her own creation. She had Cathy. Most of all she had her students. She was fortunate. She imagined what it was like for those who had no one, alone for whatever reason in the cold fight, in the emptiness.

She spotted the string of lights off the driver's side, a glowing thread. It could have been a night mirage. As she drew closer the lights separated into clusters, the homes of Settlement City. She had passed the end of the lights when the sky over them seemed to open with a white cone. From that distance she could just hear the dull rotation of the blades. In a moment the sound was gone from her window.

She punched the radio again until a jazz station came in, smoky and cool. In her mirror the cone seemed to be moving down the line, making its way over the bivouac of refugees. She tilted the reflection down and away. Under the merciless light, itinerants were lurching from a few hours of sleep. Children were crying in their beds. She felt rage rising like a personal explosive in her chest.

Margo resolved not to give in. Instead she would tune to the improvisatory cool, and to her necessary things. She was aware of her aura, which rage could puncture. She had not gone out too far, she understood. It was not any fault of hers. She checked her dashboard clock and then focused on the road in the headlights. She took two deep breaths and trusted to she knew not what. She dropped her hands to her thighs and let fate take it, spiriting her through the dark.

Chapter 9

"In five heads you can get fifty guys to piss in ten minutes." It was Roeneke. Walker didn't need to see him. They were in the same cell.

"How do I know? I'll tell you. When I was a louie, I had to time the breaks. And when I was a buck private I had latrine duty like everybody else. I cleaned those goddamn holes. Nobody knows better, believe me. That's when I knew grunt was not the way to go."

A loud laugh from Karpos, a suck-up-and-sell laugh. Walker heard nothing from Mayes, Roeneke's poodle, although he knew they were all in the same space. Walker wondered if the programmer from their side had a rank, or some other half-civie tag.

"Reminds me of the Guard," Karpos said at the sink. "Bangor, Maine. Froze my balls off."

Walker saw Roeneke's back in khaki through the slit at the stall door hinge. Mayes crossed the line of sight. Walker tried to focus on Karpos's tone as he went on, his normal voice adjusted to Roeneke's vibration. Suck up and sell. The towel dispensers buzzed twice for each. In a minute they were out the door.

He listened until it was safe to stand. In earlier years he might have dedicated a demoralizing moment or two to wondering how it had all—meaning the quixotic chain reaction of his career—come to this. Now he was beyond that. He was focused on the finish line and what it would take to get there. He caught a glimpse of himself in the mirror over the top of the stall door.

Under merciless tiny recessed halogen bulbs, his scalp reflected white through his hair. He envisioned it as a software simulation of his future state. He looked like another person, an old man. The image could not be true. It was the lights.

At the sink he surveyed his features. Out of the overheads, his scalp lost some of its sheen. Below the base of the forehead where the lines were deepest, his eyes seemed okay, not yet weary and wondering. Questing perhaps. Pale blue and five decades old, they seemed younger than the rest of his face. Pencil lines hatched the corners of his eyes, work of the eternal sketch master. He raised his chin, reasserting a decent jaw line. He turned his head left then right, aware of the ways the years had pushed and pulled his Janus face, capturing the trace of every forced smile. He looked closer, trying to get back the stark overhead clarity of the years to come. For the first forty years or so you play offense. Sometime later you switch to defense. So what. Do what you will, destiny tints the chromosomes.

The door opened. He splashed water on his hands and checked the mirror. One of the new kids. He had seen him before but didn't know his name. Bronze t-shirt and chrome earphones. One of the influx of testers hired when Xynapse went public. Most of them hoped to make developer, and a few probably would. Alpha and omega they were, he thought as he tore off a hand towel. Not alpha and omega. The kid at the start of his career. Not now, but soon enough if all went well, competing with programmers in Bangladesh and Zaire. He thought of Sophie, international studies major, and felt better about that direction, although he was less than sure how he would defend it.

Walker punched the door and checked his BerryPod then started the inevitable march to Sausalito. The conference room was toward the end of the hall, and as he reached the open door the lights were already down. The only illumination was the projection from David Montoya's notebook.

"Walker!" Don Karpos said. "Glad you could make it. Colonel, I believe you've met—"

"The colonel and I go back to the beginning. Good to see you again." As Walker shook Roeneke's meat pad he was thinking of the first presentation in D.C. He and Ivan and Dave to the Council of Colonels in a cold auditorium of Mussolinean proportions. In those days *Spectrus* had a different name, an acronym he would have to work to recall. They showed a loose combination of three games with car chases, two in decimated inner cities. High velocity three-D rotations to tweak simple minds.

The colonel, aside from his regular gray flat-top and khakis with shoulder bars, did not look the part. He was less than imposing, perhaps six feet but no taller, and medium weight. His face had an Okie randomness, slightly bugging eyes and a space between his incisors. He introduced his code monkey Lieutenant Mayes, who was not in khakis but a crisp blue button-down and slacks. He seemed more like an usher in a megachurch, sandy-haired, pale and scrubbed looking, not yet thirty. They had met before in D.C. but Walker didn't mention it, just shook the kid's hand. He could see that Mayes remembered too, although his boss did not because no interaction of a geek lieutenant would make a dot on his superior radar. Mayes looked depressed, and that was not good for an usher.

His counterpart, Dave Montoya, sat back toward them at the demo machine. With gleaming black shoulder-length hair and trimmed beard, Dave could have been a lead player in a Texicali band. He had condescended to wear a sports shirt for the occasion.

"Colonel, and Lieutenant Mayes, we asked you to come out to our turf to see what Dave has done." Karpos was beginning softly, tactfully. He would frame the demo, maybe more. "Instead of a Qcast we wanted an f2f because we felt it was important for you to get the real feel that field personnel will have when it's deployed. We can answer your questions right here. If you want to see some what-ifs, maybe Dave can do some things to the program real-time. He loves it when I volunteer him like that." Karpos grinned as though they shared the joke. Dave rocked back as though he was laughing but Walker knew he was not. He doubted they had exchanged six words.

"The last version you saw was scaled to the headset. Today we'll see all new content on the big screen. Any questions before we start?"

"Where's the popcorn?"

Roeneke's wit. Karpos was grinning widely, to the cracking point. Walker forced a chuckle, hating himself. Karpos attempted a rejoinder about last week's popcorn from the break room. Walker felt the effect of tiny bursts of acid in his stomach and turned to the blank screen in front of Dave. It was like a reprieve, a Zen garden of silica dust and temperance.

"Dave," Karpos nodded surrendering the floor. He stepped to the wall and dimmed the lights. Roeneke and Mayes sat in the front, and Walker was finally free to migrate to the back. He sat quietly in the center of a row, appearing perfectly positioned to critique the presentation. In a moment at the opposite end of the room, the screen filled with *Spectrus*.

The view was uphill, a street of bricks, some broken. Time-worn facades two and three stories high flanked both sides. Whether they were businesses or apartment buildings was hard to tell. All looked deserted. Steel grates covered the ground floor windows, and the sky between the buildings was steely and menacing. Walker had seen it all before.

He retrieved his BerryPod from his pocket and pressed the Dolby Disc onto his neck behind his ear. On the screen at the end of the room, he noted the shadow move on the roof of the second building right and admired the craftsmanship, precise. They missed it, he assumed, and the next seconds of no reaction confirmed it.

He scanned the menu and went to the title and the end-stop marker. He mashed the button with his thumb and was rewarded. He sat back in a state of near perfection in the semi-dark.

On the tiny screen Barbara Stanwyck reclined into the sofa in her liquid satin gown. Fred MacMurray focused on her anklet, weighing his chances.

There was a white flash from the roof and then a fugue of flashes and staccato pocks. The sniper's shots whined past them and circled the room in the demo speakers. Walker saw Roeneke and Mayes recoil instinctively in their seats.

As sudden as the sniper's shots, another shot answered. A backbone of sparks arced toward the roof, and a bloom of white burst on the roof of the building.

"Yeah, shitchyeah!" Roeneke erupted in the front row, and both senior and subordinate were pumping their fists. As close, Walker imagined, as they had ever been. Dave Montoya had pressed the red button on top of the joystick and brought them both to ecstasy. Such was the power of *Spectrus*. It pleased Walker to see them reduced, dominated by a well crafted illusion, an act of imagination.

He refocused on the small screen where Barbara entertained Fred. In the black and white grotto of her living room, the air between them crackled, even in the micro format of the BerryPod. It was *Double Indemnity*, the first meeting between Walter and Mrs. Dietrickson.

A third of the way up the hill, two guerillas broke from an alley on the left, black jackets and ski masks, white rapid-fire pocks straight at the player. Dave tossed two ropes of fire, incinerating them. Easy shots.

A dull cheer went up from Roeneke and his poodle. They were still hooked, that was the important thing.

Walker jumped to the start and scanned the sequences. He punched one of his favorites, when Barton Keyes introduces the little man inside.

"Because my little man tells me," Edward G. Robinson said behind Walker's ear.

"What little man?" the unwitting Garlopis asked.

"The little man in here." Keyes tapped his belly. "Every time one of those phonies comes along, he ties knots in my stomach. And yours was one of them, Garlopis." The scam artist was caught, chilled. "That's how I knew your claim was crooked."

"Oh, shit," Roeneke declaimed. Walker knew he had seen the Bad Max car. Edward G. Robinson was going on as he glanced up to confirm.

It could have been an ancient Pontiac Le Mans spray-painted with soot. The windshield was a steel cage around a hole of darkness. The car had crested the hill and was tilting down, shovel-nosed. White flashes began from either side.

"So what did I do?" Keyes went on. "I sent a tow car out to your garage this afternoon, and they jacked up that burned out truck of yours."

"PSA on the visor now," Karpos put in energetically. "Persistent Shared Awareness. On all the visors."

Walker saw a light in the PM's eyes as he surveyed Roeneke and Mayes. He was testing, checking his audience. Roeneke nodded distractedly, still riveted to the screen. Walker went back to the fireplug genius, tie too short, in black and white.

"And what did they find, Garlopis? They found what was left of a pile of shavings."

The renegade Le Mans was blasting now, overwhelming the dialog. Bass flooded the conference room, alien and thrilling. Shots flashed outside the windows like pom-poms.

"Fire!" Roeneke commanded.

The pom-poms flooded brightness over the deafening bass.

"Fire, goddamn it!" he shouted.

As though from his throat, a vomitous burst of fire arced to the target. The pom-poms merged with a shock-burst of light. White filled the screen.

"Yes!" Roeneke crowed.

"Yes," Mayes echoed. Walker was laughing silently.

The Bad Max car was smoking wreckage in the street.

"A high-value moving asset," Karpos pointed out. "Now imagine a hostile convoy…"

He was sensing blood. The PM knew his man. He could get on his wavelength. His jargon had already worked its way into Walker's project profile, concept and strategy sheets. Simulation platform, dynamic deployment, high-value target, tactical superiority.

He shuttled back to Keyes' speech, turned text flagging on, and searched on the words as Keyes spoke them: "little man." He jumped to the final instance, the scene with MacMurray as insurance agent Walter Neff when he realizes the game is over.

"The little man is acting up again," Keyes said. "Because there's something wrong with that Dietrickson case."

Neff searched him for a moment.

"Because he didn't put in a claim? Maybe he just didn't have time."

"Or maybe he just didn't know he was insured." Keyes was watching his agent carefully. Neff was holding his breath.

"Listen, Walter," Keyes went on, "I've been living with this little man for twenty-six years. He's never failed me yet. There's got to be something wrong."

"Maybe it was suicide, Keyes."

"No, not suicide…but not accident either."

"What else?" Neff asked.

Walker grinned at the hardboiled deliveries, Neff's heartbeat pauses that confirmed guilt.

He rechecked the demo. Dave Montoya's player had crested the hill and made the fateful right turn. The street was narrower, little more than an alley. Two pigeons flushed from the sidewalk. Walker saw the tiny white flash in the window opposite the car and wondered if they did. Birds reflected in the windshield. He counted the seconds under his breath, five. He held his breath for one more beat, just long enough.

Across the street a dumpster lid rose a foot. Dave responded. A fiery arc landed under the lid and it blew back, smoke billowing.

"Kill," Roeneke confirmed. "Excellent kill. That's how it is, Mayes. You can piss around—"

Roeneke was hung up, suspended. The snipers were answering with a pocking burst. On the right side of the alleyway a garbage can lid flipped into the air and banged into the gutter. Across the street a window shattered into glass chunks that showered down. Bullets screamed off the bricks, and tiny explosions of red chips were closing in.

"The roof!" It was Mayes shouting this time, and Walker had to laugh. It was the roof indeed, in fact two roofs. Snipers on opposite sides had them triangulated.

"Take him!" Roeneke commanded ambiguously. Only Walker noticed the door near the back of the conference room opening.

"You got him, you got him," Roeneke confirmed, and Dave had. Smoke and flames rose from the rooftop on the left, and the sniper had vanished. But on the right the firing resumed. Shots echoed between the brick walls and bullets whined.

Walker was confused to see Rob in the doorway as light from the hall dropped into the back of the room. Hands in his jeans pockets, he was focusing on the blazing pixels on the big screen. He did not see Walker. He seemed to be weighing whether to interrupt.

"Goddamn yes! Excellent kill!"

"Excellent," Mayes echoed.

Walker wondered whether to flag him, and at that moment Rob saw him. Walker felt half-fool, half-traitor. He understood full well what it meant between them. Rob was heading toward the front of the room.

"So now, in the network-centric theater, personnel can train in the real target geometry. From the satellite data we can interpolate three-D models, basically build out the city." Karpos was on a roll, but he stopped when he saw Rob approaching.

He towered between the front row and the screen in a Wallace Beery shirt and jeans, a head taller than Karpos. He acted oblivious to the guests in the front. Finally he bent down to Dave Montoya.

On the screen Dave's player was moving on. Walker picked out "Street of Bad Dreams" graffitied on a brick wall.

"Sorry?" Karpos directed at Rob. He was talking to Dave and seemed not to hear. Walker wanted to alert him, as though a beam was about to fall. Rob looked up at Karpos slowly, conveying that he had heard him well enough.

"Sorry," Rob replied.

"We're in the middle of a demo here."

"I needed to ask Dave about some files on the server. We have a fix to get in."

"A game."

"Right, a game. That's what we do here, games."

Muscles were working in Karpos's jaw. His face seemed suddenly blank. Walker was on his feet.

"That's what *you* do," Karpos said, tight as a cable. "Xynapse has other customers."

Rob took a step toward the PM. He glanced at the front row and then back to Karpos. A grin flashed across his face. Suddenly his hand came up to his forehead, and Walker thought he was set to parody a salute. Instead he scratched his head.

"You're quite right, sir," he said. "My mistake." He crossed back to the side of the room and appeared to head for the door. Walker slipped in behind him, partly to make sure he would keep going.

"Hey man, sorry to crash your affair," he said at the door. Walker heard the quiver of rage.

"Not mine," Walker said.

"Uh-huh."

As Walker followed Rob into the hall, he heard Karpos again.

"Sorry, gentlemen, we need to educate some of our *artistas*. Dave, can we go back a little..." He pushed the door shut.

Rob shook his head and tried to grin.

"It's gone, man. It's all death science now. Gone. I'm out. I don't have the lapels."

"No, it's not. They're in another world—let them have it."

"*You* can do that," Rob said, and it felt like a punch. Walker was not about to try a justification. Retirement was close for him, not so for Rob. He tried another tack.

"What are you working on?"

"What, the fix for *Biosphere*?"

"No, your work I'm saying, *Edenvale*. This is a game, correct? It's still here. The distribution's still here. It will be a monster and you can walk then."

Rob stared at him. In a few seconds he seemed to see something different. He held up one thumb with mock enthusiasm.

"What's that smell in there, baby powder?" He grinned easier and the thumb morphed into a two-finger peace sign. He turned and Walker watched him go back down the hall.

As he reentered, Walker knew *Double Indemnity* was no longer an option. He went down to the second row and slipped in behind the guests of honor. All eyes were back on the screen, the segment with the woman on the sidewalk pushing a baby carriage, clearly exposed to any sniper or return fire.

"Tell her to get the hell out!" the colonel instructed. Dave displayed the talk window on screen, but it was late. Walker was still replaying his words with Rob, coming down. It felt anticlimactic to him when the stroller detonated, flooding the screen with white.

It took a few more seconds for all of them to realize they had lost.

Chapter 10

"It wasn't pretty," Walker summarized.

Lynne had finished before him. He related the last of the *Spectrus* episode with Rob.

"That was great," he concluded, meaning the pesto fettuccini with shrimp and scallops. *Ensalada verde.* Pinot grigiot, the third glass of which he had nearly finished.

She rolled the last olive on her plate with her fork. He watched her mulling it over, wrinkles in her forehead above the nose.

"You haven't talked since?"

He shook his head.

"How do you think he is?"

"I imagine he's okay. Karen's probably dragged it all out of him by now and he's a toke over the line. How many people do you think remember that song? Only fossils."

"You're not a fossil," she assured him. "Just a fan of fossils."

"Fossil aficionado," he clarified. He took another sip.

"Think you should call him?"

Walker stared out the window into the yard in the evening where the blue jacaranda stood, insouciant. A few stars had appeared.

"And tell him what? That if I had any guts I would have told Karpos where to get off?"

She stared at him. He knew he had crossed one of the many lines. Could he blame it on the wine?

He got up and took his glass with him. He felt heady and blessed by a vaporous buffer that shielded him from pettiness and the pebbles of lousy events. Unfortunately, it was also alienating her. He moved to the sofa.

She was getting up from the table. In her white Indian blouse and purple pants, she took the first steps toward him. He was relieved to see she was joining him instead of walking out. She dropped a pillow behind her and curled into the end opposite him.

"I think what really got to me was after. It's hours later, mid-afternoon. I'm back in the office working on *Breakout*, Steve Halo's game, the Japan launch. Our favorite shithead shows up. I smell that cologne before I even hear him. He wants to know if Rob has Secret clearance, the highest one. As though I'm the authority on that, and of course he knows already. I tell him I have no idea. He says he'll follow up with HR. The implication of all this is obviously that Rob should never have been in the room and that I should have been responsible in some way for keeping him out. The bastard won't give up, I guarantee."

"Rob knew he shouldn't be there?"

"Maybe, but it's not that clear. This whole DoD clearance thing is so new that people don't know...is it to the letter, or...? You remember what we went through to get mine. Can you imagine Rob?"

Lynne looked hesitant. She wasn't getting what he was trying to say. He would try again.

"Rob isn't the point. It's a different company now. I wonder sometimes if it's worth it."

"Compared to what?" she said. It wasn't what he wanted to hear.

"I don't know. I'm not making a comparison."

"It sounds like Karpos has a problem. Xynapse isn't all like him, is it? I mean, suddenly?"

He could feel his blood pressure rising. He didn't know where to go from there.

"It's different," he said quietly, as though placing the words upright on a glass table. "Different."

Getting it across would be a challenge, one he was not sure he was up for. In the uneasy silence he wondered whether going on would be better or worse. The void between them was his doing, so he was obliged to try. Pinot grigiot had the pieces floating above him at the proper distance. He needed to get them in focus like rising quail and pull them down. He could start with the required security trainings in export controlled data. He could go on to the privileged information shared only by the cognoscenti—the executives, including himself, plus Karpos. The next proposal, for a high-speed flight simulator, also for the DoD. He felt tightening in his stomach. The phone rang like cold water.

Lynne headed down the hall to hear the speaker answer. Her job, they were both sure. The Gaviotas duplex was the nightmare of the month. Walker could barely hear the voice.

"It's Soph!"

He reached the remote and punched, and Sophie came into focus on the TV. Their camera LED lit red.

"Hi, Sweetie," he said to his daughter's wonderfully young image. "You okay?"

Lynne joined him on the sofa in the range of their camera.

"Oh definitely, I'm fine. I just have something I have to ask you guys because I just found out, and it's kind of exciting."

"We like exciting," Lynne said. "I think."

Seeing her always fascinated him. How long since they had talked, two weeks? Was her face a bit more mature, with Lynne's eyes but dark-haired like him? National Merit Scholar. Quick kid, heart of gold. Proud of her always, even if they were not always on the same page. Behind her on her wall was a poster of a black Amazon in dominatrix gear, cap of silver peach-fuzz hair, virgin biker hardbody. A musical artist, no doubt.

"You know I told you about Mister Pullen. Andrew Pullen, I have him for Regimes and Revolution. He's offered me an internship—it's a research assistantship—for this summer. The stipend is like, nothing," she laughed, "but I would have my own dorm room absolutely free at U.C."

"U.C.?" Walker asked, thinking California.

"University of Chicago. I forgot to tell you—it's in Chicago. He's working on a book on the Austrian School of economists, back in the early nineteen hundreds."

"Ludwig von Mises."

"Right! I'm not going to ask."

He laughed. It was one of their standing jokes: How did dad know so much weird stuff?

"Chicago," Lynne said. He knew what she was thinking. It was what they were both thinking.

"It's fine," Sophie intoned the two syllables, one high, one low. "Kids do this all the time, if they get offered."

And not many do, Walker understood. It was, he knew and needed to admit, junior year. They would not, when all consideration was done, raise an objection. He and Lynne would need to come to terms with it.

There was a time, he recalled, when their concerns would have run to muggers, a stray junkie financing his habit. Now the fantasy was stray gunfire from a secessionist holdout in a dark marble portico in the Loop or the pale guardsman firing back. He saw Lynne's hand on her purple leg, tight. What it meant to trust.

"So this would start right after spring term?" Walker asked for both of them. She was just twenty, on the doorstep. If she didn't seize opportunities, her own story could be over in ten years. He watched her image that only seemed near. A ball of light with wondrous potential. He rejected the idea of her being taken offline by some adoring young supplicant before she had her chance to take to the top step and fly, maybe her only chance.

"I think it starts about a week after classes. Just a minute." She was checking papers, looking down, her hair dark and straight on top.

He saw her reading, doing her homework years ago at the table they had just left. He saw braces and softball and Sophie at the piano and the first time he had ever let the seat of the bicycle go when she had pedaled away in front of him down the block. Now she was outward bound again, one of the chosen. *Don't go*, he was thinking. *Stay and be safe.* He might as well be saying don't ever go.

"It starts June twentieth. That'll give me some time to get settled. And Ron and Sam are still there, right?"

She had saved her best argument for last. Lynne's brother and his wife Samantha did indeed live in Winnetka. To any reasonable outsider, that would suggest a buffer of safety. An outsider did not have Walker's perspective, which was that Ron was a glamor-pussed wholesaler of straw baskets and other imported clutter from penny merchants in the third world who attacked with a shit-eating grin and nothing at all behind it. Lynne's eighty-old-year-old mother, whom he trusted much more, was also close in Oak Park, although severely arthritic. Not a safety net for Sophie.

"You guys are looking tense," she reflected from inside the monitor. "I'll be absolutely fine, I promise."

"I'm sure," Walker said, nodding, believing nothing.

"Just let us talk it over, okay?" Lynne said. "We could call tomorrow, how about noon your time?"

"Let me see." She was leaning out of the picture, flipping pages. "Yeah, that's okay. I just have an Arabic study group thing, but it's not until one."

Be safe, he was thinking. How we need to outlive ourselves, to go on saying and doing when all is said and done.

Love you, they said. Love you too, she said, and then she was gone.

"There has been a major development today in the Arkansas standoff." The TV had reclaimed its own after Sophie disappeared. "A source has told NBC News that Arkansas State Police will allow free transit out of the state in return for Carrie Whittaker's release. The journalist for The New Yorker magazine was taken hostage last week by the states' rights coalition calling itself the 'Militia of the Redeemer'.

"Turn it—" He clutched the remote and mashed Off with his thumb. The blanking of the screen felt like a tourniquet staunching blood.

They sat in silence. Outside the broad window, the flat space of the yard seemed to take them in. Old space, flat as time. They started to do what they inevitably did after an "issues" call, which was process it.

"Do you think she'll be okay?" Lynne said.

"Of course. It's not exactly Kabul. And she has good sense, basically." He put her totaled car on a shelf in his mind. It was almost three years ago. "We can sleep on it."

He patted her leg, taking the moment to do so. It was as long a moment as he could offer. He needed to get up. He was walking to the window. He felt uncomfortably fueled by vaguely formed hunches and hauntings. He was thinking back, trying to recapture.

It seemed there was a time, not necessarily innocent or simple, imperfectly clear but clear enough.

"Doesn't it make you want to go back?"

She was looking at him. She seemed a little out of focus.

"I mean to the place in time..." They didn't visualize their daughter caught in crossfire, he thought about saying.

"What?"

"Somewhere simpler."

She was staring back. Was his question so far gone? Was he inebriated, dislocated, shirking his dutiful role? Was this his true nature? Where was she, watching him, the mother of his child?

"Yes," she said. "And that's exactly what we're going to do." She was off the sofa and she had him by the hand. "Just think, in fourteen months we'll be—"

He was losing track of her words. She was on his retirement, he understood, and their dream house project. Her eyes showed concern for him. Did it matter that she had no idea what he meant? Her eyes appeared loosened a little by the wine. Generosity, he saw, the currency of love. The great generosity of women. She had switched from Sophie to him. He was delighting in the selfless disquiet in her eyes. She was leading him back to the sofa.

"Okay?"

He nodded. She sat down beside him and in a minute they were talking again about Sophie and Chicago and the things they could say to try to keep her safe.

It was later, when they had surfaced every idea they were capable of, that the beginning of the evening returned to him. He recalled how the talk at the table had started. Priorities were what they were, with their own specific gravities. Sophie had displaced Rob, no contest, but only temporarily. He knew Karpos would return like a contagion. At Xynapse they all shared the same zone of exposure. Immunity was impossible.

Rob didn't call it his sanctum, but it was nonetheless. In the dark cave of his home office, an Ennio Morricone score was playing softly on his Vib channel. The cool air held a comfortable hint of sweat and electronics. The sole source of illumination was the dual monitors, and he sat between them in the helmsman's chair. In his sacristy of calm, he was downloading all the ammunition he could find.

He scanned the few remaining links in his list. He had narrowed the context of irrelevant hits to their own Donald Karpos. He focused on the orange link. Clicked.

Karpos, Donald, U.S. Technologies. Project Manager responsible for Terrain Master Multimodal Assault System implementation and training.

He skimmed the bio page. It was a stain dropped on the Net, its subject having moved on months ago. No photo, but he didn't need one. The mug of the mogul was clear in memory, inexpungible.

He clicked another. His heart was pounding. Court record. Misdemeanor battery. He prayed for the word "female."

Knocking on his door. A hand on the knob.

"Can I come in?"

Karen was already in, partly. The light from the hallway behind her was too bright. In her black nightshirt, she would have distracted him any other time.

"Hey" he said.

"What are you doing?" She stepped behind him. He swiveled back to the monitor that was now diluted by too much light.

"I am...viewing the semantic Web."

Ready to slap the back of his head, she considered instead. Was he really being dismissive? He was doing his cool burn. It was too soon to give up. She focused on the screen.

"You're casing this guy? Come on."

"He's a thug, exactly what I thought. Look, he has a record."

Karen leaned in, reading the court record.

"How did you—"

"I subscribe to Sage. It's part of my—look at this." He had hit one of the related links. A newsline article opened. Karpos's face appeared in a one-inch square, protesting. "...arrested today in Washington, D.C., for assaulting a reporter who tried to interview him regarding the federal contract case—"

"So you're going to—"

"I don't know. I didn't say I was going to do anything, did I?" Too intense, he knew. He smelled her wonderful patchouli scent, sensed her pull back. He took a breath, started over.

"I just hope he fully disclosed before they hired him."

"And if he did, do you know how it would look if you—"

"Of course they knew about it! They're not that stupid. Do you think I'm that stupid?"

She took a breath.

"So what are you looking for?"

He tilted his head, stared at the screen. Silent.

That, she knew, was that. She left the office and pulled the door quietly shut.

So, he thought, disgusted with himself. At the same time he savored the return of his precious space. No way to win, he knew.

He focused on Karpos's newsline photo, looking for weakness, a spot to strike. The same beef-headed consciousness stared back at him in a younger package, frog face pulled taut, as though zipped tight from behind. Vulnerability zero.

How, Rob wondered, had Xynapse embraced this guy? How had it changed so much?

The marquee scrolled at the bottom of his screen and halted. He clicked the luminous green link, and a video opened in a new window. An Internetwork newsman at a desk with a perky blond sidekick trying to look concerned.

"There has been a major development today in the Arkansas standoff. A source has told NBC News..." In the background a dark-haired woman in her thirties, serious eyes, appeared on screen. "...in return for Carrie Whittaker's release."

He killed the window. He didn't especially care about the victimized reporter on the make. How much brain did it take to muck around with the hicksters? They were not, he knew, ready for self-government. One more horror, more or less. They were all in it together, wherever the great experiment—in capitocracy, democratism—was going.

"Bye bye, Carrie," he said, and it reminded him of the brothers Everly. He returned to the main screen and the job at hand.

What could he do with Karpos, smear him? Kill him? He searched the scrappy face of the junior PM.

How had it all come to this? His Xynapse? The great experiment? In a smoky back lot of his mind, Rob wondered as he searched the brutally dull countenance of his opponent, if that was the answer he was really looking for.

Chapter 11

Odd but true, Walker thought as his foot hit asphalt in the Xynapse parking lot. Working was better than a day off. He was on familiar ground again, producing his smart badge. The one-story imitation Spanish Gothic office complex was his other home. It struck him as strange that two days earlier he had been with the same people he would see again in minutes or hours, but in another world.

The company picnic on Saturday had been the obligatory playing out of the contract between the executives and all others. He never felt easy in the executives camp. He was required, but those on the other side were not. He could not recall exactly when that understanding had been reached. It had been different in the early days. Picnic, as known by all—no expectations. Now it was such that Rob, for one, chose not to attend.

Walker had spent most of it with a plastic beer cup in hand, tenuously sustaining conversations with Melinda Hanley, his only non-contract direct report, her boyfriend with a scaly neck tattoo whose name he did not recall, and Tim LeFevre in Finance. He was Lynneless. She had a project she couldn't miss, painting townhouses for her main client. He managed to stay across the party from Don Karpos, who had a way of shadowing Ivan.

The one visit he enjoyed was with Catherine, not Cathy, Kuntz, game programmer. A short awkward dumpling with hair like Harpo, she was a quick study with infectious enthusiasm. She reminded him of the start-up days, and while he could have indulged in the sad irony that Xynapse seemed to be moving in a far different direction, he focused instead on the fact that Catherine was still there. It indicated perhaps that the old spark was still there, that the creative nexus still held promise. The little dynamo going on about her game built on randomness could nearly reassure him that imagination was still their chief asset and would retake the high ground in the long run. If that happened at all, odds were it would be after his retirement, but he refused to let that detract from his one positive at the picnic. In all, he was glad when he had done his duty and his shift was up.

Not hot yet, he thought a few feet from the door, but it would be soon. He recalled the radio weather—a high of eighty. He pulled the brass handle of Xynapse and entered the air conditioned lobby.

"Hi, Gwen." He always greeted the young lady behind the desk when he used the main entrance. He was raising his badge to the hall door when he realized dimly that she hadn't answered.

"Walker," she said, and he looked at her for the first time. "There's a Leadership Council meeting." She sounded different, looked different. Invisible weights behind her cheeks and eyes. "It's at nine. Ivan's asked everyone to be a few minutes early. There's a message in your Inbox. It's encrypted."

Gwen glanced down then back up at him, the disarmingly innocent look in her eyes clouded by something. She was simply one of those people he had always favored, and he was sure she knew it. He had made the only appropriate gesture of appreciation he could, which was to put in a good word for her boyfriend when he applied as a tester. He had graduated to developer.

"You can't talk about it," he confirmed.

She looked at her keyboard.

"No problem," he said, "I'll check the mail."

"Walker," she said, and her eyes nailed him. "Can you *do* something?"

Sure, he almost said, then realized she meant nothing trivial, something about *it*. A few steps into the hall, he thought of using his BerryPod to check the message but decided to wait for the stability of his desk. As he passed

Melinda's office she glanced up with a routine "good morning." He was hoping for one more sign from someone, but Melinda was an early starter, and he saw no one else before his machine booted up and he was opening his mail.

He scanned quickly. From: Ivan...Confidential...changes in response... Games Division...Tao Matrix...names of our people... Leadership meeting.

He glanced over the list of names. Contractors, weren't they? No, he realized, not at all. His heart was going too fast. He began again from the top.

To: Leadership Council

From: Ivan

Subject: Leadership Council Meeting — Confidential

Team,

As you know our market share in our key sector has been eroding due to cost pressure. These are challenging times. To remain competitive and maintain our high level of quality in the Games Division, the Board has decided to make a change. We have committed to leveraging global resources. We will be partnering with Tao Matrix, who have assembled a very exciting array of talent. The transformation of the Games Division will begin immediately.

The names of our people who will be affected are below. Of course, contractors on the list will be transitioned first. Our direct people will be given a one-month notice, and a severance package will be provided based on length of service. During this transition your assistance will be critical to facilitate cooperation and knowledge transfer.

We will discuss the go-forward plan at our meeting this morning. I know I can count on your sup-

port as we face this challenge and take Xynapse to
the next level.

He scanned again through the names. Melinda wasn't
there; he didn't expect her to be. Marketing cut across the
divisions. Catherine was in the middle of the list, her energy
and enthusiasm like a ghost. But he wasn't focused so
much on Catherine or Gwen's boyfriend or the litany of
names he knew. When he saw the only name, he wanted to
look away, but it was like watching a wreck, an irresistible
target. He needed to get to him first.

He checked the time—eight twenty-five. Was he on the
road? If he called the apartment, Karen could answer. No,
she started earlier. He decided on Rob's cell.

One ring and he had not begun to frame the words.
Another and he was trying to trust that they would come.
Another. He picked up.

"Hey, it's Walker."

"Hey-hey."

"See me when you get in, all right?'

"Okay, I'm in. When? I'm pulling into the lot right now."

He was not ready for that. "Okay, I'm coming out. Stay
there."

He turned right in the hall and took the side door to the
lot. Rob was out of the van, slipping his laptop case strap
over his shoulder.

"So," he said, "Lynne's pregnant and you're not the
father." He was deadpanning behind gray shades, chrome
wraparound frames.

Walker paused, collecting himself, too long he knew. The
shades came off.

"Ivan's called a meeting for nine. The subject is sourcing. I'm going to fight it, but it sounds like it's already gone
down."

"They went through this drill before, right? Support was all they could do...conversions"

"This time it's different."

Rob just watched him.

"They want to go all the way in Games."

"All the way what?"

"All the way, all development."

"Direct?"

"Contract and direct."

"No shit." His brow clenched. "What do you think the chances—"

"I said I'll fight it." He came back too fast. He knew Rob heard it, but he didn't mind because he could have heard what was behind it for the first time. "I'll get with Jerry before the meeting. I'm sure at least we can buy some time."

"So it's when, not if."

"The board is saying do it, according to Ivan, but that's all I know."

"Did he say a timeframe?"

"The going-in is a month, but—"

"Okay okay okay." He was looking away, somewhere over the roof of the building. "Well, hey, thanks for letting me know."

Walker looked down into the asphalt. It revealed nothing. No good way to go.

"We'll get more time," he said. "We can work it."

"Yeah, yeah. It was Xynapse," Rob said in the direction of the building. "Now it's...fill in the blank."

Walker glanced at the same building he had seen thirty minutes before. It did not look the same.

"You okay?"

Rob nodded.

"I'm blowing this one off," he said. "Can't let all my vacation time go to waste, right?"

"I'll call right after the meeting, let you know."

He was climbing back into the green van, and then he was in the seat behind the door. Walker could feel the distance. Rob was in another category. His shades went back on, and the VW van caught and purred. They were one piece. Walker turned and headed for the door on different legs. They could be fluid vessels, cans of acetylene. He glanced back at the van that was out the exit gate and rolling.

Over, he realized. Whether it was four weeks or ten, it would be Xynapse without Rob, Catherine, Gwen's boyfriend, others, many others.

As he pulled the door again, he told himself to focus. He could do that. Jerry's office would be the first stop. There could be hope, although he didn't want to imply as much to Rob. They had discussed outsourcing before and had even experimented with certain kinds of work, low level, but never new development.

One door from the end of the hall, he saw what he did not want to see. Jerry's was closed. He knocked to the right of the poster of *Revel*, beside the toxic yellow splash from the galactic battleship. He knocked again. How could it be happening to Games with one of its three project managers missing? A strategy? He dismissed it. Was he in Ivan's office already? The conference room? It was ten to nine.

He headed back down the hall past his own office. He thought of trying Ivan's, but what could he do in ten minutes, or five? He needed to focus on the meeting where all would be present. He would make the case for outsourcing conversions but keeping the division. He would fight for a deadline extension only as a fallback. He turned the corner and headed for the small conference room, Tamalpais.

Tim LeFevre was coming from the opposite end of the hall. When he was close enough, Walker saw a new looseness in his face, as though he had aged since the picnic. He was collateral damage, a product of the shockwave. Finance would remain. Focus, Walker thought. He would need the defensible argument. He would need the data, which he did not have at his fingertips. He could ask for time. He could have it by the close of business, whatever it took. As he reached for the door handle, it felt like the kind of dream when he was about to take the big test and his mind was blank, the notes gone. Tim raised his head one tick and Walker did the same. He turned the handle and the door was open.

Tamalpais conference room featured indirect lighting and leather swivel chairs. From the door Walker saw Ivan in his place at the end of the table, Don Karpos on his right offering hushed input. Bob Landis and Jason Maki, the other two Games project managers, sat opposite Karpos. No Jerry, but they were a few minutes early. Ivan's administrative assistant Arlene sat at his left, laptop open.

Who was missing besides Jerry? Walker tried to place them, people he had met with in the same room for years. The names would come to him in a second, naturally. He would pull out of what felt like free fall. More critically, he needed the data that were far back, tiny and tumbling at the edge of his memory. But standing in the door, he was not possessed with irrefutable argument. Instead, *Can you do something?* came to him again in Gwen's young and tremulous voice, somewhere behind him in what seemed like another time. He followed LeFevre in and closed the door.

Chapter 12

On the way home, as he had through the wobbling vortex of the unreal day, Walker kept replaying the meeting from the morning. It was a worm in his head, a compulsion he could not shake.

Ivan went first. Somberly he restated the main points, then threw up the data. The projector showed revenues and trend plots. Xynapse versus T'ang Wa and Digital Arts. The market share numbers were what they were. Shareholder, the one and only God, was displeased. Distribution needed cheaper to turn SKUs. Cheaper was the solution.

Ivan wasn't finished, but they had all gotten the message by the time Jason Maki interrupted. The youngest PM in Games, and a live wire on a good day, he was first with the most obvious question. Why did it make sense now to try to source an entire division when it never had before? Jerry, who entered last looking like a cold case, laid out cogently what they had already learned—success in sourcing depended on choosing projects that met certain criteria. They could be specified simply and clearly. Little or no collaboration was required. They were not a core competency. Bob Landis echoed the theme of projects over divisions. Walker added the communication issues that could balloon cycle time and marketing cost.

As Ivan took it all in, Walker knew full well that he knew all of the issues before any of them had opened their mouths. He was doing the exercise, providing the forum. Otherwise the rage and fear would turn inward and injure the capitalist organism. It was like the employee survey that rolled up into bar charts and vague statements of approval or dissatisfaction which were dutifully processed and then ignored.

As he ended the clearing session, Ivan assured them that the options had been considered. To change what he called the "perception" of Xynapse, they needed visibility and impact. The move would give them both. Karpos appeared satisfied.

Of the Games PMs, Jerry was senior and he took it hardest. He continued to make his case, but it was the same case. Eventually he could only declare that it was unacceptable. Walker saw him trembling with rage and thought he might bolt from the room. As bad as things were, Jerry could make them worse, but he stayed.

At some point they all came to understand the nature of the new wall. It was solid and thick, impermeable. As Karpos had said, some were outside the wall and some were in.

It was only after the fact of the wall had settled in that Walker asked for more time. He argued a transition in four weeks was unrealistic. Too much would be dropped. They could only begin to implement a change of that scope in a month. Two at least would be required, more likely three.

He had acknowledged the inevitable. He was going for the easiest concession, one that Ivan would be happy to make. Instead he responded simply and with cool precision that commitments had been made. Contracts had been signed. He was an android Walker no longer recognized. It had been in the works for how long? Karpos had known.

Ivan turned the request into his own. He needed the support of all for the transition ahead. *Their* jobs were secure. They were the core, anchors in the storm, et cetera. They could expect challenges. He went over some predictable reactions and the ways to respond. At the end of the hour, he announced the follow-ups. The general announcement e-mail would go at ten with an all-hands scheduled for eleven. In the intervening hour, the managers were to meet with their reports.

As they were leaving, he called Walker aside and asked him to talk later in the afternoon. He knew it was about Rob. Some accommodation would be made for one. Walker tried to imagine it would make a difference. Something felt broken in his chest. He did not remember leaving the room.

He held his meeting a 10:05. Unlike the contractors and other "purchased labor," they were not at risk. But Melinda felt it. He could reassure his handful of direct reports, but all the others were sitting around them, their futures abruptly skewed two days after the company picnic.

Following the meeting he called Lynne. She absorbed the shock wave and then they tried to strategize. Of course he, not she, would call Rob. They started about Karen, but she had to break for a client meeting.

Ivan wasn't free until after two, and as soon as their meeting ended, Walker called Rob. Two more weeks had been arranged, if he agreed to work remotely, undetected by his colleagues. Plus, he had accrued vacation time that would be paid and his severance based on six years of service. Walker was less than surprised when his voice mail answered. In his message he said only that they had bought more time and that he would call later.

On the way home it was like a sickness. Ivan's voice droned in his head, the accented delivery like a long addictive jingle, Ukrainian pop. Halfway home he realized he had gone miles without the least awareness that he was behind a wheel.

"Hi," Lynne said simply as she met him at the door. She presented him with a glass. It was the first time she had made the grand gesture, and as he set his laptop case down in the entryway, he could almost laugh. He took the first bite from the frosted vessel, golden and cold. "How are you doing?"

He could have gone into it all, and she was expecting him to. Instead he took another drink and raised his free index finger as though to say he would be only a moment.

"Shower," he explained. It would give him space, maybe slow the cycles in his brain.

Lightly buzzed, he stood under the cone of water. The ski machine in the rec room is where he would ordinarily be. He should have hit it first. He could have channeled rage and confusion from his stomach lining and adrenal glands and spasmodic control booth of his brain into miles, maybe more than he had ever done. He could have burned calories and heightened his serotonin. It would have made everything better in the long run. As he dried off he told himself there would be other days.

"Does it make any sense at all, the way they're doing it?" Lynne asked.

Walker stuck a tortellini with his fork.

"No, none." He could amplify, but he had already recounted the arguments. Another tack seemed more appealing.

"What did Karen say?"

She had already explained that she had called Karen. He could tell she knew it was borderline. He had asked her not to call Rob, and it was not Rob, but not her mother either.

"She was upset." She checked him and chewed. He could have nailed her, he knew, but he took pinot grigiot by the stem and drank to his magnanimity. "It was funny, though. She wasn't as bad as I would have thought."

"No?"

"She said in an odd way she was relieved. She said things hadn't been good for Rob and she mentioned that guy—"

"Karpos."

"Right, and she thought that Rob was even looking for some way to get to him."

"What did that mean?"

"I don't know. I told her I thought it was crazy. I told her what you said about the whole department, that it wouldn't work." She checked him for a second. "I have no idea what it must feel like to be her, really."

He set the glass down on the coaster and admired the disc like a water ring at the base of the crystal stem. He felt that, as a fifty-one-year-old wage slave with no bullet abs, he could rocket through the ceiling.

"You don't believe what she said?"

"Of course I do."

"Well, she said he was burning out." He had tried to explain it before. He had told her it wasn't the same company.

"It's just hard for me to believe. Rob loved Xynapse, the whole culture. One guy could ruin it for him? He doesn't even work for him."

"It's more than Karpos." The PM was a symptom, Walker thought, maybe for the first time clearly. "Xynapse is going in another direction," he said quietly. "It's moving away."

"But you're safe. It isn't moving away from you."

He glanced at her, searching her face for clues. Why had they not connected? Why was she refusing to hear? That was concern around her eyes. It must be caring. She was trying to reassure him, or get reassurance?

"No, I guess not."

His tortellini had no taste. He got up and excused himself and snagged his glass. He glanced at the soundless TV where a blond female was reporting the news. She looked customized, remanufactured, suitable for framing. He headed for the bathroom or bedroom or both, he was not sure.

He remembered a bit of the bathroom, at least the mirror where he had looked for confirmation of normalcy. He recalled cleaning his teeth. He was standing in the bedroom before the plate glass, studying the blazing horizon where the sun had gone to die. Another call to Rob would be possible. He would repeat the time extension, their small reprieve. Knowing full well that Rob was out there in the web of loss, and that Lynne was probably still waiting at the table, he went to the bed, placed the glass on the night table, and lay fully clothed on his back in the dark.

Chapter 13

When he awoke she was lying beside him. It couldn't have been that long, he thought, an hour or two. He refused to check the clock. He was fascinated by her contour, the hillside slope of her shoulder to hips. Somehow waking made it seem new.

She had given him room and had come to bed quietly. He might have heard something, but he had absorbed it and fallen back to sleep. How had he gone out so fast? He gave up and checked the clock. Ten-ten.

He rolled on his side away from her. At first rising seemed ridiculous, then inevitable. He would not sleep in his clothes. He put his feet on the floor. He would simply undress quietly. But the cool of the house was like a slow slipstream. He followed it to the hall and the living room. It seemed to make sense to check the lights and the door, but of course she had turned them all off and locked.

Scents of dinner, basil and vinegar, remained in the cool air. Through the wide plate glass, the front yard lay bathed in moon glow. The jacarandas were silver-white ghosts with black shadows. Under the gibbous moon, all was silent, unworldly. It seemed suddenly plausible that he could be sleepwalking.

To test, he picked up the remote. Controlling a television would prove he was conscious. He pressed On, then Mute.

It could have been another screen, another day. A white building, one story, shabby. A wink of flame then decimated chunks of wall in a burst of white. Then an orange burst of flame and roiling black smoke. A terrorist cenacle in Indonesia or a shack in the Florida Keys? The only identifier was the Eyewitness News banner. He couldn't raise the volume.

The scene was repeating, in slow motion this time. He could absorb more visual information, to what purpose? He could tell that a dark twisted polygon looping off the building was a metal window frame. Another piece could have been a steel chair. Over the dark billows of smoke he picked out a bird, a flicker of black careening toward a corner of the sky.

He could have been in Sausalito watching *Spectrus*. It started over. This time it zoomed in before the blast. Through the window he saw the chrome arm of a lamp. It could have been a clue in a simulation game. A burst of orange and a flood of white. He killed the picture.

He felt polluted, guilty by the association of images, *Spectrus* and the nightly news. He was in the conference room, then the hall. *You can do that*, Rob had said. He drew the line between them in one sentence. Walker wondered if he could stand himself, whoever it was that he had become.

He watched the jacaranda as though it might walk on the field of moonlight. He went to the sliding glass door at the end of the room and quietly lifted the latch. As he slid it back, the complicated aroma of the night air met him. He stepped out into the earth smell and the fragrance of blooms and a trace of distant smoke.

He moved out into his yard of silica and dwarf blooms and away from the reigniting blast in his living room and the wireless network of living rooms. In the light his property was the silver-and-gray ghost shade of the lunar surface. He started to walk, and in a few moments he was moving away. He was heading diagonally away from his station, his climate-steady home and his upright self.

A squeal bit off in the distance, a coyote or the brakes of a semi. A dog's yip followed. Both sounded pure and sweet. He was tempted to howl back but thought of Lynne in their bed. He walked out farther on the sand to the end of their property. Down the gravel road a quarter of a mile, lights were on in the Dobson's ranch house. No headlights down their private road as far as he could see.

Above, the moon was bulging over its median. It hung before him in the southern sky. Outside the moon's aurora there were stars, pinholes in the black admitting the distant light. He felt an odd kind of balance as he stared straight up, rocking back on his heels. The unknowable number of years that the light had traveled settled him. He tried to open himself and it seemed that he could, and he let the traces of time flow down through him.

In a few moments he was light-headed. It felt impossible to keep standing, head tilted back, but he was compelled to stay open. At some point his body was deciding for him. He was bending at the knees, going down, flat palm on the grass stubble and hard-packed sand. He felt the slab of earth on his hip, and then on his shoulder that had never quite healed years after a dumb heavy bench press. He rolled onto his back and stuck two fingers between the buttons of his shirt, testing for his heart. He detected some repeat, and it was enough.

He stretched out his legs. The stars were where he needed them, coating the heavens broad and vast. He extended his arms. He was the Christ of five decades, *las cruces* in the sand. His body was naked, flesh and bone, his feet waxen and bony—how close to death they seemed.

He thought of Lynne and the line of shoulder to hip in their bed, himself flat on the bed of the earth. Would she wake and find him gone? He refused to think of that or any responsibility to anyone. He needed this place. The stars rained down.

He closed his eyes, and the dust and stone perfume of the close earth came to him. Something in that scent, the complete otherness of it, triggered the recognition that what he was doing was not sane. He was not the only creature on the night earth. Tourists knew about scorpions; they had been warned. Locals had no excuse. He imagined the ignominy of being stung. One could hit the side of his neck.

What would it be like? An injection, a jolt? He checked one side, then the other. Dark flats, nothing moving.

But there were rattlers, whether you saw them or not. They were nocturnal hunters out of the heat of the sun. He knew what not to do. A fast heart pump drives the venom to the brain. He thought of the distance to the house, the phone. One of his legs could make a pretty discovery for a mouse hunter. But it didn't work that way. He would hear the rattle. He tuned to the steady jabber of crickets. He could survive like any creature if he would trust his senses.

He tried to trust and listened. He would not panic or stray. He took in every scent and tried to empty his thoughts. For a quick black moment he thought of Rob, and he could not block it—the trap door that had opened under him. He felt his insides start to churn. He pressed his left hand to his chest and felt the firing against his palm.

His eyes were open again and he checked the stars for bearings. The earth under him was warmer than the night air above. His skeleton had settled, adjusting to the flat table. With no plan or effort he was surrendering to his position, becoming a flat shadow in the shape of a cross on the earth. He was not conscious of closing his eyes again.

At the head of the room, Rob was bending over Dave Montoya then challenging Karpos. Walker breathed, counting the breaths, his mantra. After ten he had put Rob away. After twenty he was aware only of the air above him. Almost cool, it was barely moving, like water in a pool disturbed by a stone. The earth smell mixed with the fresh scent of verbena.

He was not sleeping, but not fully conscious. He was in a transitory place, a state like predawn or dusk. Memories and senses crossed and faded.

There were stars again, but they were not the same. It was a different night and time, far back. A warmer night. North Carolina sky. He lay flat on his back, but on steel this time. The curving shield beneath him was the still-warm hood of a '66 Pontiac. He was a sprite of fate in the darkness, totally alive. The burnt sugar cotton candy and popcorn smells of a fair came to him. Cigarettes also and the lingering scent of poison from the fogging truck. The white billows of mosquito fog had been legal then.

It was there in memory, a linkage as thin as a thread. Above him flowed a vast river of white light, wide and higher than he could see. Moths piloted through it and seemed to flame out, purged of their tiny bodies. The moths came back to him. The white light absorbed it all, the ghostly flights and points of stars and voices in his head from the speakers in the car window and the other windows.

This, the pure flaring river of light from the projector seemed to be saying. This was it, if only for him. He wanted to stay with them there in the Crest Drive-In Theater in Hopesborough outside Durham in 1969. The Carsons or Missus Bigham, his first grade teacher, or Mary Sue Valhaber, he had no way to know. They were there or they were not on any particular night, and if they were there, they remained anonymous in the light's river, floating above Hopesborough. They were neighbors in the same town, in their other lives, the ones Walker tried to cling to, even as he was being summoned back to his own.

He was being raised, tugged back to the surface against his will. It was the brightness, singular and sharp, a craze of light reflected from metal and chrome. Rob's van was pulling out of the lot, and the sun off his mirror was like a shot.

Rob was lost. Karpos had taken him down. His reflection burned to a blind spot. Nothing Walker could do. No appeal. This was not who he was. He worked problems, resolved them. Can you *do* something? Paralyzed. Powerless. Xynapse was an engine of imagination. Had been. Now it was an imploding white box, a puff of orange fire and billowing smoke in Koala Lumpur or Kandahar. Who was he, Walker asked himself, but an accomplice? *You*, Rob had told him, *you* can do that.

He rolled to his feet. Too fast. He bent over, hands on knees, waiting for the blood to return to his head. He watched the sand under the ghost light until the dizziness cleared. In its place the dim shape of an understanding was forming. What he had seen flat on his back on the earth and smelled and recaptured was not accidental.

Walker pushed himself erect and stood, clear-headed. He did not believe in visitations or callings. It was a chance. The Dobson's light seemed like a marker from another night. He was turning, moving his feet in the direction of home.

At the sliding door he stopped and tilted his head back again. The stars were still in their nets, unconcerned but constant.

He slid the door and stepped into the cool of thermostatic space. As he latched it he felt like a stranger, an intruder in his own home. How alien was he about to become? His head suddenly filled with a story. He had seen it on some video magazine, about a man who had made of his own stucco house a glittering monument to audacity. He had covered it with remnants of bottles, colored glass and shards of mirrors and tile. Bicycle wheels and wheel covers. Somewhere in California.

He undressed in the living room and carried his clothes as quietly as he could down the hall in the dark with his head full of the night outside. He could not wake her, towering in the door in his underwear like a creature from another land, aboriginal.

He laid his clothes on the bedroom chair and decided against washing his face or rinsing his mouth. He would leave the dust of the night on his skin. He lowered his weight carefully onto his half of the mattress and lay on top of the sheet, listening. He wondered if she could be pretending to sleep and had really heard him returning,

lumbering and familiar. She was lying on her same side,
and he watched but did not see her shoulder move. In a
moment he heard a low suck of breath and then another.
He had not wakened her. She had not turned to his empty
side of the bed and wondered about him. She did not need
to know yet, as he did, that a different man was lying beside
Lynne now.

PART 2

Chapter 14

"But they might have kept a spare key under the carpet on the stair anyway," Lynne said.

"Two things," Walker replied. She was hooked and he was happy. "First, the inspector saw Tony leave looking puzzled. He went down the steps, went a little ways down the sidewalk, stopped when he realized, then came back and got the key. If it had been a normal spare, he would have used it right away. Then his wife would have used it, but she didn't, because she didn't know it was there."

"Right, the inspector said that was how he knew she was innocent. But another thing—what about the way she killed him? If she was trying to kill her blackmailer, would she stab him in the back with a pair of scissors?"

"Okay, that was far-fetched, but I think you roll with it because it was set up so well. And it was plausible because she was using the scissors on the scrapbook."

Walker realized they were nearly home and they had talked all the way. All had gone as planned, actually better. They had just seen the original Hitchcock version of *Dial M for Murder*. He had been inspired to take her to the Toland Festival Theater in Henderson. Named for the cinematographer of *Citizen Kane*, it was probably the only theater in the state that was not an odious mini-showroom. It was a comfortably shabby version of what had once been known as an "art theater." They had gone years before with Margo to see a Japanese cult sci-fi flick from the sixties or seventies that Walker couldn't recall. That had been entertainment only. This time he had more in mind.

When he had proposed it, it broke a ponderous overcast. It had been over two weeks since the announcement, and

Xynapse was transforming. The Dao Matrix personnel were all on site. The plan called for them to work in the States at first. When they had absorbed the processes and the time was right, a contingent would break off and return to China. They would grow the offshore presence over time. *Spectrus* development was unaffected. There had even been talk of hiring if one of the spin-off proposals was accepted.

Walker and Rob had spoken only twice, first by phone the day after the announcement and then a week or so later in their favorite cantina, the Rockaway Brewery. Rob told him he didn't miss much. He was working at home on his own schedule and circulating his resume half-heartedly. *Edenvale* was his focus, getting his game through testing to marketing. Walker thought he seemed lighter, and he was envious. But that lightness lifted Rob into the zone where they could talk again about Xynapse and his game and Karen, and Walker could finally tell him about his Concept as he had it then, compelling but unformed.

"Is the one that came out last year with Brian whathisname the first remake or the second?" she asked.

"Second. There was a TV version. Brian Paris isn't exactly Ray Milland, is he?" He was testing her reaction to the pop idol. It amused him that women thought of movies in terms of male leads.

"Lisa Domingo's no Grace Kelly either." He caught her grinning as she turned toward the window.

He was laughing to himself as they rolled into the driveway. They climbed out into the night air, and he felt a little like Tony Wendice with his plot. He wondered if that particular film had been an unconscious choice. It was the theater he had wanted to show, the experience. He did not need to be as thorough as Tony, or so smart. He was not planning the murder of his wife.

He unlocked the front door, and a trace of perfume from the top of her head distracted as she passed. Not Grace, he thought, still checking her backside in sky blue jeans, but not at all bad.

"That was fun." He heard her bag come to rest on the dining room table, which was good. She was staying in range.

"Glad you liked it. What do we have cold?" As he pulled the refrigerator door he was pleased to see the cork exposed in a half-full Chardonnay from a couple of nights before. He poured them each a glass.

"We didn't go with Rob and Karen did we?" She headed into the living room.

"No, Margo."

"We should, I'm sure they'd like it."

She sat on the sofa but he remained standing, his natural position for expounding.

"Speaking of Rob," he said, "he may have a new option."

"Really."

"It's related to tonight in a way."

"What, the movie? He's planning to knock Karen off?"

"Not that I'm aware of."

She was giving rapt attention, allowing him to be mysterious, feet tucked under on the cushion. He picked the spot to begin.

"How did it seem to you when we were in there?"

"Where, the theater? Retro, is that what you mean?"

"Partly, but more than that. It seemed like a completely different time and place, didn't it? I mean it wasn't something you could stand outside and watch. It was like being immersed."

"Escapism," she said.

"Yes, but not simple. Not stream-a-flick. It was the whole experience."

"So what does it have to do with Rob?"

"Can I show you something?"

She stared at him. When he saw her tilt the slightest degree forward, he turned and headed toward the stair and his office on the second floor at the opposite end of the hall from hers.

The sensor picked him up as he crossed the threshold. The track lights came on and then his screen. He rolled a chair next to his ergonomic own and they sat down at the computer. He clicked an icon on the desktop. A file opened.

"What's this?" she said even after reading the document title: Business Plan. She paged down through a couple of screens. Walker stood up.

"You know I've been thinking for a while," he started, "about Xynapse. It's a different company now, it has been. We talked about that before, remember?"

"You mean the defense project?"

"That was the beginning, but now there are spin-offs. It's Karpos and everybody around him. Going public was great in some ways, not so in others." He checked her, wondering if she had heard him. "There's a very dark part to it. But I've been rolling with it, for all the reasons we know." She was only watching.

"If Xynapse is guilty," he said, "I'm guilty, by association."

"Guilty? Of what?"

"Death, of a kind," he said. How could he explain that? She was looking back at the screen, hiding frustration, he knew. *Hyperbolic,* she was thinking, *obtuse.*

"What I'm saying is...for all the time we've known it, Xynapse has been in its own world. Now it's being absorbed. It's becoming part of...everything else...what we're in. There's a kind of war..."

He was glad he had brought his glass. He took a swallow and left the last one in reserve. She was watching him, indulging him, as she seemed to be doing more lately. By way of clarification, he was thinking of Glocks in the locker room, plastic explosive on the gas line detonated by remote. *The banality of evil,* he heard in his head from years past, and if he said nothing, if he did not speak out to dismiss it, he imagined it would stick, returning by night. He felt like saying it all, a synthesized and ineluctable whole. But his task was to make sense.

"Xynapse is becoming the opposite of what it was. It's been a game company, okay, a fantasy world of a kind. But it was a place that jacked people up. It fueled the imagination. Now it's becoming twisted."

She was facing him squarely, saying nothing, but her look was asking, So?

"So," he said, giving up on the back story and turning to the screen, "this is the new direction." He took the last swallow and let it settle in.

"This is something that you're doing," she said. She sat back in the chair.

"The plan is almost done. I've been running it by Ken. He sees these routinely, so he's been a huge help."

"You want to go into the movie business..."

"In a way," he said. "I've been talking about how Xynapse has changed, what it's lost. Now think of it this way. Xynapse has merged with what's out here. Think of the loss out there, the loss that most people feel." Across the suffering heartland, he was thinking. In the hearts of the spud-brained consumers of the lock-and-load cop shows and the cage fight marathons. The flotsam on the tide that slopped in the hollow skull of the televangelist. The reverend-major atomized as he touched his fingerprint to the ignition switch.

"Walker," she said. It felt like a slap. Was she stopping him or catching him?

"'There was a time', we say. I think there's something real that people mean when they say that. Behind it there's a solid real thing. We all need it. The full-up thing. Not just a movie of it, which is what? A play in the mind. We need the real thing, any way back to it. We need to rediscover it, uncorrupted."

It's the brand, he was thinking, the whole network of associations, but didn't say it. Lynne had heard him and she was processing. He sat down beside her.

"This plan is my shot at capturing it in something that can work."

She turned back to the screen. Maybe she needed to read it. He let her read. The seconds stretched out.

"It's a drive-in?"

"It's like what we had tonight, the full experience. So much comes with it. What does a drive-in make you think of? I remember going with my parents. They would let me lie on the hood of our car. The projector light over us was like a huge white river. I can see the moths flashing in it. The smell of the concession stand that was like the county fair. It brings a whole string of memories. Remember summer days, how incredibly long they seemed then, and free? Hitting baseballs in the back yard. Big league baseball when there were sixteen teams in two leagues and no divisions. The house in our neighborhood with a screened patio and a pool, the Hueys..." He paused, as much to savor the memories as to let whatever sentiments he could call up for her settle in.

"You're thinking I set up tonight, and you're right. You had to see before I could tell you. It would seem completely off the wall if you didn't—"

"Do you know how many people were in that theater tonight? Maybe twenty?"

Keep it in perspective. This was new territory, she was nervous. To be expected.

"This is more, that's what I'm trying to explain. Didn't you ever go to a drive-in when you were a kid? Maybe they didn't have any left in Carbondale."

"I don't know if they did or not but no, I never went."

She sounded warm as a handgun, but it couldn't stop him.

"It's total immersion. It's what makes a lot of business-es—like really successful restaurants. The food is only part of it. It's the total experience. The same way, the drive-in only *seems* to be a movie, it's the full experience. They used to be called 'ozoners' in the nineteen-fifties—the open air thing. It's a way to do what we can't do otherwise—get back to a time and place."

She watched, waiting for something. He watched back.

"So the business plan... it's to get a loan?"

"A line of credit."

"How much?"

"Not sure yet. The plan assumes a fifty percent level of confidence at this point. It's all you can know at the start."

"What's the location?" She was pushing.

"Don't know that either. But it can be undesirable for most other uses, that's the beauty of it. Any land that's on a main arterial, flat and away from lights. Do you know how perfect this area is, the number of clear nights a year? It's in the plan. Two-ninety plus, on average."

She considered, bit her lip.

"The collateral is what, the house?"

"No, my options, part of them. Part I'll cash out and put up directly when I leave."

"Leave Xynapse, you mean."

He saw her getting it for the first time. She had not understood. How was that possible? Perspective, he remembered. He had been living with it for weeks. She had been able to deny all but the last few seconds.

"Right," he said.

She pushed back from the desk.

"What does that do?"

"Do?"

"To our plans."

"Put them over the top. It will add a year at most, and on the other side of that year, we'll be better positioned, or much better, one of the two."

"From cashing in your options you're going to put in..."

"Three hundred or so."

"And so according to the numbers you must have in your plan, where would that leave the loan?"

"I'm confident I can hold it to four. And it's a line of credit—"

"You're going to do this for seven hundred? I don't think so. You're going to need more and you're going to have to put up the house for it."

"No no. Drive-ins can be built very economically, and there won't be any need to cover—"

"Did Ken guarantee that?"

Her face was bone-cold.

"There's a big up-side. It can be our cash cow when we might need it. I'm thinking out another ten or twenty years—"

"And what about now or a year from now when you were going to retire and we agreed we were going to start on the lake house?"

"If you'll listen to me—we've talked about this before."

"Stop it! You don't have to tell me what we've talked about, all right?"

"I thought you'd understand this."

"I think I do. I understand a million dollars. But I don't think you do." She stood up.

"What's the fallback if this goes nowhere? I really have a hard time seeing how that would help our retirement. How much do you know about this business? Who does anymore? It's a relic."

"Not so." He lightened his cadence, raised his empty glass like a mad professor, took a breath. "Actually, quite a number of people have done it since the glory days. And quite a few are now. It's in the plan." Don't be demeaning, he thought. "You didn't see it, did you...unless you hit it by chance. For example, did you know there are almost five hundred drive-ins in the U.S. today? The ideal size is at least fifteen acres. The concession adds about forty percent to sales. Consider what you could do today with teas and waters, punch, tapas, gourmet pizza...plus the old stuff."

He was trying to be affable at least, charming at most. She was not what he would call charmed, but she wasn't leaving the room. They both fell silent and it felt awkward, but he forced himself to leave space even though he was eager to tell the last part.

"There's another piece of this that really works," he said at last. "I can't do it all myself and I'm not about to hire employees at first. I'll need an operating partner. Who do you think would be perfect?"

She stared.

"Can't you guess?"

Silence.

"Rob."

"Rob? Have you asked him?"

"No, he doesn't know yet. But he's heard the concept and he's up with it."

"Are you doing this for Rob?"

"No, of course not! It fits, that's all. Well, doesn't it? Can you think of anybody more retro? And he could do it and still do his game."

She did not look convinced.

"Nothing about this," he went on, "is written in stone."

"What are you talking about? You've made up your mind."

"No, there's nothing signed at this point. I'm not going to do anything we haven't agreed on." He wanted to honor it and he hoped she would give him the chance.

Hands on hips, Lynne looked down at the screen, up at the wall.

"When did you get this idea?"

"Two, three weeks ago."

"Right after the announcement?"

"I guess so, why?"

She seemed satisfied.

"Do you think you could be overreacting?"

"It wasn't that specific event," he said, but he heard the false note as clearly as she must have. He was shaking his head. "It's what I said—it's been a long time coming."

Where was she? He had hoped it would be different. He could try again. He could just begin, and another angle would come to him. But was that the right thing?

"Why don't you just think about it?" he said.

She pursed her lips, looked at him, then the screen. She was clearly weighing her words too, and he could appreciate that. But when she turned and left the office without a word, he felt a sickening ripple.

Early, he reminded himself. It was early yet and all was new. She would process it. They would be in the same bed, he was sure. It would not be a guest room night.

He closed the plan and stared down at the panel of muted desktop light. It could hold a clue to their future. But it was withholding, blue and inscrutable. He turned and left the room, thinking of her and whatever delicate assurance he could summon for their good-night words. He let the sensor shut the office down. It would black out the space as though its occupants and their issues had been a phantasm, ephemeral as a carbon arc light projection on a screen.

Chapter 15

Walker was not going to do things they had not agreed on. He had said that. But that did not preclude discussion. He reminded himself on the way to meet Rob at his apartment—he was perfectly consistent with the fundamental distinction between talk and action. True, he had e-mailed a copy of the Plan in advance, but that was warp of the same woof, a talking point only.

Lynne would have no grounds to object. She had urged him to get opinions from sources he trusted. He understood the subtext—don't take it from her alone that the scheme was nuts. Aside from that suggestion, they had not discussed the Big Idea in the two intervening days. He had reaffirmed to himself that he would take no loan until they were ready, as he had told her. *Ready* was an open word, a marketing word. He knew that she knew and accepted what he had promised, and he was forced to admit that, given her understandable free-scape of fears, such an acceptance was probably love.

He pulled up outside Rob's building and got out. He could talk with Rob and she could not object. His aluminum mailbox was double-locked. Below it, the buzzer.

"Hey man, what does it all mean?

"Don't ask me, it's Chinatown." He didn't care that the allusion was old, and missed.

He followed Rob up the six steps to the landing. The door was open and they went in. He recognized the poster from Rob's old Xynapse office—Will Wright floating in a galaxy, signed by the Sim City creator himself.

"So, you going to Beijing with the Team? Shanghai I could take, not Beijing." Rob was amusing himself. In his rugby shirt, jeans, and sandals, he seemed to be in his groove.

"They're going in the fall. That's the threat, anyway. It depends on where they are by then."

"Do they know where they are now?"

Walker understood he needed that.

"Of course not. They're screwed and they're paying. Everything's sliding except Karpos's crap. They can't source that."

Rob looked like a man who was not required to report. Scruffy and hip, he was decidedly on the other side of the line that Walker was not able to cross. Not yet.

"Coffee?" He snagged his mug from the dining room table on the way to the kitchen.

"Sure."

Walker started to follow but the table stopped him. He peered into one of the monitors, littered with code. The screen beside it showed a webcam shot of a third screen cycling through fly-over and fly-through views of terrain, half-mountains livid green and purple dusk. "You're going to need a new apartment," he said. "You're outgrowing your office."

"It's permuting," Rob said. "What I'm doing here is color-shifting all the polygons through the color map. I can work on a different sequence from here and watch at the same time. There were some kinks—they should come up in a few minutes."

"You're going to miss it."

"They'll come up again. That's the beautiful thing— it's...eternal return. Or the piece of junk will hang. Either way I get what I need. Matter of fact, I'd rather not watch. What's up?" Rob passed him a mug, crossed the room to his chair, and sank down.

"You got the plan, right?"

"I did. It looks top-notch. Very professional and persuasive. Listen, man, I'll front you as soon as I get a bank."

"Did you see the reserve for an operating partner?"

Rob was considering.

"I think...you itemized the expenses—"

Not yet the moment of truth, Walker knew, but he had dropped it out of nowhere because he needed to cut through with Rob, to come to the point.

"For the first year, and extrapolated the next. It's a stipend basically, but there's a full partnership behind it." Walker paused. "I can't handle the whole operation myself. It isn't an employee thing. I'd go through half a dozen before I would find one that would work. It's a partnership thing."

"Uh-huh." Rob took a drink from the mug, not ready to admit what was being asked.

"So—when can you start?"

"Me? What does that mean?"

"Of course you. You've been in on the idea from the start. It'll be a gas—you said so yourself. You get it. That's why I sent you the plan."

"What do I know about drive-ins? You've done, uh, due diligence, right? You've got your figures down cold. They're all right there. You've got the whole thing in your head." He was grinning, being encouraging, but something else too.

"It's pretty much right there in the plan. You know about as much as I do. I've done the research for the key ratios et cetera, but you don't need that. We'd be learning the real stuff together, very fast I'm sure—sink or swim."

"Jeez, it's freakin' heroic. It's grand."

"Why not?"

"You don't go into business with your friends. Kiss of death."

"Not necessarily, not at all. We're complementary. That's what makes a partnership work. This isn't your main gig—I should have been clear. In no way would this conflict with *Edenvale* or whatever else you're working on. You call whatever time you need."

Rob's smile folded into bemusement. He looked down into his mug.

"Hey, what can I say but thanks? I hear you coming to me with this in good faith. But it's really your gig."

"What I'm saying is, I could seriously use your help. I can't do this alone. What other lunatic would understand it?"

"I hear you man, I thank you, but it's yours. It's not mine."

"What do you mean? What are you doing but the same?"

"No no no, big difference." Rob stood up to his full height and crossed to the table. He took a swig from the mug and set it down.

"So?" Walker said. "How so?"

"First, I'm not saying anything about rediscovering marvelous old things. *Edenvale* isn't about that, none of the games. Right, it's a getaway, outside of the here and now like your thing. But it isn't pointing back to anything. It's just a lot of little triggers for the brain. That's it, that's all. A possibility space. The thing in itself." He stomped across to the chair, focused on the carpet. He turned back to Walker with a darker look.

"The other thing is, it's outside country. No borders, no battle lines, no holy wars. No country clubs in golf shorts."

"Okay okay, this is the same. It's the antidote. Same as *Edenvale*."

"It's not at all." He turned to the TV screen, shook his head. "It's escape flicks only, you know. That's what I think of when I think of it. But then I think...it's not that, not escape. It's not going nowhere. It's exactly the same place."

"It's a way back—"

"It's not a way! There's no way. You can't step back in the river, man. Don't you get it? Even if you don't get it, the main thing..." He was standing in front of Walker, looking down at him. "The main thing is this country. Look around in a while? What have we in the U.S.A. today? Tweenies like Karpos driving their fuckin' monster trucks. Christian soldiers. Freakin' pagans on the evening news because they blew away the...crucifixionists.

"Some people are leaving."

"What are you talking about? People are always leaving. What?"

"I mean leaving in a major way...a meaningful way. They're seceding."

"Give me a break. What are you... It's a media event. What are these people doing, starting another country? If they're lucky enough to have jobs, they're keeping them. They're going home to the world's highest standard of life, et cetera. They might as well buy a bumper sticker. But that wouldn't be a story."

"They're forming a community. It's a community of consciousness, not turf, not political. Not nation state—that was coopted by corporate long ago. The movement has leaders, a constitution. A space in the heart."

"Hey, eloquent. Sounds like a manifesto."

Rob grabbed a remote from the bookcase, aimed and clicked, clicked again.

"Ah yes," he continued. "The local news is not new. One of yesterday's features. Human interest, I believe. The next installment of kid drops kid in mall. What was this one over, a frigging pair of basketball shorts marketed by some grease-head prick MBA?"

"They're selling time, you know that. We can counter—"

"You're going to fight this? I think not. These fuckers are all packin', man. Little brain, little dick, but big honkin' gun. It's the land of the free. Do me a favor—don't make me think." He stepped closer to the next scene, stared down at it. "And so now we have the funeral shot. Tomorrow it's the webcam in the casket, watch him rot." He killed the image, dropped the remote to arm's length like a dead handgun.

"What was it?" he said after a time. "Where does all this come from?" He turned back from the TV to a place in the corner of the room, then somewhere outside the window.

"We're talking about the same thing, aren't we?
Rob turned.
"I don't know."
"So anything we can do—"
"We do what we do, we do what we can. It's not *Eden-vale*, not at all."
Walker took a breath. Life, he understood, was resistant to solutions.
"The way out of this is in people's heads. You can re-create a feeling, a sense. That's all this is about. You create a way for the poor slob, the customer, the human being, to immerse him- and herself in a whole other reality. Think stained glass windows once upon a time. It isn't just a business plan."
"I know, man, I can see that." Rob took a second, looked down then back at him. "Sorry. It's your crusade."
He turned again to the television monitor where close-up images of braised ribs were gleaming bright as plastic, popping by in semi-second cuts.
Walker had been sure. He tried to balance what he was feeling. Betrayal of friendship, like a shot to the gut, knowing at the same time he would have to honor it. No balance occurred to him, none at all. He felt the moment growing stiff.
He produced words to assure his friend it was fine, he understood. He imagined that he could as he reached the front door and turned to Rob behind him. He was lighter in the head and colder, blood dropping from his brain. He enjoyed the moment in a bitter way. He detected awareness in Rob's face that he knew what he had done. Contrition, or a feeling close enough.
"Listen, I want you to do it. I hope it's a monster."
"Thanks. You can always change your mind," he added but did not wait for an answer. He was through the door and he could feel Rob receding behind him.

Back in his seat with his belt around him, he looked out on the quiet street that curved back to the main arterial. Two things lay before him. The first was Xynapse to which he was returning at the end of his lunch break, where he was still an executive and a contributing employee adding value, who had no other plans than to continue in the same role and spirit, as far as anyone knew. The other was an open question. His best friend and his wife were not on board. How did it make sense to proceed?

He put his hands on the wheel and drove. He punched to his own music bank and took the first cut that came to his tuner. Otis. Yes.

"You said you were tired," Walker howled into falsetto. "Tired. Tired."

He rolled back into the Xynapse lot. In moments he was on the carpet of the air conditioned hallway, indirectly lit. Toward the end, walking away, he saw the back of a colleague. He made his own gaze into a laser on the back of the buzzed head, the fold, visible even from that distance, like a razor cut at the intersection of the bull neck and the smallish skull. Karpos in the flesh, on the hoof, answered Walker's question for him.

Lynne examined the crinkles around her eyes that she had targeted with anti-aging cream. She was not ready to concede, not at all. She dismissed the notion that they seemed lighter because the sheen of the liquid was reflecting the vanity lights.

Dinner had been over for an hour. She had done the dishes and Walker had disappeared. She assumed he was in his office. At dinner he had been polite, quiet. Something was obviously wrong, but he had adroitly sidestepped talking about it. It was more of the same, she recognized. Since he had revealed his scheme, they had been correct and careful with each other. She was sick of it. She had considered bringing it up several times, but it had felt too risky.

It would resolve on its own. She knew him better than he knew himself. He could dream and expound and convince himself that pigs could fly, and that was a capability she cherished. But he could also wake up. It was his alarm system that tripped when he could not connect all the dots. This would be one of those times.

In the bedroom she focused on clothes for the next day, the meeting with Abizay West. She pulled a drawer and realized she was facing one of Sophie's senior year pictures shot at the lake property, one of a number of the three of them. A marker in time. She stood up. How they all smiled into the camera, their eyes, only imagining then how they might appear years later.

She pictured him in his office. Two weeks ago she might have been in hers working on the lake house. That was before the idiotic scheme took it all off line. She looked back at the photo. Sophie had his eyes and her hair. Lynne considered the possibility that she, not he, was the reason they weren't communicating. Even if he was misguided, did she want that?

She left the bedroom and headed down the hall. It felt okay, even good, to be giving in. She didn't intend to discuss the big idea, maybe just squeeze his shoulder, see if he was up for a date in an hour or so, a video, his choice.

When she reached his office door, he was sitting back in his chair, perfectly still, the screen blank. She smelled wine. The bottle of Zinfandel on the floor was nearly half empty and the glass on his desk was.

She tiptoed in and checked him. His head lay against the seat back, tilted away so that she did not see his face. She watched his chest rise a bit and fall. She could wake him. What could he tell her that she couldn't find out? She reached past him and touched the mouse.

The screen saver cleared and light hit them both. She checked him. Still asleep. She returned to the screen. It was his plan with redlining on. He had changed the section on operating partner. The partner was now an employee with a salary projection of one year. She looked closer. He had cleared a space below the employee paragraph. In the space he had typed two lines:

Your crusade

You said you were tired

She watched his chest, its slow rhythm. Clearly Rob had not worked out. She could talk to him about it, pretend she was sorry, seem encouraging. She knew what she could do and not do.

She turned and tiptoed back to the door and through. The hall felt like a fresh breath. He would be okay. She was not comfortable, but it was going her way. Time was on her side. She felt relieved to know she would be going to bed alone.

Chapter 16

"God," Margo said and toed the door shut behind her. She was glad to be home, more than glad. She dropped the mail on the kitchen table with one hand and swung her backpack off her shoulder and onto a chair with the other. For the last hundred yards she had been imagining herself as the cartoon vagabond crawling on hands and knees across a sea of sand. As an exaggeration, it was not outrageous. If the school had been another mile from her townhouse, dehydration might have brought her down. In a moment he was pulling the handle of the refrigerator and chugging from a bottle of raspberry water.

She considered walking day. Had it become crazy? She tried to leave the car at home on Thursdays until late spring when the heat became prohibitive. Today the heat had surprised her. Plus, she had taken too many papers. Was she ready to pay the ultimate price for her little monglings? Sad fact was, she might be getting old, although deep down she didn't believe it.

The bliss of the shower was her main focus as Margo rounded the kitchen counter, so when she saw the drawer standing open, it took a moment to register. The miscellaneous drawer. When had she done that? Had she been looking for a pen before work, or a notepad? Was that today? Peering into the drawer, she saw the contents were disarranged. Her peripheral vision may have picked it up then, or it may have been an instant later that she took in the hall that led to the bedroom.

Snake on the carpet twisting out of her room. That was her immediate take. But it was flat and wine-colored and motionless. As she realized it was not a snake or any living thing, she realized also that the reality was worse.

She started to push the drawer shut but stopped herself, heart racing, realizing dimly that another world had presented itself in the drawer and to blunder into another world was to disturb, and to disturb meant consequences. She took the first steps toward the hall.

She went softly, only partly aware that what she was doing was as smart as stopping for a hitcher in the night. She halted, stopped breathing, listened. She might not be alone. A car horn somewhere outside. Then nothing. The right thing, she knew, would be to turn around. But the spaces around her were still. She tried to tune to the rooms behind the walls. She breathed again, quick short breaths, then took one and held it down, stepping quickly and quietly to the end of the hall where her burgundy blouse with its serpentine, outstretched arm lay at her feet.

Confirmation came with a glance into her room. The Clue game box in the center of the floor, pulled out from its forgotten space under the futon frame. Her dresser drawers pulled open, socks and underwear disinterred onto the carpet. Along the wall the lid of the wicker closet propped open by a wedding gift she had kept only because it came from a high school friend, the linen table cloth jammed in the hinge.

Margo was feeling ill. Not alone. Possible she was not alone. As she listened again, she realized she was staring at the space at the back of the short table where the television had been. It was her guilty pleasure, the simple panel used only on rare late nights and weekends and then only when needed, like a drug. She was hearing nothing.

She glanced at her earring rack. Untouched, of course. What value could her trinkets be to anyone else?

She stepped into her bedroom as into a strange house. She stepped around Clue and her littered clothes. Her boots in the center of the closet looked like dead dogs. Her clothes were pulled away from the closet ends where someone might hide valuables.

The bathroom. She backed out of the bedroom, checked it. Medicine cabinet open, open drawers. She tiptoed forward and inspected the medicine cabinet, trying to recall if she had cough syrup. If anything was stolen, she couldn't tell. She glanced down into the drawers. Scrambled. He had reached in and touched her hairbrush, Tampax. She slammed the drawer shut.

"You little shit!" She picked up clothes from the floor and stuffed them back into drawers, any drawers. His stinking little shit fingers on her clothes. She lifted her slip to her nose, checked it. Her panties, her socks, checking for cigarette odor, his smudge, a trace of defilement.

"Shithead," she added and stuffed in a pair of socks. She stopped. A cold sense flowed through her as she recognized she had forgotten, and she could not afford to forget. She glanced over her shoulder. She had forgotten downstairs.

She stepped into the hall and went to the stairwell, looked down. She knew full well what she should be doing—dialing 911. He had probably broken in down there. He would head back to the same place when he heard her on the front steps. She realized she was carrying a pair of socks and set them on top of the bookcase at the end of the hall.

She stepped on one stair and then another. She was being drawn down against her will. But what was her will? She was stepping down into another space. It felt something like driving in the dark, letting go of the wheel for critical moments, trusting.

When she reached the last step she was not breathing. She needed to be still, alert. She was acutely alive, as though hearing with the clarity of prey.

She peered around the corner at the base of the stairs. The top drawer of the two-drawer file was open, folders scattered on the floor. Windows closed, unbroken. She stepped out onto the carpet.

The room felt warmer than usual. Was that possible? The sliding door was closed. She became aware of the smells in the room. With the domestic plastic scent, the ordinary toxins of construction, something other, foreign, musky underside, dirt and crushed green from the soles of shoes. She tried to focus on it. Was it evidence? Was it anything? It was gone.

She looked away from the windows to the closet. She imagined him in there with her boxes of old papers and photos and books, sleeping bag, ancient blankets. She moved softly toward the door. Somehow the undisturbed orientation of the ordinary knob seemed significant. It was plausible, even likely, that he was on the other side of the cheap hollow core door. She stood paralyzed by the prospect, wired for any tick on the other side. She flashed on her bedroom floor, clothes in disarray, his hands in her underwear. She could tear his hair, rip his face with her nails. She knew this with irrational certainty. Make him pay. If she had a gun.... She rotated the knob and whipped the door open.

Boxes, blankets, sleeping bag, musty smell. She was charged with adrenalin, facing the fact of what she had done and how it could have turned out. Insanity. She was breathing, coming down, coming down. She pushed the door closed.

She turned to the green file folders scattered in front of the open file cabinet, papers on the carpet. She knelt to pick up the car insurance envelopes and receipts and manuals but stopped herself. She wanted to restore order, but it could be evidence. What he had done she knew; she had no idea how.

She rechecked the windows. She got to her feet and inspected them. The amount of dust alarmed her, but she would deal with it later. Locks closed.

She turned her attention to the sliding glass door that was the only entrance to the ground floor. Closed. She checked the lock.

What she saw dropped through her. She bent closer. The display that she was expecting to show *Locked* was showing four blinking zeroes. The door itself was not completely closed, a slice of light between it and the frame. She pushed it shut then remembered evidence, fingerprints. It was the feeling of exposure she couldn't live with. She refrained from touching the lock.

So he had hacked the digital lock. She had heard they could do it now, but she had felt safe enough with the system that was state-of-the-art when she bought. Of course she would reprogram it, but what good would that do if they could hack it again? She could ask the police. She needed to call them. She wondered if he had hit any of the other townhouses. She checked the patio outside the glass. No trace. She imagined him quietly sliding the door nearly closed as he left, hours or minutes before she arrived.

For the first time she was reasonably sure she was alone. She had covered all of the rooms but the spare bedroom, and she had passed it on the way to the stairs. No sound, no movement there or anywhere. She must call. She should have the first thing. She headed back to the stairs.

A step from the corner she halted. She was thinking of the critical file. How could the cops blame her? If they were in her place, would they forget it and wait? If she waited, would it matter?

She sprinted back to the open file drawer and the papers. On her knees she pushed in the top drawer and pulled the bottom all the way out. At the back was the folder with no tab. She snatched it out and thumbed through the contents. She rechecked the papers. What was she forgetting? It all seemed to be there. Copies of her Social Security card, credit cards front and back, auto club card, health insurance card. She had copied them all in case any were lost. She had read somewhere it was a good idea. She didn't remember seeing a caveat that doing so packages your identity in one convenient spot. At least her passport was in the safety deposit box. The rest of the stuff needed to go there. So he had scored some electronics and missed the jackpot. She had almost come to admire his finesse. She could forget that.

Margo replaced the file of critical copies then retraced her steps to the stairs and climbed. Winded, she was punching 911 from the kitchen when she noticed her work desk by the back window. Papers were there, her district report and courseware. In place of her flat panel was an unobstructed view through the window. If she had missed that, what else? It could have been worse, she realized. On her walking days, Thursdays, she left her laptop in the locked cabinet at school.

"It could have been worse," she said.

"Excuse me?" a voice responded in her ear. The operator was assuming a crank.

"Oh, I'm sorry. I wasn't talking...I mean I was..." Stick to one thing, the fact. "There's something I need to report. A burglary."

"He didn't have to break anything because he could hack the lock." Margo essentially repeated what the officer had told her. "I heard they could do that but I never thought...I suppose you never do." The police had toured both floors and checked the evidence briefly. They had made no attempt to collect prints or traces of any kind. Margo had imagined a micro-capturing process for DNA, but it did not happen. She could see that recovery would be a miracle. She had completed her part of the paperwork, and they were standing in the front hall.

"They use scanners that intercept your code. They're pretty neat little devices. But we don't like them much." Margo felt that the senior officer was making light at her expense, but she could give him some slack. In general, he made her feel better. Officer Darst seemed solid and experienced. His partner could have been a trainee. "They're illegal here, but you can get them on the Web. We tell people who've had this kind of break-in, obviously, you need to change your code. But you also want to upgrade to three kilobit encryption. It's more expensive, but what are you buying? Peace of mind." She was taken by his instinctive rhetorical flourish. "The scanners can't crack it—yet, anyway. They have ten-foot ladders, you build a fifteen-foot wall."

Not the first time he had used the analogy, she understood. How many of these had he seen? Did he even tell his wife anymore? She pictured his spread, his ranch, his security. She imagined he owned rental units, townhouses not unlike hers. He was one of those cops with investments, a root system.

"And so you've shown us all the areas where you noticed any disturbance. And you've checked all your belongings?"

"Sometimes we don't think about credit cards, bank information, keys..." The younger one was trying to be helpful, but he annoyed her nonetheless.

"I checked the file where I keep all that," she said. "My cards were on me."

The young one nodded and he could have bit his lip. She hadn't meant to do that.

"Be sure to call us if you think of anything we haven't discussed today." Darst was on automatic, into his departure speech. "The phone number and my name and badge number are on the top of your copy."

Margo checked the paper in her hand as though she hadn't remembered his name from his introduction at the door.

"Do you think there's any chance—"

"We'll put a trace on your items. Your receipt for the monitor will help with that. We'll try, but it's hard to say."

The receipt had included a serial number. She had contributed a concrete thing.

"I wonder who he was," she said, wondering if she sounded odd.

"Probably some kid from the squatter camp. He's nothing special."

The remark landed like a punch. What did she expect? He was on a front line that she would never see.

From the kitchen window she watched them return to the squad car. A one-car job, she thought. Of course, nothing special. The cruiser just sat, and she could only imagine what they were doing. Playing teacher and pupil, calling in to report, discussing her and her trivial case. Eventually they pulled away through the few spare shadows that fell across the street.

What first? She thought of calling Cathy but decided to wait until she had regained order. Where to start? Bedroom, downstairs, whatever else she might discover in the living room? The prospect of doing anything was enervating. Of course not, she realized; she needed to call her security service. Three-K encryption. It costs more, of course. Fifteen-foot wall. Where was the number? She remembered the sticker downstairs on the sliding door, the pitiful gesture of deterrence. Same sticker, she realized, in the corner of all her windows. Twenty-four seven number. She headed to the closest source, back to the kitchen window.

As she rounded the counter she passed the drawer, and it felt like a switch had been thrown. In a perturbing moment she saw the young cop again, the flat-top high school fullback with his dull gaze mouthing the words. She halted, stared at the drawer pull. Sometimes we don't think. Credit cards, bank information, keys. She pulled the drawer and stared straight down into the empty spot that was like her other now-empty spots. The spot where her spare car keys had been.

Chapter 17

"It's a total cliché, but it's true. You never think it will happen to you. But why not? We imagine we're special." Margo rotated her coffee mug then looked up. "I just want to thank you guys so much."

"For what?" Walker said from behind the kitchen counter where he had gone for a refill. He had been happy to play breakfast chef with pop-up waffles. His main challenges had been slicing strawberries and peeling the caps off yogurt cups. He was also glad that Margo had called them. The two ladies were in their robes at the kitchen table, but he was dressed for work. On an ordinary day he would be there already, so it was not an ordinary day.

"For letting me bust in on you, of course."

"What are you talking about?" Lynne said. "Of course we would want you to get out. Jesus. The locks are broken. He could come back."

"When I called last night after the police were gone…You know it's twenty-four seven for the security, and they did answer…it was a person who could understand me at least, not a machine or a call center on the other side of the world kind of thing. Anyway, she couldn't promise a response last night. They would try to make it after midnight. I don't mean they couldn't make the half-hour response time in their contract. I mean sometime after midnight—maybe. What am I going to do, sue them? You deal with these companies all the time, I know. Maybe I should have forced the issue—"

"You were freaked," Lynne said. "I would be. Why couldn't they honor the contract?"

"She said they were responding to so many calls, there were so many incidents."

"What kind?" Walker asked. He rounded the counter and crossed to the table. He wanted to see her when she answered.

"Maybe this girl was fantasizing, but I listened because she's close to the action, on the front line, right? She said that some burglaries were people stealing food, can you imagine? She said there are always some of those, even old people, which I found hard to believe, didn't want to believe I guess. But those weren't the main thing. She said in most of the break-ins they were stealing stuff to sell for guns."

"Who's they, did she say?"

"I don't think she knew. She thought they were going somewhere out of state, the guns."

"I think you're right," Lynne said. "How would she know? We use Steelstream in two of our buildings. They have huge turnover issues. I got this from a tech who left. Lousy health plan, no 401K, every other weekend on call. You have BlackBox, right? It's the same, I bet. They don't have enough people in the field, so they give the phone girl a cover story."

"Sounds likely," Walker said. "But they did commit to the morning?"

"Between ten and noon is the window. I should get ready. Walker, you need to get going, you don't have to sit with me, you've done enough. I feel guilty taking off on a Friday."

"Oh right, you should go to work after you're burgled," Lynne said.

"Well at least I know the sub wants the work. Jeannine's a good one. She'll have them doing Brain Baker, the game."

"A classic," Walker said. "Ringo Levio did the original of that game in what...the last century."

"They love it."

As he started toward his briefcase, the phone rang. Lynne was closest.

"Karen, hey babe. You're at work. But you knew that."

She was grinning. As Walker watched, her eyes changed. She was concentrating.

"You need to talk to us." She looked straight at Walker like an alert. "Hey, you all right?" After a beat she nodded to them both. "Sure, when? He's right here, he hasn't left yet. You want to come over?" She was listening for a long beat. "You and Rob want to talk to us both...I'm repeating for Walker..."

He nodded sure, wondering what was up.

"You want to call tonight?" she asked Karen.

"When I get home," he added.

"Okay, how about six, Walker will be home. Do I get a clue? You need to get Margo too? She's right here! It's a crazy story, she had a break-in yesterday. Yes, she's fine. She spent the night here, and your call is a great reason that she's going to spend tonight too." She was staring at Margo. "That's an order. We all must talk with Rob and Karen at six."

Margo was shaking her head but waving yeah yeah at the same time, which Walker took to mean she would be there for the call. They would talk her into staying later.

"So no clue, huh?" Lynne listened but didn't repeat. "Okay, we'll be here at six."

Lynne went on, Walker understood, because for the two of them to recognize they had come to the point and disconnect would be a disgrace to their gender. He had his ideas about the evening's mystery subject, and he tried them out on the way to Xynapse. Karen said they were okay, and they would be calling together. The most likely involved *Edenvale*. The company had sold rights into another market, TV or film. Stranger spin-offs had happened, such as the series based on *Klub*. When he arrived he checked his mail and InsideX for any news on *Edenvale*, imagining tipping off Lynne and Margo in advance. He checked back during the day but was humbled. He would wait like the others.

"So what's on?" Walker said. "How about mysterioso starring Karen and Rob." The ladies were on the sofa when he came in. After sitting all day, Walker preferred to stand. Margo's security system had been reset, and she seemed back to her old self. When he passed the kitchen he saw salad and various cold complements—chicken salad, Havarti slices, sourdough. He was fully prepared to discuss their friends' surprise, he only hoped it would fit into a sane timeframe. Hunger would be a factor soon.

"They're tying the knot. We decided," Margo said. "Has to be."

"What else?" Lynne agreed.

"Not so sure," Walker said.

"Why, what do you know?" Margo fished.

"Nothing. My mind is open—"

The phone rang at Lynne's end of the sofa.

"Hey there," she said and pointed the phone at the TV. Rob and Karen were in their living room.

"Hey," Rob said.

"First we thought it would be best to get together," Karen said, "but then we thought it would be better to talk as soon as possible instead of waiting for a time we could all meet...and Margo was already there with you.

"What we're saying is we weren't going to do this by mail or chat or anything." She was clearly nervous.

"Okay, so you're getting hitched," Walker said to relieve her, stealing the girls' thunder. As he suspected, it was irrelevant. They looked different than any of them expected, subdued.

"We're karmically hitched, yoked to the max," Rob said, seemingly back in his usual persona, but Walker saw through it.

"That sounds lovely," Karen said, giving him an elbow. She took a breath.

"How can that be?" Lynne protested. "We were sure."

Sure as shit, Walker thought. Not sure at all.

"You've got us," he said. "What gives?"

They listened, and the silence was a long beat and then a moment that seemed to Walker attenuated to near absurdity. It occurred to him that it could still be a Rob-inspired gag, and he tried to cling to that notion as he saw his friend glance down then up and Karen's eyes seem to unfocus.

"What we need to tell you," Rob said, "is we're going to be moving."

Walker glanced at Karen, her eyes on the screen. She seemed to deflate inside.

"You found a house you like? Where?" Lynne asked.

"I meant moving, as in away."

"What? Where?"

"Canada. Sechelt, it's in British Columbia, a little north of Vancouver."

Walker felt it drop into the room and sink.

"What? What are you talking about?" Margo reacted. "You're saying completely out of the state, out of the country? You mean in the summer. Summers only."

Rob was shaking his head.

"It's a move," he said.

The moment felt long, then deep.

Walker recalled their shots of the Sunshine Coast of B.C. from a couple of years earlier. He and Lynne had heard the idyllic reports of pristine water and air and evergreen forests unsinged by greenhouse blight. He couldn't remember if Margo had seen the photos with them.

"Why?" Lynne almost shouted.

Walker wanted to be more surprised than he was. He joined them on the sofa.

"This isn't an overnight thing. We've been torn, sweating it. It's that we've come to a point... we need a new direction. Xynapse is part of it."

"Okay," Lynne said, knowing, "but—"

"So why go to another country?" Margo said. "You can work anywhere in the world, right? All you need is your connection."

"Because there's another part," Walker said like a bell and the room was silent. "Right?"

Rob looked cornered, nervous, as though he was being drawn, reluctantly, into the agony of explaining himself.

"We've talked about it," he said to Walker, "so you know." He directed the rest to the others. "There are things here—I mean the broader here—that we're not a part of, that we don't want to go with anymore." He looked out into the faces. Karen's hand was on his arm. "There's so much struggle," he said, "blindness..."

Ugliness, Walker was thinking, ignorance.

"violence..."

Loss.

"You're seceding." Walker said like a quiet bomb. Lynne and Margo stared at him. They had heard of it as most had, as an aberration, something like a cult. They had not heard Rob on the subject.

"It's a way to say no," he started softly. "*No* can be a positive, in context. Secession is people making that statement. It's making the commitment to live by it, in a different way."

Walker understood the others in the room were spinning, trying to catch up, trying to translate into a language they knew.

"Come with us," Karen said. "Walker, you'll be retiring soon. There's so much land for you guys to do your dream house. And Margo, this is the best. I know somebody in the school district there—"

"She's a best friend from college," Rob added.

"She's a supervisor in the district, it's perfect. She's at the middle school level, but she knows everybody in primary, I'm sure."

"Wait wait wait," Margo said. "I'm trying to get a grip here."

In twenty-four hours, Walker realized, she had been upside down, now inside out. He slid next to her on the sofa and put his arm around her shoulders. Some perfume, he guessed Shalimar, a name he remembered from a former lifetime, Kate Terribault. He escaped into the memory. She was his college freshman year in the TV studio room and his own room. He was glad he still remembered her name, but as to Margo's perfume, he really had no idea.

"Why is this what you have to... the thing you have to do?" Lynne said. He saw her struggling against her better judgment. "Do you have to go so far?"

"What are we going to do without you guys?" Margo added, blowing past the invitation to join them. "We're just going to persuade you to stay, that's all there is to it. Come to your senses!"

They went on in that vein, bantering to no avail. In the process they found out that Rob and Karen had already declined to renew their lease. They played most of it through again. Why so far? So extreme? So impossible? How could seceding make any sense? Walker tired of it before the others.

That night as they lay in their beds, he heard them all again. After the call, the focus was Rob. Lynne and Margo were sure he was the instigator and Karen, only the loving enabler. Rob was unrealistic, Lynne said it first. Walker felt like defending him but could not say why except that he understood it.

He couldn't tell if Lynne was sleeping. She seemed to be. It disappointed him that he wasn't sure. After thousands of nights, he should know.

His thoughts switched to Margo in the guest room. Her day had been hell. He wanted things for her, no loneliness primarily. Her break-in seemed like odd, discordant support for Rob and Karen's decision. They were, each of them—Walker allowed the thought as he had in various unguarded moments—alone in their worlds. He found himself in a position to accept it. Rob and Karen had sent them all back to their own squares.

"How are you going to stand the rain?" Margo asked.

"It's not a big thing where we'll be. They call it the Sunshine Coast. There's much more rain inland." Karen pulled the tape gun over the back of the box and down the side. Margo smoothed the end on her side. Sad, Walker thought, as he watched them working as a team.

"In the winter it rains," Rob conceded, "but it's tolerable."

"Tol'able," Margo corrected. "You have to practice your hick, am I right?"

"That's what will happen to your brain, you know," Lynne added. "You wind up talking like a clam digger."

"What do clam diggers say?" Rob returned. "I've never heard one."

"Woof," Lynne said.

"Come now, that's not Canadian," he returned with a lilt. "A little rain makes the trees grow, eh? You'll see when you come up."

The bookcase was half-empty, and the table where Rob had been working was clear. He was folding a packing box. Others sat on the floor, some taped, some partially filled.

The three of them had decided to go to Rob and Karen's that morning to begin the process of dissuading them. When they found them already packing, the inertia of friendship made it impossible to do anything but help. At the same time they argued absurdly against it. In the process they heard the departure date for the first time, even earlier than they had thought—three days before the end of the month, a Saturday, exactly two weeks away.

Over the intervening days, the undeniable settled in. Lynne took off work whenever she could to spend time with Karen. Margo tended to share the inversion of her life with Cathy, out of range of her other world. Walker went to Xynapse as usual where he knew what he would find. He had grown accustomed to the hollowness that had opened when Rob had left. He was marking time.

The Thursday before the day, he and Lynne hosted a dinner for all. Against everyone's best efforts, the evening drifted to maudlin. They all went outside at the end, and Walker had the sense that the widest possible sky that had once seemed to hold them like a net of stars was a traitor, fickle and weak, unable or unwilling to keep its charges from falling through.

On Friday the mover came, and the ladies were teary-eyed. By the next morning Walker felt he had been through it all and only wanted it over. Rob and Karen had shipped the VW van by transport truck, recognizing a blown head gasket could be the price if they drove it. Selling it was out of the question. As Walker and the ladies arrived, Kevin, a friend from Xynapse, and his girlfriend were leaving. They had said their goodbyes. All who were left hauled out the few remaining boxes. Then Rob locked the back of the U-Haul van, and the moment had come.

"So when are you coming up?" Rob asked.

"Up where? Hockeyland? It could happen."

"You really have to. It's a great place. Like green things instead of sand and rocks. You could do your drive-in thing there. They'd be into it, I'm sure."

It was clear to Walker that he thought it was nuts.

"Watch out," aiming a finger at Rob's head, "you're losing compression on number four." He was surprised to be blinking away tears.

Rob's arms were up then and they were in a bear hug, slapping backs. They stood apart and watched the women who were clenched in a three-way. After a male eternity they separated, and Rob moved to the driver's door of the van. The sun off the white door felt merciless.

"When will you be online?" Walker asked.

"A day after we're in, should be Tuesday."

Walker flashed on so many people gone, high school, college, after, so few he had kept in his life.

"Let's keep the line open, all right?"

"Of course, man," Rob said. "Always open."

They switched partners and hugged all around. Walker realized it could be the last time he would see Karen, the first time with tears in her eyes. He held her in the companionly embrace.

They were climbing in then and the van doors banged shut. To Walker the separation had seemed interminable. Ironically, when the engine caught he felt the band around his chest start to loosen. The worst was behind them.

Their hands were in the air, the three on the ground with their arms around one another. The van rolled.

"Call us!" Margo shouted. "Right away!"

Karen was waving out the window. Rob gave a blast of the horn. In one held breath they were around the corner and out of sight.

Chapter 18

On Monday Walker announced. From the moment the office door was closed behind them, Ivan was studying him. As he started to talk, the boss sat back. Walker was beginning to explain in words carefully chosen but irrefutable that the decision was his. The focus was on himself, not the company. Around his third sentence Ivan interrupted. He knew it was about the Games division and the impact on Rob. He assured Walker they would always do games, it was their core. But they also needed to diversify, leverage their strengths, and so on. Walker chose to contest none of it, but his decision stood.

The date was a month out, but it was understood that Walker would come in only if required over the final two weeks. He had the accrued vacation time, but he decided to make the gesture to support the transition.

When the exchange had happened and passed like an unreal wave, Walker felt another jolt as he learned that his old boss was prepared, if not for every eventuality, at least for his. Connie Linder would be his replacement—regional sales manager for Latin America, seasoned and savvy. Probably most important, she and Karpos had hit it off from the start. It gave Walker a sinking feeling, but it confirmed his choice. Ivan expressed regret and urged him to reconsider, but he wasted no time in simply asking Walker to keep Connie's promotion confidential until the announcement. Nothing felt real as he shook the hand that once belonged to the crazy Ukrainian, now CEO. He was saying something back, keeping it professional, getting a hug and a slap on his back and a squeeze on his arm, then exiting in the direction of HR for the papers. No one else would know until the next day.

He was first in the garage then through the front door. He expected Lynne would be later than usual. She had to travel to her building in Paradise Park. The air conditioned rooms of their home felt empty and vast. He opened the mail then started setting up for dinner. He was on the salad when her Alaire rolled into the drive.

"Hey there. How was Paradise today?" He crossed to her and was thinking about a cheekside kiss.

"You know the Cordoba. I told you about it, twenty units, absolute crap." Her bag went down on the chair and she was half-inspecting her mail. "The breaker panel has caught fire twice. The whole damn building should be rewired."

"Is that an option?"

"Yeah right. How was your day?"

He headed back to the counter.

"Okay." He thought about it staring into a bowl of lettuce. "I pulled the trigger."

She looked up at him, spinning then catching.

"You told them?"

"I did. Make all breaks at once."

"I'm surprised." *Disappointed* he could see instead.

"We said it could be any time—"

"I thought we would talk again before you actually did it." She saw what he was waiting for. "But congratulations." She took the steps, hugged him falsely. He tried to write part of it off to a hard day. She stepped back.

"Was Ivan shocked?"

"Less than I thought he'd be. He had my replacement all picked, Connie Linder. She'll fit right into the 'new paradigm.' Much better than I would have, that was probably obvious."

"What else?"

"That's it for now. I'm sworn to secrecy. Ivan makes the official announcement tomorrow."

Lynne went to the sink and started running the water. She could have been rinsing breakfast dishes although he didn't remember any.

"Hey, what's going on?"

She killed the water. There was one dish. She turned to face him.

"Nothing, everything's perfect. You've got your loan, you're ready to go, right?"

"You're having second thoughts."

"Is that an accusation? By the time it's said and done, we're going to be on the hook for two million." She headed for the bedroom and he followed. "Do you think a normal person would have some concerns?"

"Listen, we talked about this. Hey—" But she kept going. "Will you listen a minute?" In a second she was at her dresser, back toward him, removing an earring.

"First of all, we won't use the whole line of credit—it won't be necessary. In a year, two at most, we'll be building the house, and we'll be sitting on a cash flow we wouldn't have had otherwise."

"Walker, Walker, I'm sorry but I don't believe that. What makes you think people are sitting around waiting for you to open a drive-in movie theater? Jesus."

"I'm not saying people are waiting. I guess what I *am* saying is that after twenty-five plus years in marketing, I do have some sense of where people are before they know it. And beyond that I do have some small sense of how to make a project work and how to run a marketing campaign. Can you agree with that? Can you at least give me that, or is it too much to ask?"

She faced him, eyes storming, but did not answer at first.

"You want me to be happy about this? I understand you're pretty damn impervious to my feelings. It feels to me like the wheels are coming off, okay? We've been planning for a long time. It feels like the fucking end. I don't know what I'm supposed to do."

He wanted to tell her. Are you with me or not? he considered asking but wasn't sure he wanted to hear the answer. Instead he flashed on their years together, leaving work at noon to pick up Sophie from kindergarten, her room with old stuffed toys no longer age-appropriate, the haunted sense that they needed to turn a corner soon, but they seemed to be at an indefinite point on a long curve that twisted out of sight. This argument was not like the others. Perhaps it had gone too far.

"It's a lot at once, I guess," she said. She turned to the side, looking out the end of the long closet, through the wall, at nothing.

He understood. He had always imagined celebrating with Rob and Karen when he had made the move.

He saw tears. He closed the distance, put his arm around her.

"Sorry. The timing wasn't so great, was it? I guess I wanted to put all the separations behind us. I feel like we've been under a cloud since Rob and Karen."

She nodded but said nothing. He wanted more, something to patch the sad hole between them. He couldn't leave it. He stepped back to arm's length.

"How are you doing?"

"Okay," she said. Her tone was cool. "I want to shower. I may go to bed early—it's been a tough day."

It was code for the inevitability that he would be dining alone. She would be eating nothing. He wanted to change her mind but knew better than to argue. On the way to the kitchen he heard the shower start.

Dinner was a brick of veggie lasagna in the microwave and steamed green beans. He paired it with a Rogue ale and followed it with a middle-sized bistro glass of Merlot. Not the optimum sequence, he realized, but pragmatic.

He tuned to the Cards and Astros. It was the kind of game he especially appreciated, when he did not care who won or lost and he could revel in baseball's pure zone and hit the brainwave designed for floating, the indolent one. At the bottom of the second glass he had to admit it was not working.

He clicked the game off and considered bed and the time. Eight twenty-eight.

He flashed on Sophie at the edge of the door that was cracking open to the wide world. He imagined calling her, talking adult to adult, just to get balance, to touch in with a sane person. Ridiculous, he realized. She would hear it in his voice immediately—something was off. More to the point, he was dad and she was Sophie, neither of them an ordinary adult to the other, not yet and probably never.

He thought of Rob and Karen on their way and the common thread between them and his daughter. Freedom, or at least the illusion. But wasn't he doing the same, on the edge, with his own risk.

He was considering glass three. Why not? With the rest of the bottle he could plaster himself over like a guest walled up in a Hammer film, a lesser Usher. Instead he headed for his office, head high and only slightly off line.

He sat at his computer and his screen came to life. Of the various contacts strewn in his personal backwash—old girlfriends, couples, fellow parents—he thought of Dale. He needed a kindred spirit in the risk pool. Dale was a businessman, he carried guns. He was also a gadget-head, into quad audio on his tablet, GPS watches for his kids. He could easily be at his machine after dinner, cruising for distractions. Walker opened his mail window. Where would he start? The beginning would be necessary—what the project was, and that would lead to what his vision was, and that could require why. He could explain that it was like a cement sailboat; it made perfect sense against the odds and all the wrong assumptions. What was he hoping, that Dale had the perspective to see it, unlike Lynne, unlike Rob? He would not use the microphone, Lynne could hear him. He would use the keyboard. But the keys seemed untouchable. He stared at the mail window, and its blankness reminded him somehow of its complete opposite, Hitchcock's *Rear Window*. The effort to communicate, to clarify, seemed huge and repellent.

He pushed his chair back and stood. Then he waited for his owning self to catch up, the one with the information and the rules. He left the office, and the hall darkened as the electronics shut down behind him. He had reached the living room when he heard her above in the guest room. She had turned in bed, or the floor had creaked as she had crossed the room. It was like having Margo back in the house, but that had felt better. They had been awash in generosity, but now the lesser gods prevailed. He thought of going up to talk with her again, but it could easily make things worse. He was a prisoner in his house, in his mind.

This was not congruous with the view he had of himself, even the humblest version. It was not entrepreneurial. It was only meagerly human. He stared across the room at the blank TV and tried to conceive of a way out. His hand went to his pocket. Empty, but that could be fixed. He had had a few, but he could handle it.

After a quick trip to the bedroom for his wallet and keys, he was at the front door. He weighed whether to leave a note. He imagined her coming down, finding him gone, checking the garage from the window. He tested the vision against the odds. What would a note accomplish? The idea of it was suffocating. He stepped out into the warm evening and locked the door behind him.

Climbing into the Subaru, he hit his head on the door frame. While admitting that he did not do this routinely when perfectly sober, he recalled that it had happened. No cause for alarm.

As he pulled out of the garage he checked his acuity, then monitored himself to the end of the drive and beyond. No double vision, no big deal. He let the window down, and he was swimming in the balmy air. Traces of verbena.

He decided against any music. By the time he hit the county highway, he was rolling flat out in the rush of night air, alone but for a set of distant tail lights. The darkening sky was underlit by the last light, like fire glow on velvet.

He waited a while longer, until he was far enough out.

"What am I doing?" he asked nothing but the night air that whipped past him.

It was not, he thought, that the idea was crazy, just not simple. The countless ungraceful, reasonable ideas that passed without question—those were simple. If he could not elucidate his reasons clearly, even to himself, if the rationale was not available to him in so many words, was it a kind of faith? Was it like the faith he had once? What, he had asked long ago, separated faith in the Everlasting God from faith in a rabbit's foot? What was left then, but a belief in the capacity? For what, capacity itself?

He reached to the dash to start music but stopped himself. Habit. He needed clarifying silence. He checked the rear-view mirror and it was empty. He was cruising alone.

He thought of Lynne in the guest bed. She couldn't trust his plan on any level, and that surprised him. After their years together, he believed they had become increasingly blended. He suspected that sometimes, sleeping side by side, they dreamed the same dream, although they had never said as much. Not vague semblance dreams, but the same. Perhaps they were dreams they could not recall, or could not confess. What did it mean for him, given that echoing of their subconscious states, that she didn't trust it?

The straight road lay before him, its long pull. He smelled sand.

Silly, she was thinking. She couldn't relate. Didn't care was the point. Was it simply rage, his own rage and reaction? Overreaction? He had to admit that rage, however ideals-based, was not quite adult in the world's eyes. Juvenile. It was a lack of curing, maturation into the constrained, the unnatural. She was linking him with Rob. That was why he seemed perilous to her. He was ready to slide the lid off the contained and the known. She was more right than wrong. He saw it now.

He was linked to Rob, but there was a difference. Rob had simply moved, traded Joshua trees for Douglas firs. Traded allegiances, if the concept existed in the nouvelle nation. When his own plan crossed the line into commitment, he would cross into real risk. It would make money, he was reasonably sure. He had done his spade work, researched seasons, volumes, locations, capacities, costs, start-up and operating. But the risk was real. Lynne believed he was rolling their lives back to some starting point. Perhaps he was.

He punched the button and the music bloomed around him, huge, rich sound. Elvis and the Staples—*Suspicious Minds*. He started the air conditioning and began to raise the windows when he saw lights in the mirror, not just headlights. Red, blue, white jolts, again, again. Half a mile back, maybe more, and closing. He lifted his foot and saw his speed drop below sixty-five. How fast could he have been going? Not much over seventy. Enough for a ticket? The guy could be under his quota. It wasn't a speeding ticket that concerned him. The cop had been following, maybe for miles. He punched the music off and held his breath. A few seconds were silent, and then he heard the siren. It cut the night behind him, closing in.

He was off the gas, eyes half on the mirror, half on the edge of the blacktop looking for a smooth shoulder. He was about to be busted. He lowered his window all the way. He would be asked to get out, walk the line, be breathalized. No

note to trace his location. He would need to wake Lynne
with a call to make his bail. He was signaling right, gliding
toward a black space.

He was stopped. Window down, blowing out his open
mouth. The siren was close. He was dropping the passenger
window to clear the car of his breath. A strobe of lights in
the mirror. Crazed pulsing scream of the siren. Burst of
lights. He blew one last time out the window and tried to
gulp the night air.

In the next second it was on him then past him, howling
down the county highway. The sudden drop-off, Doppler
effect, then fading. Just as suddenly, his flashers cut off.
The patrolman had wanted him over, that was all, probably
for his own safety. He was responding to a break-in,
husband beating wife, burglary in progress. That was the
generous assessment. Bullshit was another. Random power
play by a bonehead, just because he could.

Walker pushed the door open and staggered out, rattled
and sweating. The last vapors of alcohol were fully
combusted.

"Fucker!" and "Thank you God" spilled out in succes-
sion. He stood beside the Subaru ticking with heat and
watched the squad car lights disappear in the distance. He
waited and breathed and gravity returned. He took in where
he had halted.

The land beyond the shoulder was more than flat. It had
been leveled. A hundred yards or so off to his right he
spotted the trace of a driveway he could vaguely recall
passing at other times. A couple of miles in from the road, a
low range sat like gray waves on the horizon. It was a place
he recognized but did not quite know.

He started in toward the far end of the drive, in the
direction of the mountains. When he spotted the wide cape
of asphalt where the drive ended, he remembered.
Seventeen years ago when they first moved to Boulder City,
a CalMart had stood on the spot. The next year Grand

Market of Dubai acquired the chain and closed a third of the stores. The building was razed, and Walker dimly recalled a big deal with a casino chain that fell apart in a bankruptcy. The land had sat vacant since then.

He got a feel for the dimensions of the old parking lot overblown with sand. The flat plain rolled straight to the low mountains. Above him the stars were bright in the blackness. He pondered the ancient connections that human consciousness had made among them, beasts and immortals. He walked out on the lot and made a wide circle, savoring the smell of the earth and the clear air. He felt charged, as though the circle had power.

When he was ready, he turned and took long strides back to the car. Then he drove, clear-headed and purposeful, toward home.

Chapter 19

From: Walker Beale <bealew@questar.net>
To: Rob Mathis <rob@robmathisphere.com>
Sent: Wednesday, June 5
Subject: Hey

Good to hear from you guys last night. Now that you're in, you can start adjusting to life in the swamp—Sasquatches, log rolling, etc. You have not made the mistake of your life—keep telling yourself that. Actually, it sounds not bad at all. Give me the best time for salmon. I want to go when we can noodle up a Chinook or two.

As I recall we were on the subject of my retirement thing when you asked about the Big Idea. I said something about the financing, and then if you thought I angled off, I did. The Big is a touchy topic right now, so e-mail is the better way to go. This is the deal so far.

I have a bid in on a location. Remember the Grand Market out on Veterans? It was a CalMart before that. It's fifteen acres—ideal for a mid-sized drive-in. There's nothing left but the old parking lot, but there's electric and water, which is huge. You probably remember it's less than ten minutes from our place, which means a little over half an hour from Vegas. Paiute Ridge is in the background. It's perfect.

The agent tells me there are no other bids. It's being offered by a holding company in L.A. They were betting on a residential developer years ago, but the zoning fell through. If we get past this step, the permit can take weeks, average of two, a month at most. After that it's putting in the infield, concession, wall, and screen. The screen is the simplest. The concession can be the most important—forty percent plus of total sales historically, and that's with traditional low-margin product, pop and candy basically. So there's a lot of potential there, especially when I add memorabilia, classics, and so on—the whole drive-in catalog. OK, and that brings us to our drive-in trivia question of the day:

What legend of rock 'n roll played the roof of the concession of the Sky-Vue Drive-In outside La Mesa, Texas? *Texas* is your big clue.

He considered where to put the answer. Maybe at the bottom below his signature in classic puzzle format, small font, inverted. He was trying to remember where the FlipText feature was in his mail tool when the phone rang.

He imagined she was in the living room. He reconsidered flipping the text. He would omit it instead, hook him like a Chinook. He was okay with that. He clicked Send.

When he reached the living room, Sophie was already on the screen and Lynne was raising the volume from the sofa.

"Oh, hi Dad," she said as he sat in the center cushion. He checked her for any issue, but she was characteristically bright in the bubble of youth, somewhere in Chicago. Lynne's expression was noncommittal, which had become her mode of late.

"To what do we owe this honor?" he asked.

"It's no problem, I'm fine. You look...I don't know."

What did she see?

"We're fine," Lynne put in. "Just curious."

Whatever cue Sophie had picked up on had come from her, not him. They had always been subtly tuned to one another, and Sophie was probably the most intuitive of the three. He spoke next.

"So what, as we used to say, is up?"

"It's a favor. Could you please send me a dress—it's in my closet, probably toward the back, the good one. Do you know the one, Mom, it's black with the gold embroidery on the front—"

"Off the shoulder—"

"Right, that's it. Can you send it to me, maybe two-day or something. I'm going with Andrew Pullen to his friend's wedding in Des Plains. It's a week from Saturday, and this way I won't have to buy a dress."

"Wedding?" Walker reacted. "That's your professor, isn't it? What's he doing?"

"Nothing! I just mentioned I had never been to a wedding, and he was going alone—"

"I'll send it," Lynne cut in. "If I can't find it, I'll call you."

"Kidding," he said. "I was kidding."

"I know!" Sophie excused him. "What do you think, I'm going to marry my professor? Anyway, how are you guys? What's happening with your drive-in thing?"

"It's good, actually." He described the location and Sophie remembered the spot. It had been on the frontier of her bike range in grade school days.

"What are you going to show?"

"How about *The Blob*, the original, 1958, with Steve McQueen? *Jaws*, the uncut. *Blue Hawaii*, *Follow That Dream*, maybe both. A Jayne Mansfield retrospective. *The War of the Worlds*, all three versions. And the film that made drive-ins thick as fleas in the Carolinas—*Tobacco Road* starring the great Robert Mitchum. And so on."

"Cool! I'll come."

"You'll need a car first. Or at least a date with a car."

"I don't date cars. Ha-hah. No prob. Do you think people will want to see those?"

"You just said *you* would. But you're not the target market. It's the rest of us fossils, mired in reality."

"You're saying I'm not in reality? I'm perfectly realistic, more or less."

"'Reality—I'll only go as a guest.' Who said that? No hints," he added to Lynne, hoping to engage her if only a bit. "Jason Robards in *A Thousand Clowns*. One of your mom's favorite films, at least when I met her."

"Is that right, Mom?" she asked a little hesitantly. Walker could tell she could see what he knew. Lynne was not happy.

"I liked it a long time ago. It's hard to remember."

"Hey, you okay?"

"Sure, why?"

"I don't know, you seem—"

"Preoccupied, maybe. Work stuff."

"Why don't you come out here and visit? That's what you guys should do." She looked sincere, expectant.

Walker recalled Chicago in summer in a former life. Oak Street Beach, music on the pier, days of the Earl of Old Town. Scrounging as a pizza delivery driver into the vast West Side. He appreciated that their college senior daughter would not mind her parents hanging around, at least at some appropriate distance.

"It could happen," he said. Lynne glanced at him as if she knew it would not, at least from his side. Her mouth looked stiff. He suddenly imagined she would bolt from the room.

"Why don't we talk about it?" she said to Sophie instead, leaving it open.

He asked about Sophie's research project, but he could only half-concentrate on her answer. He wanted to hear more, but he had the nagging sense they should conclude the call before Lynne boiled over. In minutes they did, Sophie reminding them of the urgency by thanking them again for the dress.

"I'll get it," Lynne said, already past him. The screen was dark. He considered a moment. Against his better judgment he followed her to Sophie's room. She was fingering through hangers at the end of the closet.

"You said you were preoccupied."

She extracted the dress, a black nylon raiment of youth, and brushed at the midriff.

"About what, you mean? What did we used to call it, future plans?"

He could answer. What else were they? Was "plans" too grand? In what way was it insufficient? Instead he gave up. He could not say it all again, try to bridge to his reality, which she would only deny.

"I'm thinking of going out to see her," she said. She looked straight at him then down into the dress and picked at an invisible spot. "What do you think?"

It took him a moment.

"It's good. I think you should if you want. We both miss her, and she opened the door. Right now I—"

"I know," she said quickly.

"I wish—"

"Of course, it's your business. You've just started, she knows that."

She was nailing him, excusing him, patching it over as best she could. He had nothing to add.

"I'm going out for a while," she said, replacing the hanger, the dress over her arm. "I have to go by the Gleason house and then I'll overnight this."

He didn't know if it was true or not. The Gleason place was empty, and he knew her contract required a visit a week. Did it matter? As he headed back to his office, he heard the front door close.

He stepped in and his screen lighted. Rob was on line.

            alamogordo, yucca flats, the friggin' end of the
      wild west as we knew it. i remember it well. it's per-
      fect for your lost empire drive-in thing. go for it! as
      the lions said to the christians.

yup, we're in and we love it but it's going to be a work in progress for a while. the septic, for example, is not shall we say, up to code. like it's not a real system—the stuff goes right in the bay. would have been good if our inspector had picked up on that. needless to say, thousands. we'll get it back but it's a lawyer just to write the friggin' letters.

on the plus side, the view out the back is two gorgeous humpbacked islands in the sound, mist in the morning, birds. yesterday we saw an eagle feeding.

i didn't tell you this. the first night we were here they freaked us. three bodies the size of soccer balls were coming over the deck rail then up to our glass door. raccoons with eyes like little black marbles and their masks. scared us shitless but made us fans forever. now we put apple slices out and watch for them.

karen has studio space and the office is coming together. like we're in a weird chinese landscape, realm of the clouds. it's better, i can say that. i'll send shots.

about your biz as a hot button—margo called yesterday. she talked to karen mostly, said she's concerned because lynne's bent out. just so you know although I'm sure you're aware anyway—the natives are restless.

and now the answer you've been waiting for. janice joplin.

"Great," Walker said as he rescanned the words. He imagined berating Margo savagely. He understood where her sympathies would probably lie, naturally, but it felt like betrayal, one more vote of no confidence.

He had come this far, but nothing would be real until he closed. Would he be testing his vision or his sanity? Even Margo was concerned about his impact, his toxicity. At the bottom of the screen in the status bar, an icon was cycling through colors, seeming to flash. One of his subscriber alerts. He clicked it and the news window opened.

"This demonstration in favor of secession is not the largest in Los Angeles to date, but it seems to be the loudest and now as we have seen, the most violent." The reporter stood before a street ganged with police on motorcycles and on foot under the chopping lights of a Fire and Rescue van. Beyond them a crowd was milling on open ground, a mixture of what appeared to be demonstrators and gawkers. "The Mayor's office has confirmed what Chief of Police Riordan stated, that no permit had been obtained for the march that began a little less than six blocks from this spot. Several witnesses have confirmed that a few of the demonstrators threw objects at the line of police who were blocking the street. There was one report of a demonstrator using a slingshot.

"From what we have been able to determine at this point in time, and I stress that first reports are subject to error, police opened fire and three demonstrators were hit. We do have confirmed reports that one man was wounded in the head, and a witness told us the victim had expired by the time medics reached him. In the park area behind me as you can see, a number of demonstrators and others remain, although police have requested that the area be cleared. It may be significant that they have requested, not ordered, an evacuation of the area at this point. As more is known and the identities of the victims are released, we'll continue to bring you this breaking story. Cassandra?"

Cassandra appeared in the frame behind the anchor desk with sculpted cheekbones and a moony ring of blond hair. Walker was feeling tight in the chest and hung over with anger toward Margo. He clicked the news window shut. In a moment he opened another.

As he scanned the long list in the titles pane, the effect was mildly narcotic. He stopped in the M's and clicked the one that seemed most likely to sustain relief.

Gable was ambling over a dry patch of range land. A close-up showcased the age scars of the old warrior, one eye clenched shut against the sun, his cowboy grin crooked, bemused. But it was Marilyn who stole the shots as she stole all of them, like a supernatural source of gravity bending all light into herself. Soon they were picking up Monty Clift at the bus stop, and he was in the back seat on the verge of DTs and they were all heading for his gig at the rodeo. Walker was feeling at ease with *The Misfits*, their loose adhesion of lost lives, corny but emblematic of a certain American experience, fantasy riders. It was set in Nevada, one he could nearly fantasize that he lived in when it was provisional, unscripted and shambling and free.

He watched until his head returned to a cool place and he could key in his answer to Rob.

Bonus points for Janice of Beaumont, Texas, but we're sorry, no. Buddy Holly and the Crickets.

Chapter 20

Walker had no sooner spotted her on the stool before the open window than he was compelled to watch. She was leaning forward, reaching across the small table to the side of the frame. She was engaged in some domestic act, but from his position behind her he could not identify it. She extended her other arm. He sensed he should fight it, but standing was irresistible. He moved closer.

Her torso inclined forward, her summer dress taut against her hip. He saw blue cotton flowers on a field of white. He followed the line of her arm. It was not divertingly toned or tanned like a swimmer's, but naturally long-boned, its reach languid. She was younger than he by two decades, even three. She could have been from a former lifetime.

The curtain pull, he realized. She was untwisting it. Through the window glass, he saw fog in the yard. Tilting, body folded, the solid fullness of her hip on the stool against light cotton, blue cornflowers on white.

He was beside her, slipping his arm under her, the weight of her breast in his palm. She glanced back at him, bluish eyes neither surprised nor reproachful, elbows on the table. Behind her head breeze stirred the curtain. His other arm wrapped around her. He tested her weight, preparing to lift her, but she turned in his arms, rotating to face him. The years between them had mercifully closed. He was back wherever they had met. He had forgotten, but he would remember. She was a timeless distraction in a classroom or a hallway or in an airplane seat beside him. The memory was recoverable in her eyes, pale blue with gray. He was searching them and then he was closing the few inches to her lips.

She did not pull away. She stayed in the kiss, her mouth opening. The cotton dress was off her shoulders, below her breasts, and her nipple hardened on his tongue. They were slow, relaxed with each other. He sensed time accommodating them, backing off.

His hand rode down her thigh to the back of her knee. He grasped her calf and lifted, her leg light in his hand. She was young and accepting and it seemed she was happy for him, and he was struck by the sense he had had before, so distant that it seemed a former lifetime, of the great generosity of women. In the room of memory, he tasted her leg. His tongue met the perfect slope of her calf, and there was no flavor at all, only a sensation like satin. He could have been tasting moonlight.

Glitter caught his eye. A tattoo wrapped her ankle, black vines, an Etruscan garland. Inside it tiny flashes showered in the window light. Grist of rhinestones, worked in like ink, jeweled thread of brightness in her skin.

He heard a whishing sound. Again. It could be a swiping blade. Again. A pulse, robotic. Again. It cut into their dream together, insistent and unrelenting, like a sinister toy.

Walker's eyes were open and he was lying dazed, between worlds. He realized he was on the sofa in his office, sweating.

He rolled on his side and checked the screen. At the bottom an icon was rotating. The whoosh accompanied each rotation. One of his alerts, a pestilence of his own making.

"Piece of shit," he addressed it as he rolled off the sofa. He killed it with a click, then opened the message.

The Motiograph projector—his transaction had cleared. He checked his watch. Ten to midnight. Where in electronic hell were they processing his order? Not St. Louis where the machine was. Pakistan, most likely. He closed the message and faced the one behind it, the one he had been writing to Rob.

From: Walker Beale <bealew@questar.net>
To: Rob Mathis <rob@robmathisphere.com>
Sent: Saturday, June 22
Subject: Status

Signed and delivered is where I believe we were are. Yes, as of last week the hallowed ground is mine. Polluted by CalMart and Grand Mart and every form of detritus of squalid capitalism, blah. I was, as you might guess, shitless, but now it's in the mirror and so, onward!

The grading was done the day I signed, and now we're lining off the infield and blocking the foundation for the concession. I mentioned the concession is a cash cow. I didn't tell you we're going to use the old-style speaker poles. Remember them? Of course not, you were an infant. The pole is outside the driver's side when you drive into a stall. On the pole is a box about the size of an old water canteen. It's connected by a spiral chord to the pole. Now picture this—you lift the speaker box off the pole and hang it inside the window. You crank the volume knob, and that's how you hear the audio in your car. Imagine what freaking genius invented that. Sometime back in the 1970s or 80s they went to radio instead. You just tuned to a frequency—no more poles. But I'm combining the two—I'll have the old poles and the hulking big box speakers, but the signal will go from wired poles to the speakers—no radio signal, which can fade. And the speakers are really Grose inside the boxes, super fidelity.

So that's the speaker thing. But first will be the parking area—the infield it's called. The contractor assumed we were going to pave it, but no. I'm just having him pack it, and I'm putting gravel aggregate in the drives. That way I'll get exactly what it was in the old days—grass needling up between the stalls and no grass where the cars go. It's a self-maintaining system. That is, as you well know my friend, the idea.

Lynne doesn't get any of this. I'd give a lot if she would because even if I feel strongly that it can work, the odds are always against anything you try to do on your own, so some support from her would be highly okay. I'm hoping she'll get there. She's back from Chicago tomorrow.

"Fading fast," Walker added at the end. "Later." He clicked Send.

"That's it," he confirmed to no one and headed down the hall toward bed. The alerts could alert each other.

He brushed his teeth with eyes closed then worked his way with no lights to the bed and lay on his back on top of the cool blanket. He looked forward to picking up Lynne, but at the same time he was glad she had been gone for this part. Startup was the hardest. He was tired in the bone and disoriented, out of his element.

He let his attention drift off Lynne to no attention. He was sick of their struggle, and the idea of struggle. Even as he was getting to nowhere, he knew where he wanted to go.

He was imagining Carolina, a window just off the beaches. He needed an onshore breeze that stirred the curtain. He reinvented her hair like a shadow. He was sinking into the memory. He was waiting for her to reach toward the window.

The next evening he was at the baggage claim in Las Vegas International with half an hour to spare. He had come directly from the site, circled the parking garage, and cleaned up in the men's room. Instead of the heavy traffic he had allowed for, the commute had been light, and he had plenty of time to alternate between cable news too far away to hear and his own image on the overhead monitors, shot by concealed videocams. Baggage claim was their place to meet, even if she had only a carry-on. For her four days in Chicago, she would have checked one bag.

He paced among the greeters. A guardswoman, M-16 on her back, clopped past him in combat boots. He scanned the arrivals board again. Still not showing Landed. He was tight with anticipation as he always was at airports. After easily half a dozen, he was repeating the robotic admonition to leave no bags unattended or they would be confiscated. The first passengers began to appear on the escalator. Soon he picked her out in the stack of human crayons.

She gave him a solid hug, and he was buoyed by two things—her smile that lightened him as always, and her perfume, cultured by body heat, musk and spice with the Italian name. He could picture the faceted bottle. She seemed a bit winded, understandably, but in good humor.

"Amazing," he said, "only half an hour late. You look great. The board says carousel six."

"O'Hare's a mess," she said, "construction everywhere. We boarded late then sat on the runway forever. Half an hour's good, considering."

They headed toward the merry-go-round. Six was rotating with a box long enough for skis and an overstuffed, flowered bag that looked abandoned.

"How's Sophie?"

"Great, I think. She's doing great. She introduced me to a couple of her friends. Here they come." The first bags slid down the chute and plopped onto the carousel. "We had a wonderful time, actually. We went to one of her favorite haunts—the Café Medici. And we got to the Art Institute—I can tell you later."

"And her spouse?"

She grinned.

"I did meet him. The professor's all of thirty. Very nice, very academic in a funny, nervous way. He reminded me of Woody Allen."

He recalled the long-ago days when he discovered Woody and his old Manhattan. Drive-in material? No. Unless he could remember the early ones, like the Japanese detective flick with the insane voice-over.

He started to ask about her mother but was not displeased to see her bag hitting the wheel. He angled in among the hopefuls and caught the handle.

"I didn't dislike him at all. I just had to keep reminding myself not to laugh. I'm sure attraction was a factor in her getting the job."

Walker had the air on, but it was six-thirty and cool enough to leave the windows down. The wind was in Lynne's hair, and the ride had a pleasantly familiar feel to him of other times on other roads. It was what he wanted. Her hemline was above her knees and her legs were open. He felt hopeful. Before she left they had been less than close.

"She's keeping him in perspective, right?"

"Of course." She was confident. They had shared secrets. "So, you said the construction started?"

He detected a note of interest and no rancor. More hopeful still.

"Well, the grading's done and we're doing the infield layout. The concession could start on Monday." She seemed to be listening. He could save the rest.

"I have to get gas. I thought I wouldn't have time." He banked off at the Excom sign and descended and they pulled up to one of the green pumps.

Walker had swiped his card and was lifting the pump handle when he caught sight of someone across the island. Her back was turned. Then he spotted the car. Of course it was. He flashed on Karen on the phone. The topic was psychic damage, and he was the perpetrator. They hadn't communicated since. Silly, he thought. He tapped Lynne's shoulder and pointed. They came up behind her.

"Hey Margo."

She clicked off the handle and turned looking surprised, but he wondered. Something in her shoulders or the micromusculature of her face. Had she seen him first?

"Hi guys! How *are* you?"

"Hi yourself," Lynne said. "We're fine. You come here often?"

Walker saw she had a passenger.

"I'm driving a friend home, a coworker, she's a school counselor, actually. Her car's in the shop." The woman half-turned to them in the open window. "Cathy, this is Lynne, and Walker. I told you about them. I've known them forever."

She had a quick smile and a firm grip, and Walker noticed her tan like a tennis player's.

"You're back from Chicago, right? Did it go okay? You look like it did."

Lynne confirmed they were on the way from the airport and rolled into an account of the visit with Sophie. Walker imagined a reluctance on Margo's part to look him in the eye. He took the opportunity to recheck Cathy in the passenger window. She was late thirties, maybe forty, lean and athletic looking in a sailor-stripe pullover with short sleeves. Overall, a turn-on.

"How are *you*, Walker?" Margo caught him off guard, and he wondered if she meant to.

He considered his options. Have mercy or nail her? He sensed her stiffen. Fate had dropped her in his lap. I'm great. I enjoy making others—especially your buddy and my wife Lynne—miserable with a quixotic and boyish flare for irresponsibility. That is what you think and babble to our mutual friends without my knowledge, correct? He was fixed on the crows feet at the corners of her eyes. The same master was etching them all, all of the precious, including Margo.

"I'm doing okay," he said. "Working on getting this show business off the ground. It's scary at first, as you can imagine. You know where you want to go, and that's the inspiration, but they say—who's they?—it's the perspiration, and the persistence, that get you there."

She seemed to ease a bit.

"So. Keep on sweating, then." She grinned, almost sheepishly, it seemed, as though looking for confirmation.

Margo was back. At least he had gotten that right. He thought Lynne looked less easy, not contrary but simply regarding him somehow from farther away.

They chatted a while longer, and then Margo finished pumping and she and her passenger were on their way. Walker and Lynne were also, in the opposite direction.

"Well, that was different," he said when they were in the high-speed lanes.

She looked less cordial than he had hoped. He thought of bringing up the subject of Cathy, whoever she was, but he recognized he was still slightly buzzed by her and thought better of it.

"So how do you feel about it now?" he said. "The business, I mean. Margo thought—"

"Okay. I'm...hopeful."

She was using his word. They had exchanged the thought. He played through what she could mean by it. Hopeful for an implosion at the earliest possible time seemed like an option.

"Really?"

"I hope it goes well," she said and turned to the window.

"Thanks," he said. And if for any reason it turns out otherwise, we have a strategy to back out, he wanted to be able to say but couldn't. The conversation shifted to her mother and back to Sophie, and he tried to convince himself the tone was positive. In all, it was less than he wanted and needed.

That night they revived sex, which had been a memory, and he had to admit that was nothing but good. At the same time it felt expected, and for no good reason he wondered if she was enduring him. Their closeness afterward actually felt better, which, he realized, was unusual for him. When they separated he drifted, waiting for sleep, but soon he was thinking of the project. In the days she had been in Chicago, he had shifted to late hours. Mailing or messaging Rob had become the norm. He hadn't checked his mail since they arrived home, and progress the next day depended on the availability of conduit, which was still unconfirmed. Tiptoeing to the office wouldn't be necessary, he just needed to reach his phone on the dresser. It wasn't that he couldn't wait until she was asleep or do it without waking her. It was a matter of perforation. It could rend the thin fabric between them. It could bring bad luck. Instead, on the backs of his eyelids, he replayed the girl of the night before. An infidelity, he knew. He could no longer see her clearly, but he had the supple weight he once held, memory in the touch. He gave up to the touch, and its weight tugged him under the edge of sleep.

The next morning Lynne was up and out before him. She wanted status from her backup for the days she was gone. Walker got the confirmation he needed in his inbox, and by ten he was at the site. Pulling up beside his contractor's pickup, he checked the scene which was not reassuring. He climbed out into the cloud of white dust from the driveway. The sun was already high and unfiltered.

"It's a mess now," Jay Lopez said. "It'll look better with key aggregate on here. We'll do a three-pass roll." He projected intensity when he talked about grading and rolling and concrete. His aviator shades glinted and his black mustache trimmed razor-clean said perfectionist—a quality Walker appreciated in his prime contractor.

"We got a break on the conduit," Walker said as they headed toward the stack of tubing. "Is it right?"

"Yes, no problem. We've got fifty sixteens. That should be enough."

The backhoe was working a trench that began at the concession foundation and extended toward the screen zone. It paralleled three that had already been dug. The wiring for the speaker poles would follow three main arterial conduits and branch off to the car stalls.

"We could get back some time here, but it depends on the electrician. He says his job was on schedule, but this is back-to-back—"

"Could you follow up?"

"I'll do that today, no problem." Jay popped his phone off his belt and set a reminder.

They headed back past the car to the concession foundation. He surveyed the perfectly smooth cement polygon, poured and hardened to match the drawing. He may have heard it before it caught the corner of his eye—behind Jay, another vehicle rolling in the driveway.

A white Hyundai Phoenix, a fat-tired, short-backed four wheeler, trailed a rooster tail of dust. It pulled up behind Jay and halted, close enough to see that the driver was a woman. The door swung open and then she was heading toward them.

Walker tried to guess which inspector she was, county or possibly state. He could show where the permit was posted. At the same time, nothing about her fit the profile. She wore a white cotton safari shirt, khaki cargo shorts, and hiking boots. Her wraparound shades looked Aspen.

"Hi," she said, smiling affably enough.

"Can I help you?"

"Suzanne Canady, *Great Basin Light.*"

Walker recognized her, not the woman before him but the name. He had seen her byline a few times in the southern Nevada rag. He nodded okay to Jay who headed toward the backhoe.

"I hear you're building a drive-in. Maybe I could do a story on it." She removed her glasses, squinting into the light, but he could see her eyes, gray-blue, wolf-colored. Her full dark hair was drawn back—touches of gray and too dry, he noticed, probably from chasing mediocre stories like his in the merciless sun.

He wondered how she had gotten the lead. He had sent out no releases; it was absurdly early. County records—public document, he realized, his permit. Not so far from his first guess.

"If all goes according to plan," he said.

"What is it, X-rated?"

"Excuse me?"

She refitted her glasses and opened the notebook she had been carrying.

"I was just wondering how you could do it. Make a go of it. It's a hooky idea, but why do you think people would drive here?"

He nodded, trying to regroup. To alienate the press, any press no matter how humble, would not be sane.

"It's an experience." He continued to nod. "It's one I think there's a market for." What angle did she have in mind, if any? He was seeing his reflection, slightly distorted, in her opaque lenses.

She flashed a quick grin, wrote nothing. She was tanned and fit, hiker-style, he guessed somewhere in her forties.

"How big will it be?" She walked to the concession foundation and around it to the far side.

"Fifteen acres, more or less," he said following. "That's space for eight hundred thirty cars."

"That's a healthy number." She wrote it down. "You said an experience. What experience are these people going to have?"

"Did you ever go?"

"You mean to a drive-in? I think I remember one time. I was maybe five or six. My father had what they used to call a station wagon, and there was a drive-in outside Bakersfield."

"How did you like it?"

"I loved it, I think. Okay, but kids love everything."

"But I think there's something in that. And it's something we're missing now—that vintage experience, the 'surround'. And the film is at the center. We're using basic old-style projection technology, before it was 'technology'. One of our projectors is going to be a classic model from the sixties, restored. We'll transmit the sound to the speakers, but they'll be the old box-style on poles—detachable ones they can hang in their windows. They're just FM tuner boxes, so they can take them in and roll up if they want."

She was scribbling.

"You said 'the film'. That sounds high-minded."

"Good point. The drive-in shouldn't be an art house. Drive-in movies are movies, but that doesn't mean they can't be well made. Look at all the genres, screwball comedy to epic to horror to... screwball epic." She was watching him. It felt odd but pleasant. "They all have classics, and some are just fun—what we used to call 'camp' when that was a concept. They're all part of the experience."

She was scribbling again when her phone went off.

"Dammit! Sorry." She pulled it out of her cargo pocket and stepped away a few paces, but he could still pick up her tone, business-level tense. He turned and watched Jay in the infield talking to the driver.

"Look I *am* sorry," she said. Her glasses were off, the wolf-colored eyes again. "I have to go, but I do want to do a story. Here's my card. Let me know when's a good time to talk, if you don't mind—"

"No, of course, no problem. A story would be great." He understood that he was sounding like a lummox. He checked her card briefly. Suzanne Canady, Senior Reporter, phone. *Great Basin Light* logo, a lighthouse that was never perched on a stout mountain.

"Good, thanks. Talk to you." She stuffed her phone back into her pocket, heading for the car.

He stepped down from the concession foundation in the general direction of her Phoenix. As she climbed into the high driver's seat, he could not ignore her dark legs and wondered how he had missed it. Above her ankle before the short white sock, a gold anklet. The tiny flat facets caught the light, a glittering illusion of threaded sun in the skin. She pulled the door shut.

White dust billowed back down the drive, and he realized he was elevated, buzzed, and not just by the prospect of a story. He slipped the card into his shirt pocket and headed toward Jay.

"Derailed," he said under his breath. He tried to refocus on the task at hand. Six hours to quitting time, and the high sun reminded him he was nothing but behind.

Chapter 21

That night while Lynne was in the shower, Walker took his wallet to the office. He opened it and checked her card again. Looking past the lighthouse logo, he focused on the number. He sat down close to the phone.

He had not conveyed his message. Instead of communicating—supposedly his area of expertise—he had drifted. He had reacted, not led. Now that he had time to consider, he could be effective. He needed to sell the story to the journalist. He knew how it should go, but as he rehearsed, he seemed to be slipping around it. He imagined his audience, he talking and she listening, the face he remembered in the glare.

If he didn't have his golden version of the message firmly in mind, did it matter? He would get her voice mail anyway.

As he stared at the phone he became aware of the sound of the shower. Would a phone call be a betrayal? A trivium, or the worst he could do? Why was he asking the question? He watched the phone for clues. He was blocking his own message. His ducks were in no rows, and they were not about to be that night. He slipped Suzanne Canady's card back into his wallet and left the office.

From: Walker Beale <bealew@questar.net>

To: Rob Mathis <rob@robmathisphere.com>

Sent: Monday, July 1

Subject: Next

Hit our first bump. Two of the crew were pushing meth on the site. Jay found out and cut them both. So now we have no backhoe operator and a ton of trench to go. He's calling around and we're running an ad, but there's an immigration sweep going on, so a lot of drivers are laying low. The driver he fired always seemed hyper, now I see why. He was a big dude too, and he did a lot of shouting when he left the lot. Empty threats I assume, mostly directed at Jay, but it's hard to know. Retaliation I don't need.

From: Walker Beale <bealew@questar.net>
To: Rob Mathis <rob@robmathisphere.com>
Sent: Saturday, July 6
Subject: Yes!

It's great that *Edenvale*'s ready. You'll have a string of monsters after it hits. Send me the preview.

Down here we're inching forward again. Jay got a driver, a transplant from San Diego. He's Navy, had two years in Indonesia. His boat was in the Sunda Strait fiasco, the friendly fire thing. He wound up with PTSD and lived on the street for most of a year. But he seems to have it together now—he told me this whole story himself. He can drive and I like him. He's slow but motivated.

Margo was over for the first time in a long time. We've reconciled. She promised to come to opening night, which is a date I can't assign yet. But it *will* happen.

On Thursday Walker was passing the library when he remembered the *Great Basin Light* published on Thursday. He tried to remember the last time he had read it. Within the year, he guessed, or at least the year before. How many papers were still on paper? In the lobby he held his card up to the dispenser and pulled a copy. He lifted it and smelled newsprint like an ancient perfume. He wanted to be a regular reader, but that depended. He skimmed the contents block then rifled through the pages.

Drive-in comes to the Basin—Carry me back

When was the last drive-in movie theater inside a hundred miles? Guess within five years and win two tickets to Liberace at the Sands. Local entrepreneur Walker Beale is developing the old Grand Doobie Market property into a popcorn time machine. It's early yet, but it may just be the sleeper of the year in our sleepy little corner of the slipstream. For the latest, keep watching this space.

Yes, he would be a reader. A writer of letters in support of Suzanne Canady's positions, whatever they may be. He would subscribe. One year, maybe two.

From: Walker Beale <bealew@questar.net>

To: Rob Mathis <rob@robmathisphere.com>

Sent: Friday, July 12

Subject: The Wall

The poles are almost all in, the trenches dug thankgod. Hughie, my PTSD sailor, is gone but Jay hooked him up with another contractor and a longer gig.

We're into the wall now. As I said, it's going to be the big hook—the namesake. It *is* the ring of stars, and it requires its own contractor. Jay has never worked with upright concrete molds, and the experts are tough to find. I was thinking huge public projects, but we found our guy through a home contractors network. Apparently the thing is big with super-mansions for the super-rich, the outré ones that look like knock-off adobes. Our genius is from L.A.— Japanese. Wears tooled boots like Angelo the Rock Jock.

Actually, molded is the most cost-effective way you can go. It's going to encircle the infield, eight feet high and four and a half at the base. On the outside face it's going to have the star effect I told you about. Broken glass, mica, shards of mirrors, reflective tile all over. Anything I can get that will sparkle like stars in the Ring of Stars. It's cornball as a teepee-shaped restaurant. I have tons of stuff from a demo-lition—the old MGM Grand.

I think I can work with our genius. It's the scope that concerns me. He's never done a project this size. I could wait for a guy in Denver who's done a few, but we would lose at least two months. I'll try Kenji first. His subcontract is tight, and I bet he wants this one for his portfolio.

From: Walker Beale <bealew@questar.net>
To: Rob Mathis <rob@robmathisphere.com>
Sent: Monday, July 22
Subject: Keeping on

More false starts. The first section of the wall col-lapsed. It's almost funny now. My Colonel Kenji was humiliated. I had to talk him out of an honorable death. He re-estimated his curing time. Even with the ideal drying conditions, the mass needed sixteen hours more. His second try went okay. We knocked off the molds and stared at it violating gravity like Stonehenge West. Eventually we just accepted it.

So, we get the process down and one of the crew splits to L.A. Nothing against us. He went back to try to spring his brother who was picked up in Orange County with fertilizer and a substance that could make it explode. They thought he was linked to a secessionist group that had the plot on B of A, maybe you heard about it. What the hell kind of country are we running? Is somebody running...

We could go trolling for a replacement, but I'm sure Kenji would rather use Carlos than start over, and so would I. We'll wait it out for a few days.

Meantime the concession walls are up and we're roller-packing the infield drive.

Lynne is more into it these days, I think. I took her out to the site yesterday for the first time. So far so good, but I can't say all is warm and cozy. What I *can* say is she's hanging in. Hope all is good with Karen, btw as always give her my love.

From: Walker Beale <bealew@questar.net>

To: Rob Mathis <rob@robmathisphere.com>

Sent: Monday, July 29

Subject: Screw heads

Jesus fucking Christ, can anybody do anything anymore? The concession sign arrived today. It's a big deal—twenty-foot back-lit fluorescent. I hired an outfit in Sacramento to do it because they have a great portfolio of vintage signs. The art for the logo—the name and cloud swirl—was done here by Zon Dezign. The Sacto bozo got that right, but I spec'ed very clearly the Coca Cola logo on both ends—1960s vintage. They gave me the chai Coke from a couple of years ago, the one with the green ring around it. The painter said it complemented the yellow aurora he used behind the stars. Jesus. I'm supposed to argue the color wheel with Sacto Rafael?

They say they can expunge and redo the logos. How do you totally leech paint out of white plastic? What choice do I have? We're behind now. If they start over I know we'd be at the bottom of the queue. I could be looking at weeks. If I had some shop in Vegas do it, they could screw it up worse.

On the plus side, we're moving on the wall again. Carlos showed up two days after he left. He said there was insufficient evidence to hold his brother, but that wouldn't have made any difference if not for the happy coincidence of an overcrowding release. If you're thinking déjà vu, you're right—it's the second in L.A. this year. So I guess no political prisoners for a while.

Walker clicked Send and took a slug of Zinfandel. He checked the system tray: 12:26. Lynne had been asleep for about two hours. He had hung around then slipped away. He needed to get to bed. He needed to handle the sign return.

He migrated to the office sofa.

Obsessed? Yes, he could confess to that. Obsessed in the service of a greater good. He emptied the glass and lay back. He pulled the blanket up from the foot. Yes, he was obsessional, in relation to Lynne, remiss. He clicked the remote and the room went dark as a sub in an oceanic trench. He pulled the blanket up to his face where it caught on his chin. He was trying to remember when he had shaved last, yesterday or the day before, when he lost consciousness.

"You're up bright and early," she said behind him. He was staring into the bathroom mirror, only his right cheek cleared of shaving cream. It was almost eight and she was leaving.

"The concession sign, the one I told you about—I have to ship it back."

"Oh," she said on her way out of the bedroom, "there had to be a reason."

"What does that mean?" he said, following her, razor in hand.

"It means you're seldom up when I leave. Simple, isn't it?" She grabbed her bag off the kitchen chair.

"No, not simple. I think you're saying...more."

"Like what?" She faced him at the door.

"Like you're pissed about something."

"I'm not angry."

"So what are you?"

"Why don't you tell me."

"I think you're mad about me doing what I'm doing, basically. You think you're the only one working, but that's because you don't get what I'm doing."

Instead of responding she pulled the door behind her hard, but he caught it. He pursued her across the asphalt to the garage.

"Listen," he said.

She was opening her door.

"Listen!" He caught the door, then pulled it open.

"Listen to what? You listen. I have a job to go to and I don't want to be late. Why, I don't know. Maybe it's habit. Or maybe it's the 'way I am'. What would you say that is, overly—something? Like overly into the future?" She seemed to sink from enraged to sad under a passing cloud. "Let me go."

"What are you talking about? I want the same things you do. We'll get the house. We'll do it exactly the way we said, and we'll be in a better position five years from now than we would have been with no business."

She was just studying him, quizzically it seemed. It occurred to him that he was standing shirtless in the garage, face half-slathered in aerosol cream. Could such a man rally support for his dreams?

"Look, I'm sorry," he said. "I know I've been acting obsessed—"

"Possessed," she said.

"Okay," he said, downshifting, thankful to be communicating. "Yes."

"You look idiotic," she said deadpan.

"Yes."

He stood back from the door and she got in. He bent down.

"You are overly...great."

She permitted a cheekside kiss, eyes straight ahead, and he contorted his neck to avoid smearing her with white. She pulled the door shut. He watched her roll out of the drive. He had salvaged what he could.

He headed back in. The confrontation first thing in the day had burned all sugar in his blood. He needed the human comforts packed in cereal and roasted beans. No more late nights, he conceded. That was the thing. Nights in the office, that was her problem. He was glad the sign was the only other battle on his schedule. He could rescue the day.

From: Walker Beale <bealew@questar.net>

To: Rob Mathis <rob@robmathisphere.com>

Sent: Wednesday, July 31

Subject: Next next

So the sign may actually work out. They say they'll turn it around in a couple of days. Believing is seeing. There's a trucker strike, what else is new, but it's in northern CA and Oregon now, so we might get lucky.

The wall's moving along—pretty dang exciting. Kenji may have it nailed after all. I want to see it after dark with the lights—that's the idea. We'll get there.

The roof is on the second floor of the concession—the projection booth and office. Exterior painting starts tomorrow.

Signing off. Damage control for wasted nights. I'm sure you can relate.

From: Walker Beale <bealew@questar.net>
To: Rob Mathis <rob@robmathisphere.com>
Sent: Thursday, August 1
Subject: Long day

Kenji put in a full ten hours today to finish up. The last six wall segments are in the molds. The frame of the screen is ninety percent. The screen seems like the crowning jewel, but it's one of the easiest parts.

The sign's in work. Minor issues, they say. I told them pentimento is not acceptable. They swear to ship in two days. If not, I'm going to Sacto.

From: Walker Beale <bealew@questar.net>
To: Rob Mathis <rob@robmathisphere.com>
Sent: Monday, August 5
Subject: Hallelujah

It's actually here and looking good. They started over. I'm sure they couldn't scrub off the chai version. You'd like it—very sixties. The logo is pure

Jetsons. Remember who produced that? Time's up: Hanna-Barbera.

The screen is up, very majestic looking, even arrogant. A big white rectangle pasted on the panorama.

The coolers and sinks are in and the bathroom's finished. Next week we bring in the projectors. I'm using the state of the art for most, but I have a gorgeous old Motiograph for some of the classics. It's an original from one of the Pacific Theatres lots in L.A., totally restored. Here's the link to the vendor. The picture of it is still up even though I've had the box for weeks. Denial that it's gone, I bet.

So we're coming down to it. Right now I'm thinking Sept. 7 for opening night. It should be a little cooler, and they'll all be back after Labor Day. That will give us six weeks to work out bugs before Halloween, which is a big night for drive-ins. Next up after we finish the concession will be dry runs. We need to test every speaker. Also the security. Didn't tell you—every speaker has a perimeter trigger code and GPS RFID. Let 'em try to take those home!

The next day Walker supervised the last of the stucco and tile work on the wall. At the end when the crew was gone, he leaned back against his fender and surveyed his domain. Evening light lay on the infield and showcased the screen in orange and gold. They were down to the finish work on the concession. In two days Jay would be on his next project. The scope of the infield with its hundreds of spaces and speaker poles seemed as intimidating as the light was magical.

He had resisted calling. His rationale had been that he was timing the call to coincide with his press releases, which had now all been sent by U.S. mail and e-mail. He knew the real reason was the time it had taken to refocus on digging the trenches after watching her Phoenix unwind its way through the white dust. It was fitting to call her from the same spot, now that he had a story she could report. It was more than fitting.

He had her card out of his wallet. He punched numbers with his thumb. At six-forty it would be voice mail. It rang twice.

"Suzanne Canady."

"Hello, this is Walker Beale," he heard himself saying. "You came to my drive-in." He sounded absurd to himself.

"Oh hi, sure. How's it going?" He thought she was moving. He imagined her wet, drying off.

"Sorry to bother you after hours. I thought I would get your—"

"No, that's okay. I have no after hours, only hours. It's by choice. You're about ready to go, aren't you?"

"You got my release—"

"I did, you're opening—"

"The seventh."

"Right, Saturday the seventh."

"Look, I also wanted to invite you personally. I don't know how the first night is going to go, but I had the feeling when you were here that you were interested and I think you would—"

"Definitely, you're right I was interested, and I am, and I can probably do that. It would be exciting to see it. Lights off, right?"

He didn't get it.

"Headlights, you turn them off before you drive in, right? For some reason I remember that."

"Right, you're absolutely right, good memory. There'll be a sign."

"Good, thanks. See you."

And then she was gone. He felt a buzz from the desk or the bath robe of Suzanne Canady. She had sounded pleased, he thought, at least not annoyed, nothing like annoyed.

Exciting to see it is what she had said. For the first time the fear of failure was real. It hit him, a sudden and annoying twist in the gut. The first step was to admit it. Then he could ride it out, put his feet back on the ground. He simply hoped it would not disappoint. It was perfectly reasonable to want a positive experience for a reviewer. He would feel the same about any press. He had sent releases to other papers, she had simply taken the initiative. That was deserving of his attention.

He took in the spellbinding light and the smell of cooling earth in the evening air. He would not dwell on the images, but he did not resist them. He was seeing the Nevada hill silver behind the blue in her eyes, then the tan taper of her calf to her ankle as she stepped up to the driver's seat, and last, the ribbon-thin glint of her anklet that caught the sun.

Chapter 22

Walker was not holding his breath, but he wasn't far from it. A million and a half into it, give or take, he could do no more. He could see the sign clearly down the straight stretch of highway, but if he didn't already know what it was, it could have been any outsized roadside enterprise. How would Lynne react?

He had turned on all the lights and powered up the ticket booth and concession where Manuel, his only employee, was waiting. Walker had already paid him for two days in which they had exercised all of the equipment from toilets to projectors. This was to be the first run-through after sundown, and he had saved it for Lynne and Margo. He was trusting that in the fifteen minutes it took to pick them both up, Manuel Cespedes would not abscond with the empty register or be stuck up. In a few seconds the sign came into focus, a retro gold and aqua prow inclined toward the highway.

"Ring of Stars," Margo read from the back seat. "Opening soon. My god, it's impressive. Really."

They were turning into the drive bordered by low white LEDs. In a moment they saw the walls.

"Walker, it's beautiful," Lynne said, a hint of awe in her voice.

"It sparkles," Margo added. "So that's the ring of stars."

He had what he wanted.

Floodlights spaced evenly around the perimeter struck a thousand flecks and shards of mirror, tile, glass, and mica. The tessellated wall dazzled. They rolled up the hard-packed white drive to the ticket booth.

"Good evening and welcome to Ring of Stars," the attendant said. White-toothed and smoothly quaffed, he wore a navy t-shirt with the ring logo. His name tag said Adam.

"Oh, he's great," Margo enthused.

"Three adults," the attendant confirmed.

"How did he know that?" Lynne asked.

"He's an Animatron Premier," Walker said. "He's taking feeds from his eyes plus the two cameras at the corners of the booth."

"He's staring at Margo," Lynne observed. "He's thinking something—"

"Yeah, right. He is cute, though. I could take him home. Is he insured?"

Walker held up his pass card and the gate lifted.

"Thank you, and enjoy the show." Adam gave a fluid combination of nod and wave in classic Animatron style.

"Bye, Adam," Margo called. "I don't think he heard me."

They rolled in and the drive opened. The concession glowed before them, a cool white fluorescent apron on the ground in front. He was relieved to see Manuel inside behind the long window. Above it the retro sign glowed—on the left end the vintage Coca Cola logo, and on the right, a red and white striped bag bulging with popcorn. In the middle the gold Ring of Stars type floated like a planet with a ring, a silver dust cloud speckled with candy-colored space debris.

"Take me back to the sixties," Margo said.

"More like the fifties," Lynne countered.

"No way, it's Jetsons."

"Which is it?" Lynne asked.

"It's what you want it to be," Walker said. "Here, that's the point. Let's go in."

He held the concession door and they stepped into the burst of cool air. Old movie posters lined the walls. Machine handles sparkled. The twin white doors of the cooler were invisibly clean. Manuel was polishing the counter.

"Hey, nice work," Walker said. The kid looked up and grinned. Walker introduced him, and then Margo focused on the posters.

"Look at this one. *Cleopatra*. And *Vertigo*."

"*To Have and Have Not*," Lynne said. "Bogie and Bacall. Isn't that the one—"

"Her first role," Walker said. "'You know how to whistle, don't you, Steve?'"

"'You just put your lips together and blow,'" Manuel finished from behind the counter. They all burst out laughing.

"An aficionado. That's why I hired him. He does a great Brando. The Godfather to the undertaker. 'What have I done...'" He was trying to cue him, but Manuel was shaking his head, grinning nervously.

"Maybe later." Walker rounded the counter and joined him. "What'll it be ladies? On tap we have vintage Coke, Sprite, sugarless and regular, a couple of fizzy waters, Dr. Pepper—"

"Dr. Pepper!" Margo effused.

"No question, Dr. Pepper," Lynne echoed. She was into it. Walker rejoiced in her tone. If he was reading in more than was there, didn't he have the right? It wasn't luck. It was vision and days in the baked flat of an Arab big-box store where a creation of pure inspiration, however crazed, now stood.

"Why don't you guys go out in the middle somewhere, not too close to the screen." He handed the drinks and the keys over the counter. "Put the speaker in the car. The window can be down or up, either way."

He retreated to the back and climbed the cement stairs to the projection room. Through the broad window he watched Lynne and Margo roll into a stall in the middle of the huge lot. He stepped back behind the console in the middle of the room. The fat red Start button was waiting. From his vantage point, which could be the highest before the mountains, he glimpsed the first stars over the humpbacked horizon. He tried to imagine that their long-ago light was with him, kindred spirits which, in their inevitable flaming out, did have, nonetheless, their shining time. He let a full breath rise and settle and pressed Start.

Inside the car Lynne and Margo saw the huge pearl-gray screen fill with color. From the booth Walker saw a fusillade of white fire over the infield. The jingle started. Fifties-style *Refreshments* lettering sprawled in red on a yellow field. A waiter in a paper hat bowed and introduced a bucket of popcorn, a spinning pizza, and yellow and red squeeze bottles that squirted the length of a hot dog. A perky waitress in a white shirt with a V-taper gave a six-foot wink.

Walker watched the crazy cartoon colors with fists on his hips like the captain of a great ocean liner. The final banner was *Enjoy the Show!* He counted the seconds, and the screen darkened into a charcoal monolith only a little lighter than the new night sky. From a dot, *Feature Presentation* zoomed out. Walker stepped behind the console and checked the tracking display.

"Okay," he said. Normal so far.

The banner faded to black.

They heard it first—the symphonic blast across a galaxy. Then out of a corner of blackness, the glorious stage—the captain's deck of the Enterprise.

An arc of plasma, concussion, then tumult. Roiling smoke and chaos in the engine room. Ricardo Montalban like a falcon with an artificial chest. The illogically tempting young Vulcan, Savick. Kirk facing annihilation. Magnificent on the screen that seemed to float like a huge window on the true dimension of space. The *Wrath of Khan* trailer went black.

The screen refilled with old Hollywood black and white. Jack Lemmon, Tony Curtis, and the only Marilyn, females every one. Train engine firing steam as they clicked along in their nylons. The curious cupolas of the old Coronado. All degrees of silver from dark to brilliant. *Some Like It Hot.*

Walker stepped back to the front of the booth. Full Technicolor again, and he was watching through double windows, his own broad window and an apartment window in another century. A New York apartment window on a courtyard where a Scotch terrier rummaged in a bed of geraniums. Miss Lonelyhearts, Miss Torso, the newlyweds, and the cave of the invalid. Jimmy Stewart's binoculars were scanning. Grace Kelly materialized behind him in gold and white. A killer in the door frame and a burst of something once known as flashbulbs. The trailer said *Rear Window.*

A subway ride half a dozen stops and up into a crack of light tied to a flute note that hangs and lifts and banks into a gull over uptown skyscrapers, floats to tar-roofed tenements and unwashed streets. Settles in a concrete court in a box of chain link and the snap of fingers like a pistol shot. Tony and Maria on the fire escape and a rumble in a dance. Cornball romance to the arbiters of taste and the guardians of chic. To the rest, *West Side Story.*

Natalie Wood steps back in time and throws up her arms, a chevron of white on black. She whips them down and engines throttle up. Pure anguish wails from the complicated demi-god, the godfather of Plato and errant son. A time flaring out like three rockets, and there are sirens in the night.

The best place, Walker felt, for the trailer to end, with *Rebel.* The screen went dark, but it seemed to crackle with the afterimage. When he had let it sink in, he headed for the steps.

"Beautiful, beautiful," Manuel said from the front window. If the kid was brown-nosing, Walker didn't care.

"Got a winner?" he asked. "All right!"

The intermission music started automatically—Dick Dale, the King of the Surf Guitar. He went outside and started down to the car, but he saw tail lights, and then their headlights were on and they were rolling back.

"Walker, it's marvelous!" Margo shouted to him from the passenger window.

"Was the sound okay?"

"Fabulous."

"It's great," Lynne added, "the whole thing." He walked around to her side.

"Thanks," he said so she would see that he meant it. "Let me take a second to close up."

"Can we drop Manuel?" Lynne asked.

"His hog." Walker pointed to the motorcycle at the end of the building.

He was starting to leave, but he needed confirmation that what he seemed to be seeing actually was, and was not a projection on his own screen, and he needed it from Lynne of twenty-four years and the mother of Sophie.

"I guess we're ready," he said to her.

"I guess we are," she said.

Chapter 23

"Margo, how the hell are you?"

"That's what I was going to ask *you*."

Walker was making light of what he guessed, from the moment he saw her number on his display, would be heavy.

"You have to start somewhere, and you have."

He was heading out of the kitchen with his phone to the living room window which, he hoped, would expand his range.

"Okay—yes." He knew where she was going. Feet shoulder-width apart before the window, he was ready.

"It's like any business. It takes time for the word to get out."

"Right, absolutely," he said. She was atoning for past sins of unbelief. Now, when all, including Walker, had more reason to disbelieve than before. Or maybe she would have done the same if all had been simpatico and she had never bemoaned his nuttiness to Karen. And then there was Karen. He never really knew what she had thought about Margo's complaint. And there was the light of the flawless mid-morning, too bright, as though the sun had become over-productive. All too much. He held the black pastille a critical inch farther from his ear. She was saying something, he knew.

"It's just, but what am I telling you—"

"Hey, Margo. Babe."

Silence.

"Thanks." He knew more was required. "I'm okay. This isn't a Hollywood premier. It's more like a mom 'n pop store, if you remember those. Indy, you might say. You'll get a few pioneers, but most will wait and see. You said it—the idea is to build on it."

"That's good, you're exactly right. I just wanted to hear you say that."

"Hey, consider it said. Want me to put Lynne back on?" Lynne had taken the call and passed it to him then headed for the nether regions of the house. She was leaving them to what she no doubt pegged as rapprochement, an extension of healing, rebonding, whatever concept from which he naturally recoiled.

"I'll talk to her later. I just wanted to check in—"

"Thanks. It's okay, really. All on course."

He was so appreciative and so glad to disconnect. Beyond the window, in the yard, he saw nature teeming in the flat earth interrupted by scrub trees. In the soil nematodes struggled by the thousands, dwarfing human wishes. Past the road a covey of eight or ten birds dropped into view and banked away, slate bodies flipping their white sides to the sun. He didn't know what they were, only some of the species they were not. Were they like his supposed audience and all the others he did not know, even after his marketing instinct had worked so flawlessly in his field? Different field, yes, but the same sloppy pool of wants and needs. Were his target audience really a species out of his range that flew by day but sucked back into their caves by night?

"Eyes on the target," he said to the glass plate, imagining a long shot at the white-bellied targets that were already specks. He recalled using the vacuous expression with a client at Xynapse. That could be who he had become, a cliché machine with diminished capabilities. Too many years pushing the fresh energy of others.

Lynne cut through the dining room behind him headed for the washer-dryer.

"She told me to keep my eyes on the target," he said. "She was being supportive."

"She's on your side," she confirmed.

He thought he heard something in her tone, and he was ready to ask, but she was off.

"I'll do the shirts," he said but she was out of earshot. Sunday was his day to wash them. He was being paranoid. Why couldn't she have meant just that, clearly and simply?

"Great, loved it. You've got a real time machine here. One of a kind."

Walker recalled the guy calling to him where he stood by the exit waving to the patrons of opening night. He was leaning on his arm out the window of a burgundy Riviera, restored and waxed. His wife was a bulky shadow on the passenger side. Revved up he was, too far and too fine, and Walker wondered if speed had been popped on the premises the very first night. For an unnerving moment, the guy seemed possessed by the star of the evening, Richard Dreyfus, manic and intense. Or he had been unhinged by the fearsome glory of the mother ship shuddering down the screen, descending from the real night sky that wrapped them all. Whatever his intoxication, his thrill was real. Walker could believe him. He was seeing his crazy-for-whatever-reason face. Could he be a spark? Sparkie. That was his name.

Sparkie was the driver of one car. One of a total of nineteen, including Walker's, occupied by Margo and Lynne. Eight hundred thirty stalls and nineteen cars. They were the select ones, he told himself. They had witnessed opening night.

He was back in the kitchen, pouring the last of the coffee into his mug. He mic'ed it until it fumed.

He returned to the window and embraced the glare. He mixed it with the dark bitter carrier of caffeine, thankful to have both. Together they made the opposite of night, which had unfolded like a nightmare and which would inexorably return.

Suzanne's car had been one of the nineteen. He saw her leave with her lights courteously off. What could she report but a disaster? Should he invite her back? Time would have to pass. It seemed like a possibility. He wanted to show a positive trend. With a baseline of nineteen, that seemed achievable.

He had sent thirty releases to web journals and placed four display ads. Of course he had included the *Great Basin Light*, and Suzanne had mentioned the opening in her column. It wasn't a full feature, but a couple of nice paragraphs tailored from the release. He wondered what his people were reading and watching. Unlike Xynapse, he had no research to go on. He lacked the stomach for a marketing campaign.

He wondered about Xynapse. He hadn't told any of them what he was doing. Could he target them? Absurd. A kind of humiliation. A few might show out of duty for one night only, which would be worse. Or he might see a repeat by a couple of marginals. What would that say?

Jogging was an option. He evaluated the bright, clear sky and his customary running trail, curving past the Dobson's out to Crescent Drive. The sun squealed out of every rock. To his caffeinated brain it seemed possible, even desirable. The memory was dropping through him again like steel balls. Nineteen cars.

Should he change the film? *Airplane III* was on the marquee. Should he go with *Viva Las Vegas* instead? Did it matter? He caught his reflection in the window, older, oddly fragile.

He turned away and headed toward the heart of the house, drawn by the domestic murmur of the washing machine. He remembered his shirts, but he would let Lynne finish her load. He owed an e-mail, and after caffeine and the chrome-bright light, he could face it.

From: Walker Beale <bealew@questar.net>
To: Rob Mathis <rob@robmathisphere.com>
Sent: Sunday, Sept. 8
Subject: Day after

Hey buddy, thanks for the call on opening day. Sorry I didn't get back. It's been a zoo, of course. The good news is it's behind me and nothing broke. Beyond that, not exactly spectacular. If you said two dozen tickets, you'd be high. And yes I know it's perspiration over inspiration, et cetera. But it's hard not to cry over how different it is from Xynapse where there's a whole machine you can rely on. Here it's everything from a standing start.

It's also hard not to wonder if it's insane. Which means if I, Dr. Frankenstein, am insane. I understand full well that few share the Vision, off the top. No surprise. We're creatures that need evidence, and such we hope to have. Time will tell. One a day at a time, the pros say. Hanging in.

He didn't eat at home, and he had his excuse. Until it was on automatic, he needed to be there early. But as he was driving in, he knew how Lynne felt about it. A couple of weeks, he guessed, hoped. He had assembled a dinner in a sandwich—layers of tuna salad, salami, turkey, Havarti, clover sprouts, and Walla Walla onion. He missed the wine but that would be later, and sweeter if things improved. He made a right at the sign that said *Airplane III.*

"Good evening, may I..." Adam said before Walker could shut him off. He had tried punching his code before the booth, but it failed until he was in range of the cameras. He would need to adjust it, which meant at very least a hunt through the online knowledge base and most likely an absurd chat with tech support.

"This is your freaking bliss," he said rolling in. "Follow it."

He opened the concession that still smelled of new paint and cleaner. The clock said 6:05. He had an hour before Manuel arrived. If he arrived. Nice kid, but how many flakes on the best of days? He had eyes, he saw the first night. He took a seat at the front counter and unwrapped the sandwich.

If the kid didn't show he could handle it. A single operator could run it. No drink. He headed for the cooler and collared a bottle of Tomato Brilliante.

Back at the counter he chomped the sandwich and drank spicy tomato and surveyed the infield bounded by the curving wall and the tall screen, the mountains in the distance. A quiet space with evening coming on. It felt like, if not confirmation, at least reinforcement. It seemed to be trying to remind him why he was doing it.

Two more bites into the sandwich, he picked up motion in the corner of his eye at the left end of the window. A moving shadow or a glint, he couldn't tell which. He pressed his face against the glass and searched the drive on the left end of the building. It was somewhere around the gate.

His phone was not in his pocket. For the first time he missed it with its programmed remotes. He had left it on the car seat or the dresser. Instead of being able to punch it on in an instant, he bolted across the room to the perimeter monitor and jumped to hit the power button.

Surprise, a ripple like nausea, then a feeling like mild electric shock. In the upper left quadrant of the screen, a car was waiting at the gate. It was clearly hers, bird of light, bird of fire, her white Phoenix. He could barely see her face through the windshield. Waiting. She could leave at any second.

He scrambled behind the counter, hit the boss button, and watched the monitor as the gate lifted. She had already started to reverse but halted. He was rounding the counter. Her car rocked forward, and then it was rolling in.

"Hi," he said in the last steps to her door, feigning casual. She flashed a smile and climbed out. Jeans and sandals this time and a light blue work shirt with sleeves rolled. She slipped the strap of a tote bag over her shoulder.

"Hi, again. Look, I'm sure you're busy setting up. I was thinking about doing a piece for the Vegas *Sun*. I can because it's the same owner as the *Light*. I wanted to get some background—how you got the idea, what you were doing before, all that. If this isn't—"

"No, it's fine, great—"

"You sure? Ten minutes, fifteen max—"

"Definitely sure. After opening night... Please, come in."

"Oh, sorry," she said as they entered and she spotted his sandwich.

"No problem, really, please, have a seat. What are you drinking? All Cokes, the fizzy water, Tomato Brilliante? Don't hold back."

"I'm good, thanks."

He led her from the cooler to the counter. As he wrapped up his sandwich he was struggling against her scent, floral and musky. He needed to start.

"So, the idea."

She laid the flat silver recorder close to him on the counter.

"Is this okay?" Open face, moon face. Under the fluorescents, in the dark waves of her hair he detected a reddish cast, and the traces of gray he remembered from before, unadulterated, like a reporter's badge of credibility.

"Sure, it's fine." What could it be but perfectly fine? "So about the idea, I guess it goes back a long way."

"You went as a kid..."

"Right, you remember. And I guess you could say that was the source."

"Okay, but what was the trigger?"

"I was in software marketing for a games company."

"Xynapse?"

"The only game in town. It had changed quite a bit from the early days when I joined the company. Some for the better."

"They went public, didn't they, when? We did a piece on it...this year?"

"A little over."

"That must have been nice."

"It's not the reason I left, to cash in. I would probably still be there except there were changes happening that I couldn't agree with. And then there was an offshoring...basically the games work was gone. It hit a lot of people I knew."

She was watching him, waiting for the connection, he realized.

"For the first six years, Xynapse was like a world to itself. Whatever you think about games, there was a lot of creativity. When it changed it became...more like the outside. People were thinking about a lot of things, mostly themselves, about what could happen to them. Fear got in. It's like an assassin. It kills creativity.

"And as Xynapse became more of a business as usual, it made the IPO possible, but it was..."

"So you were ready for a way out. How did you find it? Or did it find you?"

"Exactly, it found me. For better or worse." She was fast, he thought, breathtakingly so. "The idea was, I wasn't the only one. As in there would be appeal, sizable appeal, I thought. I do think." He checked her. Skeptical? Inscrutable. What did he expect? He was watching her eyes, losing track.

"So, when I left Xynapse I wasn't alone. It was an exodus of sorts. I left and got hit by a thunderbolt and the rest is history." He took a breath. "What I mean is, I had a strong memory...a sense. That it was the thing I would do next."

"How did you learn the business? Any experience as a kid?"

"None. Research, basically. And I talked to one owner, outside Indianapolis. He and his wife live on the property, which wasn't that unusual in the old days. Their house is behind the screen—it's basically the back wall. I won't go that far. Some of the drive-ins that are still around are family-run like theirs. Some are real monsters—very successful. There are a couple of megaplexes, one in Hollywood, Florida, the other in Dallas."

She was asking about the films and the vision they had discussed on her first visit. He was trying to minimize the effect of her eyes, which were hypnotic as a fire. He glanced away to concentrate, and as he did he caught sight of the monitor.

Outside the concession, behind Suzanne's white Phoenix, another car rolled the last few inches to a stop. He would have been surprised to see any car. One from his own garage locked him up.

Suzanne was watching him. An answer was what she needed. She had asked. He should answer.

"Excuse me just a minute?" On the monitor Lynne was getting out. He was rising, then he was opening the door into the heat that he connected suddenly with perdition.

"Hi," she said, already coming toward him.

"Hi," he said, and he hadn't meant it to sound like a question.

"I thought I would just bring you..." She held out his phone.

He hadn't pulled the door all the way. Why should he? Suzanne would be visible inside. He saw that Lynne saw. Then she was in the door. He motioned her down.

"Suzanne Canady, this is my wife Lynne. Suzanne writes for the *Great Basin Light*. I told you, she did—"

"Right, you did a note on the opening. Glad to meet you." Lynne was in her professional mode with a near-smile, extending her hand. "Note" was not lost on him. Suzanne seemed unfazed. They shook.

"I was telling your husband I'd like to do a story with wider circulation, for the *Sun*."

"Right," Lynne acknowledged. "That's great. So, you did the one piece. You must think this is really promising."

Walker tested her tone for cynicism but could not quite find it.

"Well, it's a novelty, certainly. But beyond that there's a real sense of...Americana. I think there's a story in that—recapturing a time. And your husband's going from hi-tech—"

"That's good, because...probably a lot of people won't see it. I mean they won't get it. But that's what you do, isn't it? As a journalist, I mean, or is it a critic? That's what critics do. Point out things that people don't see."

"I wouldn't say I'm a critic, or a reviewer."

Lynne was only standing. She seemed to be looking for what exactly Suzanne was.

"But I do think it's a story."

They were both nodding.

Walker felt the air between them filled with microcharges, nano-explosives.

"Well, I have to get back. It was good to meet you. Good luck with the story," Lynne concluded with a lilt, and Walker hoped only he could heard the hollowness.

"Thanks," he said, holding up the phone.

She smiled briefly and then she was in her Alaire and down the drive.

"So, where were we?" He turned back to the concession, pretending to be working the appliance in his palm.

"Look, I don't want to stir anything up." Suzanne was not following.

"What do you mean?"

She was refusing to say the obvious.

"Not at all, no problem. Really. Please." He held the door open. She regarded him a moment then took the three steps and reentered past him with her trace of perfume.

He told her all the rest that he could remember or invent. Some was a reprise of their earlier meeting, and some he hoped was new. To his disappointment, she kept the interview to twenty minutes. If they took the story, which she thought they would, she warned it wouldn't run immediately. He should count on at least two weeks.

After she left he had ten minutes to finish his sandwich. He was relieved to see Manuel arrive. With the apocalypse of opening night behind them, night two settled into something like a business. The common thread with the first night was the attendance. As he looked down from the booth over the two dozen or so cars, Walker projected Suzanne Canady over them. She was seated at the counter. Standing behind him, then stepping up, she was nearly brushing him as he held the door. He was buoyed and distracted by the visions. It was what he needed to make it through to ten-thirty.

In his last private space, he played through the images again as he rolled into the drive. Lights were on in the kitchen and living room. As he left the garage, he decided not to call out. He opened the door into silence then tiptoed down the hall to the dark bedroom. As his eyes adjusted he could make out her hip and shoulder under the light blanket. She was either asleep or it was the way she preferred to seem. Her body was the evidence, simple and eloquent. Lynne did not need to ask him how the night had gone. She already knew.

Chapter 24

From: Walker Beale <bealew@questar.net>
To: Rob Mathis <rob@robmathisphere.com>
Sent: Wednesday, October 2
Subject: Status

So, here we are on Day One plus three weeks and more. I thought by now I'd have an up-trend to report, but we're in retrograde. Fourteen last night. I'm dying down here. There is a ray of hope.

I told you about our local news lady who did the short piece before opening. She followed up with a thing for the *Sun*. Here's the link. So I hope to god this does something. Funny how fast be your own boss can chew up money. I'm thinking of letting Manuel go. He's a great kid, into cinema all the way. But I can't justify him with a dozen concession customers a night. Plus, I know he wants it to work. What the hell do I do with that?

After his third time through the article, Walker was still delighted, somewhat amazed, and completely grateful. He rechecked his photo with the Ring marquee in the background. He had thought better of telling Lynne about the shoot. The photographer had framed from his knees up with the sign behind him. The effect was magisterial, triumphant, inflated like a band on an ancient album cover, punks into kings.

Drive-in offers trip back in time

Walker Beale is a dream merchant. The former Xynapse marketing executive is a magician but he isn't working the Strip. Instead he's conjuring up a time before we were all hyperconnected, when music made grooves on a vinyl platter, and there were muscle cars called V8s—case in point the Pontiac LeMans (my personal favorite).

"When it comes down to it," Beale said, "we won't make it if all people want is OnDemand. But I don't believe that. I think they're ready for something different."

Walker laughed again, the third time. He loved the audacity. He had never said any such thing.

And unless you've been practicing time travel, Ring of Stars is definitely something different. The focus of this classic drive-in theater in Boulder City is on the movies—sci fi, comedy, adventure, horror, classic—which now change nightly.

The theater's wall is the ring—an eight-foot cement circle arrayed with bits of tile and mirror that shimmer in the lights. The effect is a glittering halo with Paiute Ridge in the background.

For most of the films there is state-of-the-art projection equipment, but for some classics that are still available on sixteen millimeter reels—Beale mentioned *2001*—there's also a vintage film projector from the glory days.

Just as they did fifty years ago, speaker boxes hang from the windows of the cars. But the sound is digital and crisp, and it echoes around the yard. There's a retro concession with classic movie posters, and the aroma of popcorn seems to be everywhere, as though it's being piped in from your memories, or your parents' memories.

The experience is a giant step back into a tunnel of American dreams. Just as the virtual worlds that Beale helped to create at Xynapse were digital escapes, Ring of Stars offers a special brand of Neverland. He has thrown away the plasma screen and thrown up a world that even the most wired of us can enter in a restored GTO and leave restored ourselves—rebalanced and more alive for having taken a strange and wonderful trip.

He was trying to think of a closing to Rob's mail and was drawing a blank when he heard the front door. He clicked Send and left.

"Hey, babe." He met her in the kitchen.

"Hey, did you see this?" Lynne looked good in her gray blouse and black skirt, and he picked up a trace of warm perfume from her day. She shed her purse onto a kitchen chair and spread out the *Las Vegas Sun* on the table. The photos covered two-thirds of the first entertainment page. The marquee shot was there, plus others of the posters and the screen not included in the online version. He studied the article, as though he had not read every word, sensing where she was with it. He detected no quills. She was presenting it, was she not?

"Right, I just saw it online."

"The photos are great. When did she shoot those? You look like..."

The Amazing Colossal Man, he thought. Maybe mid-sixties, American International. Still available?

"A monument," she concluded.

"Momentous," he confirmed. "She had a photographer follow up a couple of days ago. I forgot to tell you."

"Right," she said absently, fingering through her mail. "I haven't had time to read all of it so I wanted to finish it at dinner." She was halfway to the bath.

"Okay, about twenty minutes?" He had become the assembler of dinner on her work days. He was still eating in the shop although he once had plans for Manuel to open alone. It would work better if Manuel was still his employee. Not the main reason for keeping him on, he understood, but it was a factor.

He scanned the article to the end one last time then drifted up to her byline—Suzanne Canady, courtesy *Great Basin Light*. He rebounded the sound of her name, a river and a cloudburst. Enough, he acknowledged. The Colossus went behind the counter to make dinner.

Frozen dinner, Margo was thinking. Mattar tofu or Pad Thai. Not enough time to do her Wednesday stir fry. There would be if she didn't call the Beales, but of course she had to. She passed Salon Brandi Hair and Nails, which marked the end of multi-use zoning. Two more blocks, the home stretch.

There would have been time for both if she had not had Hearts and Minds that day. But then she would not have walked Kelli Moffat to the office after class to meet her grandmother for her ride because her mom was recovering from foot surgery. And she would not have seen the *Las Vegas Sun*, which grandma had left open on the chair when she left, and the photo of Walker with the sign behind him.

As she reached the last block, she was testing her memory on parts of the article. Walker thought people wanted more than OnDemand. He was living his dream. How Lynne felt about it was not covered. She recalled in a general way the description of the drive-in and the old cars. She was trying to remember the name of the car she had read. She thought of taking the paper out of her backpack to reread that section but resisted. Backpack on and feeling it in her feet, she was in the zone between thought and no thought as she entered her drive.

Not Thunderbird and not Corvair, she knew as she presented her card key to the front door reader. Entering the living room, she was still distracted and a bit annoyed. The elusive car had to be the reason, but she had the odd sense that it wasn't all. She settled her backpack on the sofa and took out the paper. She might need it to refer to when she called Walker. She skimmed. GTO, of course! What the hell was it? A model with no make, a punk with no surname.

She was heading for the shower when she remembered the mail. She returned to the door and the box, flipped through nothing but junk, and dropped it on the dining room table. As she turned back, she caught a glimpse of the parking lot on her side of the building. She had passed it as she always did when she came in through the front drive, and in the instant that she saw it again, clearly this time, she understood that was where her annoyance had begun.

She went to the window and stared down at the garage. Her door was open. Her stall looked hollow and dark. Somehow she had pulled to the back out of sight. Of course not. She had forgotten. She had parked on the street, or at the end of the lot. There had been a special reason.

She pulled the front door and flew down the steps. As she rounded the end of the lot, the memory of passing the same place minutes before was a nauseating phantasm. Third from the end of the garage, her open door.

She entered the stall smelling of oily concrete. Empty. She ran back out and checked the doors of the other stalls, all closed but one. In the evening sun that was low and painfully bright, she ran the extent of the parking lot, all the way to the end of the dogleg. Empty. She checked the street in both directions. What if, for whatever reason, she had parked there and it had been towed, temporarily moved? She was imagining street cleaning, painting on some building close to cars. No other explanation. No explanation.

Obilawaje. Obilawaje, she repeated under her breath as she punched the number five speed-dial on her phone. She had challenged herself to remember it when she first read it on the condo agreement, and even though she had called him by his first name on the two occasions she had spoken to him on the property, she had remembered. A refugee from Botswana.

"Raymond," she said, surprised and relieved that he answered. "Hi, this is Margo Sellman in number four. I'm down in the parking lot and the door of my garage is open and there's no...car in there. Right, my car is not there. My car is gone. It's nowhere in the garage or the lot. Do you know if it was moved for any reason...towed...any work on the garage...

"Okay. It's just...it's hard to believe it's stolen or... No, there's no sign of tampering at all. No, you don't need to come over. Let me check around some more. I'll let you know what happens. Yes, yes, thanks."

She thought of knocking on her neighbors' doors, the two she knew. Len would not be home yet; he worked four tens. She would bother Sandi only as a last resort. She had her own challenges with two teenage boys. Margo's heart was pounding as she jogged in the hot sun to the one other open garage door. When she stopped she could hear it inside her head and wondered if it was dangerous. She stood panting behind the car she had never liked. A wheel cover was missing on the right and it had a craze around the wheel well. A bright lemon Hyundai Kite.

"Hello?" She did not know the owner. She did not really want to meet him, but the priorities had changed.   No response. She stepped in. The same concrete smell. "Hello."

"Hello!" one last time to satisfy herself. "Fuck!"

She strode back toward her building and punched speed-dial one. After two rings she knew. After four she got her professional voice.

"Hello, this is Cathy Voracek. Sorry I—"

As she waited it out, she returned to the front of the drive and combed the street in both directions. She expected to wake up and find it simply there where she had left it when she had run back upstairs to retrieve her wallet or her sunglasses.

"Hey. Give me a call when you can. Crazy thing, I get home and my car's gone. As in maybe stolen. Doesn't make any freaking sense. Call me."

She was inside her front door and ready to press two when it came clear. She went into the kitchen, to the end of the counter, and stared at the top drawer. She did not open it and did not need to. She was seeing it perfectly clearly in memory, the space inside as empty as her garage stall. He knew which stall was hers, she realized. She had been cased.

"Walker," Lynne called from the bedroom. He had heard the phone, but he was focused on the night, heading for the door. "It's Margo. Pick up." If it had been innocuous, he knew, she would have simply let him go.

"Hey there," he said. "Gone?" was his response. He could hear her wobbling inside. Lynne joined him in the kitchen with her phone.

"Have you reported it?" Walker asked.

"You have to," Lynne confirmed.

"You don't know when it happened. It could have been just before you got home. The quicker you make a report the better your odds are."

They stayed on the line until Margo agreed. They both offered to join her, but she assured them she would be fine.

"I'll call her again in an hour," Lynne told him. "I might go over later anyway. She could need a ride."

"Let me know if you need anything. Manuel can take it for half an hour if I leave."

Sadly, he thought as he headed for the car, Manuel would have no problem with the volume.

Margo went inside to call the police. She was hoping they would send the last officer. He was someone she had confidence in. The phone went off in her hand and she almost dropped it.

"Hey, just got your message. What's going on?"

"It's you. Jesus, you scared me to death. The phone I mean. Never mind, I'm a basket case right now." Cathy's voice was so soothing, earth-bound. Margo went over it all again, and she knew Cathy would come, and Walker and Lynne. They would all come if she asked them, and that was enough.

"No, if I need you I'll call," she said. "Yes, I promise. I'm going to report it now, and if I need a rental I'll get one. It's all insured." As she ended the call she was thinking, for no logical reason, not about the car but about the officer she trusted, the drawer in the kitchen, and the missing keys. The mixed memory forced her to sit down.

Theft, she admitted finally. A stranger had her car. Why? Because, she ventured, he needed it more than she. She was trying for magnanimity but falling short.

"Fuck it," she said. Was it the same punk who had broken in or an accomplice, or had he just sold her key and address? Regardless of his lousy position relative to hers, did the anonymous scumbag need the heartbeats that she would expend, had already expended? She pushed 9 hard, and then 1-1.

It was a new one this time. Officer Mendez, in her twenties, stolid and dark with policewoman's arms. How many women did they have on the force? Margo wondered.

Before her two incidents she had never noticed officers apart from their squad cars.

Mendez had no background on her prior break-in, and so Margo retold the story, which felt like a grim collapse of dominoes. The young weight-trained officer listened so intently she seemed to be giving off heat. Margo felt like tickling her to get a real reaction. She wanted her car back. Serious was good, but she wanted action, and she knew the odds.

She accepted a new report and was tempted to say she would add it to her collection, but on this one, she knew, it would be wasted. As she watched the car roll away, she was not thinking about Mendez anymore or even her car. She was back on what the police operator had said—911 was not appropriate to report theft unless it was in progress. She was given another number, which she refused to write down.

"Bitch," she said. She would need to call insurance next, but she headed for the bathroom instead. "Bitch!" She could use a shower.

Walker stepped inside the house as quietly as he could at eleven fifteen. He had spent a few minutes longer with Manuel, trying to let him know he was appreciated, anticipating the day soon when he would have to give him bad news. For another night the prognosis was grim. Sixteen cars to be exact, but precision was not the issue. Data would not save the patient on tubes and going under, no matter if he had memorized the number of ceiling tiles.

As he stepped into the foyer, a sheet from a yellow pad lay before him. He carried Lynne's note to the one living room lamp that was on low.

Rob called. He said check your mail then call him. He'll be up.

He had been looking forward to a quiet shower, and he could taste the cold Chardonnay he would take with him. Before heading for the office he filled a glass with Chateau Saint Jean. He would not be denied that.

He bit down on a cool mouthful as he waited for his mail to open. Rob's subject line was Call Me. The message was a link. He clicked and NetNews opened.

"Two Shot on North Side" was the headline. He scanned for what he should be seeing.

His breath stopped. He read and read through again. He took another swallow before picking up the phone. He stared at the pad, trying to remember the right speed-dial key.

"Hey man," Rob was saying. "Crazy, isn't it? Pretty hard. But I can't say I'm that surprised."

"Jesus, so he was there for ComCon?"

"He and a couple of the suits. They walked out into a protest thing that was going on outside the show. Probably not a great decision, but I'm sure they didn't expect our resident hotshot to act out.

"I talked to Dave Montoya. He sent out a blast to the old developers—we're all gone now but him. He said Karpos went off on them shouting 'fags' and other original things. It didn't happen then. Somehow they got our stud into a taxi and up to a bar on North Halsted. What they didn't pick up on was that a carload from McCormick Place tailed them. They were jumped right on the street, and it's still light, like it's an ordinary thing, right? Karpos was the target. They were all over him. Tough hombres, these fags. A couple of the Chinese had gone with him to demo and it seems they threw themselves into it in some way to try to protect his wretched hide may he RIP." Walker saw the Chinese programmers' skeletons bent by massive thugs. "Then there were shots. Karpos got it, and somebody in the doorway of a store. The wrong spot at the right time, or is that the other way around? Turned out it was Karpos' own gun. He was packing, the freaking maniac. Dave almost went. I'm glad he didn't."

Walker saw Karpos in the hall in Xynapse, and on the sidewalk. He couldn't put them together. His family. Where were they? Did he deserve what came at him out of nightmares?

"What about the others?"

"Minor stuff. Treated and released."

"Did they catch them?"

"They uploaded a few, but who knows? The pressure's on. We've got rich boy down for a change."

"Who were they?"

"It was a street people demonstration at McCormick. The homeless thing is huge there, much bigger than you get in the media mud. There's one of the biggest camps in the country on the West Side. Stories have been done on it. But it's like a lot of cities, they can't document it all. It's a nomadic population wandering the streets. They're hard to count. That's why the shelters are overwhelmed in the winter. They don't really know what's going to hit them. As far as Karpos goes, I don't think the street people were exactly capable. It was some family thing, maybe race, a matter of honor and that shit."

Walker was going to ask if they were secessionists but thought better of it. He didn't care enough. He didn't know what more to say. He was smothered by the horror, less by Karpos's murder itself, which was encapsulated in a few sentences on screen and Rob's report, than by the context and weight of it. More than the late Don Karpos was tugging at him.

"Lived by the sword, died by the sword," Rob added.

"Where's the funeral?"

"Nowhere close to you, back east somewhere. Dave may have said, but... You should get out of there, man, I'm telling you. Get your family out."

We've been over that before, he was ready to say, because if there was ever any consideration, the Ring made it out of the question. "I'll think about it."

"Don't think too long. The door's always open here. You and Lynne could have a totally new life. There are colleges up here too, you know, for Sophie. Vancouver's an hour away. It's a great city..."

Walker thanked him. He treasured no friendship more, but he was relieved when the call was over.

He licked the last drops from the lip of the glass and went back to the screen. He refocused on the words he had skimmed twice, beginning with the first sentence. Karpos was a shock, but that was not what had stopped his breath. It was the names of the places he did not know but knew now. McCormick Place and Halsted. Chicago.

Chapter 25

It was a few minutes past seven, not their usual time to talk. Walker had a thin sleep. As soon as he heard Lynne stirring, he told her. In a few minutes they were arguing about what to do.

"It's a murder for Christ sake." They were sitting on the end of the bed. "A little too close to home, don't you think?"

He knew where she was going.

"We'll talk to her. She knows how to keep herself safe."

"She shouldn't be there."

"What do we do, pull her out? Not pay her last tuition in senior year?

"She has no real experience, she's a kid. The guy from Xynapse was a grown man with a gun—"

"Remember me telling you about Karpos? He was a juvenile with a gun. Let's call. We might catch her before her first class."

"Hey, what's up? It's early—for you guys especially. Anything wrong?"

"No, we're fine," Walker said to Sophie on the screen, her hair pulled back, seeming younger, more vulnerable, than he remembered.

"We've been hearing about some things happening in Chicago," Lynne said.

Sophie looked surprised.

"Someone Dad knew at Xynapse was killed in Chicago two nights ago. It was after one of the demonstrations."

"Do you check the news?" Walker knew the answer.

"We don't read news, Dad. We live in a bubble. It's called class and more class, nothing but class."

"Great. Aren't you going to college to make sense of the world?"

"Impossible. So you're calling because you're worried about me. Where did it happen?"

"North Halsted," Walker said.

"That's nowhere near—"

"We think you should come home," Lynne dropped.

He hated that she stepped over the line, but he said nothing. He didn't need to. He felt more sorry for her than mad.

"Mom, it was nowhere near me."

"That isn't the only place. There are things happening—"

"It's a huge city. You lived here once, in Evanston, anyway. Why are you so weirded out?"

"Because people getting shot to death is weird," Walker picked up. "We don't want it to be you." He got the two seconds of sanity he was after. "Your internship is over, right?"

"Of course, but I told you, the first term can be virtual."

"So why don't you make it virtual here or in Madison?"

"Because you know why. I m'ed you."

He did know why but was waiting for her to repeat it, for Lynne's benefit.

"My senior project is on von Mises and microfinance. All the best stuff we have about him in America is right here. And it leverages my internship perfectly."

Plus, Walker imagined, there was probably a new guy on the scene.

"*Leverage* is a noun," he said.

"A lot of nouns become verbs—"

"Not *leverage*, please. And don't *impact* me either."

"Okay, then."

"Not a good time to ride the el, okay? Or to go on random car rides. Don't go out at night in less than a pack. I know I'm insulting your good judgment. I know I'm telling you what you already know. And I'm doing it for a reason. Okay?"

"Okay." She was grinning. He was home, he had registered and was satisfied. Lynne did most of the rest of the talking, confirming with an underscore.

"I'll definitely try to be as paranoid as my parents. Now I've got to run. My dub-r starts in ten minutes."

"World Relations," Lynne translated for him.

"Take off," he said. "Take care."

They signed off and he sensed the pressure lifting. Lynne had been shocked, understandably. But Sophie's projection in the room, the illusion of solidity, had reassured them both. Plus, he had voiced Lynne's concerns in a way that respected their daughter's intelligence, basic integrity, and sense of style. Where was his medal? At least pulling her out of school would not be required.

"Well, I didn't see a picture of Professor Right in her room," he ventured.

"I have to get going," she said, headed for the bedroom and her preparations for work. He started to follow but weighed the option against his need for sanity. Instead he decided on a retreat to the kitchen, looking forward to one, breakfast, and two, the nap he would need to make it through the night.

Local Software Executive Killed

A vice president of Boulder City games software company Xynapse was shot to death in Chicago on Wednesday. Don Karpos, who was recently named vice president of the company's Integrated Defense division, was attending a trade convention.

"My god," Margo said under her breath as she scanned the rest of the *Light* story on her laptop. Her first thought was to call Walker, to make sure he knew, but she didn't have time. She was grabbing the morning news at her desk in the minutes before her students would stream in. Of course he knew. She would try to call in her first break.

After the reading lesson, which focused on diphthongs, came teamwork breakout. They were playing a long geography game of continents, climates, and natural resources. Fundamentally she was in favor, but in practice part of her recoiled. The activity was created to match the expectations of corporations, mirroring teams of specialists: one kid who was quick on joystick, a couple who had the spatial geometry to see how the pieces of continents and countries fit like an old jigsaw, and rarest, the ones who had some preciously critical, mysteriously seeded interest in climate or resources. She thought of them all as her monglings—monsters/darlings—each with special gifts which were her challenge to spot and nurture. The teamwork breakout subjects were not her choice. They were was mandated by the state for two through twelve. But breakout itself was a tried and true format, and it gave her a chance to observe her students, plan and catch a breath, or in special cases, make phone calls.

She went to the back of the room where she could step out the door if she got Walker at home, which she expected to do at that hour of the morning. As she opened her phone, she saw a message. It was a local number but not one she knew. She punched Listen. A female voice, recently high school, rattling on automatic.

"This message is for Margo Sellman. This is Boulder City police. We have some information for you. Please give us a call at two nine three, nine two two four, extension two-fourteen."

Her car was the first thought, then her townhouse. She was tired of surprises. She stepped into the hall, punched the numbers, then set up with a full view of the playground through the window in the door. An answer on the first ring.

It was the same voice, asking Margo to hold. She glanced back into the room. Ricky Stevenson was performing at his table. Leah Sukaro would shut him down. Margo could count on her.

"Christ," she said to the door frame. What did she expect, hold music?

"Miz Sellman?" A man's voice.

"Yes?"

"We have..." She heard papers. He was searching for her file. For the high probability of his being unprepared for her when she had already been through her waves of shock and overly prepared, she could despise him. "We have a report here...on your car. It's been recovered by the Atlanta police department."

You mean Atlanta, Georgia? she almost said.

"That's a long way," she said. "What's it doing there?"

"That we don't know."

The equivalent of the editorial *we*, abnegation of personal responsibility. One more in the anonymous landscape of services.

"Did they get the thief, I mean arrest him?" She pictured him with a tile cutter, waiting for her behind the bedroom door.

"Your car was found abandoned on a street at the city limits."

He said it all, she understood.

"We need a location from you. To take it."

"Can it be—"

"Is it drivable? It hasn't been visibly damaged, but that means nothing, really." He sounded like the emperor of defects. "We recommend in cases like this that you have it delivered to a mechanic who can check it over. You want to look for..."

The telltale critical signs of abuse. Infiltrator, regulator, she wanted to inject. Aspersions. Instead she waited without listening.

She asked politely for time to decide and promised to call by the end of the day. She considered having it delivered to her address, but in the end she conceded to the emperor, somewhere in the process of demonstrating carrying to the tens place. It was lunch time before she could make the calls, starting with insurance.

"Hey, I'm glad I caught you," Margo said. "I never know about your lunches."

"No kidding. No supervision today. How are your monsters? Monglings, I mean." Cathy's voice embraced her. Margo took a breath and told the story.

"And you'd have loved the officer, the domineering prick. Anyway, I'm having them take it to Dale's garage."

"He's the redneck one."

"He is, but he's really very professional when it comes to cars and that's what I need."

"When does it—?"

"It's supposed to leave tomorrow. If it does it should get here next Tuesday. It goes on some huge truck with others. I'm not counting on anything."

"You've suffered enough. Everything will work fine now. You need help with anything?"

"It's under control, I think."

"Okay, you still coming over Friday if you get a rental?"

Margo didn't so much evaluate it as surrender to Cathy's voice.

"Sure, around eight?"

"No, come for dinner. I have this Dungeness crab thing I want try out on you. Bring a nice Chardonnay or something." Margo heard the delight in her voice.

"Okay, sure. See you six-thirty."

She ended the call feeling better and pulled her drawer to wolf a handful of trail mix in the last five minutes of lunch break. The one regret was that after making arrangements with her insurance agent and Dale and talking to Cathy, she hadn't called Walker about his coworker. She had to accept it. Casey Blomberg would be the first in with his playground report of victories and catastrophes. And her car was coming home.

At the end of the night as Walker headed toward his car, he stopped and took in the clear air, inhaling the majestic darkness of the empty theater. Amphitheatre, he thought. Coliseum. What happened when Caesar Augustus put on a show and nobody came? He did not have the problem. Competition was not ZuToob or OnDemand. Plus, as well as printing coins with his own face, he had the power to crucify no-shows. The empire, Walker realized, had much to recommend it.

He added a moment of appreciation for the night's movie, *The Fugitive*. It was a personal favorite, yes. Decades after it was made, no effects scene, in his opinion, had matched the train sequence, airborne, jumping the tracks, breaching over the runaway who dropped into the ditch, showered by sparks of steel wheels wrenched from their rails. Yes, it was personal. That was the point, precisely. He had shared his appreciation with sixteen others. For a Thursday night, the turnout had met his expectations, which had become indistinguishable from resignation.

The new October air blanketed the infield. The ground inscribed by the ring was potential. He and anyone else could claim it. Like all simple things, it was there for the taking. He glanced up and there they were also, just as clear and accessible, the stars that would preside long after his ring had crumbled into undemarked earth. He opened his door, settled in, and rolled out past the ticket booth.

He would tell Manuel tomorrow. He would need him on weekends only. They could start with Friday through Sunday, but he might have to cut to two days later. It hurt, but he couldn't be responsible for Manuel. The kid could pick up some hours at Plaza Paz. Walker could not dwell on the scores of others who would be on the waiting list for those jobs.

That was the beauty of the Ring as a business, he reminded himself as he turned left out of the fluorescent bath of the highway sign. One person could run it. In the bigger picture, it was small comfort. It was, rather, a lethal indicator.

The road unrolled in his headlights, no lights oncoming, one set of tail lights miles ahead. Yes, he might be able to run it alone, but if he could it would mean a gross too low to survive. He could approach the Veridian Group in L.A. They ran a mega. They could make the Ring work. Having paid their dues, they knew the business. They could go mainstream.

But what was he thinking? The Ring was less than a month old. Of course it could take months. Any sane person would expect no less. He reminded himself of the value of sanity.

He thought of Sophie. The morning call had been weighing on him. He was feeling something like the haunted, sorrowing feeling he had after she had left for her first year of college. How real loss was. However irrational it was, he imagined them both gone, Sophie and Lynne. Focusing on loss could become an obsession, a hot iron he could not but take to his heart. It was not impossible. He took their life together for granted. It was habit, nothing ultimately substantial or shielded in any way from the pranks of fate.

He was only partly conscious of driving, skimming on layers of reflection and recollection. Lynne had tried for the best when she came home. The truth was, their daughter was seventeen hundred miles from them, and there were no guarantees.

He killed the AC and lowered the front windows. He was surprised to feel tears burning. The distant tail lights were swimming.

What was he doing? Even his first night fanatic Sparkie had failed to return. Who were his customers? In his former lifetime he had the luxury of knowing. Now he could guess who they were. He was picking up stragglers, random strikes. Captains of otherness, odd as himself.

He was in San Diego again, three decades or so ago, on one of the piers with Lynne beside him. They were standing under electric stars that only youth could reveal. He tried to see her face again, but he could not quite recall it. The famous restaurants and viewpoints and zoos of San Diego he could not remember clearly. It was the state of being he remembered, being there with her. If he were asked in the ultimate interview, all or nothing, where in his drifting, now seemingly untethered, scattershot of life choices his anchor was, he would say it was there. In San Diego or the other places that were only real in memory because of her.

It was time to fold. He took two breaths of sweet air off the desert and settled on the second like a resolution. The asphalt rolled under him. Lynne could have her world back, which meant a husband within range again with goals they shared. She could work on her house plan again as a believer. He imagined telling her first thing when he got home. She would have been asleep for an hour at most. He saw himself shaking her shoulder. On the other hand, what was the reason to wake her? If he trusted the decision, it could wait until morning.

He returned to Sophie. What would she say when he told her? He knew already. He could see her saying it. You can't quit. Weren't they giving her the same message? See it through, but look out for yourself. Be careful. He should take his own advice. It was a big decision to make on a wave of emotion.

He took another breath and held it, expelled. He checked the black sky at the top of his windshield. What was he looking for, a comet to seal the deal? He needed to decide.

He thought of them both again, how he treasured them, Lynne perhaps already in her dreams, and Sophie outward bound. He settled back on the road, and it seemed to be pulling him along in the journey they were all taking, together and separately. Together and alone. There was a balance, and he would find it. He would not be forsaking them by waiting. He had opened his eyes. He had rediscovered them, that was the main thing. He could tell Manuel weekends only, but he would live with the big decision for a while.

Chapter 26

"Be your own boss. Christ." Walker peered into the detached drain trap in his hand and tried to identify the substance. Chewing gum was a component, but it was sitting on top of something, only a wadded chunk of hand towel, he hoped. He upended the U-bend and banged it inside the trash can. The obstruction plopped out.

Intentional, he realized. The vandal had lifted the drain filter to do it. He tried to recall likely suspects from the night before. Whom and how had he offended? Who had a lousy time? Why was he thinking any of this? Because the beloved public was his boss. Kids. Punks. He would cement the filter down.

Manuel had told him it was plugged the night before. He had lacked the will to deal with it then, and now he was glad. He had his reserves back and he could concentrate, even in the sad context of the small business bathroom. There was another plus. By coming in early he had avoided new debates over Karpos's killing and Sophie. He had left a note for Lynne. It was like a bitter reminder that the goal had been to have Manuel open on weeknights so they could at least share dinner.

He ducked back under the sink and reattached the trap, tightening the couplings by hand before using the pipe wrench. He dropped two paper towels under his shoe and dried the floor. At least Manuel would have three nights, he thought as he opened the faucet and checked under the sink for leaks. He washed his hands. That was why he must tell him tonight. The next weekend could be two. It would depend. And the whole arrangement could be temporary anyway. That was how he would explain it to Lynne. It wouldn't preclude their dinner together, just defer it until he could bring Manuel back for five nights.

He would arrive in twenty minutes. With the pipe wrench, Walker climbed the stairs to the booth where he had left his sandwich. He would eat in peace and prepare. As he opened his bag he weighed whether to tell him at the beginning or end of the night. The beginning seemed nobler, but it could only demoralize. What would prevent three nights, or two, from becoming zero? He chomped on tuna and Havarti and closed his eyes and tried to replace thought with taste. That worked for seconds. It was all about volume. How to change it? New ads, aim higher, bigger papers and hyper-local web, local radio? All could work. He had already targeted with coupons, one from a cell spammer, another from a dating mashup. Two had come back. Once an ad budget had seemed to make sense. It was the one corner of the business where he had felt confident.

"Shut up," he said. This was not the conversation he needed to be having. He needed to get ready for Manuel.

Halfway through the sandwich, he was resisting going back downstairs for the drink he had forgotten, but the wad in his mouth could not be chewed. He could almost taste tangy tomato juice. As he stood up, he caught sight of the driveway through the window.

There were cars at the ticket booth. He counted four. He made out a Chia Sun King and a Morris Mini, but he focused on the first and last—a burgundy Ford Fairlane and a white and chrome Camaro. He checked his watch. Six-fifty, not eight.

Could *Grease* still have its cult, rabid enough to arrive seventy minutes early? He bolted to the door and nearly stumbled down the stairs. Get them inside, into the concession. He hit the button to power Adam on, and the boot light came on in the monitor.

He doubled the stairs back up to the booth and started the concession pitch and previews. They would run for thirty minutes. After that he wasn't sure. Rerunning it could alienate them. Or drive them to the concession. He couldn't

ure early. He chomped the sandwich. Carrying
....a, he checked the monitor from the stairs.
Another car, maybe a Khia, was pulling up behind the
Camaro. The first in line was already inside, rolling to a
center row in the infield.

He took a bite, scrambled onto the floor, and pitched the
last of his dinner into the trash. He jammed a cup under the
plastic spigot and gulped enough Sprite to slick the dough
wad down. Then he hit the popcorn switch and powered on
the hot dog carousel. He pulled the buns next, only two
boxes.

"Christ." Not much change in the drawer. He started to
head up the stairs again for the office safe, but the couple
from the Camaro were the first inside.

The guy looked sixty or so and stocky in a black KMQX
oldies t-shirt. His wife came in a pale blue cowgirl
combination, and her big hair was salon blond with a flip.
Walker learned they were retro collectors—20C music and
movies. His target audience, he realized, then tried to focus
off the fact. He passed their popcorn tub and tall soda cups
over the counter and was about to ask how they had heard
of the Ring.

"Great article in the *Sun*," the man said.

"We had to see what this was," his wife confirmed, and
Walker was aware of her eyes for the first time, blue and
sketched around by the phases of experience, some of them
ungentle.

"Great, thanks for coming in." Walker extended his
hand, thinking of what the article might have meant.

"Bruce Ringle. This is Lynette," Walker heard him say.

"Really, my wife's name is Lynne," he said absurdly.
"Pretty close."

"It's *Wyne*tte, with a doubleya," Bruce said.

"People make that mistake all the time," she added.
"One of these days I'll just change it."

Walker waved them out, and two more groups were coming in. As he started a pizza for a family of four, he spotted Manuel on his motorcycle rolling around the cars in the drive to the concession. There were at least five others in line half an hour before showtime.

"Hey, boss." He arrived from the back still tying his apron. "Early rush tonight, no? *Qué padre!* What's up?"

"Not sure but I have an idea. Pull me three Dr. Pepper, and I need a large Diet Coke."

Within minutes a stream of customers had migrated from their cars and were queuing up inside the concession. As Walker handed a card back, he caught sight of the screen. Empty. The trailer had ended and the screen was dark.

"Back in a flash." He left Manuel facing the line and took the stairs one more time. Inside the booth he hit the play button on the console, overriding the scheduler. The 3-2-1 countdown circle wrapped around, the lion roared, and as he returned to the counter, the rocking piano and sax of *Grease* hit the speakers.

"Yes, sir," Walker said. "Yes, ma'am, may I help you?"

He was suddenly saying it a thousand times like some person he did not know. He and Manuel were bagging popcorn, pulling Nutty Buddies from the freezer, popping Tombstone Pizzas into the bar oven not built for volume. He pulled two handfuls of hot dogs to restock the roaster, and one landed in the dishwasher. They were down to half a box of buns.

Call Lynne, he thought first, but she would be showering or eating, and even if she could leave in ten minutes, it would be too long. Food Circus was close, seven minutes, eight at most. He couldn't send Manuel—his bike had no rack or saddlebags to carry bun boxes. Since the film had started, the march to the concession had slowed, but he could see a line of cars still rolling in.

"Boss, I'm low." Manuel held up a bag of chips.

Walker didn't even check the stock. He knew he hadn't reordered since opening night. He was caught short. No matter what the reason, you could not be. You had to have product. Repeats were everything, and a customer told sorry did not repeat.

"Look, can you cover a few minutes, maybe fifteen. We're low on a few other things. I need to hit the market."

Manuel's face froze.

"Okay," he ventured. "The register—"

Walker had laid down the rule—he rings the sales. He went behind the register and popped it open.

"Just leave the drawer open and do the best you can." He knew what he was hitting the kid with out of nowhere. "Hey, you get a paid vacation for this. One day at least, all right?"

"Okay," Manuel said on an up-beat.

"Glad you came in?"

He laughed. Walker dropped his apron and was out the door.

He tried to estimate. The lot looked more than half full. He didn't have time to open the back gate, so he left by the front drive on the shoulder, trying to miss the halogen mini-lights. Three more cars were rolling in. The driver of a shiny yellow Cutlass stared at him. Walker waved, trying to show how great, how perfectly welcome he was.

On the road, picking up speed, he thought for the first time about burglary and assault. A punk in a jumpsuit and Calvin Klein sneakers with a handgun and Manuel behind the counter. Where was his head? It wasn't that he had left the kid alone, it was that he hadn't considered the worst case. Not the fantastic, but the reasonably possible worst case. He blinked back to the road under his lights. He could turn around. What were the odds? Who didn't live by the odds? The faster he could get back, he thought. He pressed the pedal.

In Food Circus he was jogging with the cart. He had planned the route. Aisle six buns. Two pizza. One chips. Checkout. He jammed his card into the pay slot that operated on its own time, democratic time, all customers the same time. Interminable. Freaking interminable.

Hitting the button to vend a bag, eight seconds at least. Vend another.

"Christ fuck!" He dumped the collapsing plastic into the passenger seat and the boxes splayed out. Back on the road he checked the rear view for squad cars then gunned around a smoking pickup. A punk with a handgun, he saw. One of many.

When he swung back into the drive, there was one car at the booth. He mashed the button on his remote long enough to suspend Adam and open the gate. The lucky customer paused for an honest moment then rolled through without paying. Walker tailgated him in.

He snatched at the two bags and settled for the buns and pizza that had not spilled on the floor. He bounded up the steps to the door and pulled it.

Manuel was passing a popcorn bucket to the only patron, a heavyweight black man in a green golf shirt. Walker caught his breath while he rang the sale and made change like the twenty-minute pro he had become.

"Hey, you did it." Walker noticed a few white number four bags strewn on the counter and others on the floor and a pizza box sideways in the sink.

"Sure, boss," grinning triumphantly. "No problem."

"All right." Walker grinned back. He saw the spot across the counter vacated by the hooded ghost with the gun. "All right." They both started picking up bags.

"About the vacation..." Manuel said almost laughing.

"Right, take Monday off, okay? What do you want, Saturday or something? I'll be back." Walker remembered the spilled contents in the car. "You get it paid."

"Paid?"

"*Si si*, really. Great job."

Outside he started for the car but turned back for a moment on his creation. The infield could be two-thirds full. Six hundred cars instead of a dozen. He spotted a blue and cream Chevy Bel Air, late fifties, and a deep green Olds Cutlass. The standout was a silver '62 Thunderbird, the long "Bulletbird" convertible. The evidence was there. He was not gone, not off the charts. They got it. They were out there hungering, as he had known they hungered, bet his wad they hungered. He retrieved a shrink-wrapped pizza and two boxes of buns from the floor in the front, scrounging like a menial, grinning like a madman. As he reentered the concession, four more were coming in.

At the end of the night, with the line down to two waiting for pizzas to take home, Walker went outside again. He wanted to wave his thanks to the last of the departing cars. He asked a couple of drivers how they had heard of the Ring and he wasn't surprised. He took it in. He felt like the proprietor of Chez Mirabile, beloved of his patrons, patrolling among the tables. He stayed in the moment, let it linger.

It was ten before midnight when he pulled into the garage. The crowd had meant a longer cleanup by half an hour, and there was more to go in the infield, but they would handle it Saturday. On the way home he had tried to catch up on what had happened. He was stupefied. His biggest relief may have been that he wouldn't have to cut Manuel, at least not yet. As for tomorrow, he was counting on nothing but open to all.

He entered quietly, hoping somehow that she would be awake. Leaving the single low light in the living room, he followed the hall and stepped gingerly inside the door. She lay on her right side, knees drawn up. He had no reason not to wake her. It was a big deal, of course. He had a vague sense of all the years she would demand that he wake her for any datum of great importance to them at the time. He tried to make a connection to that agreement they once shared but he could not. This, as they both understood, was different. He would tell her in the morning.

He carried a full celebration goblet of Pinot Noir from the kitchen to the office and suppressed the smart light. The blue glow of his monitor invited him to sit. He knew a phone call would be wrong. Even at midnight he was not sure he would be talking to voice mail. Either way, he couldn't trust what he might say. After two ample swigs, he started to type.

From: Walker Beale <bealew@questar.net>
To: scanady@greatbasinlight.com
Sent: Friday, October 4
Subject: Thanks
    Suzanne,
    Thank you! It was a terrific night—the first one. Everyone I asked said they had read your article. A good number came in from Vegas. There were great old cars too. They got the whole idea. I didn't see your LeMans but I'm hoping there will be another chance. One night doesn't make a business, but your article set a spark. We'll try to keep the flame going. Will let you know how it goes. Much thanks again.

"You must be on top of the world. I'm surprised I didn't even hear you come in last night."

"I was going to wake you—"

"I wish you had," she said, but he was less than convinced. He had given her the story at Saturday breakfast.

"It was great. But it was one night."

"I bet you're off and running." She turned in her robe and carried her coffee into the living room. He followed and sat on the sofa, but she stood looking out the picture window. His insides were starting to wind.

"What are you thinking?"

She took a sip and he waited. Resolution could be in the brew. She looked down into the mug and then through the window out into her own space. She turned to him.

"It's what you wanted. It sounds like your reporter did the trick. Or maybe the photos—you in the Ring of Stars." She smiled and he tried to read it.

She crossed to the sofa and sat down, staring back into her coffee. He studied her, fully appreciating the fact that she had come to sit by him.

"Something seems to be working for a change. It looks like I won't have to cut Manuel. He was great in the pinch last night. If the volume holds I can add another employee and we can get a life back. It would only take one more, I think."

"Really?"

She seemed partly wondering, partly something else.

"Yeah, why?"

"I don't think so," she said, and it dropped like a rock in a well.

"Don't think what?"

"That you're suddenly going to go back in time. The more the Ring succeeds, the more...seductive it will be."

"What are you talking about? It's a business, that's all. It's not me."

"Isn't it?" She was staring at him, mockingly innocent.

He couldn't respond. She couldn't trust enough to believe him.

"No." He had more to say. He could fucking say more. She thought it was all about him, the delusional child. *Puer aeternus*. She missed it completely, she had always missed it. He was tired of her checkouts. He would be first this time.

He got up and headed for the far end of the house. He would shave and then leave, go to Renu and work out. He didn't care whether she came back to talk or not. He took off his shirt and in a moment was looking into the mirror with a dripping face. Lines across his forehead scratched by time and doubt. Bunches of gray at his temples. In a minute the shaving cream was on and he was breathing through it all. He had the razor in his hand, wondering if she was right.

From: scanady@greatbasinlight.com

To: Walker Beale <bealew@questar.net>

Sent: Saturday, October 5

Subject: RE: Thanks

Glad things are looking up. You deserve it. I want to see but I don't want to jinx it! Maybe tonight or Sunday?

From: Walker Beale <bealew@questar.net>

To: scanady@greatbasinlight.com

Sent: Saturday, October 5

Subject: RE: Thanks

Suzanne, no jinx possible. Please come by whenever you can and call me when you're close—I'll turn off our doorman.

The sight of her mail in the box gave him a thrill, and responding was the last thing he did before leaving. It was not yet noon, but odds were even that Lynne would be off on errands. He left the office and confirmed.

He did half an hour on the machines at Renu. That was all he had time for because he needed two trips to markets to stock up on anything they could possibly run short of that night. If necessary he could repeat on Sunday. One day at a time. Don't jinx it, the lady had said.

That night he set his phone on vibrate and intended to check it periodically in case somehow he missed her call. Even before the night started, he had no time. Cars were rolling into the drive half an hour before opening. He had asked Manuel to come in fifteen minutes early in case of a repeat, and they hauled from that moment on. When *Saturday Night Fever* was over and they were breaking the equipment down, he asked Manuel if he knew anyone who was looking for a job.

From: Walker Beale <bealew@questar.net>
To: Rob Mathis <rob@robmathisphere.com>
Sent: Saturday, October 5
Subject: Update

Hey, haven't bugged you in a while. Now that it's been two nights in a row, I can tell you. It could really be happening. It started on Friday—an invasion from Vegas. The lot wasn't full but it was well over half. Many retro mad dogs in attendance—chrome and fins and wax to the max. Total blowing of the mind. Wish you could have seen it. I'll send some pics from the gate cam. Tonight was a little better, and I'm finding that as hard to believe as night one.

The lady from the *Light* started it—her piece in the *Sun* I told you about. They actually read it. I'll send you the link but now I'm dead. This may be a gig for youngsters. I'm trying to hire another.

Later. I'm going to shower and die happy.

He used the downstairs shower and slipped quietly under the covers at twelve-thirty. He lay on his back, cool sheets against his skin, and sank into a space of softening bones and muscular collapse. His thoughts were unlocking. A cool night outside and a breeze in the curtains.

"How was it?"

"Jesus, you scared me. I thought you were out." She had hit him like a power line but he didn't mind. It was great to hear her. "It was a winner." He reached over and squeezed her firm hip then snuggled up. Lynne felt warm.

"Great." She sounded clear-headed, and he guessed she had not been asleep. "Lots of cars, right? I told you." He heard delight in her tone, soft but undeniable.

"I'll start working on another employee tomorrow. I can free up some time." He kissed her ear. "Get a life back. I know this has been a hard time but it's starting to come together." He slipped his hand over her breast.

She rubbed his arm in a way that meant no action would be forthcoming. He was relieved. He was dog-tired.

"There was something on the news tonight. In Phoenix—an explosion in a hospital. The report said seventeen people were killed and they couldn't be sure how many injured, they said dozens."

"What happened?" He rolled onto his back, ready to block the content, but he wanted to hear her voice that was a warm sensurround sound.

"It was an explosion in a stairwell. They said it brought down the ceiling onto the third floor where they were doing tests, clinical trials. They think that was the target. Gene therapy trials. Some group is claiming responsibility, some fundamentalist...they're murderers. Then somebody reported a church—you know that Living Body of whatever it is—had been set on fire." She took a breath, focusing above them on some point. Her words hung for a moment like fireworks consuming themselves in the dark. It took a

settling of seconds dropping like ashes for her to realize he
was asleep.

Thank you, Walker said under his breath as though he
could be thanking God. Thank you, Margo. If she were there
he would give her a squeeze.

Her call had been perfectly timed. They had been most
of the way through Sunday breakfast and he had asked
Lynne three times what was wrong. When she finally
informed him that he had checked out while they were
talking, he apologized. He had been exhausted. What did
she expect? He had not decided to sleep. He was sorry for
slipping away. He was sorry for everything.

Margo had called at that moment and Lynne took it. Her
car had arrived early by transfer truck from Georgia. It was
on Dale's lot and he could inspect it the next day. Walker
put it together from Lynne's end of the conversation and
then escaped.

He could cool off with low-stress projects and save
himself for the night, which was unpredictable. He started
in the back hosing off the patio and chairs then moved on to
the garage where he segregated the empty paint cans,
insecticide aerosols, and two studded tires from the late
Volvo. He wasn't ready to haul them to haz-waste recycling,
but he was closer.

It was October but still into the eighties in the afternoon.
By the time he had finished the garage, he was sweating.
The air seemed bathed in honeyed light. He headed into the
air conditioning, heard Lynne around the utility room, and
considered whether to test the waters. He decided on a
shower instead.

After that he holed up in the office and brought the
spreadsheet up-to-date. Then he faced the inventory
decision. How much was enough? He saw panic runs for
pizzas and buns and ordered on the high side. If the lucky

streak ended, he could move it over time. A few minutes before four, he heard the phone again. As he entered the living room, Lynne was standing in front of the TV, arms folded and remote in hand.

"Who called?"

"Margo again. There's something happening in Chicago."

All he could see was the front of the stadium and the classic lettering: Soldier Field. Bears game. She hated football, and post high school and North Carolina Friday nights, he was indifferent. It was trivial compared to baseball, at least baseball in the old days. In the foreground he saw Chicago cops in black leather jackets behind yellow tape. Their cap bands were black and white checks. Lynne boosted the volume.

"...we're seeing. This area was filled with fans who had just left the game against the Ravens. They exited here into a demonstration on the street and on the sidewalk in front of this gate. It had started as a march by a secessionist group. It's unclear why they stopped here outside the stadium, but it may have been that the street ahead of them was closed for traffic exiting from the main parking garage.

"We do know that the march had a motorcycle police escort, although it may have been as few as two officers. Then, as we reported earlier, with the march stopped in front of the stadium, a group of—we aren't sure how many, perhaps a dozen—tangled with several of the demonstrators. A few of those demonstrators were reportedly pulled out of the crowd, and as they tried to escape they were taken down by their attackers in this area you see that is now cordoned off. We've been told at least one was severely beaten. Then a kind of general melee started with fights breaking out over the area. Stadium security tried to intervene, but they were basically outnumbered until police arrived here in force. Soon there were a hundred or more Chicago police officers on the scene.

"Dozens have been arrested. We know a number were injured, and most of those were taken to Cook County Hospital. But as we've been reporting, the most serious incident in all of this happened at the edge of a parking lot reserved for tour buses and V.I.P parking."

The shot cut to a helicopter view. A ring of police and what Walker took to be plain-clothes detectives stood in a semicircle around a stained patch of cement lot. A man in a Ravens fan jersey pointed toward the stadium entrance and then to the sidewalk.

"Witnesses say one of the officers was attacked by fans who had been involved in a fight with demonstrators. He was pursued to this spot. Here he fired on his attackers, wounding two, who were taken to Cook County Hospital. One died on arrival, and we're told the other is in serious condition. The officer is receiving treatment for his injuries, none of which are considered to be life-threatening. All of this occurred less than half an hour ago where an investigation is under way and will continue into the night. This is Len Silber, WLS, reporting from Soldier Field in Chicago."

The scene cut to the BCN news anchor of the week. Her caption read *Megan Fleming.*

"Thank you, Len. We're learning there may be other dimensions to this story. We go to news analyst Kevin Schwerner in Chicago."

"Megan, we understand that the officer, who has been identified by Chicago police as Alejandro Velez, is a Cuban American. The wounded victim whose name is currently being withheld is African American. As we reported on WLS, over the summer several incidents between these two groups erupted into violence in the West Side zone known as the Kimball Corridor.

"Today as news of this shooting began to break, we received reports of a fire in a church in the Kimball area. We have a reporter en route to the scene."

The shot cut to a satellite map and zoomed in.

"Where—" Lynne started to say. Red circles appeared around Soldier Field and the Kimball Corridor to the west.

"It's southwest," she said and trailed off. He was half-ready for what came next. "We have to get her out of there."

"Look, we just had this discussion. You heard her—"

"Of course she doesn't want to, what do you think? She doesn't know what's going on. You heard that, right?" She threw the remote on the sofa. They were not watching the report anymore. "There are bad things happening, okay? Have you noticed? Not just in Chicago. You're in some kind of... denial."

"She knows enough to be—"

"She doesn't know enough at all, that's the point! I'd like to hear you say we're her parents and we're responsible for her safety. I'd like to hear you—"

"I'd like to hear something too—you admit that your daughter has her life. Have you thought about how she'd feel if we shut her down in her last term? What does that say? Instead of standing behind her we give her our... paranoia." He hated that. Fat words, sloppy ones.

"Paranoia! What the fuck are you talking about? It's responsibility! We're her parents, we're responsible for her. This is not a school issue. It could be her life, don't you realize that? Where are you?"

He was stopped cold. He hated her face like that, locked in rage. All of their history was suddenly ignored. They were strangers. As though they had not parented the same daughter, as though she thought a critical piece of him was horribly missing.

"Where am I? That's my main problem, I guess. You don't know where I am."

He was pounding inside. He needed to restart. Of course he had considered it seriously the last time they had argued over it. He was seeing both sides, taking the long view. Hadn't he communicated that? Why didn't she get it? What had she been thinking then, that he was self-absorbed, myopic? His hands were cold and his chest was pounding. He could try all over again when he had been planning to get ready for the night. He was tired of being blamed for being sane.

The news had been replaced by a car ad. It was flashing through views from different angles with nauseating rapidity. It dissolved to a wireframe that glowed emerald, then gold.

"Let's talk about it tomorrow," he said. He intended it as a sincere overture, but he couldn't judge how it sounded. He was focused on getting to the Ring, and although it was early, he could think of a list of errands. More to the point, it was difficult for him to imagine what more there was to talk about. Even if she could find something, tomorrow was the best he could do.

They went to separate zones of the house, and he changed as quickly as he could. Through the front door, his breath started to unlock. From experience he knew a heaviness would linger. But he was free now.

As evening approached, uneasiness returned. He had been conditioned by a two-night run. By the time Manuel arrived half an hour early, there was no line at the gate. They went to work stocking and setting up, and it was only when Walker had climbed to the booth and begun to check the play sequence that he felt relief, however prematurely. The first car had arrived in the drive.

Sunday night proceeded with its own version of the previous two. The pre-opening was light, followed by a rush two minutes before showtime. The last arrivals were inside half an hour into the Silver Edition of *Rear Window*.

Suzanne arrived as promised a few minutes late, bringing a tide of confusion. He was feeling weighed down, sick at heart, but he stepped out to talk to her, leaving Manuel with a line of four. She urged him to go back in—she only wanted to tell him she was glad. He acknowledged again that her article was the reason. He waited and watched as her white Phoenix rolled down into the infield.

She left at some point while he was hauling through the night with Manuel, who had become as fast or faster than he in everything but pizzas. At the end he was calling them a machine.

Sunday, he decided on the way home, still seeing Grace Kelly in her negligee, could be his favorite night. If it continued, the cars would arrive close to start time and be cleared out by ten-thirty. It justified it all. It could be five hours or less, in and out. Maybe no hours soon. Lynne would see it finally, undeniably.

He entered the house early, a little after eleven, but all lights were out, even the living room lamp. It could have been that, even though he tried to deny the pettiness, that tipped it. He appropriated an open Merlot bottle and a large bistro glass and headed for the office. He went through the motions of checking his mail, but in a few moments he had downed the glass and was on the sofa pouring the second. He was in his clothes with no shower because he was there to keep his moment whole. It seemed to him it was his only way to do it—presided over and nourished by the muses— the radiant white and gold Grace Kelly and the chestnut-haired, gray-eyed what was she? He lay back in his own work smell and caved into the cushions. Reporter? Dangerous diva? Friend?

He got up once to hit the bathroom outside the office and peed a river. His teeth felt fuzzy, and he envisioned brushing, flossing also, in the morning. On the sofa again under his ancient ratty camping blanket, he was out in seconds.

When he awoke his first thought was that he had slept too long. He reached his watch on the floor. Nine-forty.

He rolled out and padded softly into the shared area of the house. Of course she had left already. Her bed was made.

The domicile all to himself, in the master bathroom he took pure pleasure in flossing and brushing. The mirror was flecked with toothpaste. Why should she clean it? He had more time at home than she. He would hit it after breakfast. He followed up with a long and perfect shower then headed for breakfast. Frozen waffles, he was thinking, trying to envision how many strawberries were left in the carton in the refrigerator. On the kitchen counter, he saw her note.

PART 3

Chapter 27

Sorry about the price of a last-minute flight. I don't want her to be alone. I'll stay in touch with Darrell—he can spare me right now. We don't have anything big going on and he has a new guy he wants to get some experience. Sophie knows I'm coming. I'll be at Mom's tonight.

There was no "Love, Lynne." He rushed to the closet where they kept the suitcases. How many medium-sized did they have? Sophie had hers. There had been two left. He rifled through all the bags, raked his hand on a latch. One medium. One was gone. How had she done it all after he left for the night? The reservation, packing? Then up and out before he was awake. She must have counted on him sleeping out of the bedroom. Or would it have made any difference? Maybe she had planned to get up and pretend to leave for work as on an ordinary Monday. Either way it chilled him.

His heart was tripping as he jogged to the foyer, past the note he had slapped face down on the table, and out the front door. In the painful brightness he faced the garage. Closed.

He needed to see for himself. He opened the side door. Two cars. Lynne's Alaire and his Subaru side-by-side, substantial as coffins. Who was the accomplice? He knew she would not have taken a taxi or a shuttle.

He stormed back to the house, focused on the obvious suspect. But Margo had no car. He was back inside, closing the door like a robot.

What did that matter? She had her rental. He refused to go on. He would seize a thread of doubt to let Margo off, not just because it would be too hard to face—he believed she was undeserving. He had an idea who deserved the crosshairs.

He had met Arliss Bennett only once, when he had picked up Lynne after Trimz. He had the feeling then, later confirmed by his globetrotting spouse, that Arliss was anti-heterosexual. He recalled how she looked after adrenalin and endorphins, taut and packaged in spandex with real pecs and visible cleavage. Her nose and cheekbones had been busted by Dr. Genius in Rio. She had a knowing look but she knew nothing at all. Months after that she and Lynne had gone to the trail-clearing volunteer event together—Arliss had picked her up. Not Margo, Walker satisfied himself as he folded onto the sofa. It was hard-pan Arliss with the motive and the means.

So he settled that. So what? Lynne was, however temporarily or provisionally, gone. Was he going to call Arliss if he could find her number online, tweak her and freak her for enabling? Getting a grip was a better option. He tried to focus on the positives of health and family threads still intact. Finally the house seemed to commandeer him, overriding his pluses with cool emptiness.

He went to the kitchen and punched her number, envisioning her first in the plane, then possibly still in the airport.

"Hi, it's me, I got your note. You're not picking up, so maybe you're in the air. So...I understand why you want to go. You'll be at your mom's, or with Sophie, I guess. Why don't you call when you can. Or I'll try you later. But it might be too late there because I don't know when you get in."

He cut off because he had no idea how to end it.

During breakfast he put on TV NetNews and searched for Chicago. There was a replay of the Soldier Field aftermath and shots of squad cars patrolling Kimball Corner. On the Monday after, Chicago was owned by the police.

He started reading *Unwired*, an artifact subscription from Xynapse days, but soon he was flipping pages. When would she call? His nerves were humming. He could convert it to a plus. Things would resolve, and he needed to get his life back.

In half an hour he had his work clothes in the car and was heading for Renu. Inside the club he did not call her a bitch in his silent monolog. He did not go that far because he imagined it could be bad luck. It would linger in him, a smoldering word, and do nothing but obstruct. Its power could keep her from calling. Instead he drove it all into the LifeLine machines and the track.

When he left he tried to blank the cycling thoughts. Where was she? When would she call? He would take the high road, a discipline of physical and mental health. At Brownwells, a couple of miles out of the way, he picked a chicken Caesar salad, pumpernickel mini-loaf, and a near beer. He took his time driving to the theater because dinner before five would be one more oddity, and he had reached his limit.

He ate in the booth with his phone beside him on the table. He refused to call again, at least not yet. Clouds bunched over the mountains, posing no threat but confirming the change of season. He was rinsing his mouth in the bathroom when he heard the door open. He should have locked it—he had been distracted.

"Manuel," he said. "Wrong night."

"Hi, boss. I brought you some help."

It took a moment to click. Employee two. The candidate was not what he had in mind.

"This is Sandy Esposito, my cousin. This is the owner, Mr. Beale."

"*Buenas noches.*" Walker shook Sandy's hand. He could do that much while trying to understand how Manuel could have thought he would consider a girl.

"*Buenas noches.*" Polite, demure, no nonsense, solid build. Older than Manuel, he guessed, by a year or two.

"Could you tell me where you've worked?" he started, not caring what she said, wondering how he would deal with Manuel, who looked properly sheepish. Clearly he knew how his inspiration would likely be received.

She named a restaurant, then a big box store. Although he wasn't listening to the content, she looked and sounded sincere. Clean features, regarding him directly with the unapologetic gaze of the pre-imperialist owners of half a hemisphere. She seemed to have finished. Why would you like to work here? was the only other question in his bag, but he couldn't bring himself to mouth it.

"Okay, thank you, Sandy. Could you give Manuel and me a minute?"

She understood the idiom, he was relieved to see. She nodded demurely and headed for the door.

"Look," he started, and the kid shrank. "I need somebody I can leave alone if I'm not here, and somebody who can close with you. A girl—"

"*Si, si,* definitely. She is like so, *fortissimo.* Believe me, boss. At Cooper's Roost she had to bounce a *malo* by herself because her manager had split. Ask her about it, please. And she can sing too, so *excellente.* Ask her about Children's Opera. She was in it every year, grade school and middle school. She could sing here maybe—people would love her, I guarantee."

"You guarantee, huh. Why do I have trouble believing she's your cousin?"

"No, she is, boss, I swear."

Walker stared him down, trying to figure what to believe. He didn't need a girl in there, cousin or not, and he was guessing not. He didn't want to cut him off, but he couldn't think fast enough to resolve it.

"Upstairs in the desk, middle drawer, get an application. Have her fill it out and get it back—but not tonight."

"Great boss, no problem." Manuel scrambled upstairs, and when he returned Walker was going to ask him to keep looking for candidates, but he was charged with enthusiasm and grateful, two qualities an employer would be foolish to stifle. He watched them leave, Sandy on the back of his bike that looked comically small.

He regrouped for the night, and it started early. The first Monday cars arrived on Friday's schedule, half an hour before opening. The rest was not Friday, he was relieved to see, but it was steady. It was enough to keep him from checking his phone until near the end of *Chinatown*. When the screen was empty and all the cars were gone, he could admit he was winded. If not for his globetrotting wife, he would have been happily winded. He was ready to call Manuel for five nights. He might be able to handle Tuesday and Wednesday alone, but that remained to be seen.

He arrived home without a call. As he pushed the door open, the darkness surprised him. He should have left the living room lamp on. He would remember next time. The house was dead quiet, hollow and immense. Somehow one human being sleeping had tempered the dimensions of silence.

He made his way to the lamp and turned it on. It was two hours later in Chicago, twelve-fifty. Calling was out of the question.

He showered. Then with a glass full of cheap Zinfandel he surfed channels past sculpted abs on a crunch machine and the detritus of taco and pho chain ads to the one black-and-white. He downed a third and tried to guess. Billy Wilder or Preminger. Kirk Douglas, live-wire intense, was stumbling, spiraling down in a forsaken town in the Southwest. He swallowed the rest. He had it: *Ace in the*

Hole. He poured another round and took it in two gulps. He was picturing Lynne. Calling seemed suddenly possible. It took a breath and then another to clear his head. He killed the movie. Stood up and killed the lamp. He let the impossibility drop from head to heart and on to resignation. He carried the bottle with him to the bed that was wide and cool and slept the sleep of the dead.

She needed time, he told himself.

"She's had time," he answered from his perch on the top stair where he had chosen, in his new context, to be. He had gone through the exercise first thing when he woke, checking his messages in bed, as though his phone had failed to ring or he had failed to hear it a foot from the pillow. The end of breakfast meant over a full day since she had left. She had his message for twenty hours or so. It was almost ten-thirty in Chicago.

He stood up and went to the window and punched preset one. Three rings. If her phone was on, she was checking ID. He had already decided he would leave another message.

"Hi," she said.

"Oh, hi," he said. He sounded as stunned as he was. "I didn't think I would get you. How are you?"

"I'm all right." She sounded balanced, tone even, not angry. "You got my note—"

"Right, sure."

"Sorry, I had to—"

"No, that's okay."

"Get a same day flight, I mean."

"Right. No, really, it's okay. Have you seen her yet?"

"I was just going in. Her classes are this afternoon."

"So you're—" He pictured her in her mother's house with the porch in Evanston. Not her favorite place, based on past confessions. What if it was different now, if things were changing?

"At Mom's."

"Is she okay?"

"She needs to use her walker more than she does."

He was staring through the broad window at their yard, not seeing it. There was a phone silence, and it felt new and scary. He needed a way to fill it.

"How long do you think—"

"I haven't seen Sophie yet so I have no way to know. Darrell is covered."

"Look, I'm sure. Your job isn't what I'm talking about."

"I have to focus on her now."

Okay, he thought. It would be okay to focus on them some too, he did not say. He would maintain whatever peace there was. Besides, on balance, focus on them may not have been his strong suit.

"I understand," he said. "Give her my love."

"Okay."

He imagined he was not the only one holding back. He could appreciate her restraint. It felt like the positive he had been dredging for. Pitiful, he knew.

"When can we talk again?" She was quiet. Probably too much, he realized. "Or you could call me, whenever you feel—"

"Let me do that."

"Sure. Of course." He waited for her in the silence, holding the weight inside, hating it, resolved to endure it. "I love you," he said.

"Love you too," she said a little above a breath.

"Bye," he said instead of adding be careful or anything similar that he would in the normal world of body and mind because in their present alter-world he knew the end when he heard it. Then she was gone.

Better, he wondered, or worse? Clearly better to hear her finally, a world better, even if he had been the one to call.

She had answered and responded to everything he had said and asked. Positives. Stepping stones. He was watching the empty yard.

He turned away and flopped on the sofa and closed his eyes on the ceiling. He was thinking of Sophie and Chicago, and of all of them. What was happening? How much should he fear it?

"Hey, you've got to tell me what to do." Even as she said it, she did not have great faith in gaining sensitivity or insight that would surpass her own. She thought that was her reason for calling, but maybe not the real one.

"Hey, that sounds like fun." Cathy was being cute.

"Shut up. Now listen. You know Walker and Lynne. You met—"

"Yeah, at the gas station, and you've known them—"

"Right, a long time. Good memory. They have a daughter at the University of Chicago. I don't know if you heard about what happened there."

"People were getting popped, what was it, a Bears game."

"A fight outside, after. Lynne flew out there Monday morning. She's scared. I just got off the phone with her—I was in the door ten minutes when she called. But that's not the only thing."

"Okay. What?"

"It wasn't just about Sophie. She was going to see her that day—that much was under control. To start with, I thought she was a little over the top flying out. Their daughter's a sharp young lady and she could probably make good choices. So when she had another reason to go, it made more sense, although I didn't want to hear it."

"So Christ, can you come to the point? No, let me guess. Does it have anything to do with Mister Right?"

"Walker. Her husband."

"The drive-in one."

"Right. He's obsessed with it. Lynne thought it would never get off the ground and neither did I really, but now it seems to be doing something. She said it's consuming their lives. They've been living like strangers and she feels they've gotten lost as a couple. That's the other reason she's in Chicago, I think the main one."

Cathy was quiet a moment.

"Well, I don't know them beyond what you've told me, but I do know you're a very generous and caring person and you would do whatever you could for people you love. But I know you don't want to overstep. This is tough being in the middle"

"Isn't that where friends usually are?"

"Are you answering your own question?"

"Touché. That's what I was calling for, your unique and deranged perspective, oh great Zen master, or is that mistress?"

"What happened to 'princess'?"

"Okay, princess dear."

"Zen princess, baby. Hey"

"What."

"Take care of yourself. I know you're going to call him. Is Margo not going to call, whatever I say? Whatever you do, it'll be enough. No torturing yourself—that's your mantra."

"No torture," Margo said.

"No."

"No no. I might wait a day or so. Thank you."

"Don't thank me, please."

"Okay. Bye."

Walker was making a show of restocking the pop, but he was really checking out his new team. On Tuesday he had hired Sandy and given her one night's training. She was a quick study, he thought, he was hoping. They were still drawing well, even for *The Day the Earth Stood Still*, a personal favorite—Michael Renne in an elevator stopping all earthly business by an effort of will, Gabriel Heater covering the apocalypse on radio. He imagined it would appeal to the retro sci-fi freaks like himself who, fortunately, seemed to be out there. On her second night, Sandy and Manuel seemed to be handling the counter. That was the objective, was it not? To free up time to be with Lynne.

After their talk he had vowed to give her space. That lasted until the next afternoon. He had left another message, more of a check-in, sending his love. He considered a longer apology for his inattention, putting the Ring first, but decided not to try a voice message spoken to an empty room. He considered e-mail. It was cooler, but he could think to say what he meant. He was composing it in the back of his head, watching Sandy whip open a bag and shovel in popcorn when the phone went off on his hip. He flipped it and answered without checking the number.

"Hi," he said when he heard her voice. "A surprise."

"Hi, I know. Is this a bad time?"

Well, he thought, he had a business to run and a marriage on life support and nerves that were flickering like a twenty-year-old fluorescent, but otherwise.

"Margo, for you, never. What's up, babe? How are you?"

"Fine, I'm fine. How are you?"

She knew he would be at work. Why would she be asking? Why else?

"I'm doing all right. You talked to Lynne," he said.

"A couple of days ago. She said you did too, so... She's okay, she wanted you to know. She isn't calling because she's focused on Sophie—"

"I know where her focus is," he said, and he knew it was wrong. He had heard her. She was caring. "Sorry. Go ahead."

"She wants you to know she's just needing some time. I guess you know this already maybe. Just a little time."

"Okay, thanks. I appreciate it, really." You're a good friend, he almost said. Friend to them both, he was thinking.

Through the window he was watching Patricia Neal with her moon face and black eyes. He imagined what she did not say in her moment of terror, that this was all. He needed a neutral subject.

"How's your car?" he asked, sounding absurd, not caring.

"Dale's waiting for a part, something to do with the cataclysm—"

"Catalytic converter."

"Oh Jesus, yes." She laughed her high-register laugh, and Walker was breathing easier. "The catalytic converter, of course. It's in some warehouse in Saigon. And so we're waiting for this piece of crap, which should annoy me more than it does because the rental is fine and the insurance is paying. So what is there to complain about really?"

"Nothing," he said, "I guess. I remember when you could get parts," he added vaguely like an old-timer, thinking of some previous decade of fabrication before the global supply chain. He considered trying another subject and could only come up with her classes, which was too far to go. Instead they fell back into silence, and he let her break it finally.

"So, I just wanted to say hi and pass along—"

"Right, thanks," he said. "Tell her I miss her."

From: Walker Beale <bealew@questar.net>
To: Rob Mathis <rob@robmathisphere.com>
Sent: Thursday, October 10
Subject: Checking in

Hey, buddy. I see ads for *Edenvale* everywhere. Even last night on UHF—some nose-bleed band. I hope X is working the distribution for you. It is, as you'll recall I said from the beginning, going to be huge.

The Ring seems to be rolling, amazing nobody more than me. It's steady during the week and fast Fri. and Sat. We haven't sold out yet, but I think it could happen on Halloween. I have a lock on some drive-n classics from the golden age—*Blood Demon, Green Slime,* and *Mad Doctor of Blood Island* with Christopher Lee.

I put on my second employee—a young lady— and she seems to be working out. I'd love to trust everybody, but it's a cash business, so I let her know the camera is on all night. It's hanging together, but I'm not uncrossing my fingers yet.

That, as they say, is the good news. On the downside, Lynne's gone. Sunday there was an incident in Chicago after a Bears game—don't know if you caught it up there. She convinced herself Sophie could be in danger. It was like she was seeing Chicago in flames. She left for the airport before I was awake. She's at her mother's. I talked to her for a few minutes. Sophie's fine, of course. Two nights ago I get a call at work from Margo. She's acting as Lynne's proxy. The message is basically we'll call you. Great, huh?

So yes, I expect this will resolve. The thing that bothers me is I'm the reason she's there, whatever she says. It's not just Sophie. I want to know this is a thing that will settle down. I'm starting to

Walker saw the red light come on in his Inbox. He laughed when he checked it. Coincidence, most would conclude. He knew better. We contact in many ways, he believed, in dreams, or sometimes when we dream-behave, appearing awake and functional. We send our thoughts, clear as e-mail, or as the inchoate messages of our hearts, often to those we love. Rob's mail, high-priority red, was not coincidental.

From: Rob Mathis <rob@robmathisphere.com>
To: Walker Beale <bealew@questar.net>
Sent: Thursday, October 10
Subject: Harpers Ferry
    Hey man, looks like something's happening down there.

That was all, followed by a link to NetNews. Walker clicked and a video started, streaming live.

A shot from a helicopter showed low office buildings ringed by squad cars. A short convoy of jeeps and Hummers rolled in and halted. A male reporter spoke.

"What you're seeing is the deployment of five squads of U.S. Army troops arriving to reinforce the D.C. police who have surrounded this block. We've heard these buildings may be evacuated as a precaution, but that hasn't been confirmed. There have been no reports of gunfire or explosions. At this time we don't know what has triggered this event, and as we heard from our security consultant earlier, the police will likely be moving very deliberately, possibly transporting these personnel to a secure site where they can be interviewed.

"Again, if you have just joined us, a little over an hour ago, at approximately eleven-ten Eastern time, World NetNews learned that the Arkanet, the top security communications network used by the Pentagon and other security agencies around the world, was severely disrupted, possibly taken down. Because we do not have access to this classified network, we don't know if communication has been restored. These buildings you're seeing are part of the Pentagon's Potomac Communications Center, known as PotComm. They contain the servers and routers—the technological infrastructure—that Arkanet runs on. There is much speculation—and that's all we can call it at this point—that whatever disrupted the system originated here. The experts we've talked to have told us that the security being dispatched to this center indicates this was a CAT 3 event—high severity with intent to compromise national security.

"Now we're taking you back to our reporter on the scene, Karla Nelson-Chang in Quantico, Virginia, with the story that has been breaking there. Karla."

She was standing in front of a link fence. Behind her and beyond a quarter mile of open ground, black smoke was unfolding over squat buildings.

"This is the U.S. Marines extension compound, which is the home of the controversial Deep Water detention facility. Within the last hour a series of explosions—we heard three or four—rocked the complex, and we have reports that some detainees have escaped. Minutes after the explosions, three vehicles described as dark-colored minivans, brown or black, reportedly left the compound area. We don't know if there are casualties. We understand the Marines are now in control of the compound.

"Although no group has claimed responsibility, we know secessionist groups have protested the detainment of some prisoners here, claiming they are being held illegally as political prisoners. As more details become available, we will bring them to you."

Karla was interrupted by a concussion. She recoiled then glanced to her right instead of back toward the compound.

"We've just heard what sounded like another explosion." Her voice wavered. "It sounded fairly close to us, within a mile maybe—but I'm only guessing. Can you give me a shot..."

The camera swung to the side across a blur of vehicles and tightened on an industrial park and beyond, a sprawl of low-rise commercial blocks.

"We don't see any sign of the explosion yet..." she reported, excruciatingly tense, having made the call to pull the shot away.

"Karla." The anchor, her senior, cut in.

"Yes, Jon."

The shot framed Jon and Karla, side-by-side.

"We're getting reports that the sound you just heard *was* an explosion." The two frames resolved to one, filled with Jon only. "An explosion in the area of the Quantico arsenal."

An unsteady telephoto shot showed another bloom of black rising, then a brilliant flash. It was followed by another.

"The arsenal is a storehouse of conventional weapons—service weapons and ammunition, not what the military considers..."

An awkward pause as the shot held on the first smoke bouquet and then two others.

"Considers state-of-the-art ordinance. We have this just in."

A *Briefing* banner appeared flashing below Jon in the lower right quadrant. He went on.

"A group calling itself the Harpers Ferry Coalition has claimed responsibility for the attacks on the Potomac Communications Center and the Department of Defense installation in Quantico. This is not a group that we've heard identified with the secessionist movement, but we have information from Dr. Evans Perth, a history professor at the University of California, Hayward. The group may be associating itself with the raid in Harpers Ferry, Virginia, in the days leading up to the Civil War."

Perth appeared in his own window.

"Thank you for joining us, Doctor. Do you think that the group responsible for this attack may be sending us a message through its name?"

"I believe that may be the case. The raid on the arsenal at Harpers Ferry, Virginia, which was carried out by the abolitionist John Brown and a small band of followers, took place in 1859. The outpouring of sympathy for the raid in the cause of ending slavery was one of the factors that led to secession by the southern states. In the case of these attacks today on very similar kinds of targets, I think we could conclude that the Harpers Ferry Coalition are identifying with the original raiders, but in a reverse sense—that is, they are probably in the secessionist camp. Underscoring the linkage is the fact that the raid in 1859 took place in the same month of October, on the sixteenth."

"Thank you, Doctor Perth. What you're telling us would seem to be more than coincidence."

The doctor's window minimized to black.

"So it seems that the group claiming responsibility may be linked—and we underscore *may*—to the secessionist movement. We return now to Karla Nelson-Chang on the scene in Quantico."

Walker watched Karla struggle to maintain. She was redescribing the situation, turning for a moment to the three columns of smoke that were merging in the distance behind her. She went on about the arsenal. The local affiliate had a reporter on the way.

He clicked his link to Chicago news and scanned furiously. Nothing. He left the office and jogged to the living room remote. All the news channels were on Quantico. No word of anything happening in Chicago. He checked on and off over the next half hour to be sure.

Chapter 28

Back in the office Walker added a line to his message, thanking Rob for the news, then clicked Send. At any other time he would have composed a response about Harpers Ferry, but he wasn't up to it. He needed something else. He wandered back in the direction of the living room.

On the sofa again, he acted like someone reading, but he couldn't concentrate. He avoided the bedroom. The hollowness of the house was ticking in his skull, riding along his spine. He saw the empty space on the bathroom counter where her hairband had been. He picked up the palm-sized remote. Harpers Ferry could not be on every channel.

Americans and Chinese on the International Space Station. That warmed his heart.

"If you're like me..." the overstuffed ex-exec said with green hillock golf links smooth as buttocks behind him.

"Right, I am fucking just like you, shithead. Drop dead." He killed the ad.

Three hours plus the drive, four to showtime—that was what he had to cover. He did not want to go out at all. He wanted to haul Sophie and Lynne back on a long lifeline. They could hole up in the house until the aftershocks of all the breakage—family and public contract—had passed. They could subsist—make night runs to the market or grow their own vegetables. He could buy a long gun for prairie dogs. What caliber? Or better, a twelve gauge like Dale's that could take down anything on the wing. How did Marianne make the quail? He should have stayed that day.

He was at the kitchen table. He knew perfectly well what he should and should not do. He was weighing her request for no more contact against all they had lived through in twenty-six years and all he had every right to expect. Why invoke the name of anything—of some angel between them

that was nothing but an accidental sharing of years
together, uncountable seconds together? Because the name,
whatever it was, a poor label at best, was gut-hooked deep
in his soul.

The phone was in his hand. The four key was her mom's
house, two was Sophie. Calling his own daughter would be
reasonable in every way. He was concerned about her
himself, to a reasonable degree. But he knew what he would
be doing. He would be putting her in the middle, and that
he could not do.

He was ready to call Lynne. Her cell first, then mom's
house. He reflected on their last conversation, unembel-
lished by hopeful interpretation. He replayed the call at
work from Margo, Lynne's appointed messenger. The
memories merged into something steely and cold.

He was in the bedroom, shielding himself from the
room's new occupant, emptiness. It smelled empty. Her
perfume was gone. He searched for the card in his wallet on
the dresser and retreated to the office with his phone.

Of what he would say next, he was anything but sure.
He punched keys on his keypad regardless. He should have
a pretext, he knew, but it was ringing. Then he was
identifying himself.

"Is this a bad time?"

"No, hi. Not at all. How are you?"

He was suddenly neurotic, hyperattuned to inflection
and tone. Suzanne was not annoyed, he was reasonably
sure. Quite possibly pleased to hear from him.

"I'm doing okay," he lied. "And the Ring is doing fine,
thanks again to you. I was just wondering what you're
hearing about this Harpers Ferry thing..."

"God, it's screen one, isn't it? If you've been watching the
video, I probably don't know much more than you. We've
had WNN on here in the office, and we're getting feeds that
there had to be complicity inside the facilities—it couldn't
have been done otherwise. Meaning basically Marines or

other personnel aiding the secessionists. But who knows? It's clearly marked *opinion* on the feeds."

"And there's speculation this was supposed to be some kind of spark."

"Well, they're all jumping on that, that we're on the brink of a civil war or something."

She said the words skeptically, but there was something else in her tone. A kind of war was not as crazy as he had believed it to be when Rob went off the deep end.

"I haven't heard of anything else happening," he said, then realized she had no way to know what he meant.

"It's across the country at least."

"Right. I was thinking about Chicago. My daughter is in college there. Our daughter. But it's a long way too—from Virginia, I mean."

"Yes," she said. The phone in his hand was quiet, and he knew she was wondering about him, why he was really calling. "You know, if I hear anything I'll call you. It's your cell, isn't it? I don't want to disturb—"

"My wife? No, no—she's in Chicago. She felt that she needed, she wanted, to be there." He hadn't intended to talk about Lynne. "Right, it's my cell. And thanks so much."

He wound up the call and sat back, chest pounding. He had mentioned Lynne but it was no betrayal. He felt better for having shared it. It was enough.

That night when he arrived at the Ring, he was checking the sky. Dark clouds were shouldering in over the mountains, perhaps the first, he thought, of the fall storms. By the time the feature started, lightning was pricking down. He and Manuel stepped outside, drawn by the magic of the new season. The air felt humid and charged. Half an hour from the end of the film, Walker was thinking of the kid on his bike heading back to his family's place. The sky was holding.

"You need to split. Just make sure I'm stocked and take off."

"Boss, we've got cleanup—"

"Let's start fifteen minutes early tomorrow. We'll get it."

Manuel pulled enough of everything to cover opening. It was Thursday, a manageable night.

When he was gone Walker killed the pizza oven and threw cornmeal in. Sorry, they were out of pizza. He checked the clock—twenty minutes to run. The rest of the breakdown would take fifteen at most from the time he started the floor robot. He settled back against the counter and watched black-and-white Robert Mitchum glowering at the girl. L-O-V-E and H-A-T-E read the fingers of each fist. He considered boosting the volume inside the concession. The door opened.

"Well...hi," was all he could say at first. "I hope you didn't pay to get in. But of course, you had to. You should have let me know—"

"It's a perfectly valid write-off," Suzanne said. She was wearing a purple shirt that looked like silk and white jeans. Her expression was bright and expansive.

"No way." He popped open the register. "You have a lifetime pass."

"Next time," she said. "I'll bring somebody."

He wondered for a moment who somebody might be. She was smiling at the counter. He dropped the bill back into the drawer and closed it.

"How about a pizza?" he asked, remembering as he did that the oven was off. "Sandwich? Submarine?"

"No, I'm fine."

"Dr. Pepper?"

She laughed.

"Sure."

He brought it to her and they sat at the window counter.

"*Night of the Hunter*," she said. "One of the creepiest. Who directed?"

"Charles Laughton."

"Oh, right. I always thought of him as an actor. Captain Bly—"

"You're a classics fan."

"A few oldies, some I like. But I pretty much start with the eighties. My first star crush was Harrison Ford—in *American Graffiti*. How's that for deep?"

"Could be worse."

He noticed a tiny scar on her jaw, a white crescent on tan. They were sitting at the same stools, and he was fighting off the same dusky flower perfume.

"I'm glad you came in," he said, wondering why she was there.

"I wanted to let you know about something that came in after the Virginia story—in San Diego. A swat team raided an apartment building and arrested four—two men and two women. They're calling it a 'treason cell'. They think there was a plot to hit the Naval Air Station, but it's not clear if there was a secessionist connection. They did get explosives and a couple of assault guns.

"There are other reports of a vigilante group—weekend warrior types—in El Cajon. They had a rally in the downtown park, no action, just ranting basically. They know who the secessionists are and they're going to take them out blah blah. Their duty as patriots and so on. It's BS but it's news, right? That's it, up to fifteen minutes ago. There's nothing about Chicago."

"That's great, thank you, I really appreciate it. You didn't have to—"

"On the phone you sounded like... you could use a friendly ear. I lend you my ear. Ears, in fact."

Your ear, my tongue, scatted across his brain.

"You heard that," he said. "It must be true."

He had not seen her as his therapist. He did not want to get into it all, but she was watching him. He needed to take it somewhere.

"Maybe you were hearing the space. I was probably broadcasting it. It feels odd to be in a place that's empty when it hasn't been. It takes some getting used to."

She appeared to relate, or was he only seeing that? He could speculate, had speculated, about her situation.

He continued with filler about space, relating it to space in architecture, space in film. He tried to ignore both how tedious it must have sounded and Lynne's claim to the entire theme of his empty space which, if he stopped to dwell on it, would leave him with nothing to talk about at all. He paused to gather his thoughts and looked out the window, so he saw the spots on the glass first.

"It almost held off to the end," he said.

"It's felt like rain all evening. The first of the fall."

"I wonder if they'll stick it out. I don't see any lights coming on yet. It's maybe five minutes to the end."

"I should go. You're going to be closing." She was rising, leaving Dr. Pepper. He had blown it. Or was she simply acknowledging the end of the night?

"Can you stick around? This will take me ten minutes. Maybe we could have a drink at Tula's. I'd like to talk about you for a change."

They were standing three feet apart. She was considering it, he was sure. He knew what he had said, and it was not without a message that seemed to be gaining in weight and velocity with millisecond.

"I really should go."

He saw that she meant it.

"Okay. Thanks for listening."

"Thanks for the pop," she said and waved smiling, and then she pulled the door and was gone.

Okay, he thought. She had appeared and he had rolled with it. To chase her and try to change her mind would distort the experience, unbalance it. "The End" came in black and white and Robert Mitchum was back in memory.

The first headlights came on. He killed the hot dog roaster based on his experience of none to go since opening night. The exit lights came on over the infield, and Walker saw the constant flickers of rain. The cars were in the tributary lanes then filling the lane to the exit.

"Damn it," she said in the open door. He heard Suzanne first and then the rain. She was shaking her head, hair glistening. Her blouse was dark purple on her shoulders. "It's not starting." She stuffed her hand into her bag. "It did this a couple of days ago and then it started." She retrieved her phone. "I thought maybe it was some... I should have had it checked."

"Mind it I take a look?" Battery, most likely. Corrosion. Did he have cables?

"I can just call—"

"Let me check something first. May I?" She passed him the key.

He was out the door into the cool rain then popping her trunk in the infield lights and the lights of the cars. Battery poles clean. Transducer clear.

They both got in and he turned the ignition. Lights on the dash but no fault lights—starter or alternator.

"I remember when you could jump a car, hot-wire it even," he said without thinking how ancient he sounded. The vintage models rolling past them must have cued him.

"I'll call triple-A."

"The last time I called them they took over two hours. Look, let me give you a ride. Lock it up, it'll be fine here for one night. I know a great mechanic. He can tow it in the morning and I bet you'll be running by afternoon. Do you need it early?"

"No, but—"

"Let me, please. You wouldn't be stuck here if you hadn't been trying to help me. Just give me a minute."

He led her back inside and finished the breakdown. He was less than a minute from leaving when he realized he should have locked up. A weedy character with a mountain man beard and John Deere cap came in. Walker knew somehow when he saw him he wanted hot dogs, three to go. He settled for two subs.

"Jesus," Walker said as he pushed the door again and they were hit with a heavy clutter of rain. They huddled under the awning for a moment then made their break for the car. The rain was beating into puddles, raising bubbles, nickel-sized.

"Nice," he said as he plopped into the driver's seat and pulled the door, hair and shoulders soaked, as were Suzanne's. Her scent had mixed with the rain—naturally, it struck him, the flowering aromas rising, released from the dust-dry flats. The windshield streamed. He put on the wipers and they cleared views of the headlights hitting white bullets of rain.

"Amazing," she said when they were on the highway. The storm had become a heavy drone on the roof and a smear of distant tail lights in the wipers. "Thanks so much for this. I could be spending the night in the car." She was combing out her hair with her fingers.

Another time he would have a reasonable response, if not clever at least pleasant. He was squinting, trying to focus on the road.

"You said it's about a hundred fiftieth." It was the opposite direction from his usual drive home.

"Right, one fifty-second, it's a dog-leg right."

With the wipers on high and ten under the speed limit, they rolled on for an interminable minute or two. Between passes of the wipers he picked out a sign and then the lettering.

"One fiftieth," he decoded from the white smear of numbers.

"It's next on the right. You angle off. Take it easy—it's clay. But after that it's just a little over a mile..."

He heard guilt in her voice.

"No problem, just let me know if I'm going to miss it."

He took the diagonal, a two-lane packed clay road with no sidelines or center line, only a dark swimming surface. The highway lamps were gone, and he saw no other cars in front of them or in the mirror. He tried to make out tire ruts to follow.

They both fell quiet, avoiding distractions. Less than a mile in they heard it over the rain, indistinct but undeniable, a subtle rushing, and in it a purfling like folding water.

"There's an arroyo over there," she said. "It runs parallel to the road."

Flash-flooded, he realized. Arroyos funneled water into power channels. Flash floods killed prairie dogs and coyotes, the occasional dog, even cattle. People had been caught and drowned. He knew who those were—the ones who showed up at the end of the yard, the foraging ones from the sprawling tent city you passed on the way to the mountains.

"It must be full of water already. How can that—" It was the last thing he recalled her saying.

He glanced to the left, where the shoulder should be. A wet flash on a slate-colored ripple. Water over the shoulder, rushing them broadside. He snapped his attention back to the road, and the future was swimming before them.

It felt like driving on ice. He had done it once, when they went in for his father-in-law's winter funeral in Chicago, but the lessons of that were gone. He spun the wheel, correcting. In the headlights inches of flood water were breaking through the shoulder, making a slipstream over the road.

He was trying to gun through. They were slipping sideways, out of their lane. He sensed Suzanne freeze beside him. They bucked up and over the rise of the shoulder and slid down. In seconds it was over. They were on the back side on a downslope, headlights angled up toward a lone jacaranda on the far side of the arroyo.

"Oh my God, I'm sorry." She was panting.

The engine was still running. They were sitting like astronauts tilted back in their seats. He wondered. For a moment the rain on the window lightened, and it felt like an opening. He shifted into low and accelerated gently. They began to climb. Then he felt the rear sink slightly and they were done.

"Fuck!" She would only feel worse. "Sorry," he said. "Hang on."

He was out the door into the steady rain. Mud sucked at his shoes. He checked the back tire, knowing what he would see. Sunk halfway to the wheel cover, but the passenger side looked to be on firm clay.

"We need something for traction, right?" Suzanne appeared around the back, hair slicked down.

"Why don't you get back in—I've got a mat in the trunk."

"You'll ruin it—and it's probably not enough."

She had turned, and before he could respond she was trudging away.

"Hey, where are you—"

"There was a sign," she called back. That was all.

He slogged a distance behind her. She was bending over, reaching into the mud at the side of the road. When he caught up she had it partially out of the muck, hauling it up on its side. The black-on-white sign read 35 MPH Limit.

"It had to be around here." She was straining, triumphant.

He grabbed the edges smeared with mire and began dragging it backward. She followed on the ancient wooden pole which must have been chewed by termites sufficiently for the flood to topple it.

"Okay, thanks. I got it," he said. They rounded the back of the car and he tried to angle the sign face down under the front of the tire. He heaved up on the pole and stomped it in.

They piled back inside, soaking the seats, and wiped their faces with wet sleeves. They caught their breath for a few more seconds, and then it was time.

He turned the key and eased on the pedal until he felt the rear hold. It seemed to rise. He gave it more, and the Subaru was climbing in slow motion like a whale on its tail. He was full forward in the seat, chest against the wheel. The front tires found the shoulder. The tread churned, getting back inches. The headlights hit the top of the jacaranda. Then all of the tree was lit again, and they were over the hump, back on the level clay.

"Yes!"

"Dammit," she said, "good job!"

"Dammit yourself," he said, "good job!"

Then they were laughing silly, Suzanne with her hand over her mouth, wrinkled nose. A pin had been pulled out of them both, and they were free. Instead of leaving the car where the weight of the world had downed it, they were rolling again. The washout was behind them. His stomach hurt from laughing, and he labored for breath. The windshield was starting to fog.

"How far?"

"Right up... just here, off to the right."

He saw a pair of modest houses and swung into the first drive. He pulled to the end and they sat recovering as the enormous warm flood of relief caught up with them. The headlights glared against the white block and her front window and he lowered them.

"Jesus, thanks," she said. "That was a nightmare. I can offer you a towel."

Her forehead glistened. Her fresh scent, foreign in his car, came to him with their humid heat, intoxicating.

"We're fogged up," she said and reached the windshield with a Kleenex she must have produced from her pocket or bag. She was clearing the window, reaching the inside of the glass on his side. He knew she could have been getting out instead.

She was close enough that he could smell her hair, moist, new water fresh from the sky, desert flower perfume. He had fought it from the start, but the reasons were slipping away.

His arm went around her shoulder and their faces were inches apart. He kissed her cheek. She turned to him. Their lips met and she drew back, but not in offense.

"What are you doing?" she said, a mild reproach, looking almost confused.

"I don't know. Do you?"

"No."

He saw a trace of a smile and then it was gone. They kissed again, longer. He knew well enough what he was doing. He knew by all he had put into fighting it. He felt her hand on the back of his neck. He killed the engine and they were enveloped by the dark.

He undid her top button. They kissed deeper, and the silky fullness of her bra filled his hand. There was a flutter of lightning, and then a rumble. Her hand was on his leg. He had been hit by the narcotic muddy redemption and the sparking wire. He was the monster revived. He was seventeen in the back seat of his hand-me-down Ford Galaxie with Norma Roebuck in the Carolina summer night. They separated and her voice was different, throaty.

"Let's go in."

They were out in the rain again and then at her door like kids, she with her blouse open and he in a spell, barely hearing the sound of keys in her bag.

They were inside with her door closed to the world. He was on her throat, deep in her perfume. They were moving together, backing into a hall. His shirt was open and he felt her hands on his chest. She was padding backwards and their mouths locked again. He heard thunder closer. They were in a room that held a hint of her scent, the shape of a bed behind her in the dark.

She lay back and he struggled to pull off her white jeans soaked to the skin. They were both laughing. He imagined it ending there in the moment, open to each other, defenseless but still uncommitted. A flash from her window lit them.

He was in her bed, softer than his, her alien sheet smelling of flowers. The next white flare exposed them both naked, marble-white form and shadow. Suzanne came to him with humbling generosity and in the warm flavor of her skin.

A splash of the lightning covered them, then dark again. Their bodies, revealed starkly then lingering in afterimage, made it seem to him that they had been cast together in a shadow play, like a film out of time. His tongue was on her leg. Her anklet turned a bright facet, like a trace of lightning.

Chapter 29

"Thanks," Walker said, buzzed and unfocused, smelling of Suzanne's soap. He signed the form and watched the driver climb into the cab of the Rosie's Towing truck and then take off.

He may have been incapacitated in most everyday ways, but her Phoenix was on its way to Dale's garage. That was the objective. She had volunteered to meet the driver herself, but he would not let that happen. He would have to drive her back anyway, he explained. Plus, she had to work. He had called Dale to set it up. The least he could do, he thought, under the circumstances, all of them.

As he stood in the Ring in the late morning sun and watched Suzanne's car leave the drive, the circumstances dominated his thoughts. In one package they brought elation and grief, and they were taking their turns with him. He had betrayed his wife, and every moment of his betrayal was incontrovertible. And even as he turned to the wet infield, absorbing his worthlessness. and picked a smashed paper cup out of the mud, he was slipping back into the obsession he had fought since leaving her house, tumbling images of the night before. A woman's body, not a girl's, before him in her bed in a cool white pass of lightning. Her hands on his chest as he rocked on her. Her hands behind his back, binding her to him like an act of healing. Lying together afterward, her hair on his shoulder, wondrously strange.

He had spent the night in and out of sleep, and at some point in the morning, she had risen quietly. When he rolled out, he heard her in the kitchen. He stepped gingerly into her bathroom half the size of his—theirs—one sink, alien soap and toothpaste, skin cream that was not Lynne's. How did he feel? Cool and quick and light as Scott Le Faro on bass.

Breakfast was toast, strawberries and yogurt, an orange, and strong coffee. He expected she would allude to it if not ask outright—how he was doing, the betrayal implied, what it all meant. But she didn't. She was open and cheerful, accepting. While he called Dale to arrange the tow, she was checking her laptop at the kitchen counter in her nightgown. He fought the impulse.

Up to the time for leaving, he was struggling with what he would say. He was, what? Grateful for the waves of confusion. They had pulled him in and pounded him down and soon he would be on the shore again, looking back.

"Thank you," he said beside his car. The dip in her drive was under water, but the sun was already brightening the beads on his roof and hood.

She hugged him, kissed his cheek.

"Go home," she said lightly. "Thanks for handling the tow," she added, handing him the keys. "I'll follow up with Dale." Her smile acknowledged both their places and what they had shared.

"You'll like him." He climbed in and backed out then waved to her standing like a visitation, apparition, in front of the ordinary white house they must have occupied together but which seemed impossibly foreign in the light.

The clay road was different too. Stretches that had been flooded were gleaming patches in the sun. In the spot where they had slipped over the shoulder, he drove through puddles in the ruts and hatches. Off to his right where the flash flood had raced down the arroyo, he saw only bright traces trickling on the stones.

He dropped the smashed cup into the can and refused to do any more cleanup until the evening. As he approached his car he noticed the mud, gray smears dried on the blackwalls. Marked. Guilty. How far it had strayed.

On the way home and into the garage, elated and grateful, humble and self-loathing, he floated on images of the night before. He needed to catch up on sleep. He dragged to the front door trying to recall what the morning after had felt like in earlier days. Past fifty, he had to admit it was not the same.

Their bedroom was not an option. As he headed for the sofa in the office, he glanced at the kitchen phone almost as an afterthought. The light was on.

"Hi," her message was saying. Of course, he thought. She picks last night to call. Flawless sense of perforation. Not just Lynne, he knew. Women. "I didn't want to interrupt you at work." Didn't want to talk, he understood. "I'm okay, Sophie's okay. I just wanted to let you know I asked Margo to send a few of my things." He sat down. "I think she's going to be busy getting her car soon, so it might be later in the week. I just need a few more clothes than I brought, and it's silly to go out and buy new." An appeal to good sense. "If you could make an arrangement for her to get in, that would be great. She'll call you before she comes.

"That's about it. Anyway, I'm concerned about how things are getting. I'm sure you've heard what's been happening in Virginia, so... I just hope you're all right. Talk to you later." Margo would be in the house collecting her belongings, is that what she was saying? He replayed.

On the way to the office he was imagining a shower that could make sense of his wife in Chicago asking to have her clothes sent and a woman who had him suspended in space with her healing touch. He would check his e-mail later.

The shower helped. Lynne, he understood, was rescuing their daughter from nonexistent peril. Suzanne must have the instinct to rescue him. Where was it all heading, this chain of rescue? Where under the shower head was he, dumb and staring? Where should he be? What if he had been blind, and they were actually in the heart of danger, so far from him? For the first time he considered going to Chicago.

Paranoiac, he told himself as he dried off. Get real. In the next moment he was distracted again by images of Suzanne and things she had said and the cadences of her voice. The choice was between arousal and sleep. In seconds he was on the sofa under the camping blanket, blacking out.

He had set no alarm. When he woke he sat up immediately, checked the light around the shades, then lunged for his watch on the floor. Yes, he had slept hours, but it was only two-thirteen.

"Christ." He rolled out. Suzanne, he thought. Then Lynne and Sophie. "Christ, what is my fucking intermixed life?" he said to his blank-faced computer and the sun framing the blinds with its hint of radiant normalcy. Dominated by women, he completed. The realization came to him at the same time how self-indulgent he was, how self-loving. Was it all about him? No more than necessary. He had intended to check his mail and now it promised escape. He tapped the touch pad.

As the screen opened, his eyes flashed the involuntary Z-pattern across it, upper left to right, down the diagonal to lower left. It was littered with alerts. He had never seen so many. He opened the first, from the Washington Post, and skimmed. He went to the next. The story repeated in different formats until he began to accept what he was reading.

Miami Herald
Police Move on Cocoanut Grove
An hour before daylight, a Miami Police Department swat team entered three houses in Cocoanut

Grove believed to be the homes of secessionist leaders. The community, long known as a haven for alternative styles, was targeted today as a community of traitors...

OpenDoors.org
Police State
In the City of Brotherly Love today, the attempted arrest of a reported secessionist group led to clashes with police. In the south side of the city a number of fires...

Dallas Star.com
Homeland Security Strike
Agents of the Department of Homeland Security have seized the headquarters of a secessionist cell. A raid before dawn on a complex of townhouses in Glen Oaks led to nine arrests. The seven men and two women are being held on unspecified charges. Two of the suspects are Canadian citizens...

San Francisco Chronicle.com
East Bay Under Fire
Neighborhoods in Albany and Berkeley have been hit by what may be bands of arsonists. Early this morning fires broke out in four homes in the Berkeley hills.

The Berkeley Fire Department requested and received assistance from firefighters in Oakland and Emeryville. The Emeryville volunteers were redeployed when two fires broke out in their own community.

There are unconfirmed reports that the fires were the result of coordinated arson. Sources claim that groups of conspirators from Richmond and Hayward set out before dawn with the intent to set the fires.

In August the fundamentalist Kingdom Come Church in both of those communities was the subject of stories in this space. As we reported then, the reverend Garrett Felson of the Hayward church stated on his blog, "In the dark den of the profane and foreign, the day of the cleansing crucible has come." Following this post the Castro district fires consumed fourteen homes and businesses in a single day. Several members of the Kingdom Come Church were questioned and released.

No alert from the Chicago Tribune. He opened the site and scanned. Child missing from Grant Park. Cubs sold to Beijing group. No arson. No police action.

Wide awake, he replayed the alerts. He got up, returned to the sofa, sank back, and waited for his head to normalize. With eyes closed, he balanced Lynne and leaving against Suzanne and the Ring.

To Margo it felt odd but exhilarating to be in her own car again, in the passenger seat with a man driving. Dale was doing the test drive, and perhaps because it was the end of the day, she didn't know, he had invited her to come along. She detected cigarettes and a male smell she wasn't sure of, probably oil.

"It was so nice of your wife to give me a ride," she said. "I really appreciate it."

"We didn't want you to have to walk out here."

Dale had arranged for Marianne to pick her up at Caravan when she returned the rental. They had arrived at Roadrunner Motors as he was finishing her car.

He angled toward the ramp and banked onto the highway. He accelerated then leveled off, holding steady in the inside lane. She watched him as he switched among radio, air conditioning, and heat. He braked lightly, focused on the dashboard.

She thought she had imagined it, but in a moment it was clear. They were decelerating. Dale confirmed before she could ask.

"It's running hot."

Her heart sank.

"Hot—what is it, do you know?" She felt she shouldn't have said it. He obviously felt bad, possibly worse than she.

"Heat sensor, a hundred to one. They do what thermostats used to do." He said it as though she would understand. "We need to go back." He slowed onto the off-ramp. At the base of a hill he pulled off on the shoulder and opened his phone.

"Hey, it's Dale. I need a heat sensor for a Scalia. Right, I know it's late. Where is he—Enterprise? Christ, well look, can you get anybody else? I got a customer. I need to do this tonight... Yeah, okay right, all right."

She heard him give the year and repeat the model.

"I can get the part first thing in the morning. It's right here, local. I'm going to take you back to your house. I should have done the drive before you—"

"That's what test drives are for," she heard herself explain. "Better now than when I'm driving somewhere." She tried to sound male-compatible, mechanistic.

"When we had thermostats I could have put one in for you in five minutes and you'd be on your way. I'd have all of them in stock. Now all the electronics is model-specific."

"Tomorrow's fine, really. I don't even need it early. It's one of the days I walk to the school where I teach," she lied.

She was already seeing the silver lining. It wasn't hard to find. The thought of arranging with Walker to pick up Lynne's clothes had made her dyspeptic. No car, no can do. For one more day at least. As Dale drove back slowly, she was thinking of them both, at opposite ends of the country, it seemed. How absurd it was. When they arrived at Roadrunner, Dale pulled up beside a white Phoenix in the lot.

"You mind if we take the truck?"

"Of course not."

Reprise she read on the side of the gray and chrome beast. She thought it was a Chevy. It reminded her of the *Road & Track* magazines in the office and of plastic models on boys' dressers and desks of executives. The door popped open and she climbed up into the gray leather bucket. The air was already blowing cool and she heard music. As she pulled the door she recognized the anemic derivative of what had once been known as country.

"Wow," she said. "This is new?"

"About six weeks. I drove the last one into the ground pretty much. At least they still make Chevy. It's a good write-off."

In China, she thought. Small business owner, that's what he was, grossing a million or two, netting enough with write-offs. She was seeing Marianne again, imagining their kids. Part of her was glad Chevys were still around.

"You're over close to that school on Prince."

"Boulder Ridge. That's right, fifteen-ten."

"We'll go the back way." Dale turned off four-lane Dilson Drive onto a neighborhood street.

Margo wanted to ask for a news station instead of the pop molasses, but it wasn't her place. She had heard about police actions in several cities but had missed the details. Not knowing was giving her an unruly floating sense. She couldn't ask him.

efocused on her car and the plus of leaving instead of her own. Delay, yes, but she morrow after school. Then the promise to send Lynne's clothes would be waiting for her. She tried to picture better times for all of them. How exactly to broach the subject with Walker? Which words? She was staring absently out her window, only partially aware of the autumn shadows in late afternoon, already fallen on the street and driveways from the light poles they were passing, and from the golding trees.

Walker had considered the living room, but he would have been susceptible to distractions. He needed a place to clear the noise. It was about clarity. The bathroom could have been best, but he decided not to go that far. Instead he was planted on the floor of Sophie's room, back against her bed, his phone on the carpet before him. He knew the spot could influence him. His daughter's photos of high school friends and bookcases jammed with titles and trinkets of childhood and adolescence like layers of history. Sophie's history. History of memory, memory's history. He could deal with influence. Maybe he was inviting it.

In the wake of Suzanne, he needed to reclaim some rational ground. If he followed Lynne to Chicago, what would be gained? All the old pros and cons remained, and he didn't intend to repeat them. He was concentrating on what had changed, or was changing. For one, parts of some cities were burning. Some gears seemed to have slipped. What did it mean? Given a quiet space and a little time, he could grasp it. He could render it down to essentials. Then he could see how far to take it. At the farthest, he would fold his tent. After his brilliant vision, dumb and dogged resolution, and first hints of victory, did it matter? He had come to Sophie's room and planted himself on the memory-haunted square of her floor. Did he need more answer than that?

He could close for a week or two and then reopen. He would call from the living room sofa, upright and in charge. As he rocked forward and reached for the phone, it went off on the floor.

"Jesus!" The number wasn't Lynne's. It took a moment to register.

"Rob Mathis, in person? To what do I owe this—"

"Hey man, are you online?" He sounded wired.

"Not now. Should I be?"

"Listen, I just sent you something."

"Okay, I'm on my way." He scrambled up and headed for the office, seeing the mail in his box on the way

"You all right? What's up?"

"It's you, buddy. You know what's happening down there?"

"I've caught some of it. There's trouble in a few cities." Walker was getting the picture. His secessionist friend was off on a rant. In another second he was in the office chair, clicking the link in the message. The subject line was "All Hell."

"You've got to get out—you see what I'm saying?"

CIVIL WAR in fifty-point bold was the *Post* headline.

"This is not the *Berkeley Barb*, okay? It's the *Washington Post*."

"Yeah yeah," Walker said, focused on the lead story, scanning furiously.

National Guard called out in Virginia and Pennsylvania...President Clinton evoked the words of Abraham Lincoln..."All one thing or all the other"

"Go get your family and get out of there, man. You're—"

...Secessionists made a stand...vigilante groups reported...

"Hey listen a minute. You're seeing this in Canada and I know you're concerned—"

"This is world news, okay? World news. I checked into a ticket to come down. Canada's closed the border. You hear what I'm saying? Canadians can't go to the U.S. as of today. And the *Post* story was an hour ago. I'm sending you this now."

The message auto-opened. The San Diego Union-Tribune.

Mayor Shot

Mayor Daren Cordero was shot today a little before three in the afternoon while leaving a business conference in the Chamber of Commerce building. The female attacker approached the mayor out of a crowd and opened fire with a semiautomatic handgun. Mayor Cordero was struck four times in the chest and neck. The woman was immediately subdued by police and taken into custody. The mayor was taken by ambulance to Sharp Medical Center where he is reported in critical condition.

The shooter was in a group of onlookers who had reportedly gathered to catch a glimpse of Donald Rosario, the former soccer star and majority owner of Cantabile Global Investments. Rosario had left the building a few minutes earlier through a rear exit.

The suspect has been identified as Lynette Garsus Hernandez. She has no police record and has not been linked to any secessionist group. Police believe she is a resident of Campfire City, which has been the target of vigilante group raids. Residents have accused the mayor of blocking intervention. In July the protest March on the Pier resulted in violent clashes with police and the arrest of eighteen people who are still being held...

"You can still come up, but we can't come down in the normal ways. The ports of entry are closed. Get Lynne and Sophie and get up here, you hear what I'm saying? I'll meet you at the airport. We'll be your sponsors, whatever you need—"

"Thanks, I hear you. They're in Chicago, you know...let me make some calls. You'll be at your number?"

"Absolutely. Do it."

Rob was gone. Walker's phone was empty. He punched a speed-dial key.

"What's this?" Margo said. They had seen it at the same time as Dale turned a corner. Almost at the end of the block a car was stopped in the street on a diagonal, blocking the right lane.

"Accident?" she went on, although the car did not appear to be damaged. Dale rolled closer. It was a Lexus II, champagne gold. All doors were closed, and it simply seemed to have stopped there. Margo imagined it was out of gas or had stalled, and perhaps the driver had tried to angle to the curb.

"Nice parking job," Dale said, but she thought she heard a question in it. He rolled into the left lane to go around. She wondered if he was thinking of stopping.

As they paralleled the car, she glanced right at the house they were passing, a block tract home, light green, a tricycle in the yard. The front door caught her eye, ajar. She was in her childhood home in Philadelphia, the front door open on a summer night. A box fan was pulling the air into the living room. She seemed to be smelling the air in the house they were passing. As they passed it she saw something about the door. Smashed in the middle. She rocked forward against her shoulder belt. They were stopping.

She considered being assertive. 'Let's go on.' Dale's responsibility was to her, correct?

A man was approaching his side of the truck, she missed from where, maybe between the houses. He was wearing a tan sports jacket, and over his shoulder a gray shoulder bag with a stylish sheen. Dale's window went down.

"My car died there, sorry," the man said. Pleasant enough to look at, she thought. Maybe late thirties, probably sales.

"You need a tow? I've got a repair shop."

"That would be great." He smiled and nodded, clearly relieved.

"I need to drop someone off and I'll be back. Ten minutes."

"Great. I wonder, there's one other...do you have a phone I could use for one call? I can pay you. My freaking battery died. I need to let somebody know I'll be late..."

Dale picked up his phone from the center console and opened the door. Then Margo did not process immediately what she saw.

The door popped open with Dale clutching the handle, and he pitched sideways after it. Then he recoiled backward, the crown of his head driving into her arm. She grabbed it, numbness then pain. In the gaping door two others framed the man in the tan jacket. One—massive in a black t-shirt, arms like hams—was blocking the door open.

"We don't want your phone," he growled and seized Dale's leg with both hands.

Dale lunged backward, kicking with his free foot. The third man grabbed it. He hit the glove compartment and something fell onto Margo's foot. He twisted back to reach it, but the two hauled on his legs, and he slid on his back over the seat and was gone. The door was a gaping hole in the cab.

Over the edge of the driver's seat, she could see only his legs angled up, the two gripping his ankles. The heavy one hoisted him higher, and the other's head and shoulders were jerking, clearly kicking where Dale's head would be. The one in the jacket had his shoulder bag open. Then a gun, a runner of sun on the chrome barrel. The hulk in the black shirt dropped Dale and was lumbering toward the truck.

"Let's get out, lady." He was blocking any view of Dale. The air exploded behind him. The concussion hit Margo. White. Blank. The one in the black shirt did not turn. He was on the running board, grabbing the door frame.

It was under her foot somewhere. She was scratching at the mat with both hands. She clutched the metal weight, the fat grip. She pulled her knees up, back flat against the door, and squeezed the trigger.

Nothing. Frozen. He was in, filling the chair. She fumbled over the gun, hitting any button.

It went off, deafening, blowing a hole in something, synthetic batting bursting from somewhere. The recoil jerked the gun to the ceiling. The shirt dropped back. He filled the door in a blur of smoke. Both hands on the gun, she pulled it down and squeezed again. Ear-splitting blast. He fell back. The door was an empty frame of smoke. She saw the street, the one in the jacket hunkered down, the one with the gun.

She pointed into the space and squeezed off another blast. Another. Blood had dropped from her head, and she felt a balloon inside that could fill her until she passed out. She could not see Dale's face or his body, only his legs lying straight out on the road.

White dots floated in both eyes and her head was cold. She dropped the gun and grabbed the ignition key and turned. The starter screamed back at her. She realized the engine was still running. She had the head of the shift lever with both hands ramming it into Drive.

The truck jumped and began rolling, careening off to the driver's side. A shot blasted behind her and banged the open door that swung like a sail. She grabbed the wheel and dragged herself over the console into the driver's seat. The truck jumped the curb into a yard. She was heading for a driveway and a low shark-colored sports car, some kid's car.

She jerked the wheel and the truck lurched right. It was tipping. As it straightened and rocked back, she caught the door handle and hauled it shut. The front bumper popped a light pole at the end of the drive and it sucked under the front end. The truck bucked over it. Two bounces over the curb and she was rolling on the flat street. She didn't hear the next shot, just the bang behind her into the tailgate or a fender.

The steel hulk was a wounded bull, directionless. Another shot but no impact. She could barely see over the dash and reach the pedal. She pulled herself up against the wheel and hit the gas. The bull lunged, and she was hugging the wheel on the front of the seat. The truck came straight and picked up speed. Her eyes were brimming with tears. She did not look in the mirror.

"Jesus Jesus Jesus!" Margo screamed. Her voice was broken and she was sobbing, but gulping breaths of life.

Chapter 30

"Hi, I got your message. You're right, it seems like the wheels are coming off. Maybe you've been right all along. We all need to be together now. I'm going to see how fast I can get a flight out. I'll call when I know. And please call me when you can. I want to know you're safe. I'll try Sophie's phone now. I love you."

Walker called Sophie's number and heard one tone and then her voice, every precious nuance, but it was her greeting. He left a message there also and considered the Evanston number but decided against it. He texted her instead. She would see it wherever she was.

Wherever he was. He was in the house, their house, formerly home. He was positioned at the end of the hall, looking into a photo of them together in Sophie's last year in high school, one of her senior pictures of the three of them against the strata of mesa. He was weighing Rob's offer against Chicago. And he had no reason to believe they might not be safer with him at home. He replayed the options, avoiding the place in his confusion where he kept Suzanne. He needed to tell her what he was doing. He pressed his latest speed-dial number.

"Hi, I was just going to call you." He heard a new urgency in her voice.

"San Diego," he ventured.

"Right, you heard about Cordero. Mexico's trying to close their border. No more Americanos. There's a run on Tijuana and Juarez, cars backed up for miles. But that isn't the reason I was going to call."

He heard silence, like a dropout.

"There's action back here," she went on. "Vigilante groups are hitting Reno and Vegas. They're burning buildings—secessionist safe-houses, they claim, but it's really non-white, mostly immigrant neighborhoods. And we're seeing something here, I mean Boulder City. I just got a call from Don Jenks, one of our reporters. He says there are fires on the west end. And part of Settlement City may be burning. I don't know this for sure because I haven't seen any of it. There's no video. He says the vigilantes are getting a lot of support. Police may be looking the other way. People are leaving their homes. He heard some are heading for the lake, and some may be going to the Ring."

"What?"

"They know it. Some of them seem to think they can hole up there."

"That's crazy...you said the west end...where are these people—" He was spinning. Heading for the Ring. Suzanne wasn't on the west end, but she was west of his house, and west of the theater.

"We don't know yet...where all of this is happening."

"Okay, I'm going in. I'm picking you up first."

"I'll be fine."

"You don't have a car."

"I'll call Don if I need to."

"You're not safe. You said yourself nobody knows where this is happening. I'll be there in ten minutes. You'll be ready, right?" He waited. "Right," he finished and pressed End.

Before he opened the door he tried Manuel, partly hoping for backup, mostly concerned. No answer. He imagined trying to find him, but he knew the odds.

He had just turned out of the drive when his phone went off. He swung onto the shoulder, seeing Lynne, as close as he could come to praying, holding his breath.

"Walker," she said. She sounded wired, battling, hanging on. "Walker," again, as though to confirm.

"Yes. Margo?"

"Right, it's me. Thank god you...I've got...there's a problem."

"Okay, you all right?" He heard her breathing.

"No, no I'm not. I think I killed someone."

"Were you in an accident?" Silence. "Margo!"

"No, I shot someone." Her voice broke.

He cut the engine. He heard tiny spasms, less than sobs.

"What do you mean, shot?"

"With Dale's gun. He was driving me back from the garage. There were three of them. They pulled Dale out on the ground. I think they—"

"Okay okay listen, take a breath." He was seeing the pieces of Margo, of all of them, showering down.

"They were killers. I know they killed him there on the ground. One of them was coming into the truck. I shot him. There was nothing..." Her voice hardened. "I had to."

"Okay," he said, staring through the windshield over the empty, ordinary road past the Dobson's. "Okay."

"I'm driving. I'm in Dale's truck. I'm...I can't go back."

"No, you don't go back. We'll call the police together. Where are you?"

"I don't... not sure, south of my house I'm two miles, three, from home."

"I have to go to the Ring. I'm on the way now. Meet me there, can you do that? Cut over on Larrabee and come in from the east side. You might see cars coming the other way. Just keep going. Meet me there, at the Ring." Nothing. "Okay?"

He heard a sound like agreement and then she was gone. He had been craving the sound of Lynne's voice. The terror in Margo's had him seeing Dale on the ground, Margo calling from his truck.

He rolled off the shoulder, accelerated. How long to get Suzanne and circle back? What they would find at the Ring. How to secure the gate. Lynne and Sophie, when he could call again. He tried to find his focus and lock it on the road. He could do nothing about anything else. All he could do was drive.

Margo was going too fast. She realized she had been
accelerating steadily while talking to Walker. She could not
be pulled over. She let up and coasted. Dale's crossover
country was still playing, and she jabbed every button until
it stopped. The blocks slid by outside in liquid silence, far
somehow from what had happened less than a mile behind
her.

Two houses ahead on her right, a woman in a boxy
dress and straw hat was raking leaves from under her front
shrubs. Margo flashed on the jacket and the other one and
the hulk with her shot in him but still ambulatory targeting
her in the yard or jimmying a sliding door as she was
making dinner. She should be warned. Who else could do
it? She rested her foot on the brake.

How could she stop? The hulk in the door, climbing up.
Brain-blinding shot. She could still smell gunpowder. She
was past the house, and the woman at her shrubs was in
the mirror.

Her hand was not steady. She pressed hard on the
speed-dial key she had used before Walker's.

"Please, god, please." She waited two rings. The third
went by. "Where the fuck are you!" Cathy's greeting
answered.

"Hey, it's me again. Look, call as soon as you get this,
okay, will you please? There's so much craziness happening.
There's been trouble...getting my car. It's horrible. It's not
my car...I need to talk to you, okay? All right? Call
me...soon as you can."

She made sure the phone was on then placed it in the
center console. She wondered for a moment why hers was in
the phone well instead of Dale's. Where was his? He had
been passing it to the salesman in the jacket. Somewhere on
the floor now or in the street? She took a deep breath and
tried to shake it off. She was driving in silence past the
parked cars and alien houses and small yards. She tried to
focus off Cathy and the fantasies that were churning about

her. Her goal was Walker and the Ring, and she tried to clear everything but the route from where she reckoned she was, recalling his instruction to approach from the east.

She had to be close to the school, less than a mile. If she could find Camino, it would be Boyer, then Prince. Then Larrabee and the last leg. She squinted at the street sign on the corner until it came into view. Coulter. It should intersect Camino. She turned left.

In the first block on the opposite side of the street she saw two children on the sidewalk, the girl on the curb side holding the smaller boy's hand. She didn't stop to evaluate. The oncoming lane was empty. She cut across and braked at the curb. The girl shielded the boy with her arm and began to pull him back from the street and the huge gray truck.

"Kelly, are you okay?" Margo climbed down from the high cab and rolled her ankle when she hit the ground. She stopped herself from saying "shit" and kept going because Kelly Ostrander was in her class and Davy was her brother.

"Mrs. Sellman," the girl said warily, almost a question. Margo imagined Kelly was reacting to how she looked, and she had no idea what that was.

"Where are your parents?"

"When I got off the bus Mom wasn't there. I couldn't get in. I got Davy at the Cowlitz'. We're going back home." Margo was not convinced. She suspected they had lost their way. Kelly's face collapsed and she fought it but then sobbed. Davy watched her and Margo saw he was on the verge. She knelt down.

"Honey, did you call them?"

Kelly nodded, wiping with her arm.

"Come on, give me the number." She led them to the cab and climbed back up to reach her phone. She had Kelly say the numbers and punched them one by one as Davy watched. Her heart sank with each ring, and then the greeting.

"Hello Mrs. Ostrander, this is Margo Sellman, Kelly's teacher. I have Kelly and Davy with me. They were walking home and got a bit lost. I have them and they're safe. Please give me a call when you get this." She left her number. She knew what she had to say.

"It's fine. Your mom is going to call me. I need you to come with me now."

She tried to suppress the thought she had had since she spotted them, about their parents. She was reeling inside as she helped them up and climbed back into the driver's seat. She buckled them into the passenger seat and kept the phone between her legs. A scooter rider coasted toward them down the middle of the street and passed by, staring at the truck's odd angle. South side middle schooler, she thought, Enterprise Middle.

She turned the key and backed up only as far as she had to, closer to the black shirt and Dale's body. Then she shifted and cranked the wheel and rolled. Kelly and Davy forced her to clear her head again and sharpen until she was seeing only a map of the roads between them and the Ring.

"There's a line," Suzanne said.

Walker saw there was, as difficult as it was to comprehend. As they approached the Ring, he saw a vintage black SUV behind a Khia mid-way in the drive, which meant there were probably more in front of them.

"You shouldn't have picked me up. You could have been here first."

"Out of the question," he said. "Besides, probably not."

He had imagined that if any were so misguided as to come to the Ring, he would be inside first. The sight of them on his property was upsetting. He had formulated no plan. Turning into the drive, he saw people outside their cars at the head of the line, he counted five. Two men and a woman were standing at the gate, the men huddled together. One had his hand on the hinge, and the other dangled a chrome tool. Walker guessed it a wrench.

He rolled off the drive onto the right shoulder, crunching the driveway lights. A woman was staring at him behind a window. He braked at the front, checked Suzanne, and climbed out. The woman at the gate was closest to him, clench-jawed, frozen.

"Can I help you?" he said to the men. The one with the wrench looked familiar. He was with the woman. They were patrons. They had come to the counter, maybe among the few in the early days. Now the Camaro at the head of the line merged with them in memory, foggy.

The two said nothing, faces wired.

"This is my—"

"Yes, we know," the heavier one said, his hand still on the gate the way he would rest it on a fence on his own property.

"What do you—"

"We need a place. Someplace to go. My house is burned. They... they're armed, heavy metal, automatic. Like an army. These other people..." He trailed off.

"My wife called me at the store," the one with the wrench said. His face was sweaty, haunted. "She said there were men in the yard. Jesus..." He glanced back fearfully at the drive where more cars were arriving. "She got out to the neighbors. Our house is gone. Other people's." He paused a moment "Our kids are with us."

"You called the police?"

"The police are in it with them—some of them. I saw two in their cars, doing shit. You can't tell who's with who."

"I'm sorry, I don't have a way to protect anybody. You'd be better off heading for the city." Even as he said it, Walker knew Margo was on the way. His brain was firing, catching up.

Suzanne was standing outside the car. He caught sight of the other woman's face, tight, desperate. At the gate her husband was extending his hand oddly, like a supplication. It felt uncomfortable, then unbearable.

"Wait," Walker said. He went back to his open door. Suzanne was watching. He found the button behind the visor and the gate rose. The three at the gate seemed to unclench as though he had released them with the same switch.

"Thank you. Bless you." The woman was clasping his hand with her cold hands.

"Sure," he said. "We're just opening early."

The men were thanking him, squeezing his hand. The one with the wrench called down the line, "We're going in."

Walker climbed back in the car and Suzanne joined him. He disabled Adam with his remote and the cars began to roll past the ticket booth.

"They had no place," he said. Her hand was on his leg.

"Let's leave it here," he said. He wanted to be able to get to the car there on the shoulder, unobstructed by any others, if need be. He locked up.

They walked in, and as cars continued to roll past them, Walker realized there must have been more outside than the ones in the drive. They were bunching in the center of the infield, some toward the back. As they headed toward the concession, he checked the drive for Margo. She was a cork, a survivor. He tried to recall Dale's new truck. He must have seen it, but the old one was the one he remembered.

"What can I do?" Suzanne asked. She could see the situation as clearly as he. She was solid.

"They said some police were offline but who knows? Could you try 911?"

"I did twice. Busy."

He almost laughed. "That isn't good, is it? Maybe state patrol."

"I'll see." She opened a browser and searched for the site.

At least twenty cars were in, possibly thirty. He began to count. Some people were getting out and standing beside their cars.

"Walker."

He flinched. Margo was standing beside him, trailing two kids.

"Hey," he said and hugged her, not knowing how much to get into in front of them. If he needed any confirmation after the call, it was in her face. Suzanne stepped back, her phone to her ear. "Somehow I missed you."

"It's that over there." She nodded at the truck where she had left it back from the crowd, the door hanging open. He remembered it then. She introduced Kelly and Davy as though they were all out for a stroll. Walker greeted them with an adult pleasantry, pretending they had not been sucked into a situation incomprehensible to all of them. Margo explained how she had picked them up by the road.

"We're calling the highway patrol," he said. "They'll find your parents." He nodded to the three of them. The children stared back, reflecting the emptiness of his assurance.

He glanced at Suzanne. She lowered her phone. He crossed to her and spoke softly, out of range of Margo.

"No signal," she said.

Margo had followed him, her eye on the children. She had read their exchange.

"The cell towers are down," she said. "The circuits were busy for a while, then nothing."

He felt the recognition spinning, spiraling down.

"I'll keep trying," Suzanne said. "It could come back."

He knew Margo would have been curious about Suzanne in another lifetime, but they were beyond that now. His brain was scrambling. How to get through to Lynne and Sophie. No land line in the theater, of course. He had considered a retro phone booth but had decided against it.

It seemed frivolous at the time. The closest land phone he could trust was in his house, the one he had refused to remove just as he had refused to scrap his CD player and ancient Cambridge Audio tuner. In twelve minutes they could all be there.

"Are you okay?" he asked Margo softly, remembering what she said had happened in an otherworld that was somehow becoming real.

Her face trembled and she was biting her lip. Kelly and Davy had come back to her.

"Mrs. Sellman?" Kelly said. Margo knelt down.

"They need a bathroom."

"Sure, this way" he said.

As they turned to the concession building, he saw what seemed like an illusion. Two men on the roof. A car in the back, he imagined, and a ladder. They stood at the front, slate cutouts against the orange sky. Both armed, rifles cradled in the crooks of their arms. One was simple and long-barreled, a bird gun, he guessed. The other was shorter with a heavy hand grip, semiautomatic. Both men were looking behind the building to the side. One pointed to a spot Walker could not see, but he could make out traces just above the roof, smudges blooming in the sky.

"Back to the right," he said as he opened the door and the lights responded. Margo and the kids headed to the bathroom. He went back outside and Suzanne followed.

As they rounded the rear of the building, they saw it clearly. A dark wave curled in the sky for a mile or more in front of the mountains. Every few seconds orange flames flickered below it at the earth line.

"Settlement City," Suzanne said. As she had relayed earlier, as Don had reported.

"A secessionist threat, no doubt." As he watched the smoke, the message was undeniable. It was a conclusion he had been trying to resist, but Margo's young charges made it inevitable. "We have to get out," he said.

Suzanne was envisioning the smoke of cots and rugs, sheets and cotton coats and surplus store shoes, prints of leaves on paper forged by tiny hands, aspirations furious as birds on the wing brought down.

She nodded.

He turned back, aware again of where he was. Men were on the roof with automatic guns, his roof. He would order them down. Instead he stuffed the order down, held it inside like a smoldering coal. Those were the old rules. When they went back inside, Margo and the kids were out.

"How are you guys, all right?" He passed them in the bright little hall outside the bathroom, heading upstairs. "Could you—" to Suzanne.

"Sure," she said, turning to Margo and the kids. "We can try the numbers again. Here, let's use my phone." She gave it to Kelly and they moved out into the room. "Punch these numbers and listen."

Walker opened the door to the projection booth. He was not seeing clearly. Dots were swimming in the corners of his eyes. He sat down at the desk and punched the keys on his phone and heard the cold absence of tone that Margo had said he would.

He pushed himself up from the desktop, steadied, and went to the window. A few cars, he counted four, had moved into position parallel to the far wall that faced the road. Men were standing on the roofs and hoods. He saw one rifle, and the others had handguns.

At the near end of the infield, two cars were rolling slowly back to the gate. Walker fixed on them. They could be leaving. Then he saw the others. While he had been behind the building and then inside, two pickups and a Lincoln Towncar the size of a hearse had moved into position outside at the end of the drive. They were parked side-by-side, blocking it, one on the shoulder against his rear bumper. He watched the two roll to the outside and park on a diagonal between his Subaru and the gate. He tried to see how he could back out, jostle a way to the drive. He would persuade one of them to move.

He watched the last driver get out, a guy around his own age in a t-shirt with a Jose Cuervo logo and sweat pants. He could have been in his home gym when whatever it was had hit him. Walker could talk to him.

He needed to take things that could not be left. As he started to turn from the window, he halted. Two insect figures were clinging to the far edge of the screen, a dozen feet apart, on the road side. They were on the maintenance ladder, the one Walker had never used, barely remembered.

Beyond them, he saw what they saw. A convoy of trucks, no cars. Ten or more, a mix of pickups and monsters, half with cages over the beds. One in shark-colored primer, one ancient black Hummer. A couple at the rear rolled forward; the others had halted. No other vehicles were visible on the road. Walker realized suddenly that all who would be in the Ring were in.

He scrambled back to the safe. Two nights' cash and a hundred or so in change. He bagged it in the old canvas tote he had used only a few months before to stock the office. He pulled the desk drawers. Notes and office supplies that seemed like relics, contents of a time capsule.

He started for the door then remembered. He went to the tall metal cabinet and pressed his finger to the scanner. He lifted the plastic box with the flip-top lid off the shelf and settled it into the tote. He glanced once over the room and left.

Kelly and Davy were playing a game on Suzanne's phone. She sat beside them, and Margo was next to Suzanne, arms wrapped around her middle. When he joined them, he bent down to her.

"I think we should leave," he said. "It may not be safe." She looked up at him, eyes of fear and exhaustion.

Margo and Suzanne got the kids up, and he ushered them outside. Pulling the door, feeling it lock, he wondered when or if he would open it again. As they descended the steps, he saw his target.

"I have to talk to someone. You guys wait here." He caught up in the back of the infield behind the last row. He was on the ground level with the cars clumped like circled wagons. People were standing outside, some with young children who would have been home on a normal night.

"Excuse me," he said to the man in the workout clothes.

The man turned, startled. He was as tall as Walker but heavier, fleshy faced. Jose Cuervo gold on white.

"Can I ask you to move your car? I have the wagon next to yours out at the gate."

He was looking away, shaking his head. The movement seemed dull, instinctual.

"I'm the owner," he threw down like a trump card. But now it was no card, just the illusion of a card. The man who, Walker realized, could easily have undergone electroconvulsion within days or hours for any imaginable dysfunction, hung a look on him, heavy-lidded. "I need you to move your car, if you would please."

"Yes," the man said suddenly, and Walker heard the note of damage. The man looked down, then back over his path.

Walker took the lead, heading toward the gate. Suzanne and Margo and the kids huddled with Suzanne who was trying her phone again. He glanced back at the two men on the far edge of the screen. The one on the bottom wore a hunter's camouflage jacket, as though no one could see him there on the edge between the white frame and the sky.

Walker heard a siren in the distance. He could tell the direction, tried to guess how far. It could be police or state troopers. Of course it was. The United States had not gone off line. Civilization was still around. As they neared the clump of cars in the drive, he was tuned to any sign that it was coming closer. In the next second he heard the first two pops like firecrackers outside the wall.

Walker and his companion stared at each other, animal stares. Walker glanced back. The men on the roof were crouching. In an astounding moment he heard their guns burst, one ripping off a blur of shots, in the direction of the road.

Screams flew up from the infield. The ones who had gotten out were scrambling for their cars. The jogger broke away from Walker, lumbering toward the others.

"Get down!" Walker shouted at Margo and Suzanne who were already crouching, shielding the children. "Behind the steps!"

He caught up and tackled them down behind the partial shelter of the concrete steps.

"Should we go back in?" Suzanne almost whispered, and he saw fear in her for the first time. Shots were coming in bursts from the road. A louder shot and then a ripple returned from the roof above them, then pocks from the far section of the wall. The kids were behind Margo, backs to the building, eyes wide.

"We could be trapped." He feared they could be already. He was spinning for a way to unblock the car. "There's a back way out."

"Your car—"

"Blocked. I don't think it's an option." What could he offer? He was thinking of them running with two kids out the back across open field. If they could make it at all, how far? Pops of gunfire were coming quick as heartbeats. They would go back in, hole up. He was out of ideas.

"We have the truck," Margo said.

He turned to her. If it was not disbelief, what was it? There must have been a reason he hadn't considered it. Of course she had driven there. The truck she had driven. It could not have been his brain jamming, refusing to admit it was the truck of his friend who was no doubt cold on a street they had probably all driven at one time or another.

"Of course," he said. Over the steps he saw it where she had left it, door open. "Do you have the key?"

Margo was staring at him. Finally her hand went to her hip, checking for her nonexistent purse. "I think I left it in there, in the ignition, and my purse... they must be, should be, in the truck."

"Okay, if it is I'll swing back and pick everybody up. Now stay down." He checked both women's eyes to make sure he had connected. Kelly hugged Davy who seemed about to cry.

He left the step, keeping low. Across the infield on the roofs of their cars, they were firing toward the road. Shots whined back into thuds, and puffs like talcum popped out on the concession wall below the roof line. Guns on the roof exploded above and behind him, and the shock almost buckled his knees, but he was still going. He reached the truck and scrambled up. He grabbed the steering column and the keys rattled in his hand. Margo's purse was in the back. His shirt was wet against the seat.

He slammed the door and the cab was silent. Margo had left it in Drive. He shifted and rotated the key. The engine caught smoothly. As he shifted back he was looking squarely at the screen.

It could have been any of the pock sounds, barely audible. The lower man on the ladder, the one in the hunter's jacket, was clutching his rifle to his chest, tilting forward, then dropping straight down outside the wall. The other man looked down at him but made no move to rescue. Instead he raised his gun and fired, recoiled. Again.

Walker pictured the space that held the fallen man outside the wall. One of the last sections of wall. He was lying in the grass fringe of the Ring of Stars.

He rolled a tight circle back to the steps. Margo hustled the kids to the truck and boosted them up and into the back. Suzanne joined Walker in the front. As they rounded the rear of the building, Walker set his sights on the chain link gate, seven feet high.

"Are those—" Suzanne started. He saw them at the same time, thirty yards to the left of the gate. One was hauling himself up over the top of the wall. Another crouched inside, clutching a handgun, peering over his shoulder at the infield. The climber dropped inside the wall and rolled to his feet. A third appeared on the top where he had been. They clearly had a ladder and were breaching the wall unnoticed. The first on the ground was shaggy-haired, in a black vest— flack vest, Walker imagined. The others wore camouflage, militia style vestments of the fellowship. Gang gear. There could be others outside, a matter of seconds before they found the gate.

He considered laying on the horn to warn the others but couldn't risk it. The same, he realized, with the gate. He had intended to unlock it, but even if he pulled close, getting out would be a gamble. One shot could end it for all of them.

"Fuck!" Suzanne let it slip. They all heard the concussion at the same instant, muted but undeniable, behind them. Walker saw the intruders freeze, staring toward the front of the theater. A black twist of smoke was rising over the roof. He rolled forward, and they tried to see through the rear window.

Beside Margo's head he saw fire whipping up the screen. They had hit the far edge where the shooter on the top had clung to the ladder. No sign of him, only orange flame that curled into a column of smoke. The sight of the huge white canvas caught in fire sat so astoundingly inside Walker that he could not think or move. He knew nothing. Shoulder-launched missile, he guessed. He could save none of them. Suzanne was clutching his arm. Then she was shaking his shoulder.

He looked where she was looking. The shaggy-haired man was pointing, and the one on the ground and the other on top of the wall followed the line of his arm. He was pointing at the truck. Walker saw his gun hand begin to rise.

"Get down!" he shouted. He had a hundred feet or less. He stomped the pedal and the truck lurched. A pop outside and a hit on the body somewhere behind him. Pedal to the floor, engine roaring. The kids screamed. The gate flew at them.

"Down!" In the blur at the edge of his eye Suzanne ducks below the dash. His forearm up in front of his face.

Slamming in, steel on steel, belt wrenching his shoulder.

They bucked and pitched to the right, revving furiously. The driver's side rose higher and Walker felt them starting to roll. They slammed down, rocked to the left and came upright. Stalled.

They were entangled in the gate, pipes kinked under them like straws, the top hinge of the gate ripped open.

"Oh god, are we—" he heard Margo start.

He squeezed the key over. It caught. He reversed because he had to, toward the guns. Steel mesh and pipe crunched under the rear. The front wheels popped up and back down over the tangle of gate. As he braked, a burst of shots came from behind them. Hammers scattered over the rear panel on his side, one somewhere on the cab. The kids were screaming and Margo pushed them down. Suzanne stiff-armed the dash. He slammed back into Drive and flattened the pedal.

Into the fence again, smash of hollow frame and wire, a pipe canting up, banging Suzanne's door. In another second they were through it. Off to his left he caught sight of a truck, the one the intruders had used. He coasted for the second he needed to check—the blunt shadow of a driver, no others on the ground. He cut right and accelerated.

"It's all right, we're okay," he heard Margo say, dimly aware that she had been saying it over and over as Kelly and Davy were crying.

In the rear-view mirror the truck was moving, but toward the gate. It would not follow. They were rolling over tufts of brush and tumbleweed on open plain. Three hundred feet, he estimated. In the fading light he tried to focus only on the pale and darker patches of uneven ground. They jolted on, the kids whimpering, none of them able to speak. A quarter mile.

"Everybody okay?" he could ask finally. He caught Suzanne's eyes, and then Margo's in the mirror. Kelly's arm was around Davy's shoulders, and Margo was wiping her cheeks with her hand. The girl was asking something, and he heard the word *parents*.

"Walker?" Suzanne asked suddenly and he turned. She was looking at him intently. His head.

"Did they hit you?" she shouted suddenly and reached toward his face.

His hand went to his left temple at the hairline where he felt pain for the first time. Blood on his fingers. He checked his cheek with the back of his hand. Blood, but less.

"No, I'm not hit, no," he assured her, hoping he was right, unable to understand how he had been injured, scanning the visor and padding around him for a bullet hole. More likely was the joy ride over the fence. They had bucked up and slammed back down on his side. The belt retractor cover or the door frame—some edge had cut him. "No, it was something in here. That's all."

She found tissues in her purse and he pressed them to his temple. It was tender but no worse. He was still on track. He was making a long arc back to the road.

He checked the mirror again. The lights had come on with sundown—the retro neon wedge of a sign and the perimeter lights that struck the starry mica and shards of glitter in the curving wall. The orange fire was consuming the screen like paper, a third gone. The Ring slid out of the mirror, and he did not turn. They had nearly reached the road.

He was planning the most direct route to home and a land line. They rolled up onto the empty blacktop, and he checked both directions. To his left behind them, the rabble convoy of assault trucks, tiny flashes of fire from their beds, two of them advancing on the front gate.

In the other direction they all saw the reason for the empty road. State patrol cars straddled both lanes a mile or so above them. Cones on the tops of the patrol cars of the state of Nevada were firing red and white.

"They're in it together," Suzanne said before he did.

They were blocking the direct road home. Walker tried to think of any other reason. He considered a back way, over land, but he had no way to know what they might find. He had harbored, they all had. Whom? Encroachers on subsistence jobs, unwashed fellow travelers, balls of light in temporary skins, refugees from fire.

He rolled across the road and off the shoulder on the other side. Over the plain before them, evening had settled into gray. He headed for the spot in his head, navigating with lights off over open ground for the state highway. They would cut north then east. The prairie rumbled under them. He checked the sky for surveillance.

No one spoke, and for a long time it seemed there was no sense of progress or change but the vibration of tires over the desert crust and balls of brush.

"There," he said. The razor-flat band with pale lights was just visible, miles away. He held on course and soon they were taking the steep slope up the shoulder onto the interstate. The first car closed from behind and sped around them, seeming strangely normal. He locked onto the tail lights and followed, accelerating into the gathering dark.

Where were they going? he had asked before night had closed around them. They all had lives behind them and countless points of memory to return to. But what would return mean?

Suzanne had put on the radio as soon as they had reached the highway. Frequencies around the world were covering. National Guard called out. Violence spilled over. Fire in the streets. Civil war. KNX Los Angeles was reporting that all mainland international airports had been closed.

Walker could see only one direction and one target. Lynn and Sophie were there. He had not tried to explain it because he could not, but Suzanne could read him. At one point she simply said it.

"You need to go."

He checked her to be sure he understood. A long moment passed before he could accept the enormous gift it was.

"We're sticking together, then?"

In the mirror Margo nodded, her arm around Davy who had switched places with his sister, and Kelly beside him, her orphans.

Soon they killed the radio and settled into air conditioned quiet, all too tired to speak. A convoy of trucks, olive and camouflage, rolled past them in the opposite direction. Walker tried to imagine they were bringing a return to order, to a state they knew. Soon all the others were asleep from exhaustion with the secrets of their fugitive hearts. He settled into his role and his purpose, breathing easy, unobstructed.

Over the next half hour a few cars passed them in silence, each briefly heartening. He checked the gauge and tried to calculate how far they could go on the battery and half a tank. Three hundred plus miles. Five hours. The GPS was still blank, blown. What could he make, Salt Lake City? Provo? He would stop earlier, take no chances. They would need food. Suzanne might spell him then. He would see what he had left, whether he would be a liability if he did not sleep.

He glanced at her, seat reclined, facing the window. His tote bag from the Ring slumped beside her feet. *Close*

Encounters was the first night. Full screen and empty infield. That memory was vivid, although he couldn't remember what he had shown a night ago. He could only recall trying to reach Lynne. Memories of the others came tumbling. *East of Eden*, *Dr. Strangelove*. Folly, he knew, what he had tried to do. *Bonnie and Clyde*. How he had convinced himself otherwise. It was all there in the canvas bag like evidence.

He checked Margo again in the mirror. She was safe from nightmares for a while, Davy asleep against her arm. In the window above them an orange light caught his eye, distant. It was new, or he could have missed it as they passed. He knew it was like the others. He had seen three as they slept and had kept them to himself.

The first was a plaza at a cloverleaf. It had been visible for miles. The fire was tamer than he expected when they passed the gutted Arco station, bright sign intact, and the smoldering shell of an Applewood restaurant rolling great balloons of smoke. Unattended, the remains would burn for hours. No fire trucks in sight, no state patrol.

The next was well off the highway, past an exit sign he didn't remember—Bunkerville or Mesquite. Miles in, the flames stretched the width of a town. There seemed to be two large fires, silver smoke against the black sky. Warehouses, he imagined, maybe a lumber yard.

The third had come and gone on the opposite side of the road. The flames were barely distinguishable, flickering in the distant patch like a wildfire out of season. The one in the mirror was like it, and Walker wondered for a moment if it could be the same, if the highway had curved behind them. But it could not be. The other had been miles behind.

He blinked back to the highway. Its sheer perfection, lanes straight, precisely lined, seemed incongruous, mocking, like a false promise of order. But it had them now on its own terms, in its keeping, and the road, any road, was possibility.

He needed to clear his head. They had been through a storm, but they could be on the other side. He had as many reasons to believe it as not. As many as he would allow himself, and all of them. He needed to reset. He tried to flatten his thoughts to a horizon of blue sky and water. He tuned to the hum of the highway, and after a while he was there.

He was drifting to road films, and films of misdirection. *Two-Lane Blacktop. The Misfits.* He seemed to be slipping down, sinking under a great weight like sadness. He needed to pull out. His folly, he reminded himself, but he knew there had been more.

He dropped the window a third. The night air was warmer but charged with freshness. He tilted his head to the glass and peered up over the top of the window into the ceiling of stars. He took in the renewing air and held it down. Endurance, he understood, that was all now. Making Chicago. He returned to the white lines.

But Walker could not stop himself from looking back. He glanced up at the mirror again, teased back by the fire. He fixed on the small, distant light and could not turn away, unaware that he was holding his breath, as though following a falling star. But it was only one like the others, American towns burning like embers receding to nothing in the mirror, as irretrievable as time.

14909405R10168

Made in the USA
Charleston, SC
07 October 2012